CHARLES DE LINT

Novelist, poet, artist and musician, Charles de Lint is one of the most influential fantasy writers of his generation. He lives in Ottawa with his wife MaryAnn Harris, an artist.

'There is no better writer now than Charles de Lint at bringing out the magic in contemporary life'
– ORSON SCOTT CARD

'De Lint shows us that, far from being escapism, contemporary fantasy can be the deep mythic literature of our time'
– *Fantasy and Science Fiction*

'Has a unique ability to weave together a seamless pattern of magic and realism'
– *Library Journal*

CHARLES DE LINT

TRADER

PAN BOOKS

First published in Great Britain 1997 by Macmillan

This edition published 1998 by Pan Books
an imprint of Macmillan Publishers Ltd
25 Eccleston Place, London SW1W 9NF
and Basingstoke

Associated companies throughout the world

ISBN 0 330 34935 X

3 5 7 9 8 6 4 2

A CIP catalogue record for this book is available from
the British Library.

Typeset by SetSystems Ltd, Saffron Walden, Essex
Printed and bound in Great Britain by
Mackays of Chatham plc, Chatham, Kent

for Grit

luthier, musician, author;
good guy extraordinaire

ACKNOWLEDGMENTS

I'd like to thank luthiers Grit (William Laskin in his official guise) and Ed Dick for input into the luthier's craft, as well as for some general conversations that helped bring Max Trader and his plight more to life in my mind while I was writing. Needless to say, anything I might have gotten wrong is solely my responsibility.

I should also mention that the city, characters and events to be found in these pages are fictitious. Any resemblance to actual persons living or dead is purely coincidental. In other words, to the best of my knowledge, Grit, Ed and any other instrument makers I happen to know are exactly who they are supposed to be.

And if any of you are on the Internet, come visit my home page. The URL (address) is http://www.cyberus.ca/~cdl.

– *Charles de Lint*
Ottawa, summer 1995

CONTENTS

Denied our names, our faces,
we lie in the graves of our identity
with a stranger's pennies on our eyes,
seeking to reclaim ourselves
from the spaces between
what we remember doing
and what we yet might do.

– Wendelessen, from "The Graves of Strangers"

Your treasure house is within;
it contains all you will ever need.

– Hui Neng

Shift

Whatever I may be
I meet him.
He is no other than myself
Yet I am not he.
– Dōsan, thirteenth century

I • MAX TRADER

IF DREAMS can be portents of what is to come, then I had my fair share of forewarning before my life was stolen away.

Each night, for the week preceding the event, I found myself returned to the workshop of my old mentor. Janossy was ten years dead, the workshop in the old outbuilding long gone, man and farm swallowed by the past, yet here he stood before me. Here was the sunlight spilling in through that splendid skylight high overhead, diffused and muted a hundred shades of green and yellow by the boughs of the maples overhanging the workshop. Here was the long pine workbench, covered with wood, shavings, tools and sawdust, the back of a guitar the only recognizable shape amidst the clutter.

I remember that guitar. Janossy never did finish it, but I did. He was working on it when he died, the top and sides, braces and bridge, a one-piece back. It was the perfect guitar body and deserved the perfect neck. I came close, but I couldn't match his workmanship, couldn't match the neck he would have given it. In the dreams, he's still working on it.

Sandor Janossy had been an enormous man with a temperament to match, embracing everything that touched his life with a huge enjoyment that was evenly matched in its intensity by the strong contemplative side of his nature. He had lived with the immediacy of a Zen master in an ever-present now, viewing the world through the artless eyes of a child, seeing, rather than looking. Which wasn't to say that he was simple – or at least not in a pejorative sense. Instead he resisted complications, refused to be drawn into their snare.

"When you understand how everything in the world connects to everything else," he told me once, "you have little patience for more divisive points of view."

Case in point: the luthier's craft. Everything connects. Janossy was able to read the wood with a kind of *feng shui* geomancy, finding in its grain energy nodes connected by lines as invisible, but no less potent, than the ley lines or Chinese Dragon paths that dowsers have found crisscrossing the earth. Building the perfect instrument is a matter of connecting those nodes, maintaining the energy flow between back and top and sides, between neck and finger board and the main body of the instrument. When the nodes connect favorably, when the alignment of the ley lines within the wood is at the optimum, the instrument becomes a mirror that reflects the spirit of the music called up from it in the same way that the adherents of *feng shui* believe what we do here on earth is mirrored by the astrological powers of the heavens.

Heady stuff for the young man I was when I first came to study under him – more so when I finally understood the ability firsthand.

"The master woodworkers all know this," Janossy would tell me. "Perhaps not in so many words, but they know when a wood will work with another and when it won't. They know that it's not simply the design or the thickness of the wood or the varnish that gives an instrument its heart and soul, but something else that lies hidden deep in the grain, something visible only when you know to look for it. Something that connects only when you understand the connection."

I've missed working with him, missed hearing his voice, missed viewing the world with that vision peculiar to his way of seeing that he was always willing to share with me. Returned to his company, howsoever briefly, even through dreams, I realized just how much.

But I knew I was dreaming. All the time, I knew. Not because I have the clarity of moving through my dreams the way a lucid dreamer does, but because Nia was in these dreams as well, sitting in a corner of Janossy's workshop the same way she sits in a corner of mine most afternoons after school, a misplaced figure of Gothic Bohemia here, all pale skin and black clothes and dark hair starkly juxtaposed against the warm buttery colors of the workshop.

Her presence was what told me I dreamed. Nia was barely out of her diapers by the time Janossy died, which would make it impossible for her to meet him in this way. And consider this: while she loves to hold forth while I'm working, in these dreams she'd be remarkably quiet, sitting there, hands folded almost primly on her lap, listening to Janossy with the same happy interest as I did.

What did he tell us? It's difficult to articulate, because what he said faded the same way that dreams can once you waken, the way my dreams almost invariably do. But I remember he seemed to be concerned about something. Seemed to be warning me about something. Or maybe that's only the meaning I gave the dreams later. I can't be sure now. All I knew then was that I'd wake up disappointed every morning, wake up and know it had been a dream, no more. Janossy was still dead, the farm was sold and gone and all I had of him is what he left me: the tools he passed on to me and my memories. Nothing has changed. Everything remains the same as always.

Until one night I wake from that dream to find myself in a stranger's room.

I sit up slowly, taking in my surroundings with mounting confusion. I know the momentary disorientation that can come from traveling or sleeping over at a friend's, that moment of half-asleep shock that quickly dispels once you realize where you are. But this is different. I haven't been traveling or visiting anyone. I'd spent the evening in my workshop, designing the inlay pattern for a mandolin that I was in the final stages of completing; then I went to bed in my own apartment, above the shop.

The stuttering light that comes in from the red neon sign outside the window of this room illuminates nothing even vaguely familiar. Not the bed, the furnishings, the posters on the wall. I don't know how anyone could fall asleep with a poster from one of the *Aliens* movies hanging over their bed. I certainly couldn't have – *if* I'd ever been in this room before, which I hadn't.

So this is impossible. More of the dream, I think, that's all, except now I've left Janossy and Nia behind and moved on to something new. But this dream has what the other didn't: I can taste my fear. I can smell the room. A trace of aftershave I don't use or recognize. The vague locker-room odor of a room that hasn't been aired in too long.

There were no smells in the dreams of Janossy.

But it must be a dream, for nothing else makes sense. I pinch myself, but it does no good and feels too real. It doesn't help at all. I'm still not where I should be, in my own bed.

I look slowly from the grotesque poster to my reflection in the dresser mirror across the room. I can't look away. My heartbeat goes still and a deathly silence thickens around me. My ears fill with pressure. My lungs refuse to work and added to the room's unpleasant smell is the sudden sour odor of wet clay.

Deliberately I lift my arm. The reflection follows suit. I let the arm fall to my side again. I shake my head, unwilling to accept what I'm seeing. I want, more than I've ever wanted anything before, to turn away from the mirror, but my gaze is locked on the reflection I cast upon its surface with the same numbed fascination as one might view the scene of a particularly grisly accident. This goes beyond the impossible.

The face looking back at me isn't my own. It doesn't belong to anyone I have ever seen before in my life. Instead of my own features, I see those of a stranger reflected in the glass: early thirtysomething, which makes him at least five years younger than my own thirty-eight; hair, thick and dark, unruly from a night's sleep; face, handsome with chiseled features, cheeks and chin bristly with dark stubble; eyes appearing almost black in the poor light; nose, prominent and wide at the base; lips, sensual, but the mouth a bit too wide for the face.

I feel like one of Rod Serling's hapless characters from an episode of *The Twilight Zone*. Slowly I get out of a stranger's bed and walk toward the mirror in a stranger's body. I lean close up to it, fingers stretched out until they meet the fingers of the stranger reflected on the cool surface of the glass.

I have to be dreaming, but I know in my heart I'm not.

Not anymore. Janossy's workshop is long fled. So that means . . . that means I . . .

My lungs, once so still, begin to hyperventilate, drawing air in and out of the unfamiliar body I'm wearing at such a rapid rate that I sink to my knees in front of the dresser. I have to lean my head down upon its wooden top. The faint mahogany smell helps to center me. Something is wrong. Something is terribly wrong here, but the smell of the wood assures me that however alien the world has become, I'm not crazy. I might not recognize this room, or the body I'm wearing in it. The situation in which I find myself might be impossible. But it doesn't disprove what I know to be real. I have a past that doesn't incorporate this body or room. I have memories of an entire other life – my real life. I have no explanation for what's happened to me, but that doesn't change what I know to be true.

I'm not the man in the mirror. This isn't my bedroom. My name is Max Trader. I'm a luthier. I live someplace else. No matter what my senses are telling me, those are the facts and they can't be changed. They're irrefutable. The smell of the wood assures me they're true, for it was the smell of the wood that seduced me as a boy and so became an ongoing mainstay of my life, defining who I am. If I can't believe the wood, then everything I've ever known is a lie and that I refuse to accept.

No. I know this: wood, the smell of it, doesn't lie. Freshly cut, with a saw, a chisel, a knife, roughly planed or sanded as smooth as a child's cheek. The sappy aroma always rises up into my nostrils, crowding out all other impressions. And if I mean to work that wood, then I apply what I've learned from my father and Janossy. First I have to crawl inside the wood and understand it from the inside out, for each piece is particular to itself. The swirling I whisper of its grain, the resonance of its molecules vibrating against my fingers, and always the smell, the forest, the wood, the tree, distilled into that deep rich scent that rises from the smallest sliver that might lie in the palm of my hand.

Wood, its smell, working with it, handling it, taking tools to it, shaping it, once saved my life. Or at least saved what was left of my family which, at the time, was pretty much the same thing.

My mother's name was Abigail and she died when I was nine. She was found to have abdominal cancer, the growth was removed, the operation successful. But a year later, a checkup revealed the cancer had spread all over her internal organs. Her dying took several months. The loss of her broke my father, broke the bond that had knitted my family together the way disparate threads are woven together on a loom, entwined until they become one piece of cloth. When she died, the cloth unraveled into shreds.

My father's name was Jacob and he was a cabinetmaker, from a long line of cabinetmakers, but there was little work for him in his craft in those days. After the death of my mother, he returned to working on construction sites by day, a silent and withdrawn figure now, distanced from the rough camaraderie of his coworkers, but a hard worker. It was only in the evenings that he could retreat to his workbench in the basement and if not find ease, at least temporarily forget his grief through the use of his tools and the richly ornamented furniture he made.

One evening, when I was eleven, I closed my school-books, turned off the television set and went down the basement stairs to my father's workshop. My father looked up, but I said nothing. I sat down on a wooden stool in a corner, out of the way, hands folded on my lap – as quietly attentive as Nia in my dreams. My father regarded me for a long moment, then nodded slowly and returned to his work.

That was where the smell of the wood had first seduced me. That was where the familial bond was reknitted, where the distance between my father, myself and the memory of my mother was healed, not through words, but through the wood. Butternut, lacewood and mahogany. Bird's-eye maple, red birch and hickory. We worked there together, boy and man, side by side at the long bench, making the cabinets and cupboards that grew increasingly more in demand until my father could quit the chancy employment at construction sites and devote his days to cabinetmaking full time. Until I realized that it wasn't furniture that I wanted to wake from the wood, but music. I already played the guitar and, though not as well, a half-dozen other related stringed instruments; now, I slowly came to understand, I needed to learn how to actually build the objects that produced the sounds.

I could tell my father was torn between disappointment that I wanted to abandon the family business, and pride that I would continue to work in a demanding woodcraft. He was the one who contacted Janossy, a Hungarian luthier of his acquaintance, and arranged for me to apprentice under him.

I studied under Janossy for nine years, living on his farm outside the city, surrounded by wood – the forest, the log cabin, the weathered outbuildings, the firewood in winter, the shade trees in summer, the cedar pole fences, the apple orchard, and always the wood underhand in the workshop, sitting at the bench, hickory-handled tools, ryoba saw, slivers of wood curling up from the square blades of the chisels, sawdust underfoot.

I loved Janossy as I loved my father. They were of a kind; Old World men who took pride in their work, in the details. It was no surprise to me that this large and exuberant instrument-maker should also harbor the soul of a deep thinker, for in that he was like my father, too. But where Janossy shouted his emotions to the world in a voice bigger than life, my father kept his more private, and in that I took after him.

Now that I am a man myself, those that meet me will often describe me as solemn, thoughtful, even pensive, not realizing that the joy I gain from the details of my life lie inside me, like the smell of fresh-cut wood, instead of manifesting itself in boisterousness the way Janossy's did. I'm not an unhappy man. I'm not even particularly serious. I'm willing to accept everything at face value, by what it is rather than what it seems to be, which is, perhaps, why I think I'm able to handle my current predicament better than most might.

So, no. I don't panic, though panic's waiting for me just beyond the careful ordering of my thoughts as I finally lift my head to face the stranger in the mirror once more. I don't panic, though I can feel the hysteria in my chest, a swelling presence that pushes against my hard-held calm. I don't panic, but once I've assured myself again that I am in fact awake and not dreaming, I have to seriously consider the possibility that if I haven't gone crazy, then the world around me has.

I try to be objective as I study the stranger I've so literally become, but I find objectivity has slipped away. It's become a capricious fancy dancing just beyond reach, something easy to imagine but impossible to embrace. If this nightmare is real, then the reality I've always accepted as the foundation upon which the world is constructed is now proven to be a lie. The principles of what can and can't be no longer hold. Nothing can be taken at face value again. Nothing can be trusted. Because if this can happen to me, then anything can happen. And it means that fate, god, whatever it is that oversees the running of the world, is not merely unpredictable, but malevolent.

That realization leaves me unable to do anything but stare at the reflection. It renders me immobile until the panic claws up my throat, a stifled scream finally freed.

"Wake up, damn you!" I shout.

I pick up the closest thing at hand – a small Inuit-styled stone sculpture – and throw it at the mirror. The glass shatters, spraying across the top of the dresser and onto the rug on which I'm kneeling. The sculpture bounces once off the mahogany top, then hits the floor and rolls into a corner. I pay no attention to where it goes. All I can do is stare at the scattering of mirror shards closest to hand where my stranger's features are reflected back at me, ten, twenty times. Dozens of tiny strangers regard me. Their only resemblance to the man I know myself to be is the hysterical terror I can see twisting the features of each of their unfamiliar faces.

II • ZEFFY LACERDA

ZEFFY DIDN'T want to get up. The digital glow of her alarm clock told her it was just past four in the morning and while it might be June, you'd never know it by the cool breeze coming in from the window she'd forgotten to close when she went to bed. But after she woke from a second dream of searching desperately for a bathroom, she finally pushed back the covers and slipped out of bed. She fumbled in the dark until she found and put on her slippers and the oversize flannel shirt that served as her housecoat. Hugging herself to keep warm, she opened the door to her bedroom and stepped out into the hall.

The light coming down the passageway from the kitchen on her right caught her gaze. She blinked at it in surprise, wondering sleepily what Tanya was doing up at this hour.

But first things first, she told herself. Another few moments and she'd be mopping up the hall.

She turned away from the light and made her way to the bathroom. Afterward, she walked back past her bedroom door, down the hall to the kitchen. Tanya was slouched at the kitchen table, facing her own reflection in the darkened window across from her. She didn't appear to be looking at it or anything else in particular. Her dark eyes had an unfocused, distant aspect about them.

Zeffy paused in the doorway to study her, struck as always by just how pretty her roommate was. For all her diminutive size, Tanya had the elegant beauty of the fashion model and actress she'd once been, a delicate, waifish quality that in no way diminished her womanly attributes. Zeffy was a slender, five-two herself, an inch taller than Tanya, but beside Tanya she always felt overweight – a little too top-heavy, a little too wide in the hips – even though she weighed slightly less than she should for her height.

It didn't help that Tanya could wear anything and look good in it. Adding insult to injury, or perhaps it was the real reason for her inherent appeal, Tanya had also been naturally blessed with traits that most women had to struggle to attain: a glowing complexion, luminous dark brown eyes and silky hair that was always perfect and never lost its shine. Looking at her, you'd never know that she'd once been a junkie.

Zeffy herself had to put up with the odd mix made by the coppery cast of her skin set against violet eyes and a tousled blaze of thick red hair that fell in corkscrew curls past her shoulders. She was sure that her heart-shaped face, combined with the wide set of her eyes and her slight overbite, had cosmeticians wanting to throw their hands up in helplessness whenever she came for advice to a makeup counter – if only in their minds.

But tonight Tanya's glow was diminished, swallowed by the obvious downturn of her mood, and she was smoking – something she only did when she was upset or depressed. She didn't even seem to be aware of Zeffy's presence until Zeffy finally pushed a stubborn lock of red hair out of her face and stepped into the kitchen.

"Hey," Zeffy said, taking one of the empty chairs.

"Hey, yourself," Tanya replied, looking up. "You can't sleep either?"

"Actually," Zeffy said, "I was pleasantly lost in dreamland except I had a cup of tea before going to bed and the curse of the Lacerda bladder did the rest. I was actually considering having a pee in an alley off Lee Street at one point."

Tanya's eyebrows rose. "When was this?"

"In my dream," Zeffy explained.

Tanya smiled. "Oh, one of those."

"What about you?"

"Just thinking," Tanya told her.

"Deep thoughts?"

"Weepy thoughts."

"Johnny call you again?"

Tanya shook her head. "No. That's just the problem."

"You've got to put him behind you," Zeffy told her. "All he's ever brought you is trouble."

"I know that." Tanya sighed. A stream of blue-grey smoke escaped from between her lips. "At least my head knows it. The message just hasn't got through to my heart yet."

"He told you he'd call?"

Tanya nodded. "But it's not like you're thinking." She got a rueful look. "Though maybe you'll think this is worse. I lent him some money and—"

"Tanya!"

"His rent was due and he was going to pay me back this weekend. What was I supposed to do?"

Zeffy got a sinking feeling. "How much did you lend him?"

"Three hundred dollars. He *said* he'd pay me back."

"Tanya, *our* rent is due on Wednesday."

Tanya looked so miserable that, as soon as she'd spoken, Zeffy wished she'd kept her mouth shut.

"I know," Tanya said.

"Do you have any money?"

Tanya shook her head. "Not till payday."

Well, wasn't that just perfect, Zeffy thought. Johnny Devlin gets to keep his apartment while they were probably going to be out on the street in his place. She did a quick mental calculation, but already knew that she couldn't cover Tanya's share as well as her own.

"I'm so sorry," Tanya told her. "I really thought he'd pay me back."

"It's okay," Zeffy said. "You meant well. I'm not mad at you, but if I had Johnny's neck in my hands right now . . ."

Zeffy had often cursed the day that Johnny Devlin walked into Kathryn's Café, where she and Tanya worked as waitresses. They'd both been there for a few years now, ever since they'd finished college, appreciating the flexible hours which allowed them to have a little more freedom in their lives than they could find in the normal nine-to-five that most people had to face every day. It allowed them to "follow their own muses", as Wendy, one of the other waitresses, put it.

Even if Johnny had simply come in to have a meal, it would have been all right. They'd seen him out and about in the clubs, hanging around the Market and Gracie Street, just another good-looking guy with big dreams and not enough energy to actually do anything about them. He hadn't paid much attention to them, nor they to him. Same social circles, but a different coterie of friends. If he'd come in, had something to eat and then left, everything would have been different. Except he'd wanted to order something from the specials board and then he had to know who'd written it up.

There was a running joke at Kathryn's with the specials board. When they'd first started working at the café, Tanya had gotten stuck with the job of writing up the day's specials and bright though she was, she'd always been an atrocious speller. The joke had started with her "crab sandwishes" and degenerated from there to "pee soup" and the like. At first Kitty, the owner, had made an effort to proof the boards before they went up, but everyone got such a kick out of them, from the staff to the customers, that Tanya's misspellings had become a part of the café's tradition. It had gotten to the point where they'd sit around during breaks and after hours, thinking up deliberately funny variations on the next day's specials.

Tanya had gotten a lot of teasing about it at first, though not from Zeffy. After all, who was she to ridicule somebody else's spelling when her own father, in a moment of hippie bliss, had decided to name his daughter Zeffer after what he thought was the spelling for the literary term for the west wind? But it could have been worse. He could have named her after the French word for seal.

The night Johnny came in they'd been offering "breaded soul and Trench fries" for the day's special. After Tanya owned up to it, she and Johnny got to talking. Johnny was so taken by her that he poured on the charm as only he could and they were an item within a week. The honeymoon lasted for a couple of weeks after that and then their relationship went into the first of its many downward spirals. Johnny was never abusive, so far as Zeffy could tell; his main crime was inconsideration. Not being where he said he'd be. Not calling when he said he would. Shamelessly running after girls who, God knew why, mistook his innate cunning for intelligence, his ability to always land on his feet for charm.

"What are we going to do?" Tanya said.

"Besides thump him on the side of the head?"

"No, seriously."

"I am being serious."

"I mean about our rent."

Zeffy sighed. "I don't know. We'll think of something."

"I really screwed up this time, didn't I?"

"You're just too trusting," Zeffy told her. "Especially when it comes to him."

"I always think, This time he really means it. This time he's going to change."

Well, guess again, Zeffy thought. She watched Tanya light up yet another cigarette. She hated to see Tanya smoking, but it sure beat having her cranking junk into her veins again.

"We'll work something out," she said. "Maybe we can even get the money back from him. When was his rent due?"

"Last week."

"Well, scratch that idea. But we're not going to let him get away with this. We'll go by his place first thing in the morning – you're working the breakfast shift this week, aren't you?" When Tanya nodded, Zeffy went on. "Me, too. So we'll stop by on the way to work."

"You're not going to get all pissed off at him, are you?"

How someone could be as intelligent as Tanya, yet so blind when it came to Johnny Devlin, Zeffy just couldn't understand.

"What can you still see in him?" she asked. "What's he ever done for you but bring you grief?"

"I know. I guess I just feel sorry for him."

"That is not a good basis for a relationship," Zeffy said.

"I don't think there is such a thing as a good relationship."

"Sure there is. We just haven't found one yet, that's all. The thing to do is to be happy with yourself, with what's in your own life; then if a relationship comes along it's a bonus, something to enjoy instead of the thing your life revolves around."

"Easier said than done," Tanya said.

She lit a new cigarette from the one she was smoking, stubbing the old butt out in an already overflowing ashtray. Zeffy watched a thin thread of smoke rise from the old butt. By the time the top of the thread reached the light overhanging the table, the bottom of it had already come apart, disappearing like an unfulfilled dream.

Zeffy sighed. "This is true. I guess it's one of those things that only sound good in theory."

"Like being in love."

"*Are* you really in love with him?" Zeffy asked.

Tanya took a moment to consider the question.

"I don't think so," she said finally. "It's more like the equation's incomplete. It's not exactly over, but it's not really on anymore either."

"You know what I think?" Zeffy said.

Tanya shook her head.

"I think you should try to get some sleep and we'll work this all out tomorrow."

"You think I'm beng stupid, don't you?"

Zeffy smiled. "Stupid's such a harsh word. I think confused is more the way I'd describe you right now."

"I can be such an ass."

Zeffy's smile faded. "Don't beat up on yourself, Tanya. There's only one person to blame for this mess and we'll deal with him tomorrow morning."

"Okay." Tanya butted out her cigarette. "I'll try. But don't expect any miracles."

"No miracles," Zeffy agreed. "Just your money. And maybe an apology."

Tanya started to hum the old Buddy Holly hit "That'll Be the Day". When Zeffy flung a napkin at her and headed off to bed, she launched into the lyrics as only Tanya could – lines out of order, melody slightly off-key. Lying in her bed once more, Zeffy could still hear the song as Tanya washed up in the bathroom. She folded her pillow over her ears and tried in vain to get to sleep, but it was only when Tanya finally broke off singing and went into her own bedroom that Zeffy thought she could. She burrowed deeper under the covers, then sat up in frustration.

"Damn," she muttered.

She had to go to the bathroom again.

III • MAX

I DON'T wake up.

I don't wake up because I'm not dreaming. I know for sure when I finally get up from the floor. Using the dresser as leverage, I push myself to my feet and immediately cut my foot on one of the mirror shards that scattered across the rug earlier. I sit down on the edge of the bed to assess the damage, lifting my foot to my knee. The cut's on my instep and doesn't appear to be deep, but I have trouble concentrating on it. Everything's wrong: the unfamiliar shape of the foot, its toes, the ankles, the calf resting on a knee bonier than I know mine to be, the fingers of the hand holding the foot in place.

Don't, I tell myself. Don't look at the differences, don't even think about them.

But it's impossible not to. I force myself to study the cut, wiping blood away from it with my finger. A drop falls free, staining the beige carpet underfoot. I don't look at it. Instead, I lift my finger to my lips. The faint metallic taste of the blood and the ebbing pain of the cut are what convince me to accept that this is real. That I'm not dreaming. That impossible though it might be, I'm inhabiting someone else's body, bleeding somebody else's blood onto the carpet.

I get up and go looking for a bathroom. Avoiding the mirror, I find a box of bandages in the medicine cabinet and take one out of it. I lower the toilet seat cover and sit down, wash the cut, dry it with toilet paper, cover it with the bandage. When I finally dare a look at the mirror, the stranger is still there on the other side of the glass, putting a lie to who I think I am.

Maybe my memories are the lie, I find myself thinking.

Maybe I have a mental disorder, some sort of schizophrenia. Maybe I suffer from multiple personalities and live any number of different lives.

Then I study my hands. These aren't the hands of a woodworker. There are no calluses on these hands from using tools, no cuts or scrapes from all the little unavoidable accidents that happen in even the most organized workshop. They aren't even the hands of a musician – at least not one who plays a stringed instrument. The tips of the fingers are as devoid of calluses as the rest of the hands are.

But *I* know how to work wood and play an instrument. The memories, the knowledge of my craft and tools, are too clear for me to be imagining them. No one could construct an entire lifetime the way I hold the past in my head. No one could make that much up, with so much detail.

"I can't deal with this," I say.

I put a hand to my mouth, startled by the sound, by the stranger's voice that echoes in the confines of the bathroom. Panic arises again, shortening my breath, tightening my chest, making me dizzy, but this time I fight it off successfully.

I have to adapt to the situation. I tell myself. I have to keep a clear head so that I can find out what was going on, so that I can get my own life back. I think of something my father told me once. "We're an adaptable species, Max. That's how we survive. We can put up with the most horrendous, disorienting experiences and pretend they're normal, just to survive. We might not like where we are, or what's happening to us, but we deal with it. God knows, we even get used to it. Those that don't, don't survive."

I suppose it's true. It's not something I ever thought much about – never had the need to. But my father was right. I have to learn to deal with this. Or at least try. But I'll never get used to it. Not and stay sane. I can only deal with it as a stopgap measure, as a way to get back the life that belongs to me.

Determined to do something constructive, I leave the bathroom and go looking for something to tell me whose apartment this is, whose body I'm borrowing.

There isn't much to the apartment. I flick on lights as I explore, recognizing nothing I see. Besides the bedroom and the bathroom I just left, there's a living room and kitchen. Going through the fridge and kitchen cupboards, I have to assume the apartment's owner ate most of his meals out, because there's nothing much here. He also appears to be a serious movie buff, since the only decorations are movie posters, even here in the kitchen.

I go on into the living room and take in its spartan furnishings. An inexpensive Ikea couch and chair set, pine frames, striped blue cushions. A pine coffee table. An entertainment center holding a fairly impressive stereo, VCR and television set. The center itself is made of pressboard, covered with a black veneer. There are no books, but plenty of videotapes. The titles of the movies, like the posters on the walls, run mostly towards action/adventure and horror. I sift through the scattering of CDs on the coffee table. The majority are contemporary heavy metal with a few old dinosaur bands thrown in for good measure: Aerosmith. Pink Floyd. ZZ Top.

I'm not learning much, I realize as I go back into the kitchen, except that the owner of this apartment and I have very little in common. I find an empty paper bag under the sink and take it back into the bedroom, where I fill it with the broken glass from the mirror. The Inuit statue was made of soapstone and it's broken, too, so I add the pieces to the glass already in the bag. The statue was the only incongruity.

I know next to nothing of the apartment's occupant, but it doesn't seem to go with the rest of the man's taste. Must have been a gift.

I leave the bedroom and put the bag of glass beside the garbage under the sink. That task completed, I begin to explore the bedroom.

The closet seems to belong to two different people. Office wear and casual, I decide. One side holds a half-dozen dark suits, white shirts and ties, the other casual shirts with a stack of blue jeans folded on the floor. Suddenly conscious of my relative nudity – all I'm wearing are the boxer shorts I woke up in – I take a pair of jeans from the top of the stack. They look too small, but I try them on anyway. Naturally, they're a perfect fit. Returning to the dresser, I find a white T-shirt in one of its drawers, stuffed in amongst a tight wad of underwear, socks and other T-shirts, and put it on as well.

Since I only ever wear socks with my cowboy boots in the winter, I close the drawer and pick up the pair of sneakers that are standing beside the bed. As I sit down to put them on, my gaze falls on what I've been looking for all along: a worn brown leather wallet that's lying with a pile of loose change beside the digital alarm clock.

I finish tying my laces, then pick up the wallet. The first card I take out is a driver's license. The familiar stranger I keep seeing in mirrors looks out at me from the laminated photograph on the license. I read the name: John Devlin. Thirty-one years old. The address is on Grasso Street, just off Palm. A hop, skip and a jump north of the heart of the Combat Zone, which makes sense, considering the red neon sign outside the window.

The other identification confirms the first piece. There's no automobile license or insurance, so it seems that Devlin doesn't own a car, but what is here all bears the same name. Credit cards. A birth certificate. Odd to carry that around. At his age, Devlin wasn't likely to get carded going into a bar. There's seventy-six dollars in cash. Some scraps of paper with unfamiliar names on them, accompanied by phone numbers. First names, all women.

So who are you, John Devlin? Did you do this to me, or are you waking up somewhere, feeling just as confused as I am?

Waking up somewhere . . .

The implications of that hit me. Was this John Devlin sitting in my apartment, going through my wallet right now, trying to figure out what had happened to him? It makes sense – as much as anything can in this situation. Surely the phenomenon is restricted to only the two of us. Surely the whole world hasn't woken up inhabiting somebody else's body . . . has it?

I glance at the clock, then laugh at myself. What does it matter if it's just past five in the morning? I'm not about to stand on protocol at a moment like this.

Going back to the closet, I take a sports jacket off a hanger and put it on, stuffing the wallet into my pocket. Like the jeans, it looked too small, but it's a perfect fit. So I'm ready to go and then the doorbell rings.

I jump, startled at the sound, not even recognizing it for a long moment. Disorientation hits me again. I've been feeling guilty the whole time I've been snooping through the apartment. I know it makes no sense, given my circumstances, but I can't help it. Now I feel caught. Trapped.

When the doorbell sounds again, I'm expecting it, but no more willing to answer it than the first time it rang. What would I say to whoever's at the door? How can I tell if I'm even supposed to know the person?

Whoever's standing out in the hall is leaning on the bell now. The sound of its ringing goes through the apartment in a continuous, irritating peal and I get the feeling that it's not anyone that John Devlin would want to see either.

I go out into the living room and stand in front of the door, not knowing what to do. There's no peephole, so I can't even see who's out there. Not without opening the door.

When the bell finally stops, the silence seems infinite.

"Bastard!" I hear a woman say on the other side of the door, her voice muffled but still clear enough to make out.

I step closer, leaning my head near the wood to hear what else she might say. She kicks the door, making me jump again.

"I'll bet he's in there," the woman goes on, obviously talking to someone with her. "I'll bet he's standing on the other side of this door right now, laughing at us." The door shakes as she kicks it again. She raises her voice. "Aren't you, Johnny?"

I don't dare breathe. The time might come when I'll have to interact with Devlin's friends and be forced to pretend I'm Devlin – something I'll have to do or they'll think I'm crazy. But there's no way I'm going to deal with whatever woman problems Devlin might have as well.

These people . . . why don't they just go away?

But the woman at the door doesn't appear at all ready to give up. I back away from the door when she gives it another kick.

IV • TANYA BURNS

"MAYBE THIS isn't such a good idea," Tanya said.

She felt really uncomfortable and kept looking up and down the hall, waiting for someone to yell at them as Zeffy kicked at Johnny's door. Zeffy had a lot of endearing qualities, but keeping her temper in check wasn't one of them. Nor was patience.

Tanya touched Zeffy's arm. "Let's come back after work."

"No way," Zeffy told her, obviously in high confrontation mode. "I'll be damned if I'll let him think he's getting away with it this time."

"He's probably asleep."

"With all the lights on?"

Tanya shrugged. "So maybe's he's not home. Let's just go."

"Uh-uh," Zeffy said. "If I had to get up a half-hour early to get here, he can at least have the decency to bloody well get up and tell us he hasn't got your money."

"But we already *know* that . . ."

"Oh, please," Zeffy said.

She turned her attention back to the door, arms akimbo. Drawing back her foot, she gave the door a good kick with her combat boot, adding another dent to the ones she'd already put there in the cheap wood.

"Zeffy, don't," Tanya cried.

"Don't what? If he's not there, what does it matter what I do or say? And if he is, maybe it's time he learned that he can't smooth-talk his way out of everything. Besides, I think he's there." Bang. She kicked the door again. "Why else

26

would his lights be on? Isn't that right, Johnny? Are you getting off on this?"

The door took another thump. All Tanya wanted to do was leave. She appreciated what Zeffy was trying to do, but it was just no good with Johnny. He operated on his own time and besides, Zeffy was probably going to put her foot right through the door any minute and then where would they be? Johnny'd probably sue them in small claims – or his landlord would. She was considering leaving on her own and hoping Zeffy would follow when she heard a door open down the hall and her worst fear was realized.

She turned to look at the man standing there in his underwear – boxing shorts and muscle shirt, neither of which looked particularly appealing on him because he was grossly overweight. But big. And angry. His broad face had gone red and he was glaring at them.

"You want to shut the hell up?" he said. "People are trying to sleep."

"Don't get me started on you," Zeffy told the man.

Tanya could tell that all fired up as she was at the moment, Zeffy was beyond any sense of propriety – or common sense. This was *so* embarrassing.

"Started with what?" the man asked, the threat obvious in his voice.

"Zeffy . . ." Tanya tried.

"Okay, okay," Zeffy said. "Listen, I'm sorry we got you up, mister, but we've got a problem here."

"Only problem I see is you and the noise you're making."

"So we're going already," Zeffy told him, mimicking his voice. "That make you happy?" She turned back to the door. "But we'll be back, Johnny," she added, and gave it another kick.

"That does it," the man said.

He came barreling down the hall and before either of them knew what to do, he'd grabbed Zeffy by the shoulder and shoved her up against the wall.

"Punks like you need to be taught a little respect," he said.

"Hey," Zeffy said, pawing at his arm. "I said we were going."

She tried to get out from under his grip but he shoved her again, hard enough to make her head thump against the plaster. Tanya winced. That had to have hurt.

"You leave her alone!" she cried.

The man turned to look at her, holding Zeffy pressed against the wall with one hand on her back.

"Or you'll do what?" he asked.

Before Tanya could think of something conciliatory to defuse the situation, Zeffy kicked the man in the back of the knee with the heel of her boot. His leg gave out, making him stumble to one side, against the wall. This time it was his head that banged on the plaster. By the time he turned from the wall, Zeffy had scooted over to where Tanya was standing. The man's face got redder, his hands clenched into fists.

Oh shit, Tanya thought. This was way out of hand.

"Okay, little lady," the man said. There was a mean glint in his eyes now that made Tanya shiver. "I guess I'm going to have to teach you a serious lesson."

There was nowhere to run. The hall behind them ended in a closed door and the man was blocking their escape to the stairwell. Tanya could hardly breathe, she was so scared. When she glanced at Zeffy, she saw that her roommate was still mad – but there was fear in her eyes, too. Still, Zeffy was never one to give up.

"Look," she tried. "Why don't we just all calm down—"

She had to duck to one side as the man swung at her. The sudden movement made her lose her balance. Tanya tried to stop her from falling, but somehow they both ended up on the floor in a tangle of limbs with the man looming over them.

"So you like to kick people, do you?" he said, drawing a foot back.

V • MAX

I CAN'T catch everything that's being said – not without putting my ear to the door and risk being deafened as the woman named Zeffy keeps kicking at the door. Zeffy. What kind of a name is that? But I hear enough to realize that the two women aren't friends of Devlin's. All the more reason to pretend I'm not here.

I try to remember if there's a fire escape outside any of the apartment's windows. Discretion being the better part of valor and all, I figure the best solution at this point is to find an alternative exit and leave the women out in the hall to direct their anger at an empty apartment. It seems like a terrific idea until I hear a man's voice, telling the women something I can't make out. That's followed by a sound I can't identify, a kind of scuffling, and then the hollow thump of something hitting a wall.

Not something, I realize, but someone. It's not my business, but I can't ignore what's going on now. I've got no idea what any of this is about, who's to blame, but I know I can't leave the women out there on their own – not if they're being assaulted. So much for keeping a low profile, I think.

I take a deep breath and open the door. It's gotten more

out of hand than I'd thought, but my sudden appearance freezes the participants in mid-tussle. The women lie in a struggling heap on the floor, trying to disentangle themselves from each other as the man aims a kick at them. Three faces turn to me, none of them familiar. For a long moment I can't take my gaze from the redhead – I've never seen such violet eyes before – then I step out into the hall, in between the women and the man threatening them. The man has a mean look in his eyes that I've seen before on other faces. He's enjoying this – or at least he was until I interrupted him.

"Let's all just calm down," I say, startled again at the unfamiliar sound of my voice.

"Look, buddy," the man begins. "If you can't keep your girlfriends from—"

I fix a smile on my lips. Holding up a hand, I concentrate on maintaining a sense of calm, hoping to forestall the man from working himself up any more than he already has. In his present state, he won't need much of an excuse to just start in swinging.

"I'm sorry," I say. I keep my voice pitched low, my stance nonthreatening. "I was sleeping and I didn't realize there was anything going on out here until just a moment ago."

I turn slightly to help the women to their feet without looking away from the man. The dark-haired woman takes my hand, but she's quick to let go once she's standing. The redhead refuses my help. They're all looking at me a little oddly, which doesn't surprise me. They obviously expected me to know them. I wish I could play the game out convincingly, but I'm not that good an actor and I don't know my part. I can't hide my lack of recognition. I wonder which one of them is Zeffy and what their relationship to Devlin is. The man isn't too hard to figure out. He obviously came from the apartment down the hall where a door's still standing ajar.

"Let's just call it a night, okay?" I say.

The calming effect I'm aiming for seems to be working. The red flush of anger is fading from the man's face and he's beginning to look a little sheepish.

"I'm a working stiff," he says. "I need my sleep."

I nod. "And no one meant to disturb you. We'll keep it down, I assure you."

"Yeah, you'd better do that," the man says, regaining some of his bluster. He rolls his shoulders and I expect him to start flexing his muscles next, but he backs off instead and slowly makes his way back to his apartment.

I wait until the man has closed his door before returning my attention to the two women once more. Now what do I do?

"'I assure you'?" the redhead says, looking at me like I've grown a third eye. "Well, doesn't that have a nice ring to it."

I don't know what to say. I step back from the doorway to Devlin's apartment.

"I suppose you'll want to come inside," I say, ushering them in.

Neither of them moves toward the door.

"I . . . I think we should go," the dark-haired woman says.

The redhead stares at me as though she's trying to figure something out. The other woman looks like she's on the verge of tears, but there's something else in her eyes as well, a whisper of fear that makes me feel a little sick. She's a beautiful woman. There's something almost angelic about her, which makes the fear I can see in her seem all the more out of place. Had the man whose body I'm occupying treated her badly? And just how badly? I can't see any bruises. She's wearing a loose-fitting jacket over a pair of dark slacks. Who knows what they're hiding.

The redhead puts a comforting hand on the other woman's arm.

"We'll go," she says to her friend. "But not just yet." She straightens her shoulders and faces me, head on. "First we want the money you owe Tanya."

By the way the redhead glances at her companion as she speaks, I assume the dark-haired woman is Tanya. Which makes the redhead Zeffy. I can't get over her amazing eyes. They're like bright violet amethysts, made more startling by the way they stand out against the slightly copper cast of her skin and contrasting sharply with the flood of her red hair. She doesn't have the same immediate beauty as Tanya – her appeal comes from deeper inside her – but I feel a surge of attraction toward her that I don't feel toward her friend. I haven't had this kind of instant reaction to a woman in a long time. Unfortunately, the appreciation obviously isn't being reciprocated.

"Earth to asshole," she says. "Are you still there?"

I blink. "I'm sorry. What money was this?"

Zeffy gives me a disgusted look. "Jesus, you really are a piece of work, aren't you?"

You're blowing it, I tell myself. Considering what I have to work with, it isn't really surprising, but I try to recover.

"No," I say. "I know the money you're talking about. It was kind of, uh, Tanya, to be as patient as she's been. I mean, you've been kind," I add, managing to look away from Zeffy and include the other woman in the conversation. "What I was trying to say was, how much was it that I owe you? I, uh, I've forgotten the amount."

They're both looking at me strangely – Zeffy's confusion colored with irritation, Tanya's with hurt. The whisper of fear I saw in Tanya's eyes is growing. She tugs at Zeffy's sleeve.

"I just want to go," she says. Her voice is small, as though the words are choking in her throat.

Zeffy nods, but doesn't look at her. "It was three hundred dollars," she tells me.

I remember the money I counted in Devlin's wallet. "I've got – I think it was seventy-six dollars."

"That'll do – for starters."

I pull out the wallet and hand over Devlin's money. "I'm sorry I don't have the rest of it yet."

"When will you have it?" Zeffy asks.

"I . . ." Tell her anything, I think. "In a week?"

"Zeffy, please," Tanya says.

Zeffy's features are noticeably warmer when she turns to her friend. "We're going now," she says. She stuffs the money in the pocket of her jacket. The coldness returns to her eyes as soon as she looks back at me. "We'll be back for the rest."

"In a week," I repeat.

I feel safe with that time-frame. This is Devlin's problem, so let him deal with it. I can't imagine the situation I'm in lasting out the day, let alone dragging on for a week. Though I don't mind having had the chance to meet this Zeffy. I like her spunk, the way she won't back down, not to the man in the hall earlier and not to me now. I just wish I'd been able to meet her under different circumstances, that I could be myself and not have her so angry with me – or rather, so angry with Devlin. I'm just the one who has to stand in for the jerk.

This is one you owe me, Devlin, I think.

"You've got your week," Zeffy tells me. "Your tab's now standing at two-hundred-and-twenty-four dollars."

"Right."

"We should be charging you interest."

"Whatever."

She looks at me as though she's just come upon a bug, a nightcrawler skittering around the rim of her bathtub, a cockroach that scurried deeper into her bedclothes as she turned back her bed. I want to say something, to explain that I'm not this John Devlin and would never treat anybody the way he'd obviously been treating them, but what can I say that won't make me sound like a lunatic? So I stand there, accepting her disapproval in silence. Finally, she shakes her head, speaking a volume of censure in that simple movement. Taking Tanya by the arm, she leads her off down the hall.

I watch them go. Not until they've turned at the stairwell and are lost from sight do I step back inside the apartment.

Well, I think as I close the door, that went really well, didn't it?

VI • ZEFFY

BY THE time Zeffy got her down the stairs and outside Johnny's building, tears were streaming down Tanya's cheeks and she was shaking so hard that she couldn't walk on her own. This has got to be the end of it, Zeffy thought as she steered her roommate to a seat on the curb and sat down beside her, arm around her shoulders.

Johnny'd really blown it this time. Blown it big time. She didn't know what he'd thought he was playing at, acting like he didn't know them. Just mind games, she guessed. Didn't have to make any sense, did it? She'd long since given up trying to figure him out, why he was the way he was, why he did the things he did. But maybe now Tanya would finally see what a shit the guy was – understand it with her heart as well as her head. All Zeffy could think was, it was about time. Her only regret was that it had to leave Tanya so torn up to get to this realization.

She'd been there for her roommate during the countless bouts of misery that Johnny had put her through in the past and it had always frustrated her how Tanya couldn't just put the guy behind her. Love surely was blind, more was the pity. But that frustration had never stopped her from offering what comfort she could. It was no different now, sitting here with Tanya on a Grasso Street curb at five-thirty in the morning.

She gave Tanya a comforting hug, but Tanya only burrowed her face deeper into Zeffy's shoulder, crying harder, until Zeffy began to grow alarmed. She hadn't seen Tanya like this in years, not since the nightmare they'd had to live through when Tanya was kicking her habit.

"It's okay," she soothed. "I know it hurts, but at least it's over now. You know where you stand with the jerk."

Tanya finally lifted her head. Gulping for air, she turned her face toward Zeffy, eyes glistening and puffy, nose red, makeup running in dark streaks down her cheeks.

"That . . . that wasn't Johnny . . ." she managed.

"I know he was acting weird," Zeffy said, "but— "

Tanya shook her head, the anguish plain. "He didn't even *know* us!"

Zeffy sighed. "No. He *acted* liked he didn't know us. There's a difference. He was just playing some kind of a mind game, that's all."

"No . . . nobody's that good an actor," Tanya said.

"What other explanation is there?" Zeffy asked.

Though she could see how Tanya had been taken in. He'd done one hell of a job of it, hadn't he? She never knew he had it in him. If Johnny could ever learn to channel that kind of talent and energy into something positive, he might actually be able to get somewhere for a change.

She searched in her pockets for a tissue and found a wadded-up Kleenex near the bottom that was still unused. Passing it to Tanya, she waited as Tanya dabbed at her eyes and then used it to blow her nose.

"It . . . it's like he's got amnesia all of a sudden," Tanya said. "Like he hit his head and he doesn't know who he is anymore – or at least doesn't know us." She got a funny look on her face. "Or like one of those awful movies he likes so much," Tanya went on. "You know . . . where the aliens take over your brain and . . . and pretend to be human?"

Well, at least she was talking, Zeffy thought. Not making any sense, but she was talking.

"Think about what you're saying," she said. "That kind of thing isn't even remotely possible."

"I know. I guess. But what if – what if it was?"

"Oh please. This is not *Invasion of the Johnny Snatchers*. It's just Johnny Devlin being an asshole, end of story."

"Johnny Snatchers?" Tanya repeated.

Zeffy tried, but she couldn't stifle the giggle that came when she heard her own words echoed back to her. If only aliens had snatched him, she thought. Tanya gave her a look – half sad, half stern – but Zeffy laughing was contagious. Tanya was soon giggling herself, although there was a slightly hysterical note to her amusement that made Zeffy feel uneasy.

"This is just what he wanted," she said when she'd gotten

her own laughter under control. "To have us sitting here questioning our sanity. Don't ask me why."

Tanya nodded, serious again herself. "I guess. But it wasn't just what he was saying, it was everything. How he moved, the look in his eyes, the way he spoke. I know him way better than you, Zeffy, and this was too good to be acting. Looking at him today it was like Johnny's not home anymore."

Zeffy knew what she meant. Johnny's performance had been uncanny in its attention to detail. But that didn't change anything. There were things that were possible, and things that weren't, never mind what some of their friends believed. Like Jilly, who also worked at the café with them. Jilly cheerfully accepted everything from fairies to Elvis sightings – "But what if he's not dead, Zeffy? What if he really did fake it just to get away from all the pressure and bullshit?" She could just imagine Jilly's excitement when Tanya told her about this. They'd be discussing it all day at the restaurant.

"Except it's really not possible," she said to Tanya.

"I know that. It's just . . ."

"Just what?" Zeffy asked. Tanya looked so fragile and lost that she wanted to gather her up like a mother would her child and protect her from the travails of the world.

Tanya shrugged. "I don't know. I guess it creeped me out at first, but then I got to thinking, maybe this guy'd like me better. Maybe he'd, you know, treat me better."

Zeffy's heart went out to her. "Oh, Tanya. There's other guys out there for you. Nice guys who'll treat you decently."

"I suppose. It's just, there's a lot about Johnny that I really like."

"Well, of course you do."

"And I was thinking," Tanya went on. "What if he's,

you know, sick or something? What if he's got one of those multiple personality disorders, where he's got like all these different people living inside him? They'd still be like him, wouldn't they, except some of them'd be nicer."

"And some could be worse."

"Well, not necessarily."

Zeffy sighed. "You know what you're doing, don't you? You're making excuses for him again."

There was that look in Tanya's eyes again, frail and lost, the hurt so plain it broke your heart.

"Look," Zeffy said. She took Tanya's hand and gave it a squeeze. "I don't want to live your life for you, but don't you think you deserve a bit of happiness by now? You know you're never going to find it with Johnny – you've told me that yourself a hundred times. If you don't want to take my advice, then take your own. How many times haven't you told me that you'd just like to forget him and get on with your life?"

Tanya nodded. "Lots, I guess."

"So screw Johnny and do it this time."

"You really hate him, don't you?"

A small smile touched Zeffy's lips. "Hate's such an all-encompassing kind of a word. And it makes it sound as though he has a lot more impact on my life than he does. Let's just say I wish we'd never met him."

The smile Tanya gave her in return was smaller and sadder.

"I guess that's something we can both agree on," she said.

Zeffy gave her hand another squeeze, then stood up, helping Tanya to her feet. They both ignored the apartment behind them, the lights all still shining in the windows.

"You think you'll be able to go to work?" Zeffy asked.

"Oh God." Tanya dabbed at her eyes with the small ball that the tissue had become. "I must look awful."

"We'll sneak you in the back and you can fix yourself up in the washroom. No one's going to know."

"I suppose."

Tanya studied the wadded tissue, then stuck it in her pocket. From another pocket she took out a packet of cigarettes.

"Tanya," Zeffy began, thinking, That's not going to help.

Tanya paused as she was about to light up. Her gaze met Zeffy's and Zeffy could see the pain still darkening her roommate's eyes.

"Never mind," Zeffy said. "Come on, let's go."

She stole a glance at Johnny's apartment as they started off down the block, heading for the subway station at Perry Street. There was no one at the window. She wasn't sure how she was going to manage it, but she made a silent promise to herself that she was never going to let Johnny hurt Tanya again.

VII • MAX

THE ENCOUNTER with Zeffy and Tanya upsets me more than I think it did at first. I'd been ready, once I'd given them a chance to go their own way, to set off for my own place and deal with whatever was waiting for me there. But after taking a look out the living-room window and seeing the two of them sitting down there on the curb, Zeffy with her arm around Tanya, comforting the dark-haired girl as she wept, all I can do is slump down on Devlin's uncomfortable couch instead. I stare blankly at the poster for some science-fiction movie on the wall across from me. I can't tell what the movie's called because the text is all in Italian, but it has something to do with a robot and a woman with enormous breasts.

Really, the poster barely registers. I have more immediate concerns than Johnny Devlin's lack of taste. What if there's no way to reverse whatever's happened to me? What if this is my life now: a borrowed body, the depressing tatters of somebody else's life – somebody I'm sure I won't like if I ever get the chance to meet him. What if there's no going back to who I am? What if I'm trapped like this forever?

I try to contain it, but the fear keeps returning to me. It's like a wild dog circling its prey, a constant threat. The panic I've been successfully suppressing cruises in its wake, waiting for its own opportunity to strike.

I've never had anyone look at me the way those women did. The disgust in Zeffy's eyes, the hurt in Tanya's. Lord knows I'm not perfect, but I've lived a mild kind of life to date, without a whole lot of emotional upheaval. I have only one great passion and that's my work. I have no vices. I have no strong political or religious beliefs, I'm not given to causes, and I've always treated people the way I'd want them to treat me. Decently, with a little distance. It means I have far more acquaintances than I have real friends. But it also means that I don't have any enemies either – at least none of whom I'm aware. The strongest emotion aimed in my general direction has been a kind of greedy lust, and that's for the instruments I make, not for me.

I've never been given to brooding either, but right now I find it frighteningly easy to let the depression I'm slipping into simply take me away. Because really, what's the point in struggling? What's happened to me is without precedent – at least in real life. I'm not sure about fiction because I don't read much of it, but the premise has shown up in movies. Daughters inadvertently switching places with their mothers. Fathers with their sons. And then there was that film where the old man stole a young woman's life away when he kissed her on her wedding day. I can't remember the name of the movie, but I think Meg Ryan was in it.

I give Devlin's videos a sour look. He'd probably know.

In movies, everything's resolved so easily: setup, an hour or so of struggle, ups and downs, a few jokes, a few tears, and then the quick wrap-up just before the credits run. Everything back to normal. But real life doesn't work the way Hollywood depicts it. Most people's lives aren't made up of stories with easily perceived beginnings and endings. Most people have to just muddle through as best they can, coming in somewhere in the middle, leaving before the outcome's known, half the time not even aware that they're in a story.

And in real life, people don't wake up in somebody else's body either.

I sit up suddenly when I realize what I'm doing. I'm giving up without a struggle. I've never been a quitter and the easy way I've let myself fall into that kind of thinking is disturbing. I hold a hand up before my eyes. They're still unfamiliar. I still can't relate to their being attached to his body.

But when the switch was made, what else did I step into? Just Devlin's body and the baggage of his life, or pieces of who Devlin is as well? Does the physical mind follow certain patterns that hold even when someone else is using them? If Devlin is given to quick depressions does it follow that now I will, too? And what about these hands – narrow, long fingers, lots of flexibility, but soft, unfamiliar with physical work. Can I still build instruments with them, can I still play guitar, or is that something I have to teach them how to do all over again?

When I feel myself sinking back into depression, I force myself to stand up and get moving. I take a last look around the apartment, then head for the front door. Just before I step out into the hall, I pat my jacket pocket the way I always do when I leave my own apartment. There's no jingle of keys.

Wouldn't that be perfect? I think. To lock myself out. Because while it's true that I'd just as soon never see this apartment again, I have to be realistic it might be all I have to return to. Given the choice, I'd prefer to sleep here than to make do with the sidewalk or a bus shelter.

I remember seeing a set of keys on the night table where I found the wallet and change. Returning to the bedroom, I pick them up, then pause for a moment. I haven't looked in the night-table drawer yet. Sitting on the edge of the bed, I open the drawer and find it a jumbled mess, mostly stuffed with stacks of loose papers and envelopes. I sort through them, laying each one on the bed beside me after I've glanced at it. Unpaid utility bills. Credit-card statements, the cards charged to the max. A bankbook with a balance of twelve dollars and forty-five cents. A pink slip. I study the latter more closely. Devlin had been working as a salesman in a computer store up until two weeks ago when he'd been fired.

What a loser, I think as I add the pink slip to the rest of the litter of Devlin's life I've already taken from the drawer. It really doesn't add up to much. When I put what this tells me about Devlin together with the reaction I got from Zeffy and Tanya earlier, I realize that, unlike me, Devlin doesn't have much of a life to return to. I wonder if Devlin ever thought about that. Probably not – but that makes me stop to consider my own life, how easily it can be summed up. I have to ask myself, am I really much better?

What do I have except for my work? Not much. If I was to disappear – or if Devlin was to leave the city in my body – who'd miss me? People depending on me for instrument repairs or advice. My waiting list for guitars. The woman whose mandolin I'm working on at the moment. And that's about it.

I shake my head. Don't think about it, I tell myself. It's just the depression talking. Only I'm not so sure.

I stuff the papers all back into the drawer. I'm about to shut it when I notice the edge of a small address book sticking up in one corner. I take it out and leaf through the pages. You could say this much for Devlin, I think as I look for the names of the women who'd come by earlier. At least the man has neat handwriting.

I don't find Zeffy's name anywhere in the book, but there's a Tanya listed under the Bs for Burns. So she's the one who has the relationship with Devlin. That makes sense, considering her reaction out in the hall and later on the curb. Zeffy would be *her* friend then, rather than Devlin's.

That makes me feel better, knowing that Zeffy at least had the taste not to be in a relationship with the sort of person Devlin was proving to be. I can't figure out why Tanya would either, but that doesn't seem very important. I hesitate a moment, then stick the address book in my pocket and shut the drawer.

Back at the front door of the apartment I test the keys until I find the one that fits. I drop the key chain into my pocket. Stepping out into the hall, I shut the door behind me, checking to make sure that the lock has caught. It isn't until I'm outside on Grasso Street that I realize I don't have any money except for the handful of change I took from the night table. I gave all of Devlin's folding money to Zeffy and I can't even go to a bank machine with one of his cards because there's no credit left on them.

I count the change, but there's only eighty-six cents. Not enough for the subway or a bus. Certainly not enough for a cab. That means I have to hike clear across town.

Sighing, I start off. I make a point of it to avoid looking at my reflection in store windows as I pass.

VIII • ZEFFY

IN THE end it wasn't Tanya who told Jilly about the morning's odd encounter with Johnny, but Zeffy. She and Jilly had decided to get some fresh air for their midmorning break and had walked down the short alleyway behind the café, then struck out across a small strip of lawn to where they could sit by the river. Dangling their legs over the slow-moving water, they munched on apples rescued from a crumble the cook was planning for the lunch dessert menu and shared a companionable silence.

That was one of the things Zeffy liked about Jilly. She was easy to talk to, but unlike too many people Zeffy knew, she never seemed to feel the need to fill a quiet moment with some inane comment, simply to keep a conversation going.

They didn't see much of each other outside of work, mostly because they ran with different crowds. Jilly was older than Zeffy by a dozen years or so, but she always seemed younger. It wasn't so much because of the way Jilly acted as that she'd managed to maintain the youthful exuberance that most people, even in Zeffy's own twenty-something age group, appeared to outgrow – along, Zeffy often thought, with the ideals and dreams that were so clear when you were young, but that the world inexorably wore down to such an extent that if you stumbled across them in an old diary or a scrapbook, you'd barely recognize them anymore.

Jilly dressed young, too – or perhaps timelessly was a better way to put it, with her penchant for loose clothing and clunky shoes. "I go in and out of style" was how she put it in her usual offhand manner. With her, the scruffy look simply added to her charm. She was slender, with a thick tangle of brown hair often piled carelessly on the top of her head, and pale blue eyes, electric as sapphires. A half-inch or so shorter than Zeffy, she was an enchanting combination of diminutive flower fairy and street gamine.

She was also a fairly successful artist, showing up for work half the time with paint all dried on her fingers or speckled in her hair, and she'd been at Kathryn's forever, or so it sometimes seemed. Zeffy could remember seeing her there when she and Tanya were still attending nearby Butler University. With her work hanging in galleries all over town, she didn't really seem to still need to work at the café, but when Zeffy asked her about it once, Jilly explained, "I get a little claustro, cooped up in my studio for too long. This gives me an excuse to get away. And besides, I like meeting people." Which was an understatement if Zeffy had ever heard one. Sometimes she thought Jilly knew every second person in the city – and if not them, then certainly their brother or their sister.

"Remember Sophie?" Jilly asked out of the blue.

She glanced at Zeffy, so Zeffy nodded. Sophie was an artist friend of Jilly's she'd met at the opening of a show that Sophie, Jilly and some other women had put on at The Green Man. It had dealt with child abuse and made a great impact on Zeffy at the time, particularly because one of the artists, an abused street kid that Jilly had taken under her wing, had died just before the show.

"Well, she's into another one of her serial dreams," Jilly went on. "This time she's met a kind of travel agent in that dream city of hers, this woman named Ashling who runs a bureau of dreams where you can go in and reserve a dream to wherever you want to go." Jilly laughed. "So long as the place isn't overbooked, that is."

Zeffy laughed with her. "So naturally you want to go."

"Naturally. You, of course, being the pragmatist you are, can't accept the idea. I'm sure, so you'd never even get in the door, little say get to take the trip, but I'm holding out for a chance myself."

"I'm only a pragmatist compared to you. Everybody else I know thinks I'm flaky."

"Yes, well," Jilly said. "There's that. Anyway, I try to will myself to meet this Ashling every time I go to sleep, but nothing ever happens."

"Surprise, surprise."

Jilly gave her a considering look, touched with a dreamy wistfulness. "Would you go?"

"It's only a dream, isn't it?"

Jilly nodded.

"Well, I suppose I would," Zeffy said. "Only, it wouldn't be real, would it? So it wouldn't hurt to go, but you wouldn't gain anything from it either."

"You'd gain experience. Remember what the Buddha said: 'We do not learn by experience, but by our capacity for experience.' Which I take to mean that we should have a willingness to keep an open mind, no matter how strange, or even improbable, things might appear to be."

"But it's still not real."

Jilly smiled. "Well, here's the question Sophie always asks me: If you do something in a dream – let's say you kill somebody – are you still guilty of murder?"

"Of course not."

"I don't mean according to the laws of this world," Jilly said. "I mean according to one's own inner laws – the beliefs by which we live our lives. If you're capable of killing in a dream, isn't it possible you could kill someone in real life, too?"

"Okay," Zeffy said. "I see your point. But while we're on the topic of the strange and the unusual—"

"My field of expertise!" Jilly cried. "How many points is this question worth?"

Zeffy laughed. "Let me ask you this: If you meet someone you know, and they don't know you anymore..." She hesitated, wondering how to put it. "If the way they talk is different, the way they hold themselves and move, if everything about them is different ... are they still the same person?"

"This," Jilly said, obviously intrigued, "doesn't sound so much like a hypothesis as something that might have actually happened to somebody we know."

"Well..."

"Oh, 'fess up. I'm dying to hear about it."

So Zeffy related the morning's experience to her. She explained her own belief, that it was all just a really good act, and then how Tanya had gone from thinking Johnny might have amnesia to his having been "replaced" by someone or something else.

"God, this sounds so goofy," Zeffy said when she was done. "I don't even know why I brought it up in the first place. Of *course* he was just putting on an act. Why, is another story."

47

"I never much liked him," Jilly said.

That surprised Zeffy. Often it seemed that Jilly could find something good to say about anyone.

"Oh, it wasn't just because of how he's treated Tanya," Jilly went on. "It's more . . . There was something deeply creepy about him. I can't quite put my finger on what . . ."

"Maybe it's that he's sociopathic," Zeffy said.

Jilly shook her head. "I wouldn't go that far. But, he does seem inordinately focused on himself to the exclusion of everybody else around him. But not criminal."

"Not criminal," Zeffy agreed. "At least" – she lowered her voice dramatically – "by this world's laws."

"Yeah, I wonder what he dreams of."

Zeffy grimaced. "I don't think I'd want to know."

"But he has to have some redeeming qualities, or why would Tanya have gone out with him for so long?"

"He just knows which buttons to push with her," Zeffy said. "And besides, they were pretty much finished even before this morning."

"But still . . ."

Zeffy sighed. "Lord knows I love the woman, but sometimes I think she's a born victim. She's always attracted to the wrong guys. She always gets mixed up in the bad relationships."

"It's sad isn't it?" Jilly said. "I mean, for her, of course, but also for those around her, to have to stand by and watch it happen time and again. You have to wonder where it all begins."

"Ask her parents," Zeffy said. "All those beauty pageants they had her in. And then the modeling and stuff. You've got to come out of that feeling like so much meat and not much else. When she didn't place first, or she'd lose some catalogue job, they were all over her. What's that going to do for your self-esteem? One minute it's all about how much they love her and how she's the most beautiful thing on the planet, the next they're screaming, telling her how useless she is. It may not be physical abuse, but it still leaves scars."

A troubled look came into Jilly's eyes. "Yeah, I guess we've all been there, dealt with that kind of thing on one level or another. If it didn't happen to us, it happened to someone we know."

Zeffy thought about that show that Jilly and her friends had done. She'd never talked to Jilly about the source of the work Jilly had hung in the show, but then Jilly never spoke of her past. Life seemed to begin for Jilly with when she attended Butler U. – years before Zeffy went to the university herself. Everything before that was a mystery, like the part in old maps that read, "Here there be dragons."

I guess we've all been there. Where the dragons are. Jilly was so cheerful and good-natured that Zeffy couldn't imagine anything so terrible lying in her past.

"The thing that I can never figure out," Zeffy said finally, "is how that kind of thing makes some people stronger and others victims for the rest of their lives."

Jilly nodded. "All depends on who you are, I guess. Nobody can really tell how they'll react to a crisis until it's upon them." She sighed. "Jeez, listen to us. What a depressing topic of conversation for such a beautiful day." She turned away from her view of the river to look at Zeffy. "So tell me. Why'd you never let on that you've got a gig this weekend?"

Zeffy ducked her head to hide a blush. "I don't know. I just don't want to be pushy I guess."

"The only thing you're not pushy about is your music," Jilly told her with a laugh.

"Whatever. How'd you find out anyway?"

"Tanya asked me what time I was going to get to the club. When I said I didn't know anything about it, she put her hand over her mouth and wouldn't tell me anything else."

"I kind of swore her to secrecy," Zeffy said.

"Why ever for?"

"Is that even a word?"

"It's a phrase," Jilly said, "and don't change the subject."

"I just didn't want you all to feel obliged to come."

"Oh, like you feel obliged to come to my openings or Wendy's readings."

"That's not the same," Zeffy said.

"Ah."

"Okay, already. I'm opening for Amanda Blackstone's new band at the YoMan. Thirty-minute sets both Friday and Saturday night."

"So that's good – right?"

Zeffy grinned. "Well, yeah. Of course it is."

"They're really up-and-coming from what Geordie tells me, so there'll be a good crowd."

"Probably not until they come on."

"So we'll all come to give you some moral support – unless you'd rather we didn't, being so shy and reclusive now."

Zeffy gave her a light punch on the arm. "I said I was sorry I didn't tell you about it."

"Didn't."

"Well I'm saying it now."

"Apology duly noted and accepted," Jilly said. "Is our break over?"

Zeffy glanced at her watch. "We're five minutes late."

"Which is like being on time for me. Come on. Let's go."

As they walked back down the alleyway toward the café, Jilly turned to Zeffy.

"I'm still thinking about Johnny Devlin," she said. "Did you ever wonder if maybe Tanya was right? Maybe there is a space alien in his head right this minute and the real Johnny is sleeping in a pod in somebody's basement?"

She had a sparkle in her eyes, but Zeffy couldn't tell if she was teasing or being serious. With Jilly you just never knew.

"Oh please," she said.

"But what if?" Jilly asked.

"I'd think he deserved it," Zeffy said. "Being in a pod, I mean. And I'd feel sorry for the poor alien trying to make sense out of Johnny's life."

IX • MAX

I MOVED, the spring just past. For years, even when I could afford to do better for myself, I'd lived in the basement apartment of a brownstone tenement in Foxville, sharing my workspace and living quarters with roaches the length of fiddle pegs and rats that I never saw, but could often hear scrabbling about in the walls. What kept me there wasn't so much masochism as inertia, a simple inability to face the idea of packing up and moving some twelve years of accumulated tools, wood, instruments, books, recordings, furniture and other belongings.

The turning point came when I woke up one morning, face-to-face with a rat that seemed to be the size of a tomcat. The rodent froze when I blinked my eyes open, and for a long moment it crouched there, motionless on my bed, quivering nostrils no more than a few inches from my nose. I don't know which of us was more startled at my bellow of disgust when I lunged from the bed. We hit the floor at the same time, the rat disappearing into the living room in a flash of greasy brown fur, nails skittering on the floor. By the time I reached the door, it was nowhere to be seen. I didn't waste any time looking for it, but walked through to the kitchen instead, picked up the phone and called a realtor.

Within two days, she found me a new apartment in Lower Crowsea, in the old part of the Market that backs onto the Kickaha River. Packing everything I owned – the accumulation was far worse than I'd thought – and then setting it all up again in the new place had been as monumental a task as I'd imagined it would be. But now that I'm moved in and have gotten to know the area, I'm so enamored with my new neighborhood that I can't figure out what took me so long to relocate. Living here, I feel as though I've moved to Europe, instead of another part of Newford; as though I've been magically transported into one of those idyllic French or German towns, hundreds of years old, that my father and I explored on the trip we took overseas the year before he died.

For this part of the Market has a real Old World atmosphere, with its cobblestones underfoot and the turn-of-the-century stone buildings that lean one against the other, joined in places by arches, shared courtyards, overhead walkways and tiny gardens. Its maze of twisting streets is too narrow for cars, so the only traffic is by foot or bicycle – which is probably what's saved it from the yuppie renovations that have overtaken the rest of the Market. Those yuppies do love their BMWs, as Nia likes to say.

Nia is the sixteen-year-old daughter of Lisa Fisher, the

woman who has the apartment above mine. She's dark-haired like her mother, but keeps her hair long, bangs covering her forehead. With her penchant for black clothing and her pale complexion, she'd come off as just one more neo-Gothic except she has far too much good humor. If her lips aren't smiling, her eyes are. And she's decidedly eccentric – a true bohemian, though the days of the Beats are long gone. She likes jazz, poetry, art, coffee and hanging around in my shop while I'm working, discussing and partaking of all of the above. Broad in her opinions, she eloquently delivers monologues on whatever particular subject happens to interest her at the moment while I work away at my bench, repairing a fiddle, making a guitar, refretting a banjo.

When I ask her why she avoids going to school as much as she does, she tells me it's because the institution has nothing worthwhile to teach her, that there's more to life than getting a passing grade, and besides, knowledge is to be treasured, literature to be cherished. Discussion is fine – among one's peers, of course – but memorizing by rote, or appreciating something only within the strict context of the schools board's curriculum, makes her physically ill.

I enjoy her visits – it's better than having a radio – and I sense she needs an adult besides her mother with whom to share confidences, an adult who accepts her at face value. Or maybe she's simply looking for a father figure, her own father having walked out of her life before she had the opportunity to get to know him. She doesn't seem to have any friends in her own age group for all that she's quite pretty in her own esoteric fashion. For those reasons, and because I genuinely like her, she's always welcome. So long as she lets me work. And even if she does tend to lecture me sometimes about my eating habits – too many sweets, she likes to tell me – and the fact that I own a vehicle, which came up the first time she made mention of the yuppies and their BMWs. I have an old Dodge van that I park in a garage I rent on Lee Street, within easy walking distance of the shop.

"But I'll forgive you both," she informed me.

"Awfully big of you."

"It's only because I know you guys need your candy and your toys."

I had to smile. "Your mother tell you that?"

"No. That was pretty easy to figure out on my own. But you know you really should try to shop locally. Then you'd never even need the van."

"I do when I can."

"But I can't think of anything you could want that you can't get here," she said, "except for CDs, and you can walk to Flashman's from here. Is it the signs?"

All I could do was shake my head and then go back to work replacing the machine head on a beautiful old Guild I was in the middle of repairing while Nia went off on a new tangent.

The store signs seem to me to be one of the more obvious examples of the area's Old World ambience. Most are in English, in various kinds of old-fashioned script, but some of the shops still have signage in Dutch, dating back a hundred years, and the buildings are mostly tenanted by generations of the same families. My business fits right in with the old bakeries, cafés, wool shops, antique stores, bookshops, art galleries, cabinetmaker's shops, grocery stores, butcher shops and other enterprises where services and goods alike are all offered in an old-fashioned manner – with courtesy and an unfailing attention to the customer's needs. The goods are handmade, the produce, meats and poultry all come from local farms. In the cafés, the coffee is roasted and ground on the premises. In the bakeries, the dough is rolled on flour-strewn wooden tables and everything is baked in large, old-fashioned ovens, filling the air with the irresistible aroma of fresh-baked bread and pastries.

Nia's complaints to the contrary, within two weeks of moving into the area I was doing all my shopping locally. There was no more occasion to stand in long lines at the mall grocery store or fight the traffic in the parking lots. I still drive out-of-town for my wood, but everything else I want I can find within a few blocks of home. My only other needs – machine heads, fret wire, inlays, strings and the like that I need for my business – I have delivered by FedEx or UPS, and if I have to walk a few blocks to meet the trucks because the drivers won't carry my deliveries to my door, I don't mind at all, enjoying the chance to explore some unfamiliar lane or shop on the return trip.

The neighborhood is so self-contained, and I've spent so much time in it over the past few months, that the walk from Johnny Devlin's apartment in the Combat Zone leaves me feeling somewhat culture-shocked – a sensation that's amplified by the incredible circumstance I've found myself in since I woke in Devlin's body this morning. Normally the walk would have taken an hour or so, but it's closer to two hours before I'm finally standing in front of the three-story brick and stone town house where I've been living for the past few months.

It's almost nine, but the lights are still off in the workshop. Normally, I would have been in there by eight. But I'm not in there, am I? Or even in the apartment upstairs. I turn to regard Devlin's reflection in the window of the wool shop across the street from my building. I'm out here. Only my body is inside. Upstairs, in the apartment.

I cross the street with a sense of mounting dread. I feel as though I've stumbled into a dangerous no-man's-land, a place ruled by neither sense nor logic, where every step I take will be the wrong one. Approaching is the moment that will tell me the real truth: either I am who I think I am, or my mind's taken a side trip into some alternate reality that mimics the city I know but where nothing is familiar anymore – not even myself.

What if it is true? What if I'm not who I think I am?

The concept overwhelms me. When I reach the front stoop of my building, I have to turn away. I sit down on my haunches, the cobblestones underfoot, my back against the short wall that encloses my neighbor's garden. Who am I? I have only myself; I have only what my memory tells me and no real way of knowing if it's true – not when every physical sense tells me I'm someone else. And there's no one I can turn to and ask, "Who am I?" No one who knows me well enough. Both my father and Janossy are dead. Nia tends to talk more than listen. My last long-term relationship was with a woman named Donna Corey whose two enthusiasms in life were playing bass and riding her motorcycle. It's been three years now since she joined a band on the West Coast, hopped on her Harley and rode out of my life.

Everyone else is an acquaintance. They only know my surface, what I look like, not the details of who I am. There's no one I can turn to and reveal some secret that only the two of us know, some revelation that will cut through the impossibility of my present appearance to reveal its lie.

If it even is a lie.

No, I tell myself. Don't start on that again.

But it's hard to be logical. I can feel the panic welling up inside me once more, a swelling wave of hysteria and dark despair. If there was only one person I could turn to, one person to confirm that I haven't gone crazy, that the world has ... But there's not. I have nothing, no one to hold on to, not one anchor to reality except for what lies inside my head.

What lies inside my head. All these memories. So many of them, with such detail. How can they all be lies?

I can remember the inlay I was working on last night for Frankie Beale's mandolin. She plays in a bluegrass band and wanted her name to run the length of the neck in mother-of-pearl – a little bit of old-timey flash and spunk that suits Frankie to a T, tall and lanky, with fingers so long she can span seven frets on her mandolin without a strain. I can still hear the grin in her voice when I called her the other day to tell her I was almost finished with her new instrument.

I can remember the first time my father showed me how to use a saw set to bend the teeth of a handsaw to the angle needed to get a specific cut. Or the way he taught me to use a chisel with such delicacy that there's no need to go over the surface of the wood again with sandpaper, the cuts are so smooth. I still use that technique when I'm building my instruments.

I can remember Donna showing up for our first date, dark hair hanging loose, pale blue eyes laughing at the look on my face when she told me there was no way she'd show up at a club riding in my van, it was the bike or nothing. And then she just sat there on the Harley in her black leather pants and cowboy boots, tight white T-shirt and jean jacket, waiting for me to get on behind her. The engine throbbed between our legs as she cranked up the throttle and the machine seemed to bolt from the curb as though it had been cut from a leash, and there I was, hanging on tight to her, arms wrapped around her waist, her hair blowing back into my face. In the two years we were together she seemed to take it as a personal challenge to shake me up whenever she could. Leaving had been her greatest success.

I can remember any number of afternoons in the new shop when I'd be working at my bench with Nia kicking her heels against the rungs of the old oak chair by the desk. She loved to hear about Janossy, how he'd emigrated from Hungary to San Francisco, how he'd fallen in with Ginsberg's crowd and almost given up building instruments for playing them, jazzy Gitan rhythms backing up the beat of declaimed free verse, the women and the wine and all, until he turned on, tuned in and dropped out well before Leary made it a religion, eating peyote buttons and smoking the Mary J., had his moment of saton and ended up missing the Summer of Love because he moved to the farm outside of Newford to follow his true calling.

And I can remember Janossy himself, the Beat perfectly balanced with the Zen monk, his irreverence for propriety and his belief in the basic decency of all women and men, the odd mystic bent with which he approached his wood-working that never seemed odd when it came from him, when he spoke of it. And always that gentle reminder, to keep things simple. Balanced and simple.

"Everything in balance," he'd liked to say. "Embrace whatever you approach with as much enthusiasm as you can muster, but never forget that the world still goes on, whether you pay attention to it or not. There is no event so momentous that it hasn't been seen before, no trouble so grand that it won't look small from another perspective."

Try this one on for size, I think, and then realize that given the chance, Janossy probably would. And he'd thrive on the experience.

I sigh and get slowly to my feet. Walking up to the door,

I automatically reach for my keys before I remember that all I have are the ones to Devlin's apartment, not my own.

It's an odd sensation, going inside the building as though I'm a stranger, walking up to the door of my apartment on the second floor, ringing my own bell. I think I've steeled myself for what's coming next, but nothing could have prepared me for the shock of finally coming face-to-face with myself when the door opens.

To be honest, I'd been half-expecting a complete stranger. No matter how real my memories are to me, the situation I'm in is so improbable that it seems far more likely the flaw's with me. That I've misremembered. That I'm suffering from a multiple personality disorder, something that allows different personalities to inhabit the same body, some of whom were unaware of the presence of the others. Such as the entity that thinks of himself as Max Trader.

But I know the face of the man who answers the door, know it from how many thousand mornings, shaving, combing my hair in front of the mirror, brushing my teeth. Light brown hair drawn back in a ponytail with the slightly receding hairline that expands the height of the forehead. The ears maybe a little too big, nose definitely too big, face long and thin, but not really gaunt. They aren't the features to launch a film career, but it's still my face, as familiar as a friend.

The shock of recognition leaves me speechless. I can see a similar expression in the other man's eyes, but he recovers before me.

"I was wondering when you'd be showing up," the man wearing my face says.

X • LISA FISHER

JUST ONCE, Lisa thought, she'd like to get up on time and not have to suffer through this mad scramble to catch the subway with only seconds to spare every morning. She was running only a few minutes late today, but that didn't mean much. Something always came up. A run in her stocking. Nothing to wear – or rather, nothing that felt right, even though she might have worn the exact same outfit last week and not only felt perfectly comfortable in it, but attractive as well. She couldn't find her purse. She could find her purse, but not her keys. She could find both purse and keys, but not the wedding band she wore to forestall unwanted attention both at work and traveling back and forth between the office and home.

One of these days Cleaver was going to fire her, and then where would they be?

This morning she was happy with the simple dark skirt and white blouse she'd laid out last night, the black hose with their subtle pattern of rosebuds and the low heels. Her hair was behaving, but that was only because she now had it cut so short it was difficult for it to do anything but behave. The small rash of pimples on her chin had finally decided that she wasn't going to make friends with them and had found someone else to visit overnight.

At thirty-eight you shouldn't have to worry about zits anymore, but she'd never had that kind of luck. Sometimes she wanted to throttle all those unblemished models in the fashion magazines. Not only did they have flawless skin, but they also had someone else to worry about their makeup.

Her own simply wouldn't go on right this morning. She'd done her face twice now and was so heavy-handed that she kept seeing a tramp looking back at her from the bathroom mirror instead of her own face. Finally she gave up. She scrubbed her face clean for a third time – forgoing foundation, blush and the rest – and settled on some eye shadow and a dab of lipstick. She'd just have to do her face properly after work, before she met Julie for dinner.

Julie. The thought of seeing her tonight made Lisa smile, until she realized that she still hadn't dealt with the ramifications that having a date with another woman would have on the rest of her life.

Not now, she told herself.

She swept her makeup off the back of the sink and into her purse, gave herself a last critical once-over in the mirror, then left the bathroom.

"Nia, will you *please* get up," she called through the open door of her daughter's bedroom as she passed by.

"Why?"

Lisa stifled the irrational flash of anger that filled her at the sound of that one word. She'd always promised herself that, if she ever had kids, she wasn't going to treat them the way her own parents had treated her, but more and more lately she found herself turning into her mother. She paused by the doorway and took a deep breath.

"Because otherwise you'll be late for school," she said, keeping her voice reasonable.

Nia was sitting up in her bed, her long black hair messy, features still puffy from sleep. Another late night, Lisa realized, seeing the dark circles under Nia's eyes. Her daughter had embraced the current resurgence of interest in the Beats, staying up until all hours, drinking coffee, writing poetry, listening to bebop jazz that no more appealed to Lisa now than it had the first time around when her older sister had been so enamored of it.

Lisa didn't have any real argument with what Nia did – at least not in principle. But she knew it wasn't going to stop here. For now Nia played at being a beatnik in her room, but all too soon she'd be out all night, hanging around with who knew what kind of people, and there would be nothing that Lisa could do about it.

"I'm finished for the year," Nia said. "It's summer holidays – remember?"

"Well, I still don't want you lying in bed until noon every day," Lisa said.

She winced inwardly. Now that was her own mother, verbatim.

"I won't," Nia told her. "I was getting up. I just wasn't making a big production out of it, okay?"

"If you sleep in every day, you're never going to get a job."

"I don't want a job."

"Yes, we know that. But we've already been through this all before. You're sixteen now. It's time you started pulling your weight."

"Well, I've been looking," Nia said with a shrug, "but no one's hiring."

"Well, it would help— " Lisa began, then firmly cut herself off. It would help if you didn't look like one of the walking dead, was what she'd been about to say. Nia's pale skin, the black hair, the black clothes – none of it helped.

"It would just be a help," she said.

"Okay, already."

Lisa could remember when the two of them had been able to talk to each other without arguing, when they shared everything in their lives, but in the last year or so, all that had changed. Her daughter was a stranger to her now. She knew she should be able to understand what Nia was going through with this beatnik phase – hadn't she put her parents through her own hippie days? – but her reason seemed to shut down every time she and Nia talked and it was all she could do to not be constantly on the poor kid's case, lecturing and haranguing and generally being her own parents.

It didn't help that she was going through so many changes herself, changes she was no more able to articulate to Nia than her daughter could explain her own.

"I'm sorry," Lisa said, trying to be conciliatory. "I just have a lot on my mind these days."

Like how do I come out to my daughter?

"I said it was okay."

Lisa nodded. She started to turn away, then paused again.

"I won't be home for dinner," she said, "so you'll have to get your own."

Nia raised her eyebrows. "Anybody I know?"

"It's somebody new."

"Well, I hope he's nice."

"He . . ."

He's not a he, Lisa wanted to say, but she couldn't get the words out. It was one thing to finally surrender to her own feelings the way she had, but a whole different story explaining it.

"I'll just have to see," she said.

She realized it was the wrong thing to say as soon as the words left her mouth and Nia's face closed down on her. But she *couldn't* get into it now.

"Yeah, well have a good time."

"I'll tell you all about it when I get home."

"Whatever."

Nia had every reason to be acting this sullen, Lisa knew, but that flash of irritation returned all the same. I have a life, too, she wanted to say. I have a right to some privacy. But instead she did the same thing to Nia that her mother had always done to her and rather than explain herself, she went on the offensive.

"One more thing," she said. "I don't want you spending the whole day downstairs bothering Mr. Trader in his shop."

"I *don't* bother Max," Nia told her. "He likes it when I visit. He told me so himself."

"But that's just it. This whole friendship makes me feel very uncomfortable. He's old enough to be your father."

Nia sneered. "So what're you saying? You think he's putting it to me?"

"Nia! I won't have you—"

"You're going to be late again," Nia said, giving her alarm clock a pointed look.

Oh Christ, Lisa thought. Look at the time.

"We are not finished with this discussion," she said.

"We never are, are we? If it's not this, you're ragging me about something else. It never stops, does it?"

All Lisa could do was give her an anguished look. How had it come to this?

"Please don't do this to me," she said. She could feel the tears welling in her eyes. "Not when I have to be at work in twenty minutes."

Nia laid back down on her bed and turned her face to the wall, leaving Lisa only a view of one stiff shoulder.

"So go," Nia said. "And we'll talk tonight."

"Nia, I love you."

Lisa heard her daughter mumble something.

"What did you say?" she asked.

"I said, have a nice time tonight."

But that wasn't what she'd said at all. What Lisa had

heard was, "Yeah, well you've got a funny way of showing it."

She wanted to pretend that she'd misheard, that their relationship hadn't come to the point where her own daughter didn't think she loved her anymore, but it was no use. Nia and she were becoming as estranged from one another as Lisa had been from her own mother.

Lisa couldn't face it. Trying to hide her tears, she fled the apartment.

XI • MAX

IT TAKES me a few moments to assimilate what the man wearing my face has just said.

I was wondering when you'd be showing up.

He looks so calm, so accepting of the situation, while I feel as though the ground has vanished underfoot. I know I'm standing here in someone else's skin, trying to talk to someone in my skin, but at the same time I'm plummeting, and who knows where I'll finally end up. The sensation is so real that it's all I can do to keep my balance.

"You ... you were expecting me?" I finally manage to say.

"Well, sure," the man replies. "I mean, look at us. It's goddamn unbelievable, isn't it? If you hadn't showed up here, I'd have had to come take a look at you – just to make sure I wasn't going nuts, you know what I mean?"

I lift a hand to my cheek and trail my fingers down to my chin, unconsciously exploring their shapes. When I realize what I'm doing, I drop my hand to my side. I don't think I'll ever become comfortable with the unfamiliar contours under my fingertips.

"You're Johnny Devlin," I say. I'm like the country yokel on his first trip to the big city, everything moving too fast for me, nothing really making sense because I don't understand the context of what I'm experiencing. I speak slowly because it seems as if I have to search for every word before I can use it. "This is really your face."

Devlin nods amiably. "Weird shit, isn't it? It's going to take some getting used to, that's for damn sure."

"I'm not going to get used to it," I tell him.

Devlin has a cocky look of superiority in his eyes that I've never seen when looking at myself in the mirror. He wears my body differently, too – the way he stands, the way he moves.

"Can't say's I blame you," Devlin says. "I've been checking things out – you know, your business records, your bankbooks. You seemed to have made a pretty comfortable little life for yourself here."

"What did you do to me?" I demand.

"Hey, slow down, pal. I didn't do a damn thing to you."

"You're telling me this all just . . . happened."

Devlin shrugs. "All I know is I fell asleep in my own bed last night and woke up in yours this morning wearing your face."

"And you didn't do a thing?"

"Like what?" Devlin asks, the mockery plain in his features and voice. "You think I killed a chicken and went booga-booga or something, and then zip, bam, boom, here we are?"

I nod. It's not quite what I mean, but it's got to have been something along those lines. Something I don't understand but he does.

"I never bought into that crap," Devlin tells me.

"You had to have done something."

Devlin shakes his head. "Nope. I just went to bed and fell asleep. Wished I could wake up and all my problems'd be gone, but that's nothing new. I've been doing that for about as long as I can remember because, just between you and me, pal, I was not nearly as together as you seem to have been. I mean, if I could screw it up, I did."

I can't believe what I'm hearing. "So you just made a wish and here we are?"

"Works for me."

"This is ridiculous. Next thing you'll be telling me your fairy godmother showed up."

Devlin gives me a long, studied look, that mocking light bright in his eyes. "Look at us, pal. *Something* happened that should have been impossible. Who are we to buck destiny?"

"I want my life back."

"Understandable. But it's a no-go. I don't know why things worked out the way they did, but I'll tell you this: From here on out, every night when I go to sleep I'm going to take a moment to concentrate on maintaining this new status quo."

"You can't get away with this," I tell him.

Devlin smiles. "Who's going to stop me?"

Then he closes the door in my face.

I stare at the wooden panels for a long moment, then hammer my fist against them. The door jerks open again.

"Keep it up, pal," Devlin says, "and I'll have to call the cops."

I fold my arms across my chest. "Fine."

Devlin sighs. "And what're you going to tell them?"

"I . . ."

"Exactly. Nothing. Because if you try to tell them the truth, they'll laugh you off. And if you stick to your story, they'll send you to the Zeb for psychiatric testing. And if I decide to press charges because you're in my face and harassing me, well, maybe they'll just lock you away for a while or at least issue you with a cease and desist. Are you starting to get my drift yet, pal?"

"Why are you doing this to me?" I ask. I hate the plaintive note I hear in my voice.

Devlin shakes his head. "I'm not doing a damn thing to you. I'm just rolling with the punches, pal. Playing the hand I was dealt. Now why don't you get out of my face and do the same?"

He closes the door again, but this time all I can do is stand there in the hallway. I stare at the door, knowing I should be angry, knowing I should be furious. But all I can muster up is a confused sense of loss. I feel empty, drained of the strength to go on. My life's been stolen away from me and I can't do a thing about it.

XII • TANYA

TANYA DIDN'T quite make it through her whole shift. She tried. She did the best she could to put this morning's weird encounter with Johnny behind her. Pretending everything was normal, she managed to hang in until the midafternoon lull that inevitably followed the lunch rush. Then, when it wouldn't seem too obvious that she simply had to get out of there, she tidied up her section, balanced her receipts and made her escape. Her coworkers at the café were like family, especially Zeffy, but there were some things you couldn't share with family, even a family-of-choice. She needed to be alone with her confusion and pain.

She couldn't stop thinking about Johnny, but now instead

of being confused about where their relationship stood – was he interested in her, did she even love him anymore – a whole new set of questions had entered the equation, leaving her more scared than she was willing to admit to herself, little say Zeffy. Scared and in need of a fix.

She couldn't understand what had happened with Johnny. Their relationship had been pretty much on the rocks for the past couple of months, but that didn't begin to explain the way he'd treated her this morning. It wasn't like she'd been obsessing on him, constantly in his face, calling him, trying to hang around. What had she done to deserve the reception she'd gotten from him this morning?

She knew as well as Zeffy that it had been Johnny standing there in the hallway of his apartment treating her the way he had. Aliens hadn't taken up residence in his brain. She wasn't stupid. But he had been so different. Seriously, frighteningly different. The way he'd talked, the way he'd looked at her . . . She knew it was an act, but even knowing that, she still found herself feeling that he really hadn't recognized her at all. She couldn't stop searching for some kind of logic behind his actions, like he had to have been in an accident and now had amnesia.

Which was being really dumb. Because, no. It was like Zeffy said. It had just been Johnny playing some stupid game with them. What didn't make sense was why he'd have to go through such an elaborate charade. If he wanted it to be finished between them, all he'd have to do was say so. She hadn't been calling him. *He'd* called *her*. To borrow money, it was true, but still he'd made the contact. It seemed hard to believe that he'd go through all of this just to get out of paying her back. It was easier to believe that something alien *had* taken up residence in his brain.

That she could even consider such a thing with any sort

of seriousness was what probably scared her the most and had her yearning for a fix. A little hit of euphoria. A small space of emotional detachment. A well-deserved break from the pain and stress.

She settled for a cigarette as she waited for the bus to take her home. It would be so easy to go back, to let the junk swallow up all of her problems and hard times and hide them away in a warm, comforting blur. No worries, as that Crocodile what's-his-name from Australia would say. It made for fine times. Except the trouble was you always came down. And if you cranked another hit, the coming down got harder still and you were just asking for the monkey to crawl back up on your shoulder.

That she couldn't face again.

The bus came and she butted out her cigarette. People talked about how quitting smoking was the hardest thing they'd ever done. They should try going cold turkey from a serious habit if they wanted to know some real fun and games. They should try going through the days of shivering and sweating and throwing up. The anxiety and muscle spasms. The sleeplessness, and then when you did manage to sleep for an hour or so, you dreamt that there were things crawling around behind the wallpaper and you'd wake up with big claw marks and blood on the walls and all this wallpaper under your nails. You ended up feeling like a dishrag under someone's sink and the worst thing was that you knew – you *knew* – that all it'd take was one little hit to stop the agony.

She stared gloomily out the window as the bus stuttered between stops on its way up Battersfield Road. When it reached Stanton Street, she got off, but instead of using her transfer to continue on home, she walked down the street to St. Paul's. The magnificent cathedral loomed up above her in a Gothic splendor of grey stone, tall arches and gargoyles, an old architectural patriarch in a neighborhood of gently decaying Victorian houses and estates, overseeing their fading genteelness with the kind gaze of a favorite grandfather.

Tanya scattered crowds of foraging pigeons and gulls as she climbed up the wide sweep of its steps to sit down near the top. She was surprised by the day's warmth, considering how cool it had been last night. Undoing a button of her blouse, she leaned back on her elbows and took in her surroundings.

The lunch crowds were gone from here as well, but there were still some hangers-on. Tourists getting cricks in their necks as they jockeyed with their cameras, looking for the perfect shot. Street people, dozing in the sun or talking to themselves. A couple of buskers playing – for themselves now, instead of for the money. She recognized the fiddler. He was Geordie Riddell, one of Jilly's friends, a tall, lanky fellow with long hair who always looked a bit scruffier than she thought he should. She knew the red-haired woman playing the Irish pipes with him only by sight.

Usually the kind of music they played cheered her up. It was hard not to smile at the lilting spill of notes that made up a jig or a reel. But today the music's good humor only depressed her.

Everybody had something they wanted to do with their lives, she thought. Everybody had a goal, something that burned inside them, something that they not only wanted to do, but *had* to do. Zeffy wanted to make a living with her songs. Jilly was an artist. Wendy wrote poetry. Geordie and his friend had their music. What did she have? Nothing. Her life was usually defined by whoever she was going out with at the time and if she wasn't going out with anyone, then she thought of herself as between boyfriends. Not as a singer or an artist or by any other kind of career appellation. She was just someone between boyfriends.

It was so pathetic.

Zeffy was always telling people that the reason they worked shifts at the café was because it left them the time for the things they really wanted to do, the important things. It always embarrassed Tanya because if she wasn't going out with anyone, she didn't have anything important to do. She'd keep the apartment clean. She'd make herself some new clothes. She'd read. When she had the money, she'd go clubbing.

Zeffy could spend hours practicing in her bedroom. Playing her guitar. Singing. Writing new songs. The closest Tanya ever came to anything creative was being an appreciative audience for her friends' endeavors.

Tanya sighed. She put her elbows on her knees, propped up her chin with hands and watched the Stanton Street traffic go by.

She must have wanted to be something once. Before she hit puberty and got onto this treadmill of boyfriends, she had to have been enthused by something, had some ambitions. When did she become a "pretty face" and nothing more?

Before puberty, she realized, because that was how she'd always been defined. In school, at home, in college. Hadn't her parents always gone on about how she should be a model or an actress, because wasn't she so pretty? Hadn't they pushed her into trying to make her way through life on her looks? And she'd gone along with them, hadn't she? Not so much because she wanted to, but to make them happy. Because until she knew better, that was the way she thought it was supposed to be – even though she felt it should be different. Inside. Where no one cared except for her. And later, Zeffy.

The beauty pageants had been a complete turnoff. No matter how they were gussied up, they were still meat markets.

Modeling hadn't been satisfying either. All you were was a mannequin and there were too many smarmy men always trying to feel you up, too many other beautiful women who saw you only as competition and treated you like dirt.

Acting had been better, except she had a terrible memory and kept forgetting her lines in live productions. She could deliver them perfectly – but only when she remembered them. It had quickly gotten to the point where she didn't want to embarrass her fellow cast members, never mind herself.

In films she could at least go over her lines between takes, but there still hadn't been any room for her to add any creative input. Everybody decided how she'd look, what she'd wear, how she'd deliver her lines. No one wanted to listen to what the "talent" might be able to add to the role. And she always got cast as "the girlfriend," the one who clung to the lead's arm and had to be rescued, or ended up on the end of the killer's knife, when what she really wanted was the character parts. Those were the roles with the most meat to them but the producers never thought she could play them. She was too pretty. She was the perennial girl-next-door. Her face didn't have enough character. It was too much of a stretch.

Yeah? You should see me do a junkie . . .

When the time came that she had to make the choice between moving out to the West Coast, or finishing her studies at university, she'd opted for the latter. And it wasn't because she didn't think she had what it took to make it in

Hollywood, that she was scared of the hard work or the competition or any of the other heartbreaks that a career in film entailed. It was because she knew she didn't care enough about that kind of work to put the effort into it.

Because it wasn't really her, was it? Her becoming an actress had been one of her parents' enthusiasms, not her own. No, she was only good at getting boyfriends. Not keeping them. Oh no. Once you got beyond the pretty face, well there wasn't much else there, was there? But she could hook them in just fine, thank you. She remembered how impressed Johnny had been with her Screen Actors Guild card and her acting credentials, never mind that they were only cheesy B movies. Or maybe, considering his taste in cinema, it had been because they were that kind of film.

Sisters of the Knife had been the one that got her her SAG card. Johnny had bought the video of it not long after they started seeing each other and told her he loved her part in it. Sure, it was exploitative, but he'd seen worse and everybody had to start somewhere, right? He couldn't believe that she'd given up acting when she obviously had such a talent for it. Yadda-yadda-yadda.

She'd never seen the film itself – only some of the dailies. She'd hated the shoot, hated the gratuitous shower scene, hated the oppressive promise of violence that permeated even the nonviolent scenes. *Sisters* got her the card, but the shoot also gave her a habit. Here, try this. You don't get hooked if you use it in moderation. A snort here, a snort there, and the next thing she knew she was sticking a needle in between her toes where the tracks wouldn't show, mainlining that sweet oblivion because it was the only way she could deal with all the shit that had gone down on the set.

God, this was depressing.

She shook a cigarette out of her pack and lit it up.

Through the cloud of grey smoke that wreathed her face she saw that Geordie and his friend had finished playing and were packing up their instruments. She hadn't even heard the music stop. Geordie looked up and smiled when he noticed her sitting there. He said something to his companion and the red-haired woman gave Tanya a wave before setting off across Stanton Street. Geordie picked up his fiddle case and climbed the steps to where Tanya was sitting.

"Playing hooky from work?" he asked as he sat down beside her.

"I'd like to be playing hooky from life," she told him.

Geordie gave her a considering look. "You sound like you need serious cheering up."

"I'm sorry," Tanya said. "I don't mean to whine. I'm just having one of those days. I couldn't stay at work a minute longer, you know, pretending to be happy."

Geordie nodded. "I don't know how you can do it, day after day, the way you do."

"It's usually half days."

"But still."

"Don't make me feel more depressed than I already am," Tanya said.

She managed to find a smile to let him know that he shouldn't take her too seriously, that he had nothing to do with the way she was feeling.

"So what's got you so down?" he asked.

Tanya shrugged. "Just the usual. Bad luck with boyfriends. Worse luck in figuring out what I want to do with my life."

"Who says you have to do something with your life?"

"Oh right. Wouldn't that make a great epitaph: 'Here lies Tanya Burns. She vegged through life and now she's fertilizer.' "

Geordie laughed. "I don't mean anything so drastic. But really, don't you think this desperate need to scrabble out a career that most people seem to have is a little overrated?"

"It depends," Tanya said, "whether you're doing it for yourself, or for someone else. Do you feel there's something wrong with your devoting all your time to making music?"

"No. But that's different. It's something I want to do."

Tanya added. "And if you don't get rich at it, it's still okay, right? Because you're doing something you want to do."

"Sure, but—"

"I don't have anything like that. I don't have this desire to do or be anything. Everybody I know has their niche; what they do defines them. You're a musician. Jilly's an artist-slash-waitress. Zeffy's a singer-slash-waitress. Me, I'm just a waitress. I don't do anything except cheer on my friends. And the reason I don't do anything else is because there's nothing I want to do. Nothing I want to be. I mean, I *want* to be something, I want to do something that gives my life some meaning, but I come up blank whenever I think about it."

"You used to act, didn't you?"

"But that was something my parents wanted me to do. I didn't choose it for myself. Or maybe I did, eventually, but it was after they pushed me into it. They were certainly expecting more from me than becoming a wet dream for B-movie aficionados."

She sighed and then fell silent. Geordie didn't say anything for a few minutes. They watched the tourists snapping pictures, the bums sleeping, the food vendors along Stanton Street packing up their carts. At one point a stray dog came sniffing its way along the curb and they both tracked it until it went out of sight around the corner. Finally Geordie turned to her.

"I heard something when we played up on the rez last year," he said. "One of the guys asked an elder why the Kickaha never gave up. You know, they've been taking all this shit for decades, but they just soldier on. The elder doesn't even have to think about it. 'We have our instructions from the creator,' she says. 'So long as there is one to sing, one to dance, one to speak, and one to listen, we don't give up.'"

"That's lovely, if a little Carlos Castaneda," Tanya told him. "But I don't see how it applies to my situation."

Geordie shrugged. "It was just what you said about cheering on your friends. 'One to listen.' Do you have any idea how rare it is to find a person who can do that well? Most people are too busy talking, or waiting for a break in the conversation so that they can speak, to appreciate what they're hearing." He smiled. "And I'm using conversation as a metaphor here for any kind of dialogue, be it music, art, dance, theatre. Or a good conversation."

Tanya returned his smile and this time she didn't have to work at it. "So you're saying I should make a career out of being a good listener."

"Not at all. I just don't think it should be underrated. Career's a whole different thing. If you're serious about wanting to figure out a way to express yourself, my advice would be to stop worrying about it. It'll come to you when it's ready. Or you are."

"Or not at all," Tanya said.

"Or not at all," Geordie agreed. "But I don't really believe that. Everybody's got something. Everybody has a need to express themselves creatively. The trouble for some people is that the opportunity to experience what's available just never arrives; if you don't know about something, then you can never acquire the skill to utilize it."

"I suppose," Tanya said, the doubt plain in her voice.

Geordie sighed. "I'm not really doing much of a job cheering you up, am I?"

Tanya pretended to think hard, scrunching up her brow theatrically and rubbing her chin with a thumb and forefinger.

"Nope," she said. "I still don't feel cheered up."

Though actually she did feel better. Nothing was resolved. Her problems hadn't gone away. But Geordie was always good company – as easygoing as Jilly, in his own way – and it was hard to brood around him.

"Well, you know what I do when I get depressed?" he said.

Tanya shook her head.

"This is a new thing," he told her, "but it works for me. I go over to Fitzhenry Park and have my fortune told."

"Do you actually believe in that kind of thing?"

"Not really. But I like the ritual of it. You know, the laying down of the cards, the throwing of the coins, whatever."

"I'll have to give it a try."

"In the meantime," Geordie said. He jingled a pocket heavy with the change he'd earned busking with his friend. "I'm feeling rich. Do you want to go somewhere and have a tall cool glass of something cold?"

"Only if you promise to regale me with sparkling conversation – I'm a very good listener, you know."

"So I see. Sarcastic, too."

"I think sincere is the word you were looking for."

Geordie smiled. "That, too. Now come on before I

change my mind and ask some other depressed waitress to share in the bounty of my hard-earned coins."

"I'll follow you anywhere," Tanya informed him. "So long as it's to someplace air-conditioned."

She lit a cigarette and stood up.

"Can I have one of those?" Geordie asked.

"But you don't smoke."

"I know. It's just to be companionable."

Tanya shrugged and passed him the pack.

"Do yourself a favor," she said, "and don't ever start hanging around with junkies."

He gave her an odd look, but she didn't feel up to elaborating. She'd shared enough confidences for one day.

XIII • MAX

THE SECOND time Devlin shuts the door in my face, all I can do is turn away and stumble back down the hallway. The vertigo that hit me earlier returns with a rush and I have to sit down on the steps leading up to the Fishers' apartment on the third floor. I bow my head, pressing my fingers against my temples. The spinning starts to slow down, but I can't seem to lose the nausea that's churning in my stomach. A headache throbs dully behind my eyes and my breath's gone short. I start to feel claustrophobic, as though the walls are pressing in and there's no air in the hallway, but I can't muster the small amount of energy it'd take to get up and leave the building.

A part of me realizes that it's another panic attack, I just have to ride it through. But identifying the problem doesn't alleviate it. I want to lie down, right here on the dusty floor, but that's the step too far, even with how I'm feeling. I'll be damned if I'm gong to sprawl out in my own hallway like some derelict alcoholic with a hangover.

So I sit here on the steps, curled in on myself, the weight of my upper body and head supported by my knees. I concentrate on breathing normally and try to quiet the wild pounding of my heart, but all I can think about is, why's Devlin so resilient? How come he can handle it all so well? What made him pick me for this switch? How did he pull it off and how can I force him to turn things back to normal? Are things ever going to be normal again?

I have no idea how long it is before I'm finally able to get to my feet again. I stare at the front door of my apartment, but I can't face another confrontation with the man who's stolen away my life. I feel too drained. Instead, I just turn away and start wearily down the stairs. When I reach the landing between the first and second floors, I think I hear a door close up on the Fishers' floor. I take a look up past the banisters but there's nothing to see. I think of going up to talk to Nia, but I know it's not a good idea. What could I possibly say to her? Devlin's right. No one's going to believe me. I can hardly believe it myself.

But I'm not going to make the best of a bad situation.

I continue down the stairs, pausing on the street outside to look up at the windows of my apartment. The air feels so clean as I draw it into my lungs. It steadies me, puts some strength back into my muscles, clears the nausea and dulls the throbbing in my head.

This isn't over – not by a long shot. But first I have to regroup. Calm down. Work out a plan of action. I study the windows for a few moments longer, but there's no sign of Devlin looking back down at me. As I'm about to turn away, I think I see a curtain move in a window of the

Fishers' apartment, but when I look more closely I can't see anyone there either.

Forget it, I tell myself. No one can help you. You're on your own.

What I have to do now is go back to Devlin's apartment and figure out a way to raise some money. Because if this situation doesn't get resolved quickly, I'm going to have to live on something. I won't be able to get access to my own assets – not without committing what the rest of the world would consider a crime. I'd just be taking what's mine, but everybody else, seeing me as Devlin, would consider it theft. The teller at the bank would think I was forging my own name. I can't even use a bank machine, because my bank card is upstairs in the apartment with Devlin. I could wait for him to leave, but I'd have to break in and risk arrest. Only Devlin – his own finances in ruin – has access to my assets now.

Fine, I think. Devlin may be broke and up to his ears in debt, but he still has an apartment full of stereo and video equipment that I can try to sell.

The thought wakes a twinge of guilt in me but all I have to do is remember the smirk on his face and his smug declaration, *From here on out, every night when I go to sleep I'm going to take a moment to concentrate on maintaining this new status quo.*

He's stolen my life. His arrogance demands payback. At this point, whatever I have to do to get my life back, up to and including the use of Devlin's meager assets, is simply fair game. And I refuse to allow myself to feel repentant while doing so.

So I start the trek back to Devlin's apartment. I cut straight back across town this time and make it to the building in just under an hour – half the time it took me to make the trip out earlier today. But I'd been operating under a cloud of loss and confusion then. It's different now. I'm no happier about how things stand than I was when I first discovered what had been done to me, but at least the confrontation with Devlin has proved one thing to me: I'm not crazy. Impossible though the situation is, at least now I have no doubts. It's real. I can stop questioning my sanity and get on with the job at hand. I can stop simply reacting to what's thrown at me and initiate my own countermoves.

When I reach Devlin's building, I take the steps up to the apartment two at a time. That's one thing to be said about Devlin, I think as I fish in my pocket for the keys. At least he kept himself in shape. I'm not even winded.

I pull out the keys, insert the one for the apartment into the lock and try to turn it. Nothing happens. Confused, I try the other keys on the ring, one after the other, but none of them work.

Now what's going on? I tested the keys before I left the apartment for this very reason. They have to work. Unless . . . unless someone has changed the locks while I was gone . . .

My heart sinks as I remember the state of Devlin's finances. What if along with all those other unpaid bills, he hasn't been paying his rent either?

My hard-earned optimism fades. I take the stairs back down again at a slower pace, searching for the superintendent's apartment.

XIV • ZEFFY

ZEFFY LEFT the café and headed for home as soon as her shift was over, worrying about Tanya, but feeling a little apprehensive as well. God knew she loved Tanya, but Zeffy wasn't sure she had the strength to deal with another of her roommate's depressions. She knew it was a totally selfish thing to be thinking, but she couldn't stop herself. Whenever Tanya's life went downhill, Zeffy's ground to a standstill as well because she used up all of her energy in support of her friend.

She couldn't afford that right now. Not with this gig coming up. A *real* gig, mind you, not some floor spot at one of the folk clubs, but one with her name up there on the posters as well as that of the headlining band. She passed a couple of the posters on the way home, stapled onto telephone poles, and smiled every time she saw it: Zeffy Lacerda, her name listed right under Glory Mad Dog's and the words "opening act."

She wanted to be hot that night. She knew her material forward and backward, but she was still practicing hard every day because she was determined to pull off the perfect show. Glory Mad Dog had a good following in the city, plus they were being courted by a half-dozen record companies. The club seated five hundred and it could easily sell out. If she did well, all kinds of doors could open for her after this weekend. Better gigs. Maybe her own following of faithful fans. God, maybe even her own contract, though she knew that if that ever happened, it was still a long way down the road.

So she couldn't blow this show. She'd wasted far too much of her life as it was – all those years that she'd played only for herself, too scared to ever think of seriously making a career out of it. Sitting in her room, writing her songs, practicing, dreaming about being up on a stage somewhere and making it all seem so effortless the way it seemed everybody else could. People had no idea how scared she got, how much nerve it took for her to get up there behind the mike and play her music. She couldn't do it at all if she had to deal with one of Tanya's crises at the same time.

And it had happened before. Nothing major, no big gig like this, but more than once a crisis of Tanya's had her cancel a gig or not go out to an open-mike night. Hole-in-the-wall clubs, it was true, but still. At what point, she wondered, did you get to live your own life? At what point did you say, No more, I'm doing something for myself this time?

She sighed. Ah, who was she kidding? She'd never let Tanya down. She'd never let anyone down if they needed her. It just wasn't in her. She was no saint, but if you couldn't be there for your friends when they needed you, then what was the point of singing about integrity and supporting one another in your music? It wasn't like people got into trouble on purpose. It wasn't like they chose the worst possible moment to have some emergency that they couldn't deal with on their own.

But it was hard sometimes. Especially when you saw someone making the same mistake over and over again. Like Tanya. Maybe she'd managed to stay clean, but the guys she inevitably fell for . . . It was as though Tanya was doomed to repeat the same bad relationship forever. This business with Johnny Devlin was only the latest installment in a story that had been going on for as long as Zeffy had known Tanya, and Johnny wasn't even the worst, God help them all.

What was the most frustrating about all of this was that Tanya was such a sweet person. And a true friend. When she wasn't trapped in one of her downward-spiraling depressions, she seemed to live her life for other people. You couldn't find a more supportive friend, always ready to pitch in and lend a hand, the very best company, never complaining except for when some guy dumped her and the blues got way serious.

But when Tanya got depressed . . .

So it was with some trepidation that Zeffy entered the apartment. Worst-case scenario, she'd find Tanya crying. Running a close second, she'd be on the verge of tears because she'd started thinking about all the bad relationships, running them into each other, so that they stretched out in one long unbroken string – which was enough to depress anyone, Zeffy agreed. But she needn't have worried. She found her roommate in the living room, ironing, an old REM CD on the stereo playing at a low volume. She was singing along with Stipe – off-key as usual, since she couldn't hold a tune for the life of her, but warbling away happily.

She broke off and smiled when Zeffy came into the room. Zeffy returned her smile. She dropped her knapsack on the floor and sprawled out on the sofa, relishing that first rush of relaxation after having been on her feet all day. Whenever she worked a full day like this, she renewed the promise, too often broken, to hold firm and only do half days. Tanya finished the sleeve she was working on, then turned off the iron and joined Zeffy on the sofa.

"Can I guess that you're feeling better?" Zeffy asked.

"I suppose I was pretty obvious, slipping out the way I did."

"Only to those who love you."

"Yeah, well I was feeling pretty down when I left," Tanya

said. "I planned to just come home, but when the bus pulled up by St. Paul's I had to get out. I hung out on the steps for a while." She offered up a wry smile. "Feeling sorry for myself, I'll admit. But then I got to talking with Geordie who'd been busking there earlier and the next thing I knew we were having iced teas on the patio of The Rusty Lion and I couldn't even remember why I'd been feeling so down." She paused for a moment. "No, that's not quite true. I knew why, but it just didn't seem quite so important anymore."

"That's good."

Tanya nodded. "He's really quite the character, isn't he?"

"Who? Geordie?"

"Well, who else are we talking about?"

Zeffy gave her a considering look. Good lord, could Tanya actually be going for a normal person for a change? Geordie Riddell was one of the sweetest men Zeffy knew, a kind, gentle soul, shy sometimes to a fault, but not in the least a Milquetoast, thank goodness. Like most of her friends, Zeffy liked a man to be considerate, but she still wanted him to have some spunk. Sometimes it seemed to her that this whole PC agenda had taken things all the way over to the other extreme. Instead of having to fend off macho jocks, now you ended up having to jump-start a bunch of wimps. Yuck. A certain amount of shyness could be attractive, but there had to be some backbone there as well. Happily, Geordie had enough of both.

"So is there romance in the air?" she asked.

Tanya actually blushed. "Kind of early to say, wouldn't you think? I mean, he was just being friendly."

"Jilly says he's way shy when it comes to that sort of thing – both him and his brother. It's a genetic thing."

Tanya laughed. "Oh, right."

"So you sort of have to make the first move," Zeffy went on, "because they'll never do it on their own."

"Maybe we could double-date them."

Zeffy smiled. "So you are interested."

"Well, he's the first guy I've met in forever who seems to be genuinely nice. And he's certainly good-looking."

"Quite good-looking – in a scruffy sort of way."

"This is true. He is scruffy, but I'm thinking more that he's such a nice change from Johnny."

"Anything decent would be a change from Johnny," Zeffy pronounced with great solemnity.

"This is true. After what he put me through this morning, I don't ever want to see him again."

"Except to collect your money."

Tanya shook her head. "I don't even care about that."

Zeffy put her hands behind her head and looked up at the ceiling. She wore a look of satisfaction that was positively beatific.

"Well, I'm going to make sure he pays up," she said. "And I'll enjoy collecting every cent of what he owes you – right down to the last errant penny."

XV • MAX

THE SUPER'S apartment is easy enough to find. It's on the first floor, at the very back of Devlin's building. Under the buzzer someone's taped a small rectangle of paper that reads, TED PINKNEY, SUPERINTENDENT. I thumb the buzzer and wait. I'm expecting someone like the super in my old building in Foxville, an overweight balding man in worn chinos and a sleeveless T-shirt who answers every question and complaint with the same unfriendly glower. Pinkney's not even close.

The man who comes to the door is a tall, cadaverous individual possessing a full head of slicked-back hair. He's wearing a spotless white T-shirt, dark blue mechanic's overalls with sharp creases in each leg and leather work-boots, polished to a bright shine. He answers the door with a cheerful smile that lasts only until he recognizes me – or at least until he recognizes Devlin, which, all things considered, is pretty much the same thing.

"Don't start," he says before I can speak. "I warned you and warned you and all you ever did was laugh it off."

"I'm sorry?"

Pinkney shakes his head. "Playing innocent's not going to help either. We carried you for almost three months."

"But—"

"You got the notice, so why the surprise?"

"So he's—" I catch myself. "So I've been evicted. That's why the locks have been changed."

Pinkney nods his head. "Weller was by with an officer a couple of hours ago to wrap things up. You weren't there, so we figured you'd just cut out."

Weller, I assume, would be Devlin's landlord.

"And my things?"

"They've been impounded. If there a anything left over after the sale, Weller will issue you a check. Do you have a forwarding address?"

"Jesus, what do you think?"

Pinkney gives me a sympathetic look. "Don't get mad at me. They told me to ask."

"So all I get to walk out with is the clothes on my back," I say.

"It's not like you didn't get a chance to pack a bag or anything, Johnny. I gave you the final notice myself on Friday. I thought for sure you'd work something out over the weekend. If you couldn't come up with the money, you could at least have taken a few things with you. I'll tell you, I was surprised to see everything still there. You should have at least taken your stereo and TV. Now you've got nothing."

But why should Devlin have bothered? I think. Why take anything? The eviction isn't his problem because he's found another way out.

"Look," Pinkney says. "If you need a couple of bucks . . ."

I shake my head. I won't accept charity – not in Devlin's name.

"I appreciate it," I say, "but no thanks."

"What're you going to do now?" Pinkney says.

"Get my life back," I tell him.

Pinkney gives me a confused look.

"I wouldn't know how to begin to explain," I say. I put out my hand. "You seem like a decent person. I hope Devlin didn't screw you the way he seems to have screwed everybody else he knew."

Pinkney automatically takes my hand and shakes, but I can see his confusion deepening as I speak.

"You know," I go on, "the more I get to know this guy, the less I like him, and I didn't much care for him right from the first."

"Are you sure you're going to be okay?" Pinkney asks, a hint of uneasiness in his voice.

I know exactly what he's thinking: Devlin's lost it – not taking money when it's offered to him, acting differently, talking about himself in the third person. Pinkney doesn't get it, but I'm not about to explain.

'Maybe we'll run into each other again under more pleasant circumstances," I tell the super. "See you around."

"Sure," Pinkney says dubiously. "See you."

I walk away, feeling the weight of the man's gaze on my back for the entire length of the hallway. By the time I reach the front door of the building, I still haven't heard Pinkney's door close. I step outside and set off down the street.

I walk aimlessly, the blocks disappearing under my feet. I'm oblivious to my surroundings. I think of the super, standing in the doorway of his apartment, watching me leave. Scratching his head, maybe. Definitely thinking Devlin's gone off the deep end. For all I know, he's still standing there, will be standing there for hours to come. I don't much care.

I walk until I find myself deep in Fitzhenry Park. I blink in surprise at the tall trees that rise up on either side of the path in this part of the park. Beech. Some magnificent white pine. A stand of hemlock. The woods are deep here – untouched, some say, from the days when the first settlers came.

I take a deep breath, savoring the pungent smell of the pines and hemlock, the sap and the dead needles that carpet the ground; then I step off the path and walk in under the trees. Moments later, the woods swallow me from sight and it's like I was never there.

XVI • NIA FISHER

NIA LAY in bed long after her mother had left, trying to hold back her own tears. The aftermath of the argument they'd just had lay like a heavyweight on her chest and she found it hard to breathe. Though her mother had tried to hide it, Nia knew she'd left the house crying. Nia had wanted to go after her, to say "I'm sorry, Mom, I love you, too," but the words stuck in her throat, choking her. Tears blurred her sight. She hated the constant antagonism that lay between them but couldn't seem to stop herself from saying the horrible things she did.

If only their relationship could go back to the way it had been. They'd been friends before, confidantes as much as parent and child. But the turnabout in how they related to each other had settled deeply into its new pattern and reversing it at this point no longer seemed possible.

It was weird how much things could change in a year. They used to get along so well. They used to feel so lucky. But her mother had become progressively more unhappy and bitter over the last few months – with her job, with her love life, with the world in general – and Nia was left to bear the brunt of that discontent. Nia knew she was no angel, but everything she did now was criticized. They never talked anymore, only bickered. At one time her mother had been so proud of the free spirit in her daughter; now that free-spiritedness was the source of much of their contention.

She understood that her mother was making an effort to keep her problems to herself, to deal with them on her own and not worry Nia about them, but that was a large part of what was going wrong with their relationship. Her mother had always been there for Nia. Now it seemed to Nia it was her turn to be encouraging, her turn to be the one to offer comfort and support. Instead her mother was shutting her out, hiding not only her problems from Nia, but the other details of her life that they'd once shared.

That was one of the reasons she spent so much time downstairs with Max: she was lonely, plain and simple. Max helped fill the hole in her life put there by the growing alienation between her mother and herself. Having been her mother's best friend for so many years, she'd never really been able to connect with her own peers because their concerns all seemed so juvenile. She hadn't needed another best friend when she'd had her mother. Losing that friendship had been devastating because she had nothing to replace it – nothing until Max moved in downstairs and proved both interesting to be around and amicable to her daily visits.

Sometimes she thought she drove him a little crazy – yammering on about anything that happened to pop in her head – but he never asked her to leave. And they could share companionable silences, too, the way she and her mother used to be able to before those silences all seemed strained. She supposed she filled the role of surrogate daughter for Max, since he didn't have any kids of his own. Though she didn't see him as a father figure. He was just her friend.

It was funny that her mother thought she was seeing too much of him. Max was the one who, when Nia complained about the latest thing her mother had said or done, would always try to get her to see things from her mother's side.

"Doesn't sound to me like you're opening up to her either," he'd say. "How's she supposed to know how you're feeling if you don't tell her?"

"You don't understand. I used to be able to do that, but I can't anymore. Whatever I tell her now just gets thrown back in my face the next time she's mad at me. I don't want to give her any more ammunition."

Max would smile. "So why don't you tell her that as well?"

She knew he was right, but things had progressed to a point where it was too late for that kind of dialogue. She was gun-shy, having been cut down too many times already.

And while she could understand how maybe her mother felt the same way, it didn't make it any easier for her to open up. She couldn't even say she was sorry anymore. The pain in her heart created a bottleneck in her throat that only allowed the hurtful words to come out, not the ones she really wanted to say.

Nia sighed and rolled over to look at her clock. The way she was feeling now, the last thing she wanted to do was get out of bed, but she knew she should get up and face the day. It wasn't like tomorrow would be any better.

I should move out, she thought as she slid her legs out from under the bedclothes and put them on the floor.

The idea scared her as much as it thrilled her. Where would she go? What would she do?

Rummaging around on the night table in front of her cassette machine, she dug through her cassettes until she found one by Thelonious Monk. The cool sound of his piano slid through her thoughts, washing away their immediacy. She loved the sound of jazz, from big band and bebop to fusion and the more ambient stuff that was now often filed under New Age in the record stores. It was music rich with heart and soul, but still technically brilliant. Sometimes she thought it was its very dichotomy that appealed the most to her.

She slipped on a pair of black jeans and went into the bathroom to wash up. The music followed her through the ritual of combing out her hair, then down the hall to the kitchen, where she brewed herself a strong cup of coffee from an espresso blend. She wasn't hungry, but she nibbled on a piece of dry toast so that she wouldn't have to lie about skipping breakfast if her mother should rag her about it when she got home.

The Monk cassette ended while she was still eating, but

she didn't feel like putting on more music. There were times when she liked to have just one sound in her head and let it settle there throughout the day, a kind of balm against the inferior music she was subjected to when she left the apartment and had to put up with traffic noise, the muzak in stores, or whatever crap somebody was blasting from their boom box. She did the same thing with poetry sometimes, or chapters from novels, the text gathering power in her mind the longer she held on to it, the selected lines untouched by other, less meaningful words.

After a while, she got up to check the mail. She paused just outside her door when she heard voices on the landing below hers, not quite ready yet to face anybody else today, not even Max. She didn't mean to eavesdrop, and was about to go back inside the apartment, but curiosity got the better of her, and then the very oddness of the conversation made her creep over to the railing and listen more closely still.

It was Max, speaking to a stranger, but Max might as well be a stranger himself from the weird things he was saying and the way he was saying them. She shook her head as she finally started to get the gist of the conversation. What they were talking about was impossible.

She jumped when the door suddenly slammed shut below her, heartbeat accelerating. The stranger who claimed to be Max hammered on Max's door. She began to retreat from the railing, holding still when she heard the door open once more. The ensuing conversation – mostly from Max's side, this time – only muddied the waters further.

The door closed again but this time the stranger didn't try to regain Max's attention. Nia heard him move on the landing, the creak of his weight on a stair, then nothing. Pulse drumming, she returned to the railing and leaned over to see the stranger sitting on the steps coming up to her landing. His back was toward her, his face was in profile. He was no one she'd ever seen before. Strikingly handsome, a little disheveled. And a complete stranger.

When he bowed his head, his anguish so plain, her heart went out to him. She certainly didn't know him. He might well be crazy. But she couldn't help feeling for him, empathizing with the bleak despair that seemed to grip him. Maybe it was because it mirrored her own feelings this morning, only increased a hundredfold.

She leaned there on the railing watching him until he finally stirred. Afraid that he might look up and see her, she slipped back across the landing to her own apartment, bare feet silent on the wooden floor. She closed the door with a barely audible click, then hurried to the bay window in the living room. From there she could look down at the street in front of her building. She held the white sheers open just a crack with her finger so that she could peer down without being seen.

The stranger appeared after a few moments. She started to let the sheers fall back in place when he looked up, but then realized that he was studying Max's windows not her own. She'd couldn't read the play of expressions that moved across his features. It was like trying to hold the wind, they shifted so quickly one into the other. The turmoil of his emotions again seemed to echo her own earlier confusion and again her heart went out to him.

She stepped back from his view when his gaze rose up to her window, letting the sheers close. She waited a beat before returning to stand by the glass. He was no longer looking up at her window. He strode off down the narrow cobblestoned street and she watched until he was lost from view. Letting the sheers close once more, she slowly sat down on the sofa and tried to figure out exactly what it was that she'd stumbled onto. Something very strange, that was for sure.

The conversation between the two men had been surreal and she was convinced that she shouldn't take it at face value – after all, what they'd been talking about was impossible. So it had been some sort of . . . what? Code? Metaphor? It didn't make any sense at all. Then she thought of the fact that Max was still in his apartment. Normally he was in his shop by eight, already working for an hour or so before he opened for business.

She went back into her bedroom and checked the time. Just after ten. That late! She chewed at her lower lip, trying to decide what to do. After a moment, she came to a decision and finished getting dressed.

She got rid of the T-shirt she'd been sleeping in and put on a clean black one, tucking it into the waist of her jeans. Over that she put on a vest that had been a black jean jacket until she'd torn the sleeves off, much to her mother's dismay – "Nia, I just paid fifty dollars for that jacket!" Sitting on the edge of the bed, she tugged on her dark purple combat boots, laced them tightly, and finally stood up. She looked at herself in the mirror. Without makeup, her face looked like it belonged to a ghost.

"I *feel* like a ghost," she said softly.

In their kinder moments, her schoolmates referred to her as "that death chick," the rare times she did attend classes. She supposed it was preferable to "fuckhead" and "that creepy bitch," which she got more often, though really, she didn't much care what they called her. Who had the time to pay attention to cretins that didn't even know the difference between a Beat and a Goth? Her predominantly black wardrobe wasn't an embracing of the funereal look the way the Goths dressed. She had no great preoccupation with death at all, except for how it had stolen so many of the greats before their time, stolen them when they still had so much to share. Kerouac. Wes Montgomery. Lenny Bruce. Robert Johnson. The list was far too long and depressing.

But she was interested in ghosts, especially in the idea that people could become ghosts in their own lives and simply fade away because, after a while, no one could see them at all. That was the truth behind so many of the mysterious disappearances that had people so baffled, she was sure. The man on his way to the corner store. The woman who never made it home from work. It wasn't that they'd gone AWOL from their lives, or even something more sinister. They simply lost contact with who they were, with the people around them. With nothing left to anchor them, they became invisible, ghosts. And eventually just faded away completely. . .

She turned away from the mirror and picked up her knapsack from where it lay by the foot of her bed. Slinging it over her shoulder by one strap, she left the apartment again. She went all the way downstairs, ostensibly to check the mail. There was none. Turning from the mailboxes, she crossed the foyer to the door of Max's shop, but the CLOSED sign was still taped to the glass, the shop dark except for what light came through the front window.

Maybe he's sick, she thought, peering into the dark room as though she'd find the answer in there among the various tools and instruments, some half-finished, some only in for repair. The mandolin from that friendly bluegrass player who'd been in last week was lying on the worktable, surrounded by sketches of Max's plans for its inlay pattern. Otherwise everything was in its place.

Nia sighed and turned away from the door. So now she'd be the good neighbor and check up on him to see how he was doing, she supposed. Nothing to worry about. He was her friend, right?

Her uneasiness grew with each step she took up to his landing. She knew she had nothing to be afraid of – this was *Max*, after all – but she couldn't shake the creepy feeling that had settled inside her ever since she'd overheard the conversation between him and that sad stranger. It had been such weird business, so crazy. She felt a little crazy herself, thinking about it, half-convinced that she hadn't really heard them properly. Maybe it was like one of those black-and-white Cary Grant comedies that her mother liked so much, the ones where somebody would be talking about one thing, but because of mixed signals or whatever, everybody would think he was talking about something else. The conversation worked either way you heard it.

She stopped in front of Max's door.

No, she thought. It hadn't been that kind of conversation. She hadn't mistaken what they'd been talking about – it just didn't make any sense. And she couldn't even ask Max about it, because then she'd have to admit she'd been eavesdropping on him.

She had to smile at herself. She was building this way out of proportion, she realized. There was a reasonable explanation of what she'd heard this morning. She might never get to hear it, but it still existed, because one thing was for sure, people didn't switch bodies – not this side of a Hollywood screen. To consider otherwise was just being silly.

She knocked on the door, stepping back when it was flung open a few moments later.

"Hey, I was serious, pal," Max began, his voice trailing off when he realized that she wasn't the stranger he'd been talking to earlier, back for another round.

Are you feeling okay? Nia had been about to ask him. I saw the shop was closed and I got worried.

But the words stuck more forcibly in her throat than had her apology to her mother this morning. Because the man looking at her from Max's doorway, the man standing there in Max's skin . . . he was looking at her blankly, expectantly, the way you'd look at a stranger who'd come to your door, thinking it was a salesman, or a Jehovah's Witness. He didn't recognize her at all, not for a moment, and all she could do was replay in her mind the conversation she'd overheard earlier. The impossible things she'd heard went tumbling through her head until she felt as though someone had stuffed her into a spin dryer and locked the door, everything going round and round.

"Can I help you?" the man asked.

A deep coldness rose up Nia's spine and she felt sick to her stomach. With her voice still stolen by fear, all she could do was shake her head and back away.

"Are you one of those deaf-mutes?" he asked.

Nia continued to back away. Her legs were all watery and she found herself making hopeless promises to a god she'd never quite believed in that they wouldn't give way on her and tumble her to the floor. The man who'd stolen Max's body studied her a little more closely.

"You know, sweet thing," he said slowly, "I think maybe you and I should have ourselves a private little talk."

He knows he screwed up, Nia realized. He knows he screwed up, that he's supposed to know me, that I know what he's done to the real Max, and now he's going to kill me so that I can't tell anybody else.

The man took a step toward her, hand outstretched as though he were trying to coax a nervous animal to come to him. That was all it took to break Nia's paralysis. She bolted. Not upstairs where he could trap her in her own apartment – she didn't want him to know where she lived – but down to the first floor and out the front door, running at full speed, boots clattering on the wooden floor and then the cobblestones outside, chest so tight with fear she thought it would burst.

She didn't slow down until she got to where the street began a twist that would take it out of sight of her apartment building. Banging up against the nearest wall, she looked back to see that there was no one following her. She held on to the wall for support and bent over, trying to catch her breath.

She couldn't go back, she realized. Not by herself. Not with that . . . that monster still in the building. She'd have to wait until her mother got home from work and then – then what? What could she possibly tell her mother that wouldn't sound completely insane? Nia shook her head. With the way things were going between them, her mother would think the worst and try to check her into some drug rehab clinic.

Okay, so she wouldn't say anything. But she'd still wait for her mother to come home before she went back in there, except then she remembered that her mother wasn't coming home after work tonight. She had a date and God knew how late she'd be getting in.

Nia slid down to the ground and leaned back against the wall. She stared at her building with morbid fascination.

What could she do? The only course of action that seemed open to her was to try to track down the stranger from the hallway – the one who claimed he really was Max – but in a city this size, that would be almost as impossible a task as trying to convince anybody that what she'd heard was true. But the stranger was the only one who could help her, the only one who'd believe her.

Stranger? she thought suddenly. That conversation returned to haunt her again. No, that had been Max, incredible as it might be.

She stood up slowly and gave her apartment building a last searching look. The man in Max's skin still hadn't made an appearance, but she knew he was in there. Waiting for her if she tried to return. She shivered and turned, walking quickly away.

Oh Max, she thought. How am I ever going to find you?

XVII • MAX

I NEVER realized how big the wooded tracts in Fitzhenry Park are until today. You could hide an army in here. Or maybe there already is an army hidden here, for I keep coming across rough campsites, cardboard shelters tucked in under the pines, ratty blankets or sleeping bags hidden under the spreading boughs of the stands of cedar or wedged up in the branches of the hemlocks and hardwoods. More than a few of the city's homeless are squatting here.

I think I can feel them watching me at times, but I never see or hear anyone. Which isn't surprising, considering how much noise I'm making myself.

Occasionally I stumble out from among the trees onto one of the many paved paths that cut through the park, startling a jogger or in-line skater with my sudden appearance. The fear in their eyes bothers me a lot. The way they put as much distance as they can between themselves and me. One woman on in-line skates gives a sharp cry of alarm when she sees me and hugs the far side of the path before she speeds away.

No one has ever been afraid of me before and the experience appalls me. That woman had been terrified, coming around the corner to find me standing here on the path. I watch the flash of her legs as she flees and make a promise that this is one more thing Devlin's going to pay for when I finally settle accounts with him. No one should be made to feel like this, especially not while trying to cope with everything else I have to.

Later on in the day I meet someone who isn't startled by my sudden appearance, merely indifferent. He's a hobo, a homeless man, sitting on one of the many wooden benches that line the paths, bearded, long-haired, grimy. Shabby clothes, eyes unfocused and sunk deep in a gaunt face, a plastic shopping bag stuffed with clothing at his feet. The skin of his hands and face is like old leather, weathered by the elements, dirt caught in the deep creases. It's impossible to guess his age, though judging from his body odor, I can make an educated guess as to the last time he had a bath.

We study each other for a long moment when I first come out of the trees. I stick my hands in my pockets. I touch the handful of change in one of them. Not even a dollar there. Not enough to buy a subway token or a coffee in most places. The homeless man's appearance acquires a new poignancy for me then.

That's going to be me, if I don't get out of this soon, I realize. Another homeless man that no one sees and no one cares about.

"How're you doing?" I try.

Right then I just want to hear somebody else's voice, someone who doesn't know Johnny Devlin and hold a grudge against him. The hobo watches me from under his thick eyebrows, but says nothing. His continuing disinterest wakes a twitch in my chest.

The guy's worse off than me, I think, and even he won't have anything to do with me.

"Yeah, well you have a good day," I say.

The hobo finally stirs. He spits a wad of greenish phlegm on the pavement between us.

"Fuck you," he says, and offers me a toothless grin with no humor in it.

I retreat, stumbling back into the woods.

It wasn't personal, I tell myself. The guy was just some sick, old bum who wouldn't have a kind word to say to anyone. But I can't shake the feeling that it was personal. No matter who I am in my own head, the whole world sees me as Devlin. The whole world recognizes me only by Devlin's worthlessness – even people who've never met me before – and that's how it's going to be from here on out. I'm going to be met with, if not antagonism, then certainly indifference for the rest of my life.

I come out of the trees again, but this time it's to find myself on a rounded granite headland overlooking the shore of the lake. A bike path follows the shoreline, twenty feet or so below me. The traffic on it is heavier than the paths I've come across earlier, but standing above it, I'm distanced from the passersby. I could be on another planet, for all the notice they take of me.

Which is just as well, really. The last thing I want now is to be among other people.

I sit down on the smoothed rock and lean back against the bole of a tall cedar that's managed to root itself in a crevice. Putting a hand behind my head, I rub the rough bark of the tree. It flakes easily under my touch, getting under my fingernails. I bring my fingers to my nose and inhale the rich aroma of the wood, letting the familiar scent calm me. After a while I can feel my tension begin to ease. The tightness leaves my shoulders and chest and I find it a little easier to breathe.

The far horizon of the lake catches my gaze. With the growing dusk, the demarcation between sky and water is disappearing, smearing into one broad canvas of faded blues and greys. I find myself thinking of Janossy and what he'd have to say about my situation now. I smile. Probably the same thing Janossy said whenever he started a new project, quoting Yogi Berra as though he were a Zen master instead of a baseball player: "You've got to be very careful if you don't know where you're going." And then he'd tell me to meditate.

I rub the residue of the cedar bark between my fingers and breathe its scent again. I don't need meditation to regain my balance. All I need is my life back.

My stomach growls.

Or at least a decent meal.

I had supper last night around seven as I usually do – closed the shop, went upstairs and cooked a stir fry that I ate with some reheated rice. But that was while I was still in my own body. Who knew when Devlin had last eaten.

A sudden rustle in the trees behind me makes me sit up and turn quickly. I don't see anything at first; then a dog creeps forward on its belly, moving out of the brush but stopping well away from where I'm sitting. A stray. Fur matted, ribs showing. It doesn't look to be any particular breed, just a midsized mongrel with some terrier in it, some shepherd. Maybe a little Lab. Heinz 57 – that was what they called a dog like that when I was a kid.

"Hey, buddy."

I hold out my hand but make no move toward the animal. The dog watches me, tail twitching, but comes no closer.

"Wish I had something to feed you. I think you could use it more than me, though I guess it won't be long before I start looking as rough as you. But I can give a little affection and that's got to be worth something, right? Guys like us, we need to get it where we can."

The dog thumps its tail once, but holds its position, belly to the ground, submissive. I can tell it's interested in me, that the soft tones of my voice are easing its fear, but not enough for it to come any closer. I don't blame it. The sort of life a stray like this leads, it's probably had people cursing it and throwing things at it more than it ever got a kind word or a pat.

"Is that it, old fella? People treating you the way they've been treating me? Nobody's got a kind word, there's nobody to turn to, but you've got nothing of your own? Tell me about it."

The dog lies with its paws crossed in front of it, the weight of its head resting on its paws. Whenever I speak, its tail gives a weak thump against the stone.

"C'mere, buddy. I won't hurt you."

The dusk's falling rapidly now, but my eyes adjust to the poor light. I can still see the dog, know it's watching me, drawn, but too nervous to come any closer. I let my hand fall back onto my lap.

"That's okay," I tell it. "You just take it easy. We'll lie here and keep each other company. Would you like that?"

It's so dark now that the dog's only a shadow on the rock, but I let myself believe that I saw its tail thump in agreement. I lean back against the tree again and close my eyes.

I'll just rest for a little bit and then figure out what I'm going to do next.

But the long weird day catches up with me in a rush of weariness. Just as I'm drifting off I sense, more than see, the dog come wriggling forward to lay its head on my lap. I shift my arm slightly and the dog tenses, relaxing only when I lay a hand on its shoulder and absently ruffle the matted fur. Sighing, the dog closes its own eyes and I fall asleep, still patting him.

XVIII • ZEFFY

AFTER DINNER, Zeffy retreated to her room to practice. She pulled out her guitar case from where she stored it under her bed, as hidden from cursory view as was her desire to sing. Her guitar was a midprice Yamaha, the best she could afford for the time being. One day she'd get something better – an old Martin, maybe, or even commission a Laskin or a Trader. A smile touched her lips as she took the guitar out of its case. Right, like she could ever afford to actually have one built to her own specs. But a person could dream, couldn't she?

Her strings were starting to go dead, but she didn't feel like changing them until the day of the gig, so it took her a little while to get in tune. She was very aware of Tanya reading a magazine in the living room, which made it hard for her to loosen up. She knew it was stupid. In a few days' time she'd be playing these same songs in front of a few hundred people, but she had this thing where, if she knew there was someone else in the apartment, she always found herself holding back. Didn't get the ring out of her guitar the way she wanted it to sound. Didn't project much past the back of her throat.

She practiced scales for a while, hoping that Tanya would at least switch on the TV. After a half-hour, she gave up and started working on her set. She closed her eyes, pretending she wasn't sitting on the end of her bed in her own bedroom, but on stage at the YoMan, her guitar and voice booming back at her from the monitors, the PA filling the club with her sound.

She didn't have a long set, only nine songs. Having long since worked the kinks out of the material, practice now entailed running through the set two or three times a day. She started with an original, a real rouser that, with the right mix by the sound man, should have her guitar swooping and swelling in waves the way Luka Bloom's did the one time she saw him in concert. Guy didn't need a backup band with that sound. She followed that with a cover of Kiya Heartwood's "Wishing Well" – one of those songs that she wished she'd written, delicate fingerpicking, sweet melody, but the words were so resonant, at times almost grim. It was about rising from the abyss, about facing the worst and being strong enough to get through to the other side of it, if not entirely intact, then at least true to yourself.

The next song was another original, also about facing darkness, but the character in this song hadn't had either the luck, or just plain fortitude, of the one in Heartwood's song. When all was said and done, its protagonist was the one who was always left standing on her own, unable to understand where it had all gone wrong.

It had a simple chord structure, the hook coming with the change from the song's major key to its relative minor for the first couple of lines in the chorus. Zeffy sang it, almost completely transported away now – not to the imaginary club in her head, but to that place she went where the songs came from, where a good performance had chills cat-pawing up her spine.

> *What she has she is holding,*
> *But what she is holding is gone.*
> *It all fades away at the break of the day*
> *in the hush that comes just before dawn.*

The song ended on a minor chord and she let it echo and fade before she finally opened her eyes. Still feeling a little spacy from the feeling that had come over her while singing the song, she was surprised to find Tanya leaning against the door jamb of her bedroom. She hadn't even heard the door open.

"That's a new one, isn't it?" her roommate said.

Zeffy nodded. "I've been working on it for a while, but it finally came together for me last week."

"I really like it."

"Thanks."

Tanya hesitated for a moment, then asked, "Is it about me?"

"I'm not sure," Zeffy said. She honestly didn't know. "It started out from the way you were feeling after Frank broke up with you, but then it went off somewhere on its own. You know me. I never seem to be able to write about what's happening in my life or around me, except indirectly."

"I feel like that sometimes," Tanya said. "Like in your song, I mean. Not all the time. Not right now. But I know that feeling all too well."

Zeffy nodded. "Me, too."

Tanya looked at her in surprise. "I can't imagine you ever feeling that lonely."

"Lonely's such a specific word," Zeffy said. "I think I'd describe it more as a sense of forlornness that I never quite understand." She shrugged. "I don't know where exactly it comes from, it just shows up, all uninvited, and hangs around for a while."

Tanya straightened up from where she was leaning against the door jamb. "I guess I was interrupting you."

"No, it's okay. You look like you've got something on your mind. C'mon in and sit down."

She laid her guitar back in its case and moved over a little on the bed to give Tanya some room. Her roommate hesitated, then walked over from where she was standing, and joined her.

"It's just stupid," she said. "I fell asleep while I was reading and then I had this weird dream where everybody I knew treated me the same way Johnny did this morning – you, Jilly, Geordie, my mother. It was like nobody knew me anymore and when I woke up, I felt all creeped out. I mean, I knew it was just a dream, but I still had to come in here and see if you, I don't know . . ."

Her voice trailed off and she gave an embarrassed little laugh.

"To see if I'd recognize you?" Zeffy asked softly

Tanya nodded. "Dumb, right?"

"No. Everybody gets dreams like that where what happens in them feels so real that can't believe it didn't actually happen when they wake up. I mean, think of Sophie."

"But she *really* believes . . ."

Zeffy smiled. "Or something. The thing is, you shouldn't be embarrassed about feeling the way you did. I know you're not really over Johnny, so what he did this morning must've really hurt you."

"Oh, I'm over him now," Tanya said. "After what he did today, he's history. I even threw away my cigarettes."

"This is a good sign," Zeffy told her.

Tanya sighed. "I suppose. But now I can't get rid of the feeling that the only reason I'm all interested in Geordie is because, well, you know me. I don't like to be between boyfriends."

"I can't help you there," Zeffy said.

"But what would you do?"

Zeffy didn't even have to think about it. "I'd take it slow."

"But don't you worry that if you take it too slow, then maybe he'll think you're not interested in him?"

"If a guy's seriously interested in you, you can take it as slow as you need to. I don't mean you ignore him, Tanya. You just don't jump right in bed with him or declare your undying love on the first or second date."

Tanya frowned. "I don't—"

"I didn't mean you in particular," Zeffy assured her. "I meant you as in plural. People in general."

"Don't commit until they do. Jeez, guys get all the breaks, don't they."

Zeffy laughed. "What? You don't think guys have anxiety attacks about this kind of thing themselves?"

"I guess you're right."

"Can I get that in writing?"

Tanya shook her head. "No, but you should write a song about it," she said, getting up. "You could set it up like an advice column, part of the verse being the question, the other part the answer."

"I think John Prine already did."

Tanya paused by the door. "Then you should write a song about my dream."

Zeffy thought about that dream. Nobody knowing you. Taken to the extreme the way Tanya had in her dream, it really was a metaphor for how people felt lots of times, wasn't it? Not that nobody might physically recognize them, but that nobody understood the person they really were.

"Maybe I will," she said.

But Tanya had already left the room.

XIX • NIA

BY THE end of the day, Nia was spent. Her feet and calves hurt from walking around all day and it had gotten to the point where all she wanted to do was get her own piece of cardboard and lie down on it the way some of the panhandlers she passed were doing. Instead, she continued on down Williamson Street until she got to Gypsy Records, where she claimed for herself a portion of the wrought-iron bench that stood outside the store, only just beating a punky-looking guy to the seat. He said something snarky to her, but the words didn't register. She merely smiled at him and stretched her legs in front of her. The luxury of being off her feet felt glorious. The punk reacted like a cat, sauntering off down the street as if that had been his intention all along.

Nia watched him go, then listlessly turned her attention to the traffic going by on Williamson Street. It was coming up on rush hour and the four-lane street had grown progressively more congested as commuters jostled for position on the northbound lanes with cabs and buses. Every so often the pavement would shake as a subway went by under the sidewalk, but the rumble of its passage barely registered above the street noise. They were playing an old Lee Konitz album inside the store. The sound of his sax spilled out of the speakers hanging above the entrance of the store, but she soon gave up trying to pick it out.

After a while she found herself staring at a weed growing up beside one of the planters the city had placed at the edge of the sidewalk as part of its efforts to green the city. She had no idea what sort of a plant it was, but its tenacity won her sympathy far more than the geraniums and petunias trying to survive amidst the trash that littered the planter and the clouds of exhaust. She didn't quite know why she identified with it. Maybe it was because they were both outsiders. Neither of them fit in.

As she watched, a pair of women approached the planter and sat down on its edge to wait for their bus. The running shoes they both wore seemed out of place with their office clothes: nylons, tight short skirts, blouses with padded shoulders. Both carried briefcases. One of the women put her foot on the weed, flattening it under the sole of her sneaker, and Nia looked away, sighing. So much for its chances for survival.

She let her gaze wander the street, looking for a face she now doubted she'd ever find. Within fifteen minutes of deciding to track down the stranger she'd spied in the hallway of her building, it had dawned on her exactly what an impossible task she'd set herself. Some could claim to be able to find a needle in a haystack, but then some people also thought that angels danced on the head of a pin.

No, she soon realized that she was never going to find him, but since she couldn't go back home anyway – not with Max, or whoever it was that looked like Max, still there –

she'd stuck to her search for hours, wandering all over the Market, then widening the circle of her search to the downtown area. She began to feel that she'd have a better chance of winning a lottery, even if she never bought tickets, or getting hit by a comet.

The man could have passed her a dozen times without her recognizing him. All it would take was a slight change in his appearance. A hat, or a pair of sunglasses. He could have just gone home – if he had a home – or left the city. She'd gotten to the point now where she wasn't even all that sure what he looked like anymore. She'd only ever seen him in a darkened hallway up close, and then from a distance on the street below her window.

A bus pulled up to the curb in front of her and the two women sitting on the planter got up to join the crowd boarding it. The crushed weed lay flat against the pavement. Nia felt like going over to it and trying to coax it upright once more, but what was the point? Someone else would just step on it again. What was more amazing was that it had managed to survive as long as it had.

She continued to sit there, not even bothering to search the faces of the passersby, until the traffic started to die down. She could hear the music coming from Gypsy Records' speakers more clearly now. The lead instrument was still a sax, but it was more contemporary than the disc they'd been playing earlier. Everette Harp, she decided, recognizing his style from a special she'd heard on Zoe B.'s radio show, *Nightnoise*, her favorite late-night listening. He had a nice smooth sound, but she wasn't sure she liked the somewhat schmaltzy chorus of background voices.

Halfway through the next cut, the music was abruptly shut off. She started, feeling as though her ears had suddenly popped, then realized it was closing time. The staff would be leaving now. They'd walk, maybe take the sub or a bus home, sit down to dinner ... She felt jealous of the normality of their lives, which was weird, because she'd never in her life had the slightest yearning to be normal before this moment. But she'd never been in her present situation before, either.

She was tired and hungry, and if the truth had to be told, a little scared. Well, she couldn't go home, not with the chance that the stranger pretending to be Max might still be there, but she could at least have something to eat. She hadn't had a thing since that bit of toast this morning and a large cappuccino she'd bought from a street vendor in the middle of the afternoon.

She checked her finances to see what she could afford, then got up and walked down the block to a coffee bar with the unassuming name of Susie's, where she had a couple of cups of coffee – the beans freshly roasted on the premises – and a cheese and tomato sandwich on light rye. The coffee was better than the sandwich, but she was so hungry she ate the whole thing, stale bread, processed cheese and all. Splurging on a couple of chocolate-chip cookies, which were good, she settled back into her seat.

The coffee bar was filled with yuppies and wanna-be alternative types – the kinds of trendy people that she normally couldn't stand to be around – but she still stayed there, nursing her second coffee for an hour before finally getting up to leave. Once she was back out on the pavement, she didn't know what to do. It was still too early to go home.

Returning to the bench in front of the record store, she killed another hour before this seedy-looking guy started to hit on her. He made her skin crawl with his slicked-back hair and this black leather jacket that looked so cheap it had to be made of vinyl. But his mouth was the worst of all – lips so thin they were almost nonexistent and every time he smiled, all she could see were the gaps where he was missing teeth.

It took going into a bar to lose him. She got kicked out almost immediately for being underage, but at least her admirer was gone by the time she was escorted out by a surprisingly apologetic bouncer. She checked her watch – not even nine – and decided to walk around some more, just to kill time until her mother would get home, but what she thought was merely aimless wandering brought her within sight of her home before she even realized where she was going.

She paused in the shadow of an old brick house and looked at her building. The lights were off in her apartment and Max's shop, but it seemed like every light in Max's apartment was on. Her anxiety returned. She didn't have the nerve to try to creep by his door, couldn't even stand to be this close to him, so she turned and retraced her steps through the narrow twisting streets of the Market until she got to the corner of Lee Street where her mother would arrive. She'd either come by bus, or – if her date had a car – this was where she'd have him let her off.

She stood there for a while shifting her weight from one foot to the other, until she realized that this was really dumb. Her mother might still be hours, probably would be hours, considering how long it had been since she'd last been out on a date.

Only why did it have to be tonight? A horrible thought occurred to Nia. God, what if she really hit it off with this guy and stayed overnight? Except she'd call home, if that was the case, and discover that Nia wasn't home either. Which would bring her back, all worried, and Nia knew she'd really be in for it then.

Sighing, she looked around for a more comfortable spot to wait. Spotting some wooden benches farther down the block, she went and slouched in one of them, willing time to hurry up and pass.

Naturally, it wouldn't. As the minutes crept by, each slower than the last, she grew more and more irritated with her mother for staying out so late on a night like this. It made no difference that her mother knew nothing of the day's odd occurrence and so couldn't really be blamed. Nia just felt like she had to take it out on somebody and, out of habit more than anything else, her mother was an easy target.

It was unfair, and she knew it, but everything was unfair, wasn't it? That weed getting crushed in front of Gypsy's. What had happened to Max. Life in general.

Going on like this was stupid, she thought, feeling guilty and depressed, all at the same time. She forced herself to think of something else to pass the time. The last poem she'd read, she decided. Lew Welch's "The Image, as in a Hexagram." She loved the idea of the hermit in his cabin, locked away against the blizzard and winter, emerging in the spring with a book and only one set of clothes. It was so weird how Welch had gone off with a rifle into the mountains near Gary Snyder's house and just never came back. Disappeared like Ambrose Bierce in Mexico. Though maybe they didn't disappear so much as become invisible to those around them.

That thought brought back her depression, so she concentrated on the Monk album she'd been listening to this morning. She'd read somewhere that his son was planning to rerecord all of Monk's music the way it was really supposed to sound, because apparently the albums that existed had originally all been recorded in just one or two takes, not allowing Monk the time he said he needed for his arrangements. His producer described him as being somewhere between difficult and impossible, but Nia guessed that sort of thing came with genius.

She was looking forward to his son's recordings and envied his having been able to hear the music firsthand and up close the way he had. Monk had kept a piano at the foot of his bed and the first thing he'd do in the morning was get up and play. He played music all day and Nia couldn't begin to imagine how wonderful it would be to grow up in that kind of environment, although she did think it was funny that the son had taken up the drums when he started to play music himself. Still, she liked his group and meant to buy a tape or CD by them the next time she had some spare money.

She guessed her mother was right. She *should* get a job. Then she wouldn't always have to be mooching money for this and that and the next thing. She'd have her own. She wouldn't have to explain why she was broke, or what she'd spent her money on. As it was, she still got an allowance, which was so juvenile, except she couldn't not accept it, because then she'd have no money at all.

She checked her watch for what felt like the hundredth time since she'd sat down. Almost eleven now. Maybe her mother wasn't coming home. Maybe she was having so much fun she hadn't bothered to call home first, she was just going home with this guy. Maybe she was remembering the fight they'd had this morning and didn't *want* to come home. She could be putting it off for as long as she could.

Nia wouldn't blame her, considering the way she'd

treated her mother this morning. But where did it leave her? She didn't know what to do. There was no one she could stay with, and she sure wasn't going home by herself.

She could feel the beginning of a panic attack when she saw a car pull over to the curb a little farther up from where she was sitting. It stopped under a streetlight and the tightness eased in Nia's chest when she recognized her mother stepping out of the passenger's side. She got up from the bench, pausing a little uncertainly when the driver's side of the car opened as well and a woman stepped out.

What happened to her date? Nia wondered.

But then the woman came around the front of the car and embraced her mother. Nia stared, stunned, as they began to kiss. It wasn't a friendly goodnight kiss between two friends, but a long lingering kiss, hands roving up and down each other's shoulder blades and backs.

Nia shook her head.

No, she thought. This isn't real. That's not my . . .

The horror of what was happening came to her before she could finish the thought: it wasn't just Max who'd been taken over by some stranger's mind, but her mother, too.

No, she wanted to cry. It can't be, I won't let it be true. But she knew it was. That wasn't her mother. Whatever alien had swallowed Max had stolen her mother as well.

Tears welled up in her eyes, blurring her vision until she could no longer see the two women, the streetlight casting their shadow across the sidewalk in one long, entwined shape. But the image was burned in her memory.

Sobbing, Nia turned and fled into the night.

XX • MAX

I'M DREAMING of Janossy again when I wake. Suddenly, in a fright. I stare wildly up into a night sky thick with stars, the hard stone under me. I'm just as disoriented as I was this morning. My back's stiff and sore. It's dark and I'm cold and there's something warm and hairy pushed up against me. I start to panic, but then it all comes back to me. Not the dream – this time I can't remember it, only that Janossy was there. What I remember is what should be a dream.

I sit up, moving slowly so that I don't startle the stray. He starts to quiver under my hand, but I calm him down before he can bolt.

"Easy there, easy, boy," I tell him, stroking his matted fur. "There's nothing to be afraid of. Everything's going to be okay."

I'm talking as much to convince myself as him. I'm talking to hear a voice and right now even my own will do.

I guess I thought everything would go away while I was sleeping. That I'd wake in my own bed again instead of on a stone headland in Fitzhenry Park. That I'd be in my own body instead of trapped in one of some loser that nobody likes, myself included. That I'd get my life back . . .

I can see well enough in the dark to know the dog's gone big-eyed, looking at me, worried. I sense a rapport with him, as though we've been buddies for years, and find I like the feeling. We never had dogs, growing up in the city, even before my mother died, but Janossy did, Pitter and Hoo, a couple of mutts that were already ancient when I moved out to the farm. Pitter died the first year I was living there, Hoo outlived Janossy by a couple of months.

"The best animal friends," Janossy told me once, "aren't the ones you choose, but the ones that choose you. The ones that just move in on you."

"What about the ones at the animal shelter?" I asked him. If you think I'm into details now, you should have known me back then. I couldn't take anything at face value, always had to ask what if and why not. "Don't you think they deserve a chance at a good life? It's not like they can wander around, looking for the right person to move in with."

Janossy smiled. "Just because a dog's in jail, doesn't mean he can't make decisions anymore."

To hear him tell it, the dogs in lockup could *will* somebody to come in and take them home. And maybe it's true. It was true for Janossy, at any rate. Half the time he didn't so much ask questions as make pronouncements.

I always meant to get myself down to the pound to see if one of the dogs there wanted to make a decision about me, but somehow I never did get around to it. Janossy would say I was simply waiting for this old stray lying beside me now only I never knew it.

"I think I'll call you Buddy," I tell the dog. "How do you feel about that?"

I get a sloppy kiss with a big wet tongue in reply and have to wipe my face. The breath that accompanies it is even worse – almost as bad as the big lug's fur. He's seriously in need of a bath.

"We're going to have to do something about the way you smell," I tell him. Then I smile. "Though with the way things are going, we'll be a matched pair soon enough, I guess."

I lie back down again, stare at the sky, the stars, feel the warm length of the dog pressed up against my side. The city seems impossibly far away. I can't hear it, can't see it except for a hint of its glow refracted in the boughs of the trees. We could be on a camping trip, up in the mountains behind the city, or out along the lake in cottage country.

I wish we were. I wish we were just on holiday, the two of us, taking a break from the city and the shop, instead of being what we are, a couple of hoboes with nowhere else to go. It'd be easy to fall back into the depression that's been shadowing me throughout the day, but Buddy's presence makes it easier to keep at bay. It's not that I'm suddenly happy with how things are going. It's just that there's something about sharing hard times, knowing that you're not alone, that makes the hardship easier to bear. I don't wish a troubled life for Buddy or anybody else, but I have to admit I'm glad he's here now.

"It's you and me," I tell him. "So we better take care of each other because we're all we've got."

I feel the thump of his tail against my leg and fall asleep again, comforted by the even rhythm of his breathing.

The Center Cannot Hold

. . . any everywhere.
The ceremony of innocent is drowned.
W. B. Yeats, from "The Second Coming"

I'm a burning hearth. People see the smoke,
but no one comes to warm themselves.
– attributed to Vincent van Gogh

I • LISA

D AWN WAS an hour old. Through the gap between the gabled roofs of two neighboring houses, Lisa had been watching a rectangle of night sky drift from grey through pinks to a rich cerulean blue. She felt as though she'd aged twenty years overnight. Punchy from a lack of sleep and too much caffeine, all she could do was regard the perfect day that was shaping up on the other side of the windowpane and wonder how it dared present such a cheerful view when who knew what had happened to Nia? Her daughter could be lying dead in an alleyway somewhere. She could be halfway across the country, on a bus, in the cab of some tractor trailer, riding in the passenger seat of a businessman's car, a businessman who was looking for an exit at this very moment, some out-of-the-way place where he could pull over, hit the locks on the doors, and then reach for Nia . . .

She wanted to smash something, anything. She wanted to cry. When Nia got home she was going to give her such a piece of her mind. She'd ground her for life. She'd . . . she'd hold on to her so hard, she'd never let her go.

The tears were a thick pressure, welling up behind her eyes, but she made herself hold them back. She'd been crying half the night. If she started to cry this time, she was afraid she might never stop. She made herself stare at the blue rectangle of the sky, stared so hard that when she looked away orange spots danced in her eyes.

The music on the radio gave way to a newscaster with the seven-o'clock news. Turning from the window, she forced herself to pay attention. She expected the worst, to hear some horrible story about a young girl whose name was being withheld until her family could be contacted and then the phone would finally ring and it would be the police, that sergeant with the low voice saying, "I'm sorry, Ms. Fisher, but we have some very bad news ..." But the disasters outlined in the news didn't seem as though they could have anything to do with Nia and the phone didn't ring.

"Why don't they *call*?" she said.

Julie put a comforting hand over her own. "It's still early."

"Early? She's been out all night."

"I know. Bad choice of words."

But Lisa knew what she'd meant. It was the same thing that the sergeant at the Missing Persons desk had told her on the phone when she got home last night to find Nia missing. It was too early to worry. These were the difficult years. The defiant years. Teenagers Nia's age were forever testing the bounds of their parents' authority. They'd had a fight that morning? Perhaps her daughter was playing delinquent on purpose then, to prove a point. If Ms. Fisher was patient, he was sure Nia would be back on her own later on in the night, sometime in the morning, for certain, but in the meantime he'd make a note of her description and pass it along to their dispatcher. He'd call back if he heard anything at all, though he hoped Ms. Fisher understood that there were a thousand girls out there in the city matching this particular description. No, a photograph wasn't necessary.

Not at this point. She hoped it wouldn't be necessary at all. She should try to get some rest and not worry.

As if that was even an option.

"She's just never done anything like this before," Lisa said.

Julie nodded sympathetically. "But you did have a fight."

"All we seem to do is fight these days. She's been driving me crazy. But if anything's happened to her . . . "

"Everything's going to work out," Julie said. "She'll be okay."

"We don't know that."

Julie sighed. "You're right. But I remember doing this to my parents, just to make a point. I'm not saying it's right; I'm just saying it happens."

"I suppose . . ."

And hadn't she done the same thing herself? Lisa thought. Bucking a ridiculous eleven-o'clock curfew by staying out all night. And hadn't her mother said to her, I hope your children treat you the same way you've treated us. Lisa had never realized the pain she'd caused her parents. She'd only been able to see the unfairness of their rules.

"Waiting's the hardest."

Lisa nodded. The waiting was turning her into a wreck. She wanted to do something, but both the police and Julie agreed that the best thing she could do was wait here at home.

"Maybe I should try calling the hospitals again," she said.

"They already know to call you if anyone that looks like Nia is brought in."

"I know. But I feel so useless. I've got to do something."

"Why don't you make some more coffee?"

And what would that accomplish? Lisa wanted to shout,

but she understood what Julie was saying. She was amazed that Julie was still here, that she'd spent the whole night with her the way she had. How many men would still be here, would be this supportive on a first date?

"My nerves are so on edge," she said, "I don't think I could take another jolt of caffeine. But I can make some more for you, if you'd like."

Julie shook her head.

She looked amazing, Lisa thought, even after being up all night. Blouse a little rumpled as it clung to her trim torso and shoulders, dark hair all thick tangles, the point of a catlike chin cupped in her hands, elbows on the table. There was a smudge of shadow under each eye, but the tone only accentuated their deep grey and made her look even more desirable. The worry Lisa had for her missing daughter was a huge, swelling presence, lodged like big stones in her chest and stomach, an overpowering sensation of anxiety and helplessness, so the surge of attraction she felt for Julie right now came as a complete surprise.

"I really appreciate your staying here with me tonight and this morning," she said. "I don't know how I'd ever have been able to deal with this on my own."

Julie smiled. "That's what friends are for."

"I hope," Lisa began. She felt awkward, the words sticking in her throat. She tried again. "I hope we can be more than friends."

Julie reached out and gave her hand another comforting squeeze.

"Me, too," she said.

What am I doing? Lisa thought. Nia was missing, maybe hurt, maybe worse, and here she was, flirting. With another woman. She felt like a terrible mother, but she couldn't stop the warm glow that spread through her, that rose to put a sudden flush on her cheeks. She didn't want to stop it.

She made herself look away, back at the phone, and cleared her throat.

"I wish someone would call," she said.

This time Julie made no response. She seemed to know exactly why Lisa was changing the subject. She gave Lisa's fingers another quick squeeze, then returned her elbow to the table, chin cupped in the cradle of her hands once more.

11 • MAX

THE NEXT time I wake it's to feel sunlight on the other side of my eyelids and I know it's morning. The warmth of the sun puts a warm glow on my face and for a moment I feel good. This time I know where I am, what's happened to me, and for some reason there's no panic, just a kind of weary acceptance that this is the way it is. I'm stiff from sleeping on a granite bed, but I've felt worse.

It could be worse. It could be raining. I could be dead instead of wearing somebody else's skin. Lying there on the headland, I can feel a breeze on my skin. It's coming in from the lake, but it's comfortable rather than chilling. The sun's already burned off the night's chill.

I hear the sound of the lake against the shore, the footsteps of joggers as they go by on the path below. Buddy's lying next to me, still pressed close, asleep. When I sit up, he starts, stirs nervously, eyes big, a little scared as they look at me. I hold him, not tight enough to scare him, but enough to let him know he's welcome, that he doesn't have to flee. I can feel his body tremble under my hands, but I talk to him, soothingly, and finally he starts to settle down. When I take my hand away, he gives it a little butt with his muzzle, asking for more.

"Okay, Buddy," I tell him. "You want loving, you've come to the right place for it."

It feels good, putting a little happiness into someone's life, even if that someone's only a stray dog.

I wait until the path's clear as far as I can see in either direction, then make my way down the incline to the lakeshore. I wash my face, but though I'm thirsty, I'm not willing to lap the water up the way Buddy is. My cheeks are rough with stubble. I'd like a shave and a bath. My stomach grumbles, louder than it did last night. I'd like a meal, too. I have to laugh. Why stop there? I'd like to be back home. I'd like to *have* a home.

I make myself put aside that line of thinking because I know it'll take me nowhere but down. The exercise is a little easier than it was yesterday, probably because I've got a companion now. Buddy's sitting beside me, water dripping from his muzzle, an expectant look in his features. Waiting for breakfast, I guess. You and me both, fella.

I hear the sound of another jogger on the path behind me. When I stand up and turn, it's to find myself on the receiving end of one of those disdainful looks that I'm almost getting used to. But this time I don't let myself look away. I square my shoulders and meet the jogger's gaze, thinking I've got as much right to be here as you. Before he can turn his attention elsewhere, I give him a smile and a wave. He seems a little surprised, but he smiles back and returns my wave.

Welcome back to the human race, I tell myself. I watch the jogger until he's out of sight, then brush the dirt from my jeans and jacket.

"C'mon, boy," I say, and take the path myself, following the route the jogger took, but at a slower pace.

The city shows up faster than I'm expecting it to. One moment I could be up in the mountains behind the city, walking the deep woods like those around Janossy's farm, the next I see the skyline over the tops of the trees, I can hear the noise of the traffic. Five minutes later I'm by the War Memorial, watching the food carts setting up along Palm Street. I can smell the coffee from here and just thinking of the muffins, bagels and other fast-food breakfasts the vendors are selling has me cursing every bit of leftover food I ever threw out.

By noon, this part of the park will be a riot of sound and color, the pathways and lawns congested with people on their lunch break, kids hanging out, tourists, fortune-tellers, buskers, joggers, skateboarders, in-line skaters, mothers with their children, nannies with somebody else's, crafts people, junkies, old men playing cards and checkers, hookers down from the Zone on their own coffee breaks. Summertime, it seems as though everybody in the downtown area shows up in these few acres by the War Memorial. It's almost as popular as the Pier, down by the lake on the other side of town.

This time of the morning there are only business men and women, mostly in power suits, grabbing a coffee and a quick bite on the way to work, and a few homeless people like me making campsites out of the benches. A couple of them have set up complicated cardboard structures using their benches as the principal support. Others merely mark their territory with a scatter of possessions: shopping carts; a stack of coats, inappropriate for the weather and not much good for anything else at this time of year; the inevitable plastic shopping bags.

I find a bench that hasn't been claimed by anybody else and settle down, Buddy lying by my feet.

Now what?

I could try to cadge some spare change from the suits like a few of the other street people are doing, but I can't quite muster up what it takes to do it. Can't admit that I've fallen that far, I guess. My stomach's still rumbling. When a woman in a sharply tailored skirt and jacket ensemble drops half her muffin in the garbage can beside my bench, my mouth's actually watering. I'm up and digging after that half muffin before the woman's got three steps away, ignoring the disgusted look she gives me. But then, when I have it in my hand, all my appetite leaves me. I just can't do it. I can't eat what somebody else just threw in a garbage can. I'm not hungry enough yet, I guess.

But that doesn't mean it has to go to waste. I break off bits of the muffin and feed them to Buddy.

"At least one of us isn't going to starve," I tell him.

He wolfs the food down, one, two, three bites, and then he's looking for more, pushing at my knee, licking my hand.

"Sorry, Buddy. That was it."

But now I'm checking the other suits out, seeing what they're maybe going to throw away, marking the distance, figuring if I can get to the can before one of the other street people do.

"Hey, there, virgin. What's your dog's name?"

I turn so fast, it's like a cartoon. There's a young Native American guy sitting on the bench beside me, lounging there like a cat, like he's been there for hours, and I never even heard or saw him approach, never felt his weight on the bench when he sat down beside me. He's a lean, rawboned individual with black hair pulled back into a ponytail and the spookiest eyes I've ever seen. They're dark, like night shadows are dark, like a crow's wings, laughing eyes, crazy eyes, but solemn, too.

He's wearing jeans and scuffed leather workboots, a white T-shirt that makes his skin seem darker than it is. Propped between his feet are a couple of folding wood-and-canvas stools and a knapsack that looks as though it's made of mooschide.

"What did you call me?" I ask.

He grins. "Virgin. I figure you're, what? Two, maybe three days old?"

I guess the solemnity I saw warring with the craziness in his eyes lost the battle.

"Look," I tell him. "I don't really get—"

"I was talking street-old," he says, breaking in. "I can always tell. You're newborn to the world of the have-nots. Hungry, but not hungry enough to eat garbage yet, doesn't matter how fresh it is."

He looks better off than the other street people around us, but the way those crazy eyes of his lock on to me, I don't think he's saner. They're so black I can't quite make out their color. It's as though they don't have any, as though they're all pupil.

"So?" I say.

I'm not trying to be argumentative. I've never been one to pick fights, and anyway, crazy or not, he looks very capable of taking care of himself. But I don't like the way he's sitting in judgment of me. I already know I'm hard off. I don't need my face rubbed in it.

"So I'm just making conversation," he says. "I took a look at you feeding that dog of yours before you even ate yourself and I'm thinking, that's a man with principles. I like a man who takes responsibility for his companions, you know. What'd you say the dog's name was?"

"Buddy." I find myself replying before I realize I'm going to.

He nods. "Bones," he says, sticking out his hand.

I guess it's his name. His hand's there in the air between us for a moment longer than is really comfortable before I finally give it a shake. What the hell. Yesterday I wanted somebody, anybody, to talk to, so why am I complaining today? So what if there's something in his eyes that tells me he should be in a padded cell in the Zeb instead of out here on the street?

"I'm Max."

"You don't look like a Max."

I give him a sharp look, but his face gives nothing away. Then I have to smile. As if he knew anything. As if he could even be involved.

"It's still my name."

"Okay. Max and Buddy." He acts like he has to consider it, then nods. "That's good. They fit. You'll be good for each other."

"I'm glad you think so."

Bones smiles. He smiles a lot. "You're not really glad I think so," he says. "But that's okay. I know what you're going through. The first few weeks are the toughest. You want a coffee? Something to eat maybe, for you and Buddy?"

I don't even ask him why he's offering. All I can do is look at him.

"Hey, I spend a lot of time here," he says. "I get to know who's just going through a bad spell and who wouldn't earn their way if their life depended on it, which it does, but are they going to listen to me when they didn't to anyone else?"

"I don't—"

"And then there's those who'd just as soon cut your

throat as give you the time of the day." He gives me a sharp look, making sure I'm paying attention. "It's different in this world, living on the street. Different from the ones that the citizens live in – the one you just came from. And it's changing all the time. I tell you, these days I don't know if we're all the same species out here anymore. I don't mean black man, white man, skin – none of that. Just, who's human and who's not. Who's planning to give a little and who just wants to take. Who's comfortable in their own skin and who thinks they're worth more than the rest of us. Thing that people forget is, we all die, right? We all die and no matter what we do, the universe is going to go on, perfectly happy without us in it."

I've long since lost the point of what he's saying – if there even was one. He's still wearing that smile, the kind that goes too far and makes the person on the receiving end uneasy. Makes me uneasy, anyway. I have to wonder, why'd he pick me to talk to?

He looks at me now, expectant.

"So . . . what?" I say. "Do you want to know which kind of person I am?"

"I already know that. I look at you, I look inside you, and I know."

"I see . . . "

He laughs. "You want to know why I'm buying? Okay. See, the deal is, I've got coin to spare, so why not share? Are you interested or not?"

I'm not sure where all of this has been leading to, but I know one thing.

"I'm interested," I tell him. "The truth is, I'd kill for a coffee and something to eat."

"Watch what you say," Bones warns me. "You never know what spirits are listening. Maybe they'll take you seriously and the next thing you know they're waving a contract in your face and trying to stick a pen nib in one of your veins."

He's beginning to remind me of Janossy. Not in the way he looks, or even in what he's saying. It's more the attitude. It's back to the eyes. It's as though there's an invisible world that he can look into, not even necessarily because he wants to, but because he can.

"What do you do here in the park?" I ask as we head over to one of the carts.

"I read the bones and tell people stories about themselves."

It takes me a moment to work that out. Now all the mumbo-jumbo starts to make sense.

"So you're one of the fortune-tellers," I say.

It figures. The knowledge I've acquired of Janossy's mystical woodworking theories notwithstanding, I don't have a whole lot of patience with all of this New Age stuff. These days aroma therapies and mushroom teas are going to cure all our problems. That's because the pyramids and crystals didn't work.

"I suppose it depends on your definition of fortune," he says.

"No, I mean you read the future for people."

That crazy look's real strong in his eyes now.

"I know what you meant," he says. "A large coffee for my friend here," he adds, addressing the man at the cart. "And a Darjeeling for me." He looks down at Buddy's hopeful features then back at me. "What do you think your friend'd like?" he asks.

He's let the spacy stuff go, just like that. Like throwing a switch. He's on, he's off. But I'm too hungry to worry at it anymore and I know Buddy is, too, so I let it go.

"Do they sell big juicy steaks here?" I ask.

He laughs. "Maybe toast us up a bag of bagels, too," he tells the vendor.

III • TANYA

TANYA CAME into the kitchen to find Zeffy counting change, the coins clicking against each other on the wooden tabletop as her roommate organized them into piles by denomination. The biggest pile was quarters, a small hillock of metal that glinted in the sunlight streaming in through the kitchen window. The same light gave Zeffy's hair a radiant hennaed glow as though the red-gold tangle of curls had been spun from threads of fire.

It always bothered Tanya, the way Zeffy shortchanged her own looks. There was something intrinsically appealing about Zeffy, an immediacy and warmth that rose up from someplace deep inside her to give her an aura as welcoming and bright as the sun now haloing her hair. Given a choice, Tanya would trade looks with her in a moment. Who needed another fashion-magazine clone? – which was what Tanya saw when she met herself in a mirror. It wasn't anything she worked at, but there it was, all the same. It made no difference if she dressed down or didn't bother wearing makeup. That face in the mirror was the face of a clone, interchangeable with those looking out at her from the newsstand, *Vogue*, *Elle* and the like.

The world needed more angels like Zeffy.

She could look fierce, oh yes. All Tanya had to do was think of Zeffy facing down both Johnny and his neighbor yesterday morning to remember just how fierce. But mostly Zeffy carried a Botticelli nimbus about her that had everyone wanting to be her friend. Tanya would much rather be someone's friend than one more variation on this year's model.

"What are you doing?" she asked Zeffy as she poured herself a coffee.

There was enough in the pot for one last mug, which made her wonder just how long Zeffy had been up. Considering Zeffy didn't have a shift today, Tanya had been sure she'd sleep in.

"Counting my tips," Zeffy replied. "How much did you make yesterday?"

Tanya shrugged. "I don't know. Maybe seven dollars."

She looked in the fridge to discover that they were still out of milk. That figured. It had probably been her turn to pick it up and, as usual, she'd forgotten. Joining her roommate at the table, she saw that Zeffy had written the amount, seven dollars, along with a question mark, down on the pad of paper by her elbow.

"I did a little better," Zeffy said. "But then I was there for the whole day."

"What's this for?"

Zeffy gave her an oh-please look. "The rent. We have to raise – let me see – a hundred and sixty-eight dollars by tomorrow. Got any rich friends you can hit on?"

"Oh my God. I forgot."

"And I don't think Johnny's going to come through in time." Zeffy gave her a rueful look. "If he ever comes through, which I doubt."

"What're we going to do?"

Zeffy sighed and sat back in her chair. "I don't know. Maybe I can get some work with a temp agency for a couple of days. That'd help."

"Couldn't you ask Jilly or Wendy to trade off shifts with you?"

"I already did – that's why I was going to stay home. I was supposed to have the rest of the week free to practice for my gig. It's kind of short notice to ask them to switch again."

You don't need to practice, Tanya almost said, but she managed to keep it to herself. Zeffy was confident about everything except her music, which was ridiculous, considering how good she was. Still, if Zeffy felt she needed the time to practice, then Tanya thought she should have it. She was all for anything that would help Zeffy do well at the gig, so the thought that Zeffy might have to go out and do some secretarial work for a couple of days made her feel particularly guilty. How could she have been so stupid as to lend Johnny that money?

Then she had an idea.

"Why don't you do what Geordie does?" she said.

Zeffy looked blankly at her.

"You know, go out and busk. That way you could practice and earn some money at the same time."

"I couldn't do that," Zeffy said.

"Why not?"

"Because, well, where would I . . ." She shook her head. "I wouldn't even know where to begin."

"Come on. It'd be perfect. You could go to St. Paul's, or down to the park. Catch a few rays, practice, make some money. Look at that sky out there. How can you even think of not enjoying it?"

Zeffy glumly followed her gaze and looked out the window.

"It's shaping up to be a beautiful day," Tanya said. "What more could a woman ask for out of life?"

"I don't know if it's the kind of thing I could do, Tanya. I'd feel so . . . so vulnerable."

Tanya wanted to be sympathetic, but she knew that at this moment it would be a mistake.

"You've practiced tons in your bedroom," she said. "Maybe it's time you got a little more experience playing for real people."

"I . . ."

"Oh God," Tanya said. "Look at the time. I've got to run or I'll be late." She gulped down the last of her coffee, grimacing at the lack of milk. "But promise me this: You won't call some temp agency. Remember how horrible it was the last time we did that?"

"I remember."

"So promise you won't."

"I can't. If we don't come up with—"

"Promise me."

Zeffy sighed. "Okay, already. I promise."

"And think about the busking deal."

"That I can't promise."

"I didn't say do it," Tanya told her, "although I think you should. I just want you to seriously consider giving it a try."

Tanya stood by the kitchen door, refusing to leave until Zeffy gave in.

"Okay," Zeffy said. "I'll seriously consider giving it a try."

"It'll be great," Tanya told her. "You'll see."

"Oh, right."

"Just don't let the fame and fortune go to your head."

Zeffy had to laugh. "From busking?"

Tanya turned away. Calling back over her shoulder, she added, "And say hi to Geordie for me if you happen to run into him."

"Sure," Zeffy said. "Hey, maybe I'll see if he wants to form a band with me. You know, we could be an item, on stage and off."

Tanya didn't have to look back from where she stood by the front door to know her roommate was joking.

"In your dreams," she said.

She timed her parting shot perfectly so that the door closed on "dreams," leaving Zeffy unable to put in the last word.

IV • MAX

I CAN'T remember the last time food tasted this good. Bones sits there beside me, sipping his tea and smiling while Buddy and I stuff ourselves, the toasted bagel halves vanishing in three, four bites. He buys me a second coffee and I could've gone for another, but I don't ask and he doesn't offer. Besides, I should be ungrateful for what he's already bought me? Not likely. Right now, all I feel for him is a warm affection, crazy eyes and all.

When the bagels are all gone, I'm so full I couldn't eat another bite. Even Buddy is finally satiated, lying there on the pavement by our feet, stomach swollen, a sappy contented look on his face. Bones smiles some more.

"The two of you look better already," he says.

"Thanks," I tell him. "I never thought I could be that hungry."

"You don't know hungry," Bones says, "and I hope you never do."

There's a world of history in what he's saying. I think of news pictures I've seen of famine victims and I know he's right. For the first time since we've met, I wonder about him

– not so much who he is or what he does, or even why he's befriended me, but where he came from, how he came to live the way he does. He shakes his head when I ask him.

"Uh-uh," he says. "First rule you've got to learn: You never ask how any of us got to be on the street. Life's different here from the way it is where the citizens live. They're all talking, talking, talking to each other about themselves, about each other, wanting to know this, wanting to know that. Down here, we don't ask about each other. Person wants to tell you something, fine. But don't ask. That's a big no-no. Too much hurt caught up in most of our lives. Most of us, we don't want to remember."

"I'll keep that in mind."

"You do that," he says.

He looks away and I follow his gaze. The businesspeople might have gone on to their jobs, but this part of the park's busier now than it was when I first got here. The first baby strollers are congregating down by the War Memorial, commanded by a fairly even mix of older women and teenagers. Some of the girls are so young. I wonder which are nannies and which are taking their own infants out for some air. I see kids playing hooky from school, retirees strolling the paths, people walking their dogs. More joggers – I guess they don't have jobs to go to, but it makes me wonder how they can afford all that expensive exercise gear. The buskers, fortune-tellers and crafts people are starting to arrive, having their breakfasts, gossiping with each other, not so much getting ready for business as staking out their spots. Most of the street people have given up their benches. Some are making a halfhearted attempt at panhandling, but nobody here at this time has any money for them. Others have just drifted off, carrying all their belongings with them in a few plastic bags or a shopping cart.

"Think about it," Bones adds. "Nobody's homeless because they've got a choice. Nobody lives on the street if they've got a home or a job they can go to. We've got people here should be in the Zeb, or some kind of halfway house, but no one's got the time or money for them, so they're just walking through the fog of their lives, marking time. We've got others too screwed up on drugs or drink to think much straighter. But most of us'd take something better. There's just no opportunities. There's nothing left for us out here but what we can scratch out for ourselves."

"It's criminal," I say.

"Sure it is."

"Somebody should do something about it."

Bones smiles. "And what did you do, before you found yourself down here living with us?"

I want to explain that my circumstances aren't the same, but then I realize that what's happened to me is no different from what's happened to anyone else I see living here on the street. Maybe it was a little weirder, how I got here, but just like them, I didn't have a choice and that's what it all boils down to. That's what Bones is trying to tell me.

"Now some people," he says, "they make enough, get themselves a cheap room, maybe. Hotel or rooming house. Maybe they get to eat a little better. But it's a long road back to where you're a citizen again. So meanwhile, you make do. Try to hang on to a little something for yourself, even if it's just a piece of pride that you haven't given up yet. But how you got here, it's nothing you want to talk about. Mostly, that's the way it is. Nobody wants to remember the fall. You worry on that too much and it just makes you crazy. So you live on handouts and sometimes you smoke a little or drink a little, just to help you forget. You make do."

He looks back at me. "What do you think? Are you going to make do?"

I don't know what to say. I haven't really thought that far ahead. I don't want to think that far. I don't want to make do with the mess of Johnny Devlin's life. I want my own back.

"This is what," Bones asks. "Your second, third day?"

"Second."

So, you've still got a chance. Your clothes are in decent shape – you're pretty clean. Could use a shave, comb your hair, maybe."

"What're you saying?"

He shakes his head. "You're some piece of work. What do you think I'm saying? Get yourself a job. Sell hamburgers, bus tables, wash dishes. Do whatever it takes before you lose the chance."

"But—"

"See, they can smell it on you and I'm not just talking about BO. They know when you're too hungry for the job. You go now, maybe you can still get one. A few more days on the street and you won't exist for them anymore. You'll become invisible."

Get a job. As Johnny Devlin. Start all over again with no future, no hope? I don't even want to think about it. The kinds of jobs Bones is describing would steal too much time away, time I need to figure out how to get back what's mine.

"I can't do it," I tell him.

Bones shrugs. "I'm not even going to ask why."

He stands up then, hoists his backpack and the two stools. He seems disappointed in me, as though he feels he's wasted his money and advice.

"Time I was setting up," he says.

I trail along with him, Buddy at my heels. There's a free

144

space along one of the paths where the other vendors are setting up their tables and crates, a kind of obvious no-man's-land. As he heads toward it, I realize that there's more to Bones than meets the eye. He's not simply a homeless fortune-teller making do, but a big fish in this little pond. There are more vendors than there are good spots, but no one's touching the space he's heading toward. Without anybody having to tell me, I know it belongs to him – whether through respect or fear, I can't tell.

"You have any skills?" Bones asks.

He unfolds his stools, sets them up so that they're facing each other, sits down on the one facing the path. I don't make the mistake of sitting in the other, though Buddy's curious enough to give it a smell all around.

"What kind of skills?" I say.

"How would I know? I'm just wondering, is there something special you can do?"

"I'm a luthier," I tell him. "I make instruments.'

"Used to," he says.

I shake my head. "Maybe I don't have my tools or my shop anymore, but that's still what I am."

Bones is laying out a square of buckskin on the pavement between the stools and looks up with a grin that makes his eyes go scary-strange again. Too dark. Too deep.

"Good for you," he says. "Don't you forget that." He considers me for a moment, then asks, "Ever do any other woodwork?"

"Sure. Some carpentry. My dad was a cabinetmaker. I used to carve for fun – made some great fiddle heads for a fiddle-maker I used to know – but then I got too busy to keep it up."

Bones stands up and reaches in his pocket. I think he's going for some more money, but before I can refuse it, he pulls out a folding knife, maybe four and a half, five inches long. Wooden handle. He tosses it over to me.

"Careful with the blade," he says. "It's sharp."

"What am I supposed to do with this?"

He laughs. "What do you think? Carve something and sell it. You want my advice, you'll collect some wood and do your work on the spot. People like to see an artisan actually doing the work. Entertains them. Sometimes they'll toss you a little coin just because they enjoyed the show."

I use my thumbnail to pull the blade out of the handle and it locks into place. It's a beautiful steel. A serious blade, one that'll hold its edge for a long time.

"And keep the carvings simple," he adds. "That way you'll make more and sell more."

"This knife . . ." I begin.

"I know. It's a beauty."

"I can't accept—"

He shakes his head. "Who says I'm giving it to you? That's a loan, plain and simple. I'll expect it back in a couple of weeks, same shape as it was when I lent it to you." He gives me that grin again. "So one of the first things you're saving up for is a hone stone, Max, because I like my blades sharp."

I'm only half listening to him. I can do this, I think. I'm already remembering branches, bits of roots and the like that I saw coming here from the headland. I can work at this today, and maybe, if I'm lucky, make enough to give myself a stake. It's work I can live with. Work that'll connect me to what I was, that'll allow me to think and plan while I'm hopefully making the money I'll need to see Buddy and me through these hard times.

"I don't know how to thank you," I tell him.

"So don't."

Simply standing here, holding the knife, I can almost feel the wood underhand, read its grain, follow the ley lines from knot to center cut and up and down the length. I'll want a soft wood to start, I think. Something I can work with easily and fast. Cedar or pine. I'm looking forward to it, yearning to get back to it, as though working with wood is something that's a lifetime in my past instead of only a few days.

Then I have to wonder: Why can't I read people the way I can read the wood?

Bones is still watching me with those dark eyes of his, looking deep, under my skin. "Just remember how it went down with you and me today," he says. "Remember it, and when you get the chance, pass it on."

"I will."

He sits back down on his stool and continues setting up. "Meanwhile, you'd better hustle yourself some supplies and get settled before even all the mediocre spots are gone."

I want to say something more. I want to enthuse about his generosity to me, a complete stranger, but I realize he honestly doesn't want to hear it. He meant what he said. He gave me a piece of good fortune and just wants me to pass it on when I get the chance. It makes me more curious than ever as to what brought him here, where he came from, but this time I don't make the mistake of asking.

He smiles again when I give him a nod, as though while he's sitting there, he can look right into me, straight through the skin and bone, and read my mind. I give him another nod, then start off across the lawn, heading for Fitzhenry's wilder acres.

"C'mon, Buddy," I say. "We've got work to do."

I get maybe ten feet away from where Bones is sitting on his stool.

"And, Max," he calls after me.

I turn to look back at him.

"You need a leash for Buddy. A leash and a collar, but anything'll do. Even a piece of rope."

"Why?"

Bones points to a sign. I read down a list of things you can't do in the park and find the one about no unleashed dogs. Bones digs around in his pack and comes up with a coil of stiff, braided twine.

"Here," he says, tossing it to me. "Keep this handy for when you see a cop."

I catch the rope and wonder how Buddy will react to it. Will he understand that I'm not trying to steal a piece of his freedom? That it's just something we'll have to do to maintain appearances, but really, he's still going to be free to come and go as he pleases? I look down at him and his trusting gaze meets mine. I guess I'll worry about it when the time comes.

"Thanks," I tell Bones, and we set off again.

V • NIA

NIA REALLY wanted to know: What were you supposed to do when your world came to an end, when there was nothing you could count on anymore? What was the point of even trying to go on?

But there was no one to ask, no one to turn to. No one she could trust to be who they were supposed to be. She had only herself – and perhaps the stranger she'd seen in the hallway outside of Max's building. They were the only ones that knew that the pod people were really here. That there really were aliens setting up house in other people's bodies.

No one else was going to believe her. No one else could

be trusted. She was going to have to spend the rest of her life like this, hiding, trying to be invisible, starting at every sudden noise, looking at a familiar face and seeing a boogieman's eyes looking back at her.

For now she was relatively safe, hidden between a Dumpster and the back wall of an alley running off Bunnett Street, sitting on a stack of newspapers that were waiting there to be recycled. But how long would it last? How long before she had to be on the move again? Hugging herself, she stared at the graffiti sprayed on the wall of the building on the other side of the alley. The words didn't really register. Something ruled. Something else sucked. Somebody loved "A.L."

Nia stared down at her feet. She was cold and scared and more miserable than she'd ever been before. Last night she'd run for what seemed like hours, hard and far, half-blinded with tears, run until she finally stumbled up against the side of an unfamiliar building somewhere on the east side, panting, clutching at a stitch of pain that started where her thigh met her torso and went straight up into her chest, grabbing at her lungs.

The trek back to familiar territory had taken all the nerve she could muster because there weren't simply the usual dangers of the streets to worry her. There were the pod people as well. The ones that had stolen first Max and then her mother. And how many others had they taken? she'd asked herself as she skulked through back alleys and lanes, avoiding any contact with people. She didn't know how many of them were walking around with some alien *thing* sitting in their heads. Didn't know if the monsters were out looking for her right at that moment, scouring the streets for the kid who'd discovered their secret. She could only assume the worst.

The blocks around Bunnett Street weren't any safer than the east side. They were too close to Palm Street, the strip clubs and bars and Men's Mission; a combat zone of hookers and junkies, street toughs and worse. The only people in this part of town were the lost and the needy, the hopeless – and those that preyed upon them. She was as likely to get mugged or raped here, as captured by the pod people, but at least she knew where she was, knew there were dark alleys where she could hide until morning. And feeling so lost and helpless herself, she fit right in with the rest of life's losers who gravitated to this part of town. So she went to ground, here behind the Dumpster, and waited for the longest night of her life to finally be over.

Her spirits had lifted a little when the sun finally rose, but now that the morning was here, she didn't know how she could go on. All night long she'd concentrated on making it through the night. Well, now she had, only nothing had changed. She still couldn't go home. There was still no one she could turn to for help. If anything, things might now be worse. The streets would soon be full of people, the sidewalks clogged with them. There would be no avoiding them. How many of them were pod people? Maybe all of them. Maybe the whole city had been taken over, everyone except for her.

The idea made her feel sick. She had to lean her cheek against the cold bricks of the building beside her and wait for the vertigo to pass.

The whole city . . .

She knew it was impossible. But then, so was what had happened to her mother and Max. She thought of the old joke – Is it still paranoia when you know everyone's out to get you? – but it didn't make her feel like smiling. It just made her feel worse, because it was probably true. Neither

her mother nor Max was particularly important in the overall scheme of things. They didn't have anything to do with running the city, running the country. They didn't have the kind of power that the pod people would want to acquire. It made more sense for them to take the people at the top and then work their way down to those less important. And anyone who got in their way . . .

Nia shivered, hugging herself harder. She found only marginal comfort in the circle of her own thin arms.

No, she really couldn't go on like this. With only a few hours of being on the run under her belt, she couldn't imagine living like this for days or weeks or longer. She might as well turn herself over to the aliens now and get it over with. Maybe, once they took over her body, they'd store her brain in the same place where they were keeping her mother's and at least she wouldn't feel so alone.

Except . . .

She sat up a little straighter, chewed on her lower lip. Went back over the bits and pieces of that surreal conversation she'd overheard between the alien Max and the stranger who'd claimed to be Max. If she'd understood them correctly, the aliens hadn't so much taken Max, like in that dumb movie where she'd first heard about pod people, as switched his brain with someone else's.

It was all so hard to work out. Had it only happened in her building? Then why hadn't they got her as well? A vague, kind of desperate hope rose in her. If people's brains were being switched from one body to another, then might her mother not be out here, somewhere in the city, wearing somebody else's skin? If she could find her mom, then maybe they could—

The clang of a metal door opening made her jump to her feet. A tall, heavy-built man stepped out into the alley, muscles straining under his T-shirt as he manhandled a pair of large green garbage bags, heavy with refuse. Nia froze, not knowing what to do. She wanted to bolt down the alleyway, but the man was already between her and the safety of the street beyond. She tried to shrink back behind the Dumpster, but it was too late. His gaze turned in her direction, found her. Anger clouded his features.

"Got you this time!" he cried.

He dropped the garbage bags and came for her.

She'd never seen him before in her life, but she knew exactly what he was talking about. He was one of the aliens, out looking for her. And now he had her.

Fear galvanized her. She darted from her now useless hiding place, tried to slip past him, but he was too fast. A meaty hand closed on her shoulder, jerking her back.

"You think it's a riot, dontcha?" he said. "Spraying up my walls with your paint and crap. Well, let's see how funny you find it when the cops take you downtown."

"I . . . I . . ."

She'd had it all wrong – and so did he. He wasn't one of the pod people and she hadn't been spray-painting his walls. But she couldn't get the words out.

"And don't think I'm not going to press charges," he told her, dragging her back toward the door. "I've been just waiting to catch one of you little buggers back here."

"No, you don't understand," she finally managed. "I was only—"

"Oh, I understand," he said. "I understand plenty. You're too goddamned lazy to go to school and too goddamned lazy to work. Your parents can't control you and you think you own the world. But let me tell you something, little lady. I don't have to take your crap."

He'd almost dragged her into the rear of his store now.

Nia couldn't see what sort of a place it was, what he sold, because her eyes hadn't adjusted to the dimmer lighting inside, but she knew she wasn't going to let him take her in there and call the police. The police would call her mother and then that ... that *thing* pretending to be her mother would come down to the station to take her home ...

"Please, don't," she tried, grabbing hold of the doorframe.

An incredulous look flooded the man's features.

"Gimme a break," he said. "After all the crap I've taken from you and your friends, you think I'm going to let you go now that I've finally managed to grab one of you? I don't think so, kid."

His fingers dug deeper into her shoulder and he gave a sharp tug, pulling her away from the doorframe. She was unbalanced for a moment, then steadied herself. Before he could pull her further inside, she hauled back and kicked him in the shin with the toe of her combat boot.

"Jesus!" he cried.

The grip on her shoulders loosened and she pulled free, tearing off down the alleyway before he could grab her again. He followed, but fear lent her a speed he couldn't match. By the time he reached the end of the alley, she was already halfway down the block.

"You little bitch!" he yelled after her. "I'll remember your face and if I ever see you around here again I'll ..."

His voice trailed off until she couldn't hear him anymore. During a glance over her shoulder, she saw he'd given up his pursuit, but she kept on running all the same. Panic had taken over again, the same as it had last night. She kept expecting a passerby to grab her, for the faces of the people on the street to suddenly peel back like latex masks to reveal monsters underneath.

Straight down Bunnett she went, across the intersection at Perth Street against the light. Car horns blared around her, brakes squealed, but she kept on running. Panting, now. Tears in her eyes. A mindless wail erupting in the back of her head, deafening her inner ear. She made it down another block and was about to dart across Palm Street when a hand grabbed her and pulled her back onto the curb.

She spun out of the grip, eyes wide with fear, but unable to focus.

"Watch yourself," her rescuer said.

When she started to go across the street again, he caught hold of her once more. A cab came by, only just missing her, the driver leaning on his horn and shouting at her.

"Have you got a death wish?" the man asked.

She pulled free once more, but this time leaned up against the lamppost. She hugged the metal pole, gulping air. She could make out her rescuer now, just some ordinary businessman, suit and tie, clean-shaven, a look of concern in his eyes. Cars and buses went by on the street beside her, going faster than they should, the way everybody drove in the city. On the other side of the street she could see Fitzhenry Park, the long line of concession carts along the sidewalk at this edge of the park, the businesspeople crowding around them.

"What's the matter?" the man asked. "Has someone been—"

She registered the light change and bolted into the street again, this time with a green light in her favor. She heard the man call out from behind her, but she ignored him, made it safely across the street, onto the sidewalk where she almost collided with a food cart. The vendor shouted at her to be careful as she dodged it. She had a bad moment in the midst of all the businesspeople. She started flashing on monstrous faces again, pod people trying to grab her, but

154

the crowd opened up for her, the suited men and women stepping out of her path, and then she was free of them, on the lawn and running for the trees.

VI • ZEFFY

It was almost noon when Zeffy walked up to ground level from the subway stop at Stanton and Palm and stepped out onto the street. Immobile, she was an island around which the flow of pedestrians broke. She blinked in the sunlight, shifting her guitar case from one hand to the other. Across the street she could see the trees of Fitzhenry Park towering over the high stone wall that encircled much of the park, chestnuts and oaks, birches, pine and the scrubbier cedars. There was a gate here, on the corner, with stone lions guarding either post, but the path went straight into the park, south and east, away from the section she wanted where the buskers and vendors congregated in front of the War Memorial. Deeper into the park, the path branched off and eventually bore one back to the memorial, but it was a longer, more roundabout route. Easier to walk the two blocks down Palm Street and come to the memorial from the street.

Oh God, she thought, as she finally set off again, joining the pedestrian flow. Her nerves were already fluttering and she hadn't even opened her case yet. She really didn't know if she was ready for this. She was only here because Tanya had shamed her into it.

Never vain, she'd still spent hours deciding what to wear. She wasn't sure of the protocol. Did she go as herself? Did she dress as if she needed the money? Tie back her hair or wear a hat? In the end she went for comfort. Red high-tops and a Cock Robin T-shirt that she'd had made from the cover of their *Best of* album. Faded Levi's and a white cotton sweater that she'd rolled up and stored in her knapsack in case it got cool. Hair put up in a loose bun from which stray strands were already escaping. A touch of lipstick and eye shadow.

It felt wrong, but then she knew however she'd left the apartment would feel wrong. How she looked wasn't what was giving her butterflies. It was the whole idea of standing behind her open guitar case in the park, playing music and expecting people to toss change in because they liked what she was doing. As if.

She'd never confused her desire to perform with her ability to do so. The chops, she had. Hours of working on scales and chord progressions, finger-picking techniques and flat-picking. More hours honing her songs, her voice, her phrasing, her projection. The place where it all unraveled was when there were more than a couple of people listening to her. When there were strangers watching her, looking straight under her skin, right into her heart where she was a shy little girl again, in a playground, in the halls at school, ostracized from the other children for no more apparent reason except that it had happened, become a habit, stuck until she finally left that environment, that old neighborhood, and went on to university.

There she was able to reinvent herself – perhaps too well, sometimes overcompensating for her shyness with a bold-ness that surprised even herself. That became another habit, in and of itself, so much so that she, along with everyone who met her, thought that she'd always been this way. The illusion held for her until she performed. Then it dissolved, the old hurts coming back to her when she stepped onstage, as though childhood were only yesterday, held at bay by no more than thin gauze, and she knew she'd never wholly escape the little girl she'd been. The little girl, trying so hard to please her peers, yet never succeeding.

She knew dozens of musicians, watched them play, went to their gigs. Some had better stage rapport than others, some had better musical skills, but all of them made the performance seem so effortless – the way it only felt for her when she was alone, playing in her room. That was real freedom, she thought. That was when the past finally lost its hold on you and you could move on. The trick was getting there, stepping through, into that freedom.

"So how's my favorite redhead?" a voice said.

Zeffy started, then smiled when she turned to find Geordie Riddell leaning up against a lamppost nearby, fiddle case in hand, smiling back at her. She hadn't even realized that she'd stopped walking.

Geordie was his usual scruffy self, frayed jeans, scuffed shoes, ragged Indian-print vest over a short-sleeved, collarless white shirt. All charm, when he smiled. Something tender in his eyes, even when he was angry, which wasn't often. He had the same even temperament as Jilly, a laissez-faire that seemed inborn rather than cultivated.

"How would Amy feel if she heard you say that?" Zeffy asked.

Geordie laughed. "Good point. What I meant was, how's my favorite redheaded guitarist?" His gaze shifted from her face to her instrument. "Got a gig?"

This was so embarrassing, Zeffy thought. She felt caught out. Here was Geordie who made his living busking, teamed up with Amy more often than not, fiddle and Irish pipes, the two of them a unit, if not a romantic item. He was going to think that she was such a phony. But it was too late now to pretend she was here for anything else.

She shifted the weight of her guitar case from one hand to the other. "I was thinking of ... you know, playing a little music in the park."

Geordie looked away to the lunch crowd that was congregating around the War Memorial.

"You could do okay," he said. "It's a pay week and a nice day – always a good combination."

When his gaze returned to hers it was utterly guileless and Zeffy realized that she'd been projecting her fears again, deciding beforehand what somebody thought instead of waiting to see what they were actually thinking. As if Geordie would ever be so small-minded.

"Do you think so?" she asked. "I've never done this before so I wouldn't know."

"Really?"

She nodded. "I'm kind of nervous, actually." She laughed, but was unable to keep her apprehension from showing. "And that was the understatement of the year. If you want to know the truth, I'm semi-terrified."

"Don't be. If it gets bad, just close your eyes and pretend you're playing for friends. The worst people can do is simply keep on walking, which, when you come to think of it, is better than playing to a room that's sitting there, glaring at you, wondering when and if you'll do something they like."

"I suppose. Luckily, I've never had that experience. My worst gigs are those where basically nobody shows up."

Geordie winced. "I hate those. *Especially* when you're playing for the door."

"And of course they never ask you back."

"Not that you'd *want* to go back."

They both smiled at the shared experience, but only because there was enough time and distance between them and the actual events. Zeffy remembered, as she was sure

Geordie did, just how devastating those nights were. Even when you knew it wasn't your fault – bad advertising, a big sports event or concert on elsewhere, folk act booked into a hard-rock club – you still felt like such a personal failure.

"I'd set up over by the fortune-tellers," Geordie said. "See? There are some open spaces to the left of where they are. Don't get so close you'll drown them out, but don't go so far that you lose out on the spill over of people drawn to them."

"You think so?"

He nodded. "And a word of advice: If you get a biggish crowd – which, having heard you play, I don't doubt you will – play through to the end of the song and then take a break, retune or something. The cops are pretty good here about letting us busk, but they don't like having too many people crowding around, blocking the path. Irritates the people who paid for their vendor's permits, if you know what I mean, and then the cops've got to deal with their complaints."

Zeffy was still blushing over his compliment and missed some of what he was saying.

"I need a permit?" she asked.

"Officially, yes. Unofficially, just be cool about it and no one'll hassle you."

He pushed away from the lamppost. "Gotta run. Amy'll be waiting for me at St. Paul's."

"Thanks for the advice."

"No problem. Hey, if you ever feel like working the theatre queues with me or something, give me a call. I can never seem to get anybody to work evenings – mostly because they want real gigs. But it's fun, and the money can be good."

Zeffy flashed on how she'd been joking with Tanya

earlier in the morning. She could just imagine her room-mate's reaction to her playing with Geordie – never mind that she'd met him before Tanya ever had and neither of them had ever expressed any romantic interest in him until Tanya had last night. Tanya always had this fear that people were going to steal away her boyfriends.

"I don't think so," she said. "I'm just kind of doing this to warm up for a gig I've got this weekend."

Geordie laughed. "What did I tell you? Everybody wants their name on the marquee; nobody wants to play the streets."

Zeffy sighed. She hoped he didn't think that she considered herself too good for that sort of thing.

"It's not that," she started, but then she realized she didn't know how to explain.

"I understand," Geordie told her. "Really I do. Truth is, I'd rather play a club, too, but when the gig's not there, I've still got to pay the rent." He grinned. "Besides, I'm such a little music slut. I don't care where I play, so long as I get to play."

Zeffy had to laugh. "Well, maybe we could try it sometime. I'd have to learn some of your tunes."

"So call me when you're free." He looked at his watch and put on a look of mock horror. "Amy's going to *kill* me."

"I'm sorry. I didn't mean to keep you from—"

"I'm *kidding*. You know how long it takes her to tune those pipes of hers. She'll probably still be fiddling with her reeds when I get there." He gave her a jaunty wave and set off for the bus stop. "Say hi to Tanya for me. I had a great time with her yesterday."

"That's what she said, too," Zeffy called after him. "You should call her," she added, deciding she might as well do her bit to seeing her roommate's love life get back on a more even keel.

He was a half-dozen yards away, but Zeffy could still see the flush that rose up from his neck to color his cheeks. She knew just how he felt, how the shyness made everything close up inside. But she also knew you couldn't let it rule your life.

"Really," she said. "She doesn't bite."

And you'd be good for each other, she added to herself.

But Geordie only blushed more furiously and made his escape.

She watched as he caught the #12 heading west on Bunnett, then turned to face her own ordeal. Her happiness at meeting up with Geordie slowly drained away. Yes, she knew exactly how he felt, but she was going to follow her own advice, which meant she wasn't going to let the butterflies get the better of her.

Squaring her shoulders, she hoisted up her guitar case and headed for the open spot near the fortune-tellers that Geordie had pointed out to her. She felt almost sick by the time she got there, but was still determined not to give in to it. Dropping her knapsack on the grass, she opened her guitar case and took her instrument out. It was all she could do to stop her hands from shaking with all the bored businesspeople watching her from nearby benches. Their hands and mouths were busy with sandwiches and hot dogs, French fries and drinks, deep-fried zucchini, muffins, ice-cream bars and every sort of lunch dish and confection available from the food carts nearby, but their gazes were all on her. Curious. Watching her every move as she fumbled through the business of getting into tune.

Welcome to the dinner club, Zeffy thought as she finally stood up. Her guitar was tuned and there was no other excuse at hand to stop her from starting her first song except that she thought she might die. Maybe that wasn't such a bad idea. A little extreme, though. Maybe she should just wish to be about an inch tall so that she could creep away through the short grass behind her and not be seen.

Enough, she told herself. You're just making it worse.

She took a deep breath, closed her eyes and launched into a cover of "This Far From Home," a song she'd learned from the album of a Vancouver singer-songwriter, Susan Crowe. One verse in, still singing about the metaphorical temple that held the writer's past, she realized it was a bad choice. Great song, but she couldn't give it the kind of powerhouse delivery that busking required. The piece needed a sound system so she could lean into the dreamy flow of the words and music without straining. It was a late-night song, smoky club times, whiskey-voiced, a bittersweet remembering of times long gone to which one couldn't return.

Out here, in the open air and competing with the traffic over on Palm Street and the lunchtime crowds, her performance sucked. She heard her voice quaver on the chorus and hated what she was doing to the piece. It deserved better than this. She took the song to the end of its chorus, ended with a repeat of the last line.

Now what? she thought, her mind gone blank. She knew hundreds of songs, but couldn't remember a single one. It was as though she'd never spent all those hours, painstakingly learning the chords from records, leaning close to the speakers to decipher an errant phrase or word.

And then she made the mistake of opening her eyes.

She could feel herself freeze up as she looked around herself, gaze nervous, stomach doing little flip-flops. The people sitting nearby seemed way too interested, leaning closer in her direction from all sides while those on the further benches didn't seem to be aware that she'd ever begun or stopped. A couple of guys walking by gave her the once-over that had nothing to do with her music. All her guitar case held was the handful of coins she'd tossed in to spike the pot – a gentle hint as to what those passing by could do with all that loose change weighing down their pockets.

Think, think, she told herself, and could only come up with a song she'd learned from an old Elvis album, "That's All Right, Mama."

Well, why not?

She started in with a shuffling skiffle beat, avoiding bar chords so that the sound of the open strings would carry and ring, opened with the chorus, drew the air from her diaphragm, pulled it up through her chest and aimed the lyrics at the other side of the far benches. The boom of her voice startled her as much as it did the people having their lunches around her. But it was a good surprise, she realized, eyes still open, gaze sliding from one face to another. It woke smiles, started feet tapping. By the time the chorus came around again, she knew she had them.

Singing the Elvis song reminded her of Kirsty MacColl's "There's a Guy Works Down the Chip Shop Swears He's Elvis," so she segued into its opening chords, followed that song with a bouncy version of the Jazzabels' "El Diablo." To her surprise, people were actually stopping to listen. Coins were landing in her guitar case, even a few bills. As the crowd she was drawing swelled, she felt brave enough to try one of her own more up-tempo pieces and realized halfway through the song that she was actually having fun.

Busking seemed so different from playing on stage. She supposed it was the lack of pressure, the fact that people were ambling by, stopping for a bit, then walking on. She wasn't on a stage, under a spotlight, the audience expectant. She wasn't locked into the knowledge that the sound system would amplify every mistake she made along with the bits she got right. Here it was come-what-may. People could listen, or walk on. And the weather certainly helped. The day was beautiful, putting her in as much of a good mood as most everybody else seemed to be feeling today. It woke a devil-may-care attitude in her, had her playing with her phrasing, jazzing up her instrumental breaks with a bit of scat.

Tanya had been right, she thought as the crowd reacted to the finish of her song with a round of applause and smiles. She played one more song – Cock Robin's "El Norte" to go with her T-shirt – then took a break to let the crowd disperse. She tried to be casual, glancing into her guitar case, but she couldn't hold back a grin when she saw all the money lying there. There had to be at least twenty dollars.

"Don't hear many girls with a voice as big as yours," a man said as he dropped a couple of bills into the case.

"Thanks," she said, still grinning.

She wasn't quite sure how she should take that. She supposed it was a compliment, well meant for all that it seemed a little backhanded. Right now it didn't seem to matter.

"Do you know any Salt 'N Pepa?" somebody else asked.

"No," she said. "But maybe this'll do."

The crowd had lightened enough for her to feel she could start playing again and she jumped into the only rap song she knew, Luka Bloom's version of "I Need Love" that he'd gotten from LL Cool J. She'd had to change the lyrics around a bit when she learned it to make the song fit a woman's point of view, and this was the first time she'd sung it in public, so she wasn't sure it would work. It was also a little harder to project her voice on it than it had been with the last batch she'd just played through, but this time she'd had the foresight to take it up a key, hoping her voice would carry farther under the theory that if you couldn't sing louder, you could always sing higher. It seemed to work.

"I love you, lady!" a young skateboarder yelled before kicking a foot against the pavement and riding off into the crowd. He couldn't have been more than fourteen.

Zeffy blew him a kiss and those people standing close enough by to make out the lyrics laughed. She got through another short set before the crowd grew too big again and she had to stop once more. It happened quicker this time, and more quickly the next. By the time she stopped her fourth set, she'd only been able to do three songs before she got worried about how many people she'd drawn, crowding the sidewalk in front of her, swaying in place with their lunches in hand, listening.

Maybe she should quit while she was ahead. A recent glance at the contents of her guitar case had her itching to count her take. She thought she might have almost seventy or eighty dollars in there.

It seemed like she'd picked the right time to decide to stop. The crowds were thinning anyway, people heading back to their offices, lunch breaks over. But it was hard to give it up. Playing like this, loose and easy, had given her a buzz she hadn't felt in ages.

"You're not all done, are you?" a fellow asked as she turned her guitar case around, ready to start transferring her earnings to her knapsack.

She looked up at him, smiled. He was a nice-looking young man, late teens maybe, or early twenties, casually dressed in shorts and a T-shirt, baseball cap pushing down his dark brown hair.

"'Fraid so," she said. "For today anyway."

The words surprised her. But it was true. She wanted to come back. She'd had too much fun *not* to. She did realize that part of her success might be because of her novelty. She was new here, something a little different. But while she wouldn't turn down the money she'd made, she realized it wasn't the money that had given her the buzz. It was the sheer pleasure she'd gotten from playing.

"So you'll be here tomorrow?" the fellow asked.

"If it's not raining."

He got up from the bench where he'd been sitting and dropped a dollar bill in her case.

"Well, I'll see you then," he told her. He started to walk away, then paused. "You know, you should be thinking about playing in some of the clubs."

"Thanks."

Tomorrow, she thought as she watched him leave, she was taping a poster for her gig on the lid of her guitar case. Free advertising wasn't going to hurt.

She finished packing up, then hoisted her knapsack to her shoulder, the weight of all those coins surprising her. Better than tips any day. At least here she felt as though she'd really earned the money. Half the time at the café it was more like people added their gratuity by rote. It didn't matter if they thought she'd done a good job or not, they simply did it because it was expected.

Picking up her guitar case, she wandered down the path, smiling her thanks when one or two of the fortune-tellers complimented her on the music.

"Come back any time," one of them said.

He sat on a stool behind a small table covered with

astrological charts. It all looked terribly complicated to Zeffy.

"Thanks," she said.

The man grinned. "But don't be too good. You want to leave a little money for the rest of us."

"Don't you listen to him," the dark-haired woman reading Tarot cards at the next spot over said. "You were bringing us business. I did more readings in the couple of hours you were playing than I did all day yesterday."

Zeffy smiled and continued on, past the fortune-tellers, over to where the craftspeople were set up. There were people selling jewelry and pottery, sketches and paintings, clothing, baskets, painted-paper boxes – there was even a leather-worker making shoes and belts on the spot. One man had an elaborate display of handwoven cotton scarves and little finger puppets made from what Zeffy assumed were remnants from his larger weaving projects. Her gaze moved from his table to the man sitting on the ground next to him, a scruffy dog curled up against his leg. The dog regarded her nervously, before dropping its head back onto its forepaws.

Zeffy smiled when she saw the funny little stick people the man was carving. He had a haphazard pile of twigs and bits of roots stacked beside him and was busy pulling features and humorous stances out of the found material with a small knife, using judicious bits of carving to amplify a nose here, eyes there, dancing legs, a big grin . . . whatever worked.

She looked up from his hands to his face and then she stopped in her tracks.

"Johnny?" she said.

It couldn't be. But when he lifted his face to meet her gaze, Johnny Devlin's unmistakable features were looking back at her. There'd been a welcoming smile on his lips until he recognized her. Something changed in his eyes and then he schooled his features into a carefully neutral expression. Watching the smile fade, Zeffy felt a pang of disappointment that she couldn't explain.

"I don't have your money yet," he said.

Zeffy found herself shaking her head. "That's not why I'm here. I was just . . ." She waved a hand back in the direction she'd come from. "Playing some music over there."

"That was you? You're good. Really good."

There was no reason that she should care in the least what he thought about her or her music, but Zeffy couldn't help but warm to the compliment. For a moment it was as though she'd never met him before, as though he was as much a stranger to her as had been the fortune-tellers and the boy on his skateboard. But then she remembered who it was sitting there on the ground, making his little stick men.

Little stick men.

She put her guitar case down so it was standing on its side and sat on it. Looking more closely at the small figures, she had to marvel at how much expression he managed to pull out of the wood with just a minimum of carving. Her gaze returned to the dog. It returned her gaze, a nervous twitch around its eyes, as though picking up on Johnny's reaction to her. It looked like some scruffy stray that nobody'd want, little say Johnny.

Zeffy couldn't figure it out. None of this made sense. Johnny was openly contemptuous of craftspeople who worked the streets. "Talentless losers with needy faces" was how Tanya had told her he'd described them once. "Why don't they get a real job instead of subjecting us to the pathetic crap they're trying to sell?" And apparently he hated animals. Cats, dogs, budgies, goldfish, whatever kind of pets people kept.

"What's happened to you?" Zeffy had to ask, curiosity overcoming her natural inclination to simply get up and walk away.

"What does it matter?" he asked.

He continued to work as he spoke, gaze moving from the carving in his hands to her face when he spoke, then down again. Around them, the lunch crowds had thinned so much that many of the vendors were beginning to pack up and leave. No one was paying attention to either them or their conversation, not even the weaver right beside them. He'd been putting his scarves away in a cardboard box but seemed to have become hopelessly distracted by a well-built spandex-clad woman on in-line skates who was doing slow circles around the pigeons by the War Memorial.

Zeffy returned her attention to Johnny, still trying to figure out this apparent complete change in his personality and habits. She thought of Tanya's insistence that something had happened to him – personality disorder, aliens, whatever – and couldn't suppress a shiver.

"That was some business you laid on us yesterday," she finally said. "Tanya thinks you've turned into a pod person and to tell you the truth, you almost had me believing it for a while. The thing I can't figure out is why you're doing this. You trying to stiff Tanya for her money is a pretty cheap shot, but acting as though you've never met her ... that's really low, even for you."

His head lifted again. There was an expression in his eyes that was unlike anything she could imagine Johnny feeling, a lost, hopeless, despairing look. The look of someone at the end of his rope.

"You want to know the truth?" he asked.

Zeffy nodded.

"I never met either one of you before yesterday morning."

"Oh, please."

"I really don't much care what you believe," he said, resignation weighing down his voice. "You came over here to ask me. It's not like I went looking for you."

This was true. And Zeffy hadn't been looking for him. She had better things to do with her time. But now that she had run into him, she'd hoped that he'd come clean with her, not continue this stupid game. Why she even wanted to know, she wasn't sure. Because the whole business irritated her, she supposed.

She watched him lay down the knife and carving he'd been working on. The dog stirred at his side and he put an arm around it, ruffling the stiff fur under its chin. That little show of affection irritated Zeffy even more.

"Well, since we're discussing the 'truth,'" she said, "I have to tell you that I've never much cared for you. Never have – doubt I ever will."

"Fine."

"Oh, come on. Let's cut through the BS. Why are you going through with this elaborate charade? I could care less for myself, but you've got to know it's really messing up Tanya. You want to break it off with her, okay. It happens. So break it off. But don't play these games. You're not being fair to her."

"Fair. That's a laugh."

Zeffy was trying to be calm about this, but she could feel her temper fraying.

"What the hell's gotten into you, anyway?" she demanded. "You were always self-centered, but the way you're acting now goes way beyond normal."

170

He wouldn't look at her. Head bent, he stared at the ground, stroked the dog. She could see his fingers trembling in its fur and had the sudden feeling that he was about to cry. This was so not Johnny that she got the creeps all over again.

"Okay," he said finally.

Zeffy had been about to retreat from what she felt was turning into a seriously weird situation. Now she waited. Johnny finally met her gaze, a haunted look in his eyes.

"You really want to know what's going on?" he asked.

She nodded, although now she wasn't so sure.

"To start with," he said, "my name's not Johnny Devlin. I know I look like him – Christ, I woke up inside his body yesterday morning, so I can't blame any of you for thinking I am him. But I'm not. My name's Max Trader. I'm a luthier. Until yesterday morning I'd never heard of Devlin, you, or your friend Tanya before. Until yesterday morning I had a good life, but now it's all gone, shot to shit, just like that."

He snapped his fingers and the dog started nervously. He calmed it absently, fingers combing the dirty fur. Zeffy really wanted to leave now, but the weight of his gaze seemed to pin her to the spot.

"If you want to talk to Devlin," he went on, "go to my shop in the Market. He's got my life – my apartment, my shop, my tools, my money, my friends. He's got everything I spent a lifetime building and he's not giving it up, now that he has it. All I got in exchange is what you see: no home. No money. No career. No friends. Nothing. Just Buddy here."

Zeffy could only stare at him.

"You say you're Max Trader," she repeated slowly. "Of Trader Guitars."

"I was. Now I don't know who I am anymore."

"I see . . . "

Zeffy had never met Trader, but she'd seen articles about him in the papers and in *Acoustic Guitar*, lusted after one of his beautiful handmade instruments. She knew what he looked like, if only from pictures, and it was nothing like Johnny Devlin.

She shook her head. "This is insane."

"Tell me about it."

"No really. This isn't funny at all."

"Do you see me laughing?"

"So what are you trying to say? That somehow you and Max Trader switched bodies?"

He shook his head. "Devlin and I have switched bodies. I told you. I'm Max Trader."

"Jesus," Zeffy said. "You're really sick, you know that?"

He shrugged. "You asked. And nobody's making you sit there and listen to me."

He turned his attention back to the dog, leaving Zeffy to fume. She wanted to hit him with her knapsack, let the heavy weight of all those coins knock some sense into him. She wanted to grab him by the shoulders and shake him until he owned up to the truth. Instead, she continued to sit there watching him fuss over the dog – knowing that he *hated* dogs – and didn't know what to do.

"So tell me something that Johnny wouldn't know," she said finally. "Something only Trader would know."

Anger flashed in his eyes. "How the hell would I know what Devlin does or doesn't know?"

"You know what I mean. Prove it to me."

"Why?"

"So that I'll believe you."

The anger left his eyes. Only the resignation remained. And a sadness.

"There's no way you can believe me," he said. "Half the time I don't believe me.

"But—"

"Look, this is my problem, okay? There's nothing you or anybody else can do about it. And there's no point in pretending that you care about what happens to me because so far as you're concerned I'm Johnny Devlin, and we already know how you feel about him. If I'd met you under different circumstances, maybe things'd be different, because I quite like you. But we didn't. I don't have a life and yours doesn't include me except for the fact that I owe your roommate some money."

It was plain to Zeffy that he believed what he was saying, wholly and completely. He spoke with such conviction that she almost believed it all herself. The difference was, she knew the truth. What he was saying was impossible, so there were only two possible explanations. Either he was lying, or he was sick, and the longer she spoke with him, the less she thought he was lying.

"You're right," she said, choosing her words carefully. "You and I never got along. But that doesn't stop me from wanting to help you when you're in trouble. I'd do the same for anyone."

His lips shaped a wry smile that she'd never seen on Johnny's face before. It didn't reach his eyes.

"Even when you think I'm Johnny Devlin?" he asked.

"Even when I—" Know you're Johnny, she'd been about to say, but she caught herself. Play along with him for now, she told herself. "Even when I think you're Johnny."

"I guess your beauty runs deeper than the skin," he said.

She blinked. "What's that supposed to mean?"

"That you've got a good heart. It's obvious that you despise Devlin, yet you're still willing to help him. Not many people would do that. Most people would sit back and watch him take his fall."

Zeffy wasn't sure what he was up to now. She'd almost think he was making a pass, but his present charm was nothing like what she was used to seeing in Johnny. Natural, instead of oily. Or was it only because she was on the receiving end of it this time, instead of watching it work on Tanya?

"I think you should get some medical help," she said.

He nodded. "I've thought of it. I know it would be the smart thing to do. I think I'm crazy myself, half the time. But I know all these things – I have a lifetime of memories of being someone else and I've got to trust that they're real or I'll lose it completely."

"I guess." Zeffy was still trying to be careful with what she said to him, still not sure why she even cared what happened to him. "But maybe it's a disorder of some kind – something they can help you with through therapy."

"And if it's not a disorder?" he asked. "What happens if I'm right?"

"But that's . . ." she hesitated.

"Impossible," he said, finishing her sentence for her. "I know. So they'd lock me away in a padded room and I'd probably be there for the rest of my life because I know who I am and I'm not going to pretend to be somebody else, I don't care what it costs me or what people think. I'll admit I've had my doubts, but if I'm not who I believe I am, I don't think I could go on. I couldn't be Johnny Devlin. Everything he stands for is repugnant to me."

Zeffy knew exactly what he meant. She felt the same way about Johnny. Except this *was* Johnny and he didn't seem at all repugnant to her right now. He seemed lost and hurting and filled with a deep despair, but there was still a strength underlying his pain, a strength she'd never seen in Johnny. One of the things she'd disliked the most about him was the weakness he couldn't quite hide under his bravado and charm – at least not from her. Or not until now.

God, this was confusing.

She'd heard of this sort of thing before, multiple personalities, many of them unaware of the others' existence. But it was something you read about in a magazine or a book, or saw on *Geraldo*; not something that showed up in your own life. She had no experience with this sort of situation. No idea at all how to handle it. She didn't even know why she was involving herself, except there was something so vulnerable about the man sitting across from her that she was beginning to have difficulty thinking of him as Johnny.

He even looked different. A little scruffier. Clothes rumpled, two days' worth of beard, hair loose, all mussed up instead of combed back. He held himself differently, too. The way he moved, his posture, his facial expressions. Then there were the carvings and the dog . . .

"Kind of leaves us at an impasse, doesn't it?" he said.

The rueful smile was back, a sweet smile that worked its way through Zeffy's already crumbling defences. This was crazy, she thought, as she caught herself smiling back.

"So . . . how's business?" she asked, just to change the subject.

He shrugged. "So-so. But I'm actually enjoying myself. The last time I did this kind of thing was too long ago."

"You used to do wood carving before?" she asked.

"Not Devlin," he said. "Me. Max."

"Oh, right. So how much do you sell them for?"

"Whatever people want to pay."

Zeffy dug into her knapsack and came up with a few dollar bills.

"You don't have to buy one," he said.

"No, I want to."

She chose one that looked like a little toadstool of a man with a raggedy peacock's tail and enormous eyes. Afraid that it would break in her knapsack, she held it in her hand as she stood up.

"I have to go," she said. "To think about all of this."

He nodded. "I don't expect you to do anything. I just want to say thanks for listening."

"Right."

She felt as though she was deserting him, but she had to go. There was too much going through her head at the moment for her to make sense out of anything.

"Will you be here tomorrow?" she asked.

"Probably. Unless I figure out a way to switch us back. But even if that happens, I'll make a point of being here if I know you're coming."

"Right."

Why did she keep saying "right"? Zeffy wondered. It made her sound like a broken record. Then she had to question again why she cared what Johnny thought of her and started to get confused all over again.

She swung her knapsack onto her shoulders and picked up her guitar case.

"So I'll see you," she said.

"I'll look forward to it."

She left quickly, grip too tight on the handle of her guitar case, carving safely cradled in her other hand. Her pulse sounded loud, thrumming against her eardrums. Her breath was short. She didn't know how he was getting to her, she thought as she hurried out of the park, but it was working. And the worst thing was, she didn't know how she felt about it. She knew what she should be feeling, but seemed incapable of calling up that anger anymore. She couldn't hang on to it at all.

VII • LISA

JUST AFTER eight, Lisa called in sick to work. She wanted to tell her employers the truth, that her daughter was missing and she didn't think she'd be much good for anything until Nia had been found, but Julie talked her out of it before she made the call. "Don't give them fuel," she said. "If they think you can't handle a crisis in your personal life, they're going to equate that with how you perform under pressure when you're in the office."

"But—"

"And you can kiss goodbye to any hopes of advancing. Believe me, I've been there."

Lisa hesitated, hand still on the phone. "I hate being dishonest."

"Save the truth for those who deserve it," Julie told her.

There was something in her voice that drew a sharp look from Lisa, but Julie turned away as though she didn't notice the sudden hole of silence left in the wake of her pronouncement. Her gaze went distant, held by something that lay on the far side of the kitchen window's panes, and Lisa felt unaccountably bereft. Julie had so much presence, she filled the space around her with such vitality, that her abrupt preoccupation lay like a heavy veil between them, not only creating distance, but making her almost unrecognizable.

Lisa wanted to reach through that veil, to bring Julie back from whatever dark place it was she'd gone, but she couldn't find the words she needed to bridge the distance. They didn't know each other well enough for her to feel she

177

could pursue it at the moment and it was too confusing to try to deal with it on top of Nia's disappearance.

She sighed and picked up the receiver, forcing herself to approach things one at a time. Call in to work. Check off that piece of business. Deal with the next item on the list.

When the connection was made and she spoke to the receptionist at work, she realized that Julie had been right. If she had tried to explain the real reason for absence, she didn't think she would have been able to stop. So she kept it brief, cradled the receiver once more.

Julie turned from the window, the distance gone from her eyes. It was like the sun coming out from behind a cloud cover, as though, in those few minutes while Lisa made her call, Julie had confronted whatever darkness it was that she'd had to visit and now it was banished to trouble her no more. She was so much her usual, warm self that Lisa began to question what, if anything, it was that she'd thought she'd seen.

"My turn," Julie said.

It took Lisa a moment to register what she meant.

"I can't let you stay with me all day," she said.

"Can't let me or don't want me to?"

"You know it's not that. It's just, this is my problem. I really appreciate your staying as long as you have, but I can't let Nia's taking off like this disrupt your whole life, too."

"I can't bring Nia back," Julie said. "I don't have the answers, so being here with you is all I can do to help." When Lisa still hesitated, she added, "Let me at least do this for you."

"I do want you here," Lisa said. "I just hate the idea of our starting off with me being so needy . . . "

Julie shook her head. "This is a scary situation. Anyone

would understand your needing some moral support. It's nothing to be ashamed of."

"I suppose."

Julie made her own call. She was quick and efficient when she got through to her own office, spending no more time than was needed to get the information across, speaking in a businesslike tone that expected no problems and got none.

"There," she said when she hung up. She leaned her elbows on the table, steepling her fingers. "So now I think it's time we had a word with your downstairs neighbor."

The only reason Lisa hadn't gone down to Max Trader's apartment earlier was because Julie wouldn't hear of it. Last night, when they finally realized that Nia wasn't coming home, Julie felt it was too late. This morning, she insisted on waiting until the hour was reasonable.

"Your life is in turmoil," she said. "I know that and you know that. But other people aren't necessarily going to feel the same way about it and won't particularly appreciate being disturbed because of what they'd consider as nothing more than some teenager's growing pains."

Remembering the reaction of the police, Lisa had reluctantly agreed, for all that she'd still wanted to run down to Trader's floor and hammer on his door, more and more convinced, as the hours dragged by, that he was in on it, that he was harboring Nia, that maybe he'd even put her up to it. She knew next to nothing about the man except that Nia had what Lisa considered an unhealthy fascination with him. Yes, he seemed like a respectable businessman and Nia only visited him in his shop, not in his apartment, but she couldn't see anything natural about their relationship. For one thing, he had to be at least twice her age. For another there was something almost too calm, too friendly about him, as though he was hiding something.

A few weeks ago, she'd talked about it over lunch to Allison, one of her coworkers. Allison's response had been what kept her from outright forbidding Nia to spend as much time as she did in the man's shop.

"I've read about this kind of thing," Allison had said. Lisa had never known anyone to read as much as her coworker. "What's probably happening is your daughter's projecting a father fantasy onto him, which, considering her age and the circumstances, is perfectly natural. And that leaves you, who's had to take up all the slack since her real father deserted the two of you, feeling jealous that this perfect stranger can just waltz in and reap the benefit of a kind of parental relationship without having to do a thing in terms of raising and looking after her.

"I'm sure it's perfectly innocent. My own Rachel went through a similar phase with the owner of a bookshop that had me going crazy until she got over it."

"But you hear all these stories . . . "

Allison nodded, very serious now. "Has there been anything to make you think he's taking advantage of Nia?" she asked. "Anything at all?"

"No."

And the truth was, ever since she'd spoken to Allison about it, Lisa had seen that she did resent Trader's presence in her daughter's life for pretty much the reasons Allison had put forward. The realization made her feel small-minded and not very happy with herself. It was too much what she thought her own mother's reaction to the situation would have been, rather than her own.

All of which made her nervous about going downstairs to talk to him now and more grateful than ever that she had Julie here with her to see things through if she got all tongue-tied. They went down to his shop, but even though it was past nine, the store was dark. Julie held her hand as they went back up to Trader's apartment, giving her fingers a squeeze and letting go when Trader responded to their knock.

"Hello," he said as he opened the door. He wore a cheerful smile and gave them a once-over, gaze lingering too long below their necks before it finally rose to their faces. "What can I do for you today?"

"It's Nia," Lisa began.

The world felt out-of-kilter and she wasn't sure if it was because talking about Nia's disappearance brought the reality of the situation back into overly sharp focus again, or something about Trader himself. His good humor seemed relentless and totally out of keeping with how she was feeling.

"How can I help?" he asked, smile reined in now, a look of studied concern coming over his features.

Something about him rang a false note, but she couldn't put her finger on what it was. Maybe it was just because she didn't know him well enough – certainly not as well as her daughter did.

"Maybe you should come in," he went on when she didn't respond.

Lisa shook her head. She gave Julie a quick glance. When she saw her friend's pursed lips, the way Julie was studying Trader, she knew she wasn't alone in how she felt.

"No," she said. "Thank you. I was just wondering if you'd seen her today or if she came by the shop yesterday."

"You're my first visitors of the morning," he replied, "and I never even got downstairs to open up yesterday." He put a hand against his chest and gave a light cough. "I was feeling under the weather – stayed in bed the whole day."

What a phony cough, Lisa thought, and her worries

returned. She wanted to push by him into the apartment, not as an invited guest, chained to politeness, but like a guerrilla, or a member of a TV-styled SWAT team, to tear the place apart, searching every room, every cupboard.

"But happily," Julie said, "you seem to be feeling much better today."

Her voice held an ironic tone that he didn't appear to catch.

"Yeah, well . . ." He shrugged. "You know, rum-and-lemon toddies – the miracle cure."

Why isn't he asking about Nia? Lisa wanted to know. Why isn't he showing any concern? The obvious reason terrified her. Her knees got watery, as though they were about to give way under her, and the vague sense of vertigo she'd experienced when he first opened the door returned more strongly, with a dizzying rush.

"If you hear from her, or if you see her," Julie said, "would you ask her to call? I don't have to tell you how worried we are." She paused, allowing the heartbeat of silence to give significance to what she said next. "And of course, we'd like to be able to tell the police they can stop looking for her."

"The police?"

Nothing changed in his face, in his eyes, in the way he stood, but suddenly everything about him seemed alert.

"So it's . . . that serious," he added.

Julie nodded. "She's only sixteen and this can be a very dangerous city."

"You're telling me," Trader said. "Why do you think I'm living in this part of town?"

"No place is safe," Julie told him. "Some places just seem to have the odds more in your favor."

He made no reply to that beyond shifting his gaze from Julie to Lisa, back again.

"Well, let's hope for the best," he said. "And listen, let me know when she gets back."

"And if you hear anything yourself—"

"I'll call you right away," he assured her.

"We'd really appreciate that," Julie said. She waited until his door was closed and the two of them were going back up to Lisa's apartment before adding, "What a creep."

Lisa nodded. "I think he knows something. Did you see the way he reacted when you mentioned the police? He seemed to go so still."

"I don't know if he's involved or not," Julie said, "but he certainly strikes me as being capable of it."

"We've got to tell the police."

Julie stopped Lisa on the landing. "And tell them what?"

"About him. So they can – you know, search his apartment."

"Lisa, we don't even know if anything *has* happened to Nia."

"But—"

"The police aren't going to listen to us any more this morning than they did last night. If she's not back by tonight, then I think they'll start taking this more seriously. But until then, they're not going to go breaking into anyone's apartment looking for her."

All Lisa's feelings of helplessness returned in an over-powering rush. "But what can we do until then?"

"We hope. And we pray," Julie said. She led Lisa back into the apartment, but left the door ajar. "And we listen to what your downstairs neighbor gets up to. If he goes out, we follow him. If he doesn't . . ."

183

Her words trailed off. Lisa gave her an anguished look, understanding that Julie knew no more than she did about what they could do. Wait. Hope. Pray.

"What if he doesn't open the store again?" she asked. "That'd prove something, wouldn't it? We could tell the police then, couldn't we?"

Julie sat back down at the kitchen table. "Tell them what? That he's lazy? That he's only pretending to be sick?" She shook her head. "All we can really do is wait."

She got up and steered Lisa into a chair at the table. Standing behind her, she kneaded the tense muscles at the nape of Lisa's neck. Lisa leaned her head forward, appreciating the contact for all that it brought no real comfort. The possibility of any closer intimacy between them had been drowned in an ocean of worry and fear.

Oh Nia, she thought. Why are you doing this to me? Why won't you just come home?

VIII • NIA

NIA HEARD the boy long before she saw him. She was in an out-of-the-way section of the park, surrounded by old-growth cedars, their dense stands broken by granite outcrops pushing out of the earth like the limbs of buried stone giants. Here a shoulder, there a knee, grey body parts encrusted with moss and braided with roots. Her own perch was a rounded elbow that let her look down on a park path that ran by below.

She'd watched the occasional cyclist wheel by, all of them in a hurry, heads bent over the handlebars, chasing moments that they'd probably never catch, they were so busy with the chase. Less often, there were in-line skaters, once a whole covey of bright spandex, the unpleasant plastic hum of their wheels on the pavement heralding their appearance long before she saw them. Until the boy, there had been no one on foot, not even any joggers, no one walking slowly enough to look around, or up, and see her on her granite perch.

The announcement of his approach was verbal, a distant, nagging hum of a voice that turned into language, then finally understandable words as he came into sight. He was either talking to himself, or to someone Nia couldn't see yet, every second word an epithet. As he drew closer, she saw he was alone.

Unlike the other people she'd spied on from her vantage point, he wasn't dressed for sport. Baggy jeans, the crotch hanging halfway to his knees. Paint-stained jersey, sleeves pushed up on his forearms. Air-pumped basketball shoes, the laces undone. Baseball cap worn backward, with hair like scarecrow straw sticking out from under it. His face was long and narrow with the look of a fox that was accentuated by a raggedy goatee. Eyes hidden behind shades. An old army-surplus knapsack hung from his shoulder by one leather strap. Nia couldn't guess his age – somewhere around her own, give or take a couple of years.

He paused under her stone elbow, attention drawn to her as unerringly as a predator's to its prey. Nia held her breath. He cocked his sunglasses with one paint-stained hand, steady gaze settling on her face. She was surprised at how blue his eyes were, radiant with their own inner light. Or maybe he was just stoned.

"Yo!" he called up to her. "So what are you supposed to be? A nun?"

Her first intention had been to fade back into the cedars. To slip through the haven of their branches and leave only the pungent scent of the bruised leaves behind. But the peculiarity of his question held her in place, reminded her to breathe.

"What do you mean, 'a nun'?" she said.

He shrugged. "You know. The all-in-black look. Hair's too long for a Goth. The sun's out, so you're not one of the undead. You don't have wings or feathers, so forget a crow. That only leaves a nun."

"In jeans?" she asked, unable to stifle a giggle.

"Hey, why not? Who the hell knows what they do in their time off."

"I don't think nuns have time off."

"Their loss."

"Why were you swearing?" she asked.

"Fucked if I know."

He let his sunglasses drop back onto his nose. The strap of his knapsack started to slip and he shifted it higher onto his shoulder. Lisa heard a metallic sound, like cans rattling against each other.

"So what d'ya see from up there?" he asked.

Nia hesitated for a long moment before replying. "Why don't you come up and find out?"

"Thought you'd never ask."

Instead of going around behind, pushing through the cedars the way Nia had, he scrambled straight up the stone face of the outcrop, moving like a monkey. All he lacked was a tail.

"Cool," he said when he was sitting beside her.

She knew exactly what he meant. It wasn't the view so much as the sense of being outside the world proper. You could see anybody approaching you, but few people were going to look up and see you.

"Got any smokes?" he asked.

Nia shook her head.

"Figures." Long pause. "So what's your tag?"

Nia blinked in confusion.

"When you're throwing up," he said. "Tagging. I saw you earlier, the beef you were having with Stetler. In the alley."

"I don't know what you're talking about."

"So you're not a writer."

It wasn't a question and was spoken in a tone of voice that told Nia he was losing all interest in her. He looked out over the path, face blank, eyes unreadable behind his shades, then leaned back on his elbows.

"It's okay," he said. "It's a nice day. Be what you want to be, like I give a shit."

"What's yours?" she asked. "Your . . . tag."

His head turned in her direction, pushed up the sunglasses with a stiff finger. The blue shock of his eyes rattled her.

"TAMP," he said. He pulled an aerosol paint can from his knapsack and sprayed the letters in a bubble-script on the rock between them, all caps, bright red paint. "Like that." He looked up grinning. "So now you know me, right?"

She didn't know him, but at least she knew what he was talking about now. Graffiti. Like that in the alley where she'd spent the night.

"Sure," she said. "I guess everybody must know you."

That called up a smile. "Fucking-A. I got me more throwups than any writer in the city."

"The man in the alley," Nia began.

"Stetler. He owns the Radio Shack on Bunnett. I got a beef with him goes way back so I make sure he sees my tag every chance I get, front and back. He cleans 'em up and I just throw 'em back up."

"He thought I'd done it."

TAMP laughed. "Yeah, well, fuck him. What does he know?"

"My name's Nia."

"We all got problems."

"What's that supposed—"

"Yo. Hang loose. Somebody boost your sense of humor?"

Nia shook her head. She was beginning to wish she'd followed her first instinct and retreated instead of waiting for him to climb up to her perch. She didn't like the fact that he'd spray-painted his name on the rock. Didn't like the way he looked at her. Didn't like being mocked.

"So what're you doing up here, Neee-ah?"

She shrugged. "Nothing much. Just hanging out."

"Where do you live?"

"Wherever I want to."

"Runaway," he said with a smirk.

"What's it to you?"

"Hey, don't act like I'm in your face," he said. "I'm just making friendly."

"It's more like you're making fun of me."

He shook his head. "You got to not take this kind of shit so seriously. It's just talk. No beef. Nothing heavy. So happens we're driving down the same highway. I just been on the road a little longer, that's all."

"You ran away from home, too?"

"Nah. Got my ass booted, but same difference, right?"

"I suppose. So where do you sleep?"

"Squatland."

Nia was impressed. Squatland was what kids had taken to calling the Tombs, that precinct north of Gracie Street where a developer's bankruptcy had become the city's disgrace. It was an eyesore of deserted tenements, empty lots and long-abandoned factory buildings that ran on for block after derelict block. The main streets, running north and south, were kept clear as they cut through the area, but the side streets were mostly impassable, choked with litter and rubble, junked cars and appliances. Runaways and homeless people squatted in some of the buildings, hoboes camped out in the garbage-strewn lots, but petty criminals, dealers and bikers owned its raggedy streets.

You had to have nerve to dare that part of town – nerve Nia didn't think she could muster. Half the murders and other violent crimes in the city took place in the Tombs, or on its periphery.

"Isn't it . . . dangerous?" she asked.

"Get with the program," TAMP told her. "So's life."

"I guess."

"So you got any money?" he wanted to know.

She had about thirty dollars in her backpack but she wasn't about to tell him that. All she'd admit to was a couple of dollars and some change.

"Too bad. We coulda scored us some cat, had a fine time." He gave her a considering look. "A very fine time."

Nia pulled a face. "Yeah, like I'm going to stick something made with Drano and battery acid up my nose."

"What the fuck are you on about?"

"Methcathinone. Don't you even know what it's made of?"

"Who cares? You do a few lines, you get high. Better rush than coke and it lasts, so where's the problem?"

All Nia could do was shake her head.

"Yo, Miss I-Know-Better. Cat's cool. Get yourself a little ephedrine and anybody can make it. Cuts out the middle man, you know what I'm saying? Puts the power back in our hands instead of the bankers'."

"I don't do drugs," Nia said.

He looked at her in disbelief. "Like not ever?"

"Not ever."

"Why the fuck not?"

"I don't like the idea of being messed up like that."

He shook his head. "You don't throw up, you don't get high. Yo, what the hell do you do for fun?"

"I like jazz."

He thought about that for a moment. "Ever heard of The Rhatigan?"

Only one of the best jazz clubs in town, a seedy little dive on Palm Street, by all accounts she'd heard, but their house band was supposed to be fabulous and all the best players dropped by to sit in when they were in town.

"Of course," she said. "But I'm underage. I'd never be able to get in."

"I could get you in – dude behind the bar owes me a favor." He shot her a suspicious look. "You do drink beer, right?"

So rarely she might as well say she didn't, Nia thought, but she found herself nodding. And then wished she hadn't because it suddenly occurred to her to wonder why she even cared what this guy thought about her and the answer troubled her. TAMP was a jerk. The kind of guy she wouldn't look at twice if she passed him on the street. But having been on her own for over twenty-four hours now, with no one to talk to, she was grabbing on to his company because she needed someone and there was no one else. Her mom and Max had been stolen from her and she didn't have any real friends. There wasn't anyone else she could turn to, no one at all, which was way more pathetic than she wanted to admit. She was reduced to putting up with the company of a foulmouthed, petty criminal and self-proclaimed drug addict, just for the sake of human contact. He stood for everything she hated about her generation and now she was actually considering going to some bar with him just because there'd be good music and he could get her in?

What had happened to her sense of ethics? The realization that she could put them aside so easily made her feel ashamed of herself.

"Look, I appreciate the offer," she said, "but I've got to go. I . . . I'm supposed to be meeting somebody."

The shades went up and the gaze of those disconcerting blue eyes settled on her, read the lie, then looked away, sunglasses back in place, dismissing her.

Yeah, you too, Nia thought, but she couldn't seem to muster much conviction to the sentiment.

"'Scool," TAMP said, not bothering to look at her. "Lady's got an appointment."

"Well, it was nice to meet you."

"I'm sure."

As she started to get up, he turned around. He picked up his spray can from where it lay on its side by his knee, offered it to her.

"Here," he said. "Throw up your tag beside mine. Let people know who owns this spot."

"No, I don't think that's such a—"

"Yo, you're too shy, no problem."

He gave the can a shake, but before he could start to spray, Nia had crouched down beside him. She grabbed at the can, aiming its nozzle away from the rock. TAMP gave a little shake of his wrist, easily dislodging her grip.

"You don't want to be doing that," he told her.

A shiver of fear went through Nia at the coldness in his voice, but she refused to let herself back down. She couldn't. If only to herself, she had to make up for being such a little wimp earlier. She had to stand up for things she believed in. If she didn't, or couldn't, then she might as well go back home and let the aliens have her brain, too.

"Look around you," she said. "What do you see?"

His expression was unreadable behind his sunglasses. "What do you think? Trees. The park. A lot of green crap. You making a point here?"

"Yeah. All of this . . . it's beautiful. What do you want to ruin it for? What makes this special is that you can't own it – or that you shouldn't try to. If you want to spray your name onto stuff, do it on buildings, but not here."

"You telling me?"

Nia hesitated at the suggestion of menace in his voice. She cleared her throat.

"No," she said. "I'm asking you."

He stared at her for a long moment before he finally nodded. "You're one weird chick, but you've got *cojones*, and I like that." He held the spray can up between them, then made a show of putting it away in his knapsack. "Yo. The paint's all gone and everybody's happy, right?"

Nia nodded. "I guess."

She stood up, half-expecting him to stop her, but he lounged back down on the stone.

"I've got to go," she said.

"No surprise there."

"So, I guess I'll see you around."

"Whatever."

She turned and headed for the back of the stone. Before she could push through the cedars, his voice stopped her.

"If you change your mind about The Rhatigan," he said, "I'll be there later on tonight."

"I'll remember that."

She made a hole for herself in the trees, spreading the

boughs with her hands, then let them close behind her like a curtain. To her great relief, TAMP didn't try to follow. When she got down to the path he was still stretched out on the stone above, lying on his back now, arms behind his head, sunglasses pointed up to the sky. Nia hesitated for a moment. She almost called up to him, but realized she didn't know what to say, didn't want to start up another conversation with him anyway.

Settling her backpack more comfortably against her shoulder blades, she set off down the path at a brisk pace. A sense of relief settled over her that lasted only as long as it took her to realize that she still had no place to go, no one to talk to, no one to ask for help.

Her stomach rumbled.

She could get something to eat, she decided, but that was only a stop-measure. It solved nothing. Once her appetite was satisfied, the whole sorry state of the rest of her life would remain.

Deal with one thing at a time, she told herself. She sighed, hearing in that phrase the echo of her mother's way of handling problems, but minding it less than she'd usually own up to. Things were different now. All the problems she and her mother had been having were forgotten, swallowed by events beyond the control of either of them. At this moment she'd have given anything to be with her mother – her *real* mother – and wouldn't have cared how much alike they might seem.

IX • MAX

I'M SO bemused from my latest encounter with Zeffy that I don't notice Bones until he flows into a cross-legged position on the grass beside me. I have to smile at this cat-like ability he has to imply permanence and cool importance to every action, no matter how mundane or fleeting. Sitting there, regarding me with that unreadable gaze of his, it's as though he's been with me all afternoon. Buddy doesn't even stir at his arrival, except to open one lazy eye that soon droops closed again.

"Nice-looking woman," Bones says, nodding in the direction Zeffy took. If I squint, I can still see the bounce of her red hair receding in the crowd. Bones is watching me, smiles. "Has a lot of heart, too."

I nod in agreement. I know what he means, though I don't know how he knows it. Maybe his bones told him.

"I'd say I was in love with her," I find myself saying, "but I don't know her well enough to tell."

"Uh-huh. She someone you were trying to leave behind, or's she just coming into your life?"

I shrug. "A little of both, I suppose."

"Damn," Bones says. There's a birdlike cock to his head now, dark eyes studying me, amused, raven glitter in the pupils. "I knew this'd happen someday. Hand out those cryptic fortunes for long enough and sooner or later everything begins to sound like a riddle."

I smile at his confusion, but I don't bother to explain. I don't take his confusion seriously either. I get the feeling there's little he misses. Instead I ask him about his choice of oracular device, those bones that gave him his name. I saw him working earlier, when Buddy and I got back from our scavenge in the woods, the way he'd toss this handful of bird or mouse bones onto the deerskin spread out on the pavement in front of him, reading something in the pattern the bones made that neither his client nor I could see. But I guess if people could, nobody would be going to him, would they?

"You mean, where do they fit into the Kickaha tradition?" Bones asks.

"Something like that."

"Well," he says. "You get medicine men who read dreams, but otherwise there's not a whole lot of interest in fortune-telling on the rez." He smiles. "'Cept some of the old aunts like to check out the tabloids, read the predictions, cluck over the astrology column. But I guess I shouldn't laugh. You know somebody in one of those tabloids predicted the '92 quake in California?"

"Really?"

"Oh yeah. Mind you, same woman predicted about a hundred other things that didn't happen. Guess you've got to get lucky once in a while."

I can't tell if I'm supposed to read something more into what he's saying, or smile along, take it at face value.

"So where did reading the bones come from, if not from the Kickaha tradition?"

Bones grins, he's got that crazy look in his eyes again "I made them up."

"But that's—"

"Cheating?"

The man's treated me fair and I don't want to alienate him, but I find myself nodding.

"I guess it all depends on how you look at it," Bones says. "Now me, I figure all oracular devices are just a way for us to focus on what we already know but can't quite grab on to. It works the same as a ritual does in a church – you get enough people focused on something, things happen. The way I see it is, it doesn't much matter what the device is. It's just got to be interesting enough so that your attention doesn't stray. Fellow reading the fortune, fellow having it read – same difference. They've both got to be paying attention.

"What you get's not the future so much as what's inside a person, which," he adds, "is pretty much the real reason they come to you. They're trying to sort through all this conversation that's running through their heads, but they get distracted. Me, what I'm doing with my hands, with the bones, it forces them to pay strict attention to me. The noise in their heads quiets down a little and they can hear themselves for a change. It's my voice, but they're doing the talking."

"So will you read my fortune?" I ask.

Bones looks regretful, but shakes his head.

"Why not? Let me tell you, I could use someone to make a little sense out of what's going through my head."

"You don't believe."

"But you just told me that it's just a matter of paying attention. I can do that."

"It's not the same."

I'm getting a little frustrated. "You're telling me all these people you're doing it for believe?"

"Enough to give me their money."

"Oh, come on," I say. "For most of them it's just a lark, something to do to pass their lunch hour."

Bones nods. "But you're different, right?"

"No," I tell him. "What I'm saying is I don't get the difference.'

"Can't really help you there. That's something you've got to work out on your own."

I search those dark eyes of his, looking for a smile, but the gaze he returns is serious.

"Okay," I say. "The bones are something you made up and they work because the people coming to you for readings believe in them."

Bones gives Buddy a look. "The man's got it in a nutshell."

"So what do you believe?"

The dark gaze returns to consider me. "That anything is possible."

I almost come back with some smart ass remark, but his eyes make me think about what I'm about to say. They won't let me joke. They have me looking at my carvings, remembering Janossy and his ley lines that work their *feng shui* mystery on the wood, remembering how I used them in my own instrument building and repair, used it today in each and every one of these carvings I made. More to the point, those dark eyes make me think about what's happened between me and Devlin.

"Just like that?" I ask.

Bones looks away, across the park, head cocked like a raven again. I get the uncomfortable sensation that he's seeing a whole different world from the one I see. Buddy stirs nervously at my side, sensing the change in the air. There's a static interrupting the normal flow of how things should be. It's like the electric charge that sits in the air before a storm but it's centered in Bones. I look at him and I can almost hear a distant thunder.

"Just like that," Bones says. I think he's answering my question, but then realize he's only repeating what I said.

His gaze comes back to me. "Depends on the weight you want to give those words – that make any sense to you?"

I shake my head.

"Let's take the word *just*," Bones says. "Okay. Say, you see a man dancing. If you tell someone he's just dancing, do you mean 'only,' or do you mean he's doing something that he spent a lifetime learning and he's making it seem effortless?"

"I think I'm starting to get the picture."

"Are you? Maybe he's doing a lawful dance."

"I think you're being deliberately oblique," I tell him.

Bones laughs. "Maybe I am. Or maybe there's some things you can only approach from the side. Look at them straight on and there's nothing there."

"Like what?"

"Like look at yourself. Made a few bucks today, did you?"

"What's that got to do with—"

Bones holds up a hand, stops me cold, good humor gone.

"I look at you now," he says, "and already the man I met this morning is gone. He was beat, almost broken. Man I see now is thinking, maybe it doesn't have to be so bad, this new life I'm in. Maybe I can make do."

I don't say anything. I know he's right. I'd made enough to get Buddy and myself something decent to eat, with some left over that I can stretch into our breakfast. It's not like my problems are all suddenly solved, but I'm not feeling so helpless. I'm thinking maybe we can get by.

"You're getting comfortable in this new skin," Bones says. "Too comfortable. But let me tell you, it's easier to slip into than out of again."

I give him a sharp look. He *knows* what's happened to

me, I think. What Devlin did. How can he know? But we're not talking about the same thing, I realize when he goes on.

"But what're you going to do when winter comes?" he asks. "Head south? Look for that job you could get now, but you won't get then? You listen to me, Max, because this is the last time I'll tell you: You've got to get off the street now. Longer you take, harder it gets. Wait long enough and you'll never get off."

"You're doing okay," I say.

Bones laughs. "Sure, I'm doing okay." He waves a hand expansively. The gesture could be taking in the park, it could be taking in the whole world. "This is what I am. I'm living in the forest because I've always lived in the forest. Only difference is, the trees are made of stone here. And maybe this is your life, too. I don't know. I've got me a squat in the Tombs, share it with a decent lady. We don't own much, but we don't want much. We move when we have to. When the police decide to roust our building, we go on to the next. But we're nomads and we chose this life. You've got to ask yourself, is this what you want now? Or do you want that old life of yours back?"

He shakes his head. "Ten years from now, you're still living hand-to-mouth, what are you going to be thinking? That you made the right choice? Or are you going to be drowning your hurts in a bottle like the rest of the ones that can't make their lives any better?"

"You make it sound so hard."

"It is hard," Bones says. "You see these people, playing music, telling fortunes, selling crafts. They're not street people the way you're street people. They've got places to go when they leave here, they've got lives. They're here because they want to be, or because it's on the way to where they want to be."

"And you?"

"Don't look at me all wide-eyed and romantic. Yeah, I chose to live this way, and sure, it's hard. But the operative word here is *chose*. You told me you were a luthier." He points at the little carvings I made. "Is this something you want to do forever?"

"No. But it works for now. And later . . ." My voice trails off.

"Yeah," Bones says. "Later. How do you plan to buy the wood you'll need? The tools you'll need to work that wood? You're not here because you want to be and the longer you stay, the more it's going to eat at you."

"Somebody stole my life," I say, the words just coming out of my mouth. I lay a hand on Buddy's back, work at a knot in his wiry fur to stop from shaking.

Bones doesn't ask what I mean. He looks at me, eyes hard.

"So take it back," he says.

He rises with the same fluid motion he used to sit beside me, legs straightening effortlessly, doesn't use his hands. One moment he's sitting there cross-legged, the next he's standing over me.

"Why me?" I ask him. "What made you choose me to help?"

Bones shakes his head. "First day I see somebody new on the street . . ." He smiles. "Everybody gets my lecture, Max. You choose what you do with it. Whatever you choose, that's who you'll be and you won't hear any more about it from me. The only thing I'll ask of you is, don't come talking to me about what-might-have-beens. I don't want to know about how you got done wrong, how the doors are all closing in your face, none of that. We'll talk about whatever you want, but I don't want to know from hard times."

"Because you think they could have been avoided," I say.

"Because I know it." He shrugs. "Or at least I know you've got to try. Sometimes the bones deal you a bad hand. It happens. But the thing is, you've got to fight it. You've got to at least try."

"I thought you said you'd made them up."

"What? The bones?"

I nod.

"I did," he says. "But that doesn't mean they don't work."

He smiles, lifts a hand and walks off before I can say anything else. I sit there, fingers still working Buddy's fur, and watch him go. I don't know what to make of him. Half the time he seems a little crazy, the other half he's making sense, but those eyes of his look to be laughing at you for taking him seriously. Those eyes. They always seem to undermine what he's saying.

Then I realize he's like the bones. It doesn't matter if what he's telling me is sometimes contradictory, sometimes too off-the-wall. Not if it makes me think. Talking to him must be like throwing the bones. It makes you focus. It makes you remember who you are.

I'm still watching him walk away when I realize there's someone standing in front of me. I look up and she bends down at the same time. Blond hair as tangled and long as Zeffy's, dark skin, but it's from the sun. She's wearing an Indian print dress that's mostly blues, shading from robin's egg to indigo, and thong sandals. Her eyes match her dress, leaning more to the indigo. She's got a knapsack on the pavement beside her, bulging it out of shape, a small folding stool tied to it. Her elbow leans on the side of a closed-up card table for balance as she crouches to look at my carvings.

"These're great," she says.

"Thanks."

"How much are you selling them for?"

I remember her now. She was selling silk scarves and blouses a little farther down the row. Leaving early, I suppose. I'm surprised at how many of the vendors pack up after lunch, but I guess experience tells them when they can make a buck and when they're wasting their time.

"Whatever people want to pay," I tell her.

She laughs. "You're not going to get rich that way." Her gaze lifts to meet mine. "I'm Jenna."

"Max," I say as I take her proffered hand. "Nice to meet you."

"Likewise." She smiles, gaze returning to the carvings. "My daughter would love one of these."

She lays the card table against her knapsack and sits on the pavement, picks up one of the carvings, a long skinny figure, like a gnome that got caught up in a taffy pull. I found the shape in a cedar root. Kept the wild tangle of tiny roots and filaments for its hair and worked my way down from there, breathing deep its rooty odor while I carved out features, found shoulders, arms, torso, legs.

She lifts the carving to her nose. "This smells great."

"Cedar's got a heart of its own," I tell her. "For some things, it just can't be beat."

She laughs. "You sound like Crazy Dog."

"Who?"

She jerks a thumb in the direction Bones took. "You were just talking to him."

"I thought his name was Bones."

202

"Lord knows what his name really is. I've known him for years – before he got into the bones. I used to room with Cassie – his . . ." She gets that look people do when they're trying to find a tag for a couple who live together, but aren't married. "You know, significant other. He was so wild, straight off the rez that we started calling him that for a joke." She smiles. "But the joke was on us because he goes, 'That's a pretty close translation to what my grandmother used to call me.'"

"I haven't met Cassie yet," I say.

"Yeah, well she's working the Pier, these days. Got lucky and copped a booth in the last license raffle."

"It's better there?"

She laughs. "You *are* new. You work the Pier, the tourists give you money, just for being there. All it takes is to look a little offbeat, a little exotic, and Cassie sure fits the bill."

"She's a character – like Bones?"

Jenna shakes her head. "Nobody's like Crazy Dog. He give you his 'get off the street while you can' spiel yet?"

"He seems sincere."

"Oh he is. It's just . . ." She shrugs. "I don't know how to explain him. I don't think anyone can. He disappears every once in a while – for a couple of days, a few weeks, comes back with those wild eyes of his gleaming with mischief and . . . I don't know. Something else. Like he's gone walkabout right out of the world and there's still traces of what he saw, sitting there, left behind in his eyes, glittering."

I've never had so many conversations in one day about this sort of thing.

"Where do you think he really goes?" I ask.

"Who knows? If you talk to someone like Bernie – you know." She points toward the memorial. "The guy over there, selling rock T-shirts, the one with the glower? He says Crazy Dog's doing time at the Zeb when he goes away, that the doctors have him loaded up on serious medication while he's there, but they can only keep him so long. Once he's on an even keel they put him back on the street, tell him to stay on his medication."

I give her skeptical look.

"And of course, according to Bernie, as soon as he's on the street, he just throws the pills away."

"I don't think Bones is crazy," I say. "Not like that. Intense, definitely. And . . . quirky. But not padded-cell crazy."

"I don't think so either. He makes too much sense. Has he done a reading for you yet?"

I shake my head.

"It's scary how dead-on he can be. I mean, I always thought Cassie was good – she reads the Tarot – but Crazy Dog just seems to climb right inside your head and shuffle things around until your problems seem small and the future looks bright."

"Sounds impressive."

"But it's not," Jenna says. "Or it is, I guess, but it doesn't seem that way." She purses her lips. "And it's funny. He doesn't play on his heritage – never would. Dresses like the rest of us in jeans and a T-shirt when he could be doing the whole shaman bit – you know, leather and quillwork and feather, moccasins on his feet and beaded headband, shake a little painted gourd rattle. But all those people wanting to walk the Red Road, they zero right in on him. Figure what he's saying is important – which it is – but for all the wrong reasons."

"Keeps him in business," I say.

"And pisses off some of the people back on the rez I've

heard. They think he's making like the bones are some ancient Kickaha oracle, but he doesn't."

"He told me he made them up."

"He tells that to anybody who asks. Oh well. What're you going to do?" She holds up the gnome carving between us. "I've got to get this for Kilissa. How much do you want for it?"

"Like I said. Whatever you want to pay."

Jenna shakes her head and drops a couple of dollars in my hand.

"Can I give you a little bit of advice?" she asks.

"Sure. Why not?"

"Set prices for them. And fix yourself a little table of some kind. Put a nice cloth over it. Get the carvings off the ground and display them with a little pizzazz – which they deserve anyway. I guarantee you'll sell more."

I spread my hands, palms up. "You're looking at everything I own – and even then the knife is borrowed."

"I see where you're coming from. Okay. Get a plank and some bricks, then. Come see me in the morning and I'll lend you one of my scarves. I've got some nice ones at home, solid colors. I'll bring a few with me and you can pick the one you like the best."

My surprise at her generosity must be showing on my face.

"Hey, we're not all assholes like Bernie," she says.

"I don't know Bernie. Everybody's been really nice that I've met so far."

Jenna smiles. "Then don't make the mistake of talking to Bernie. It'll ruin your day. Gotta run. See you tomorrow."

She gathers her belongings and heads off, knapsack bouncing on her back, the gnome carving held carefully in her hand. I look down at Buddy.

"What do you say, fella?" I ask him, ruffling his wiry fur. "Do you want to stick it out a while longer, or should we find ourselves something to eat?"

I swear that all dogs are born knowing certain words. Walk. Eat. Good dog. The important stuff. Buddy looks up when I talk to him, interested, tongue lolling, alert. Like he *knows* what I'm talking about.

"Okay," I tell him. "We eat."

I bundle up the carvings and the wood I haven't used yet in my jacket and we head back into the park. I'll find a safe place to stash them, clean up in one of the public washrooms – maybe see if I can't make Buddy a little more presentable as well – then we'll head over to the market and get some dinner. I don't know where we'll sleep tonight. I find I don't really care. It's such a beautiful day I can't imagine the night being unpleasant. We'll sleep under the stars somewhere.

But as we head deeper into the park, Buddy running ahead, stopping to make sure I'm following, then running off again, something Bones said earlier comes back to me.

You're getting comfortable in this new skin. Too comfortable.

He's got it all wrong. I'm just getting my equilibrium back, that's all.

But let me tell you, it's easier to slip into than out of again.

He was speaking metaphorically, I tell myself. But I can feel the chasm, lying in wait, somewhere close, just out of sight. I know there's a long fall on these streets, creeping up on me, waiting to catch me off guard. I feel like I'm on the bottom rung right now, but at least I'm still above ground. I know I have to be careful. I have to fight the despair and everything that comes with it. I have to fight Devlin and get back what belongs to me. But thinking of Devlin only reminds me of my helplessness. It seems to bring the chasm closer.

I need a break from all of this.

Buddy comes running back to me and I realize I've come to a halt. I'm standing in the middle of a lawn, fists clenched in the fabric of my jacket, muttering to myself like some old rubbie. I hold the folded jacket against me with one hand, bend down to give Buddy a little loving.

"We're okay," I tell him. "We're going to be okay."

That's all he needs. He buys the lie and goes racing off.

When we're alone, he's like a different animal from the nervous, mistreated dog that befriended me last night. It's like the past just washes off him and only now exists. We're happy. He's a big goofy dog and I'm his pal. It's only when there are people around that he reverts. Withdraws into those dark places he's got to be carrying around inside him and remembers bad times.

He buys the lie, but I don't. I don't know if we're going to be okay, if we'll pull through this. I don't know what's going to become of us. If I can't get my old life back, I'll have to make a new one. And Bones is right. If I want a new life, I have to start at it now, before I get to the point where I can't wash the street from me. But if I start a new life, I'll never be able to get my own back.

I'm caught in a circle that's like the Ouroboros worm, swallowing its own tail. Not a *feng shui* dragon leaving lucky paths in its track, nor the Midgard serpent from whose body new life is born, but some dark monster that lives only to feed upon itself. I have to break the circle. I have to make a choice.

I don't know if I can. I don't know what to do.

X • ZEFFY

THE CAFÉ was quiet when Zeffy pushed open the front door. She carried her guitar case behind the counter and tucked it underneath, where it would be out of the way while she got herself a tea. The kettle was still warm and half full, so she merely plugged it in, then rested her arms on the counter and looked out the window at the traffic going by on Battersfield Road. This was one of her favorite times of day in the café, the usually busy room catching its breath during the midafternoon lull. For any of them working the lunch and dinner shifts, it was a chance for them to catch their breath as well.

Wendy came out of the kitchen while Zeffy was pouring hot water over a Bengal Spice tea bag, her blond hair bullied into tidiness by a half-dozen bobby pins and a barrette. Her initial smile at seeing Zeffy changed into a puzzled look.

"We did trade off this shift, didn't we?" she asked.

Zeffy nodded. "I just came by to collect Tanya."

"Ah, Tanya," Wendy said.

"What's she done now?"

"Nothing. You're just late. She's already been swept off and away by a rather scruffy-looking fiddler."

"Geordie."

"Geordie," Wendy agreed. "I had no idea they were seeing each other."

"It's a new thing."

"Well, I hope it's a good thing," Wendy said, "because I'd hate to see him get hurt."

Zeffy smiled. "And not Tanya?"

"Of course Tanya, too. It's just . . ." Wendy shrugged.

"You know what I mean. Grim as she makes it out to be when one of her relationships falls apart, there's always someone there for Tanya. I think there's a waiting list, isn't there? But Geordie's not exactly the most worldly of fellows when it comes to matters of the heart."

"You've such a way with words. Have you ever thought of becoming a poet?"

"Oh, please. Don't you start, too."

"Jilly been teasing you?"

"Mercilessly. I should never have told her about those greeting cards."

"Well, they are rather Hallmarky."

Wendy sighed. "But tastefully so. Aren't they?"

"What's tasteful?" Jilly wanted to know, coming out of the kitchen with a couple of plates of sandwiches.

"Your flashing eyes," Wendy said. "That shine like stars come down from on high."

"Oh, you're talking about the cards again. Ah-ah," she added as Wendy aimed a kick at her. "I have customers to serve."

She swerved gracefully out of range and aimed her way through the clutter of tables to where the café's only two customers sat by the front window. Zeffy smiled as she watched Jilly place the plates on the table. She didn't know how Jilly did it, but she always managed to serve her customers with a casual intimacy, as if she didn't really work here, they'd merely happened to drop by her loft while she was preparing a meal.

Zeffy turned back to Wendy. "I need to roll some change," she said. "Do we have any of those coin-rollers left?"

"A bag full. I'm glad to hear someone's been making good tips."

"Hardly. But I did go out busking today and have stacks of change to count."

"I'm in the wrong business," Wendy said as she left to serve a young man with a severe haircut who came in and chose one of the tables in her station.

Zeffy collected her tea and the bag of coin-rollers and carried them over to the table in the back corner that the waitresses usually commandeered when the café wasn't too busy. She took out her sweater and laid it on the chair beside her. As she began to transfer her change from her knapsack to the tabletop, Jilly slid into the chair across from her.

"Need any help?"

"Well, if you're feeling up to it," Zeffy told her, "I certainly wouldn't turn you down."

"It's this or fill saltshakers."

They both knew that the saltshakers would still need to be filled when this was done, as well as the sugar and pepper dispensers. Zeffy also knew how much Jilly hated doing it.

"I'll help you with the condiments," she said.

Jilly smiled. "Great. You know what they say, a job shared is a job halved."

Zeffy raised her eyebrows.

"Or however it goes." Jilly cupped a handful of coins and pulled them over to her side of the table, where she began to sort them. "I take it Wendy told you about Tanya and Geordie?"

Zeffy nodded.

"Do you think it's serious?"

"I don't know," Zeffy said. She felt a bit of Wendy's ambivalence about the whole thing. "I'd hate to see either of them get hurt." She paused in her own sorting of coins to look across the table. "But it's got to have more potential than either of their last relationships."

"I can't remember Geordie's last relationship."

"He was going out with that girl in The Tatters. wasn't he? The one that played bouzouki?"

Jilly shook her head. "They were just friends."

"I think Tanya could really blossom in the right relationship."

"And Geordie's no Johnny Devlin," Jilly said.

"Ah, yes. Johnny."

Jilly gave her a sharp look. "Don't tell me there's something new on the Devlin front."

"New and stranger than ever," Zeffy said. "It's so weird I wouldn't know where to begin with it."

She fell silent, trying to understand the feeling that rose up in her when she now thought of Johnny Devlin.

"So give," Jilly said, leaning closer.

"Well, for one thing," Zeffy said. She reached over to where she'd set her sweater on the chair beside her and carefully unfolded it. Inside, wrapped up for safekeeping, was the carving she'd bought from Johnny at the park. She handed it to Jilly. "He made this."

Jilly's face lit up with delight. "I love it."

She turned it over in her hands, then set it down on the table between them. Zeffy knew just what Jilly meant. She loved it, too. There was something at once innocent and worldly about the little carving's features, a dichotomy expressed with only a few judicious cuts of the knife that still spoke volumes.

"He's selling them over in Fitzhenry Park," she said. "He and this scruffy stray dog that acts like it's been surgically connected to him."

Jilly's gaze lifted to meet Zeffy's. "Are we talking about the same Johnny Devlin we all know and don't much love?"

"I really don't know."

Jilly got such a shivery look of anticipation about her at that pronouncement that Zeffy expected her to start rubbing her hands together.

"This sounds so mysterious," Jilly said. "And I love a good mystery."

"Even when you're stuck in the middle of it?"

"Especially then." She smiled at Zeffy. "So am I stuck in the middle of it?"

Zeffy shook her head. "No. But I am."

Although that wasn't entirely true, she realized. She didn't owe Johnny anything – he'd earned her dislike – and there was nothing to stop her from simply walking away. Nothing, except that she'd go crazy thinking about it until she knew for sure, one way or another, what was going on and why Johnny was suddenly able to make her feel the way she was feeling now.

"Well?" Jilly asked, drawing the word out. "Aren't you going to tell all?"

"Promise you won't laugh?"

"I only laugh when something's funny," Jilly assured her. "I can see this isn't a joke for you."

"That's an understatement."

Zeffy took a sip of her tea to fortify herself, then plunged into her story. She was reluctant to tell everything, especially this weird feeling of affection for Johnny that overcame her while talking to him, but you couldn't tell half a story around Jilly. She was too good a listener, utterly absorbed in a story as it unfolded and gifted with a knack for asking exactly the right question when things were unclear or she felt that the teller was holding some pertinent element back. Never pushy, but she invariably got the whole story.

"I know what you're liable to say," Zeffy said, finishing up, "but really. People don't just swap bodies."

"Stranger things have happened in this world," Jilly said.

"Not in my world they haven't. The world I know has always been, what you see is what you get."

"Don't you find that kind of limiting?"

Zeffy shook her head. "No, I find it comforting."

"And yet I can hear the doubt in your voice."

"I know. God, it's so confusing. When he's talking to me, it all seems to make such sense, even when I know it can't be true. My head says he's mentally unbalanced – in a nice way, mind you, because the Johnny I saw this afternoon is everything Tanya would have wanted him to be. But my heart keeps asking, What if what he's telling me is true?"

"Oh-oh," Jilly said. "Sounds to me as if he's charmed you."

"He *is* charming – but not like the Johnny we know. There's nothing smarmy about him. The man sitting there behind his eyes is simply a nice guy." She shook her head. "I can't believe I'm saying this. I can't believe that I'm actually buying into this whole 'Invasion of the Johnny Snatchers' business."

Jilly gave her a long considering look. "You like him, don't you?"

"Well, he's very likable. I don't *want* to like him, but I can't seem to stop myself."

Jilly nodded. "You know what I think?"

"Why do I have the feeling I'm going to regret telling you any of this?"

"I think you're as mixed up about how Tanya's going to react to what you're feeling as you are about whether or not he's telling the truth."

Zeffy's immediate objection died before she could voice it. Because it was true. Not only was she confused about Johnny's bizarre story and her new feelings toward him, but she could just imagine Tanya's response to her suddenly taking up with Johnny Devlin, whether he was changed or not. There'd be no end to it.

"What am I going to do?" she said.

"You could start by finding out if he's telling the truth," Jilly said.

Zeffy gave her a curious glance. "You're always telling me that I should learn to accept that there's more to the world than what we can see – as though I should be willing to take it on faith. What makes this different?"

"I do think that," Jilly said. "But I'm also pragmatic. In this case – because of who we're dealing with – you need more than Johnny Devlin's word to go on. There's a big difference between keeping an open mind and being gullible."

"Some people would say they're one and the same."

Jilly smiled. "People say and do things all the time that make no sense."

"In a perfect world, everything would make sense."

"This is a perfect world," Jilly said. "The only things wrong with it are those we screw up."

Zeffy had to shake her head. Trust Jilly to have an answer for everything.

"How come you can make a pronouncement like that and get away with it?" she asked.

Jilly laughed. "It's because I'm so shy and retiring."

"And I'm the Queen of Sheba."

"I don't believe that," Jilly told her. "See? I'm not a complete flake."

They were both still smiling, but Zeffy sensed the underlying seriousness behind Jilly's humor.

"You're not going to let me drop this now, are you?" she said.

"It won't be me," Jilly said. "It'll be you. It's going to drive you crazy until you figure it out."

Zeffy nodded. "Which means going to Max Trader's shop."

"Do you know where it is?"

"Somewhere in the Market. There was an article on him a while ago, about his shop moving there. All I have to do is look up the street address."

"You could pretend there was something wrong with your guitar," Jilly said.

"Actually, there is. My bass E-string gets a buzz when I capo anywhere past the fifth fret."

"Whatever that means.

"It means I've got a perfectly legitimate excuse to go see him."

An hour later, after dropping in at the bank and exchanging her rolled coins for folding money, Zeffy took a bus up Battersfield to the Market. She couldn't have picked a worse time to go. By the time she reached Stanton Street, the bus was crammed with commuters, the bus inching its way north through the rush-hour traffic. Zeffy sat on an aisle seat, knapsack on her lap, guitar case propped between her legs, her body squeezed between a portly businessman and a long-haired boy in a flannel shirt listening to a Walkman at such a volume that she could clearly make out the tinny melody, if not the lyrics, of the song that was playing. It wasn't anything she recognized.

She would have been quicker walking, but she hadn't felt like hauling her guitar all that way. Every stop they came to she reconsidered, briefly, as the crowded aisles accepted another two or three passengers, but it soon got to the point where she knew it would be more trouble than it was worth to push through the press of the crowd and try to get off. Turning her head, she could look through the window at St. Paul's. She half-expected to see Geordie and Tanya sitting on the steps, but then the bus made a right onto Stanton and the front of the cathedral was lost to her view. All she could see now was the grey-stoned bulk of the building, the gargoyles on the higher ledges, the dome and bell tower rising above them.

She turned back to look at the stomach of the woman standing directly in front of her and dropped her gaze to the slightly more interesting view of her own lap. She hadn't spied either Geordie or Tanya. No reason that they'd be there anyway. She sighed. The only reason she was looking for them, she realized, was that she was feeling guilty. It made no sense. There wasn't anything happening between her and Johnny and she wasn't keeping anything from Tanya. There was no big secret. She hadn't seen her roommate since this morning, that was all. She'd tell Tanya all about it when she got home.

But the feeling wouldn't go away.

The congestion at the corner of Stanton and Lee was the worst she'd seen in ages, but the bus finally made its turn and twenty minutes later, it reached her stop. Zeffy pushed her way through the grumbling crush of people, muttering, "I'm sorry," though what she really wanted to tell them was "Will you *please* get out of my way." They parted for her grudgingly, no one wanting to give up their precious few inches of space. The idea of a smile appeared to be a completely foreign concept to most of them.

When she finally stepped down onto the pavement, she let out a breath she hadn't been aware of holding. This, she thought, was the reason why she didn't want to ever get a regular job. Not if it meant fighting these crowds twice a day, five days a week.

The sidewalks were crowded as well, but they seemed positively sedate after the sardine-can press of commuters on the bus. And once she turned off Lee into the Market, all the bustle and stress of rush hour was washed away. The cobblestoned streets, too narrow for vehicles, transported her to a different time. The twentieth century didn't really seem to intrude here, where the stone and brick houses jostled shoulder to shoulder in a friendly manner, their peaked and gabled roofs like so many wizards' hats seen row upon row, the buildings connected only by small squares, gardens, arches and occasional overhead walkways. The store signs were all hand-painted, their windows beveled glass through which cats or dogs could be seen sleeping amongst the displays.

The sounds of traffic from Lee Street diminished, then disappeared far more quickly than would seem logical, the cars and buses and unhappy press of commuters exchanged for the occasional bicycle, children playing, men in wooden chairs smoking pipes or playing cards while they drank dark coffee or glasses of beer, small clusters of gossiping women who looked up and smiled at her when Zeffy walked by. She still shared the street with people, there was still noise, but it was all muted in comparison with the rush-hour streets she'd so recently left behind. It was all so . . . civilized, if somewhat old-fashioned. There was something to be said for a lack of progress in certain regards, she decided.

She made a few wrong turns – the Market streets had a tendency to turn back on themselves when you weren't expecting them to – but finally found Trader Guitars. She stood in front of the wool shop across the street from it and studied the front of the three-storied brick and stone building for a long moment before crossing over. There were no cats or dogs sleeping in the display window, no real display at all since the floor of the shop ran immediately up to the panes. Which made sense, Zeffy thought, since you couldn't exactly hang instruments where the sun would get at them and warp their necks.

Opening the door, she stepped into musician's heaven. The store held the smell of a woodworking shop, a distinctive aroma that enveloped her as soon as she entered, but it was the instruments that brought the involuntary smile to her lips. A dozen or so high-end guitars hung along the back wall – a small-bodied Martin New Yorker and a newer dreadnought model, a Gibson archtop, a twelve-string Washburn, two Guilds, a six-string Laskin and, of course, a Trader with a gorgeous spruce top that gleamed almost white in the overhead light. There were also a dobro, a banjo, a couple of resonator guitars, their metal grillwork gleaming, one of them an all-metal-bodied National. Two mandolins, a few fiddles. A stand-up bass. A workbench ran along another wall, covered with various parts of instruments and tools. A glass counter island held capos, strings, picks, guitar steels and other instrument supplies.

Sitting at a rolltop desk in the far back corner, Max Trader himself lifted his head when she came in. He looked exactly as she remembered from the articles she'd seen on him: ponytailed with a slightly receding hairline, kind-faced, tall and aesthetically slender. The desk was covered with papers that he was obviously sorting through, but he laid them aside and rose to meet her.

Seeing him like this made her realize how ridiculous Johnny's claim was. The two men weren't at all alike, not in looks or, with what she knew from reading about Trader, in how they lived their lives. The idea that they could have

218

switched brains was stupid as well as impossible. But then, as Trader drew closer, she was startled to see a look of recognition come into his eyes. That was impossible, too, because they'd never met. The questions rose up in her mind all over again.

"You look like you know me," she said. Her tone was light, but her pulse was drumming.

Something crossed his features, an odd look that Zeffy couldn't quite identify. It was there and gone so quickly she was left unsure of what she'd seen, if anything.

"I feel like I do," Trader said.

His voice was nothing like Johnny's. She studied the way he moved, the way he held his body, looking for something that might remind her of Johnny in the same way that the Johnny she'd left behind in Fitzhenry Park had been so different from the man she knew.

"Well, I think I'd remember if we'd ever—" she began.

Trader broke in, pointed at her guitar. "I know what it is. I've seen you play somewhere."

That was certainly possible, Zeffy supposed, though she couldn't imagine what he'd be doing in the small places she had played so far in her very fledgling career.

"But I can't remember where," Trader went on. He shrugged. "It'll come back to me." His gaze returned to her guitar case. "So what can I do for you?"

"I've got a buzz on my E-string," Zeffy said.

"Well, let's have a look at it."

He led her over to his workbench and cleared a space for her case. Zeffy lifted it up, then got distracted by the inlay work on a mandolin that spelled out "Frank" along the instrument's neck.

"Do all of your instruments have names now?" she asked, trying to ease her own nervousness with a joke.

His gaze followed hers and he smiled. "I probably shouldn't be saying this, but can you believe a guy that wants his name spelled out like this on the neck? Who's he trying to impress?"

Zeffy shrugged. "I don't know. I think it's kind of neat."

His smile broadened. "See? I knew I shouldn't have said anything."

"Well, it's just that it'd really make the instrument yours – especially when you've commissioned somebody like you to make it for them."

"Maybe I should put my own advertisements there."

"Doesn't seem your style," Zeffy said, thinking of how he'd come across in the articles.

His eyebrows lifted questioningly.

"Well, just from what I've read about you," she said. "You know. Like in *Acoustic Guitar* and the profile that ran in *The Daily Journal*."

"Don't believe everything you read. Some people still think Elvis is alive."

Zeffy smiled. "Or that he's just left the building."

"Exactly." He indicated her guitar. "So show me this buzz."

"Well, it's only when I capo past the fifth fret."

Taking the guitar out of the case, she put the capo on to show him, apologizing for the fact that her strings were so dead. He took the instrument from her and gave it what seemed like a very cursory glance before replacing it in its case.

"So the big question isn't can you fix it," she said, "because obviously you could. What I need to know is how much is it going to cost? I'm working on a tight budget these days."

Thanks to Johnny Devlin.

Trader made a vague motion with his hand. "The cost's not a big deal – it's not like it's a long job or anything – but I'm pretty booked up at the moment. Leave it with me and I'll get it back to you next week."

"Oh, I can't do that. I've got a gig this weekend."

"So I'll lend you a guitar."

Zeffy couldn't help it. Her gaze went to the row of instruments that hung on the back wall. She was itching to try them, but knew he wasn't talking about any of them.

"No," Trader said, following her gaze. "Not one of those. I was thinking more of an old one I've got upstairs that I can lend you. Do you mind watching the fort while I get it?"

"Not at all. It's just – I don't want to be any trouble."

"Won't take me more than a minute."

"But . . . "

He was already walking toward a side door before she could reply. She watched him go, then crossed the shop to where the guitars were hanging. Looking up, she couldn't resist running her thumb across the strings of a couple, touching the polished finish on their tops and sides. What she wouldn't give to own pretty well any one of them. She took down the little New Yorker and sat down on a stool, tucking its compact body under her arm. It was so small compared to her own guitar that she felt like a giant holding it, an adult trying to play a child's instrument. She gave the strings a strum.

Considering its size, she couldn't believe how much sound came out of the body. The neck was a couple of frets shorter than she was used to and she didn't think she'd like the slotted head in the long run – too much of a hassle for restringing – but it sounded sweet. Digging out a pick from the pocket of her jeans, she started playing the first few bars of "Wildwood Flower," then immediately wanted to hear what the tune would sound like on the National resonator. She was taking it down when Trader returned, one of his own dreadnought models held casually in his hand.

"Think this'll tide you over?" he asked.

Zeffy replaced the National and took the guitar from him. Sitting back down on the stool, she gave it a brisk strum with her pick. The sound that came out of it was so big she was almost startled into dropping the instrument. Trader steadied it before it could fall.

"What do you think?" he asked.

"I . . . I couldn't." She noodled on the strings while she spoke, falling in love with the instrument despite herself. Her regret was sincere when she added, "This is beautiful, but—"

"But what? It's not being played right now anyway, so why don't you use it?"

Zeffy shook her head. "You don't even know me. I could just walk out of here with it and you'd never see it again."

"You are leaving your guitar," he said. "Think of it as your collateral."

Right, Zeffy thought. Her cheapo Yamaha as collateral for a Trader. The difference in price between them was only a few thousand dollars.

"You're joking, right?" she asked.

He shook his head. "Look, it's not like I wouldn't be able to find you again. We're all musicians. What're you going to do? Leave the city and head off to Mexico with it?"

"To own this I just might."

"Well, don't forget to send me a postcard."

All she could do was look at him. "You really wouldn't care, would you?"

"Of course I'd care. I'm just too trusting for my own good. But I like the look of you, so what the hell."

"I've been busking . . ." Zeffy began.

He shook his head. "Play it wherever you want. Treat it as if it's your own while you have it. Like I said, it's not getting played anyway. I know you'll be careful with it."

Careful? Zeffy thought. She didn't know if she'd be *able* to play it she'd be so worried.

"Maybe I should just take my guitar with me today and I'll come back next week."

Trader smiled. "What do I have to do, take an oath to swear it's all right? Stop worrying so much. It's an old guitar." He took it from her and went over to his workbench with it. "Let's see if it'll fit in your case. There. A perfect fit."

He laid her Yamaha down on the counter and closed up the case. Swinging it down, he turned and handed it to her.

"But "

"I hate to seem pushy," he told her, "but I've still got a mess of paperwork to get through before I can call it a day."

Zeffy had to give in. "Thanks," she said, accepting the case from him.

"No problem. I'll have yours ready for you next week – say Wednesday?"

"Okay. I'll take seriously good care of this."

"I know you will. Say, where are you playing this weekend? Maybe I'll drop by and check you out."

"The YoMan, Friday and Saturday night. I'm opening for Glory Mad Dog."

He nodded. "If I can make it, I'll be the guy wearing the T-shirt that says, 'She's playing my guitar.'"

"I wouldn't need that to recognize you," Zeffy said. "If you come, I'll buy you a drink after my set."

He gave her a look that she would have taken for a come-on if they were in a bar, but here, in his shop, she couldn't take it seriously.

"I'll hold you to that," he said.

A few moments later she was out on the street, walking back toward Lee, the Trader guitar a surprisingly light weight in her case. She felt so stupid for even considering Johnny's story with any seriousness. What could she have been thinking of? But it wasn't only Johnny. Jilly was almost as much to blame, too, egging her on the way she had. Zeffy planned to give both of them a piece of her mind the next time she saw them, though with Johnny, never again would be too soon.

No, scratch that, she thought. First she'd make sure he paid Tanya what he owed. Then he could drop down a hole and be lost forever, the smug bastard. When she thought of how he must be laughing at her right now, it made her feel a little crazy. She wanted to track him down and shove his stupid carving down his throat. But no. She'd be mature about all of this. She'd wait to see if he had the nerve to show up in Fitzhenry Park again tomorrow and *then* she'd do it.

XI • LISA

LISA DIDN'T allow herself to lie down and try to get some sleep until they finally heard Trader leave his apartment. They listened to him go down the stairs, check his mail, then finally open the store.

"We'll take turns staying awake and keeping an eye on him," Julie said when Lisa still hesitated.

"You'll wake me if anything happens?"

Julie smiled. "I'll wake you in a few hours even if nothing happens," she said. "I'll be wanting to catch some sleep myself by then."

Which only made Lisa feel guilty all over again.

"Oh God," she began. "I feel so bad about dragging you along through all of this."

"Don't."

"I'm trying not to, but it's hard. You should at least have the first sleep."

Julie laid a finger against Lisa's lips. "Hush," she said. "Right now, you need it more than I do. I'm something of an insomniac, so I'm used to operating on next to no sleep."

"Really? What keeps you up?"

"If I knew that, I guess I wouldn't have the problem," Julie said. "Now go on. You're amost alseep on your feet as it is."

It was true. Lisa was exhausted. She had a headache to go with the dry itchiness behind her eyes. Her mouth tasted terrible and every one of her limbs felt as though it had a ten-pound weight attached to it. She could barely drag herself into her bedroom and didn't bother to undress once she had. Instead, she lay on top of the covers and turned her face toward the wall, away from the bright sunlight that made it through the window's drawn curtains. She thought she was too tired to sleep. Lying there, she listened to Julie close the apartment door. She heard the shower go on and fell asleep while it was still running.

"I borrowed some of your clothes," Julie said when she woke Lisa later. "I hope you don't mind."

A heavy fog clouded Lisa's thoughts as she dragged herself up from a heavy sleep. Her gaze was turned in Julie's direction, but could barely focus on her.

"Nia?" she asked.

"Nothing yet. And your neighbor's still in his store. I just checked."

Lisa sat up slowly. She looked at the bedside clock and saw that it was almost three. She'd slept for six hours, but it felt as though she'd only just closed her eyes moments ago. The taste in her mouth was worse, but her headache had subsided. The fog was starting to clear and Julie came into focus. Lisa thought Julie looked much better in the borrowed sweatshirt and black jeans than she ever had herself.

"You should've woken me earlier," she said. "You must be exhausted."

"I stole a few catnaps," Julie said.

"I guess you really don't need much sleep, then, because you look terrific."

It was true. Sitting there on the side of the bed, Julie had never looked better. She seemed rested and alert, the casual clothes suiting her – as did the lack of makeup. They gave her a softer look and made her more appealing than ever.

"The shower helped," Julie said. "I can't tell you how much better I felt after having it."

Lisa believed it. The way she was feeling at the moment, she couldn't get into one quickly enough herself.

"Well, I'm about to find out," she said.

She swung her feet to the floor so that she was sitting beside Julie. The sudden proximity made her feel self-conscious and she quickly rose to her feet.

"You should try to get some sleep now," she said.

Julie shrugged. "I'll try lying down, but I don't think it'll help."

Lisa didn't know why she was feeling so shy. She'd known all along that she was attracted to Julie, that at some point there would be more to their relationship than dinner and the long, sweet kiss they'd shared before walking hand in hand through the Market's streets to the apartment last night. She'd known, was even looking forward to it with a mixture of emotions evenly divided between nervousness and anticipation. But right now ... there seemed to be an electric charge in the air, a sexual tension that she didn't quite know how to deal with. She grabbed her bathrobe from where it hung behind the door and was about to flee into the hall, only pausing in the doorway because Julie had called her name. She looked back to see Julie stretched out on the bed, the sweatshirt riding high on her midriff.

"Call me if you need someone to scrub your back," Julie said.

Lisa swallowed thickly and gave a quick nod before she escaped out into the hall. She closed the bathroom door and leaned against it, tried to concentrate on evening out her breathing.

A cold shower, she told herself.

Stripping quickly, she started up the shower, then found she couldn't face the idea of cold water. She adjusted the temperature until clouds of steam rolled up, fogging the mirror. One foot in the tub, she hesitated, looked at the closed door. She took a deep breath, then stepped over to the door and cracked it open.

"Julie!" she called, then quickly slipped into the shower before she lost her nerve.

*

It was two hours later, while she was lying spooned up against Julie in the bed that she suddenly thought of Nia. She sat up, clutching the sheet against her breasts.

Julie turned and regarded her through heavy-lidded eyes. "What's wrong, sweetheart?"

All Lisa could so was shake her head. Tears welled up in her eyes and slowly traveled down her cheeks.

"Oh God," she finally said. "I . . . I'm such an awful mother. I've just . . . just been lying here . . . we've been . . ." She swallowed hard, tried again. "It's like I forgot I even had a daughter."

Julie sat up and reached for her, but Lisa wouldn't let herself be comforted. All she could think of was Nia, how the most terrible things could be happening to her right now, and here was her mother, not even thinking of her.

"What . . . what was I thinking?" she said. "This . . . this is so wrong . . ."

She got up suddenly and hurried from the room. Collecting her robe from where it still hung in the bathroom, she put it on and went into the kitchen. There she sat at the table, the tears still fogging her sight. Her blurry gaze settled on the phone and she willed it to ring. Her chest was so tight she could barely breathe. She held the bathrobe closed tight at her neck, trembling with a chill that wouldn't go away because it came from inside.

After a while she became aware of Julie leaning against the doorjamb. Looking up, she saw that Julie had put her own clothes back on. Lisa had no idea how long Julie had been standing there.

"Do you want me to go?" Julie asked.

Her voice was softly pitched. Lisa couldn't hear the hurt in it that she saw in Julie's eyes.

"I . . . I don't know what I want," she said.

Julie nodded as though Lisa had just explained everything. Maybe she had, Lisa thought. She just didn't understand any of it yet herself.

"Neither of us was thinking straight," Julie said. "In some ways, we couldn't have picked a worse time. But you know, sometimes it's at a time like this that we need to be close to someone else the most. You didn't do anything wrong."

"I know. Or I guess I know. It's just . . . what if while we were making love . . . what if right at that same time some sick bastard was hurting Nia?"

"I don't have an answer for that."

Lisa nodded. She grabbed a tissue from the box on the table and blew her nose.

"Nobody could," she said finally. "I'm just so messed up right now that I can't think straight. I—"

The phone rang, rattling them both. Lisa stared at it, unable to answer. All day she'd waited for it to ring and now she couldn't pick it up, couldn't face the possibility of her worst fears being realized.

It rang again. Two more and the answering machine in the living room would pick it up.

Lisa looked helplessly at Julie. "I can't pick it up," she said.

Julie nodded. She left the doorway and took a seat at the table. As she reached out for the receiver, Lisa put her hand over Julie's.

"Don't hate me," she said.

The hurt hadn't left Julie's eyes yet, but she slowly shook her head.

"I couldn't if I tried," she told Lisa.

Then she picked up the phone, cutting off the fourth ring.

XII • NIA

THIS WAS no way to live, Nia thought.

She was sitting on a bench at a bus stop on Lakeside Drive, a few blocks west of where the cedar and pine bluffs of Fitzhenry Park fall into the lake. On the bench beside her was the crumpled wrapper from a tuna-salad sandwich on a French roll that she'd just finished eating. The pair of gulls that had been keeping her company, pacing back and forth on the sidewalk in front of her, hoping for a handout, finally gave up and went looking for more likely pickings.

Nia took a sip of bad takeout coffee and wished she were anywhere but where she was. Or at least not feeling so alone. She missed her mother. She missed being able to talk to Max. She missed being able to listen to some decent music. If she were doing it over again, she'd pack herself some real necessities: a sleeping bag, changes of clothing, her Walkman and some tapes, a few books. More money.

She had twenty-five dollars left and was hoarding it against the future when she'd need it more – much as she'd like to at least buy herself something to read right now. She had a couple of hundred dollars in the bank, but she was afraid to withdraw any of it in case the thing that was pretending to be her mother was having the bank watched. The same went for all of her regular haunts. She had to avoid them all. Which only left the parts of the city that she either didn't care for, or that were too dangerous for her to feel safe in.

What she should really do, she'd realized, was leave the city. Make a new start somewhere else. But the thought of that terrified her. The idea of an outlaw life might seem like fun when you were sitting in a café, listening to, oh say,

Miles Davis on the sound system and reading Kerouac. The reality wasn't anything like she'd imagined it would be for the simple reason that the writings of the Beats and their like couldn't prepare a person for what it was really like to be on the streets, living the gypsy life, unfettered and free. Right. As if.

So far, the reality hadn't even come close to the romance.

The reality was she was dying to take a shower and change her clothes. She was lonely. She felt lost. She was scared. The sun would be setting in a few hours and she couldn't bear a repeat of what she'd gone through last night. But as things stood, she had no other choice. The very act of having run away had left her with no options beyond what she was doing now. Or taking TAMP up on his offer to get her into The Rhatigan.

She grimaced. Too bad he couldn't have been a nice guy, but true to course, the only boys she ever seemed to attract were the weirdos. Computer geeks, Beat nerds, way-cool guys like TAMP who make her skin crawl. Where was Christian Slater when you needed him? She'd even take him with a monkey heart, like in that movie *Untamed Heart*. Maybe because of the monkey heart.

Setting her Styrofoam cup down on the pavement by her feet, she pulled her knapsack onto her lap and dug around in it until she found her address book. She started to flip through its pages, discouraged for the first time in her life at how few entries there were in it. You'd think after sixteen years of living on this planet she'd have more people than this in her address book.

Most of the entries were useful in their normal context, but worthless to her present purpose. Doctor, dentist. Her mother's number at work. Max's at home and in the shop. The number for the poet's co-op that she'd always meant to join, but somehow never did. Some record and book stores. Which left . . .

Angie.

They'd been best friends up to about four years ago, when Angie discovered boys in a big way and suddenly had no more time for Nia. Nia had acquired her own interest in boys, but it never took over her life the same way as it had Angie's. Maybe it was because Angie attracted nicer guys, though Nia didn't think jocks were much of an improvement over the ones that always came her way. She hadn't talked to Angie in months and, really, this didn't seem like the right occasion to renew their friendship. At one time they could have shared anything, no matter how implausible, but now . . . How could she even start to bring up her problems without feeling like a complete flake?

Deirdre.

Moved away two years ago when her parents divorced. Nia didn't have a new address or number for her.

Chas.

Nia pictured him in her mind, tall, skeletal thin, black shock of Goth hair, skin so pale it was almost white. They'd gone out on one date, which had been such a disaster that she hadn't spoken to him again.

The other names were all the same, each had an unhappy story attached to it, some reason she couldn't call them.

She sighed and was about to close the book, when she remembered one last number. She turned to the second-to-last page. The seven digits written there in ballpoint seemed to leap out at her from the field of white surrounding them. She'd gotten that number from her mother's private papers while her mother was at work one day. Carefully copied it out years ago, just the number, no identification needed, like she'd ever forget who it belonged to, but she'd never used it. Never had the nerve. She'd had the need once, when she was younger, but not the number. Once she did have it, the passage of time had turned need into anger and there didn't seem to be any point anymore.

Daddy dearest.

She supposed she must have talked to him at some time in her life – she'd been five when he walked out on them – but she couldn't remember. Couldn't depend on memory to even tell her what he looked like. The only reason she knew was because she'd come across a wedding photo tucked away in a book, the one picture she knew of that had been spared her mother's purge of everything to do with him.

She couldn't blame her mother – it wasn't as though her father had ever done anything to make her think better of him than her mother did – but something made her keep the photo all the same, made her hide it away, taking it out only when her mother wasn't around and she was feeling depressed. She didn't know why she bothered. It never made her feel any better. Morbid curiosity, she supposed. A prop for playing make-believe and what-if.

Like now. What if? What if he came through for her now where he never had before?

Her father's phone number continued to fill her field of vision, her entire world reduced to seven digits and a swell of conflicting emotions that made her chest feel too tight. Partly fear, she knew, but if she was being honest with herself, she had to admit it was partly anticipation, too. She didn't even know if he'd talk to her, but what did she have to lose? Only her pride, and she'd gladly give up a measure of it to spare herself another night alone on the streets. And who knows? Maybe he'd changed. Maybe he'd been wanting to talk to her himself, wanting to tell her he was sorry, but like her, he couldn't get up the nerve, was afraid she'd hang up on him before he even got the words out.

There had to be some good in him. Even her mother must have seen some, or why else would she have married him?

Okay, Nia told herself. Stop rationalizing this. Just do it.

So she stuffed the address book in the pocket of her jacket, collected her knapsack, sandwich wrapper and coffee, and headed down the block to the phone booth she could see by the entrance to the park. She dropped the wrapper in the garbage can on the way, dug about in her pocket for a quarter when she reached the booth. Once she was inside, she folded the door closed behind her, dropped the quarter in the slot and punched in the number before she lost her nerve again.

The connection was made so quickly that she was caught off-guard. The woman on the other end of the line said, "Hello. Hello?" She sounded annoyed, impatient.

Nia cleared her throat. "Um, could I speak to Dan, uh, Dan Caplan, please?"

"Hang on." The woman didn't bother to cover the mouthpiece as she called for him. "Hey, Danny. It's for you." Beat. "And it better not be that waitress at Bruno's or we've got some unfinished business to clear up, you hear me?"

Nia wished there was a bench inside the booth, something, anything to sit down on. She was all flushed and her legs felt weak. Leaning her forehead against the glass, she tried to take slow breaths to still the sudden drumming of her pulse.

"Hello?"

The voice was nothing like she'd expected. Higher in pitch, almost a boy's voice.

"Um, hello?" she managed.

What did she call him? Dad? Father? Mr. Caplan? Dan?

"Who is this?"

"It . . . it's Nia. I'm . . ." Your daughter, she wanted to say, but the word wouldn't come out.

"Nia who?"

"Your . . ." She swallowed nervously. "Your daughter."

"Jesus," he said. A long pause followed.

"Are you still there?" she asked.

"Oh yeah. Well, this is a real blast from the past, isn't it? Christ." Another pause. "So why are you calling?"

"I . . . I'm in trouble. Mom's not—" Herself, she was about to say, but he broke in.

"Yeah, well now that you bring her up, I thought your mother and I had an agreement about this."

"I don't know what you—"

"So you're in trouble, huh? How old are you, kid?"

This wasn't going at all the way she'd imagined it would. She'd never expected a lot – sitting at home, looking at the wedding picture, trying to envision how it might go. She'd always had this little hope that maybe he'd be interested in hearing from her. She'd been prepared for him to refuse to speak to her. But this. It was like she was some salesman, interrupting his dinner.

"Sixteen."

"Sixteen already. Well, then you're old enough for a little advice from your old man, kid: You've got a problem? Work it out."

"But . . . but I've got no place to go."

"Ran away, did you?" He gave a humorless laugh. "Can't say's I blame you. But you're not moving in on me."

"It's just that—"

"And your old lady's going to be hearing from me – you can count on that. We had a deal."

"But—"

"Don't be calling this number again."

And then he hung up.

Nia slowly moved the handset from her ear. It took her two tries to hang it up, the black plastic clattering against the metal hook until she finally got it right. A long time ago, she'd promised herself that if she ever did call her father, no matter what happened, she wasn't going to let it upset her. She wasn't going to cry. But she slid down the glass side of the booth now and huddled on the floor, arms wrapped around her knees, tears streaming.

There'd always been an ache inside her, a pain born of not knowing why he'd left them, of being afraid that it had been her fault, that she was somehow to blame. The fantasy had been that it could be fixed. Sometimes she'd been able to pretend that it had all been a misunderstanding and one day, in the right place, at the right time, everything would get worked out. Things would be good again. He and her mother wouldn't get back together or anything – she wasn't that naive. But there'd always been this possibility, almost a promise, that when she finally talked to her father, he'd tell her how much he'd missed her, how much he regretted not having been there while she was growing up.

All that was gone now. The only thing left was the pain. And it hurt, it hurt so much. It shouldn't. It wasn't as though she'd ever really believed in the fantasy. But until she made the phone call, it had been possible, if not likely.

Now there was nothing left for her to hang on to. Nowhere for her to go. She had no father, she had no mother – at least not one she could recognize. Who knew where or how far her mother's soul had been thrown when the monsters took over her body?

The realization made the tears come harder.

XIII • ZEFFY

"I DON'T believe this," Tanya said.

Zeffy looked up from the mushrooms she was slicing to find her roommate giving her a sad look. They'd been talking about how their days had gone while preparing dinner: Tanya all excited about Geordie, he was so genuinely nice, how he made her feel interesting just for who she was, but she couldn't figure out why he hadn't tried to kiss her yet; then Zeffy telling about her success busking, how much fun it had been, how she'd run across Johnny in the park afterward, what he'd said, it was so weird, how convincing, how *nice* he'd been. Their conversation had seemed so innocuous to Zeffy, sharing the gossip of their lives, business as usual, until Tanya broke into her story.

"What can't you believe?" Zeffy asked.

"This whole business with Johnny," Tanya said. "You've been on at me for ages about what a loser he is. Yesterday you told me I was crazy to think that the way he was acting was anything but some sick game."

"It is some kind of sick game."

"Then how come you look the way you do when you're talking about him?"

"Look how?"

Tanya sighed. "I don't know. All starry-eyed, I guess."

"Isn't that a little excessive?" Zeffy asked, trying to keep her tone mild. "The word I'd use is more like curious."

Tanya shook her head. "After all the negative things

you've had to say about him, how can you suddenly be all interested?"

"It's not like you're thinking," Zeffy told her. Not anymore, she thought. Not after meeting Max Trader at his shop. "You didn't let me finish. I went looking for you at the café, but you weren't there, so then I decided to go on to Trader's workshop and—"

"You don't get it, do you?" Tanya said. "This is so unfair. I think something strange is going on with Johnny and it's like I'm nuts. But then Johnny tells you this bullshit story and you're willing enough to check it out. I thought I was the one who was your friend, not that *loser*."

"He's not my friend."

"Then why were you ready to believe him but not me?"

"I don't know. It's not . . ." Zeffy shook her head. "Johnny had me going – I'll admit that – but my visit to Trader's just proved to me what I knew all along: he's an asshole."

"But you had to prove it first."

Zeffy sighed. "What was I supposed to do? It all started sounding so reasonable and then Jilly—"

"Why don't you just admit it?" Tanya said. "Despite everything you know about him, you took a liking to Johnny. The impenetrable Lacerda defenses actually came down which proves the point that you can make a mistake the same as anyone else."

"When did I ever say I didn't make mistakes?"

"Whenever you talk about my boyfriends."

"I can't help your taste in boyfriends," Zeffy said.

"Well, thanks for that vote of confidence."

"God, will you listen to yourself, Tanya? When have I *not* been there for you?"

"We're not talking about that. We're talking about how

you were always putting Johnny down when I was going out with him, how you just couldn't understand how I could care about him, but now you're suddenly all interested in him."

Zeffy shook her head. "I don't want to argue about this."

She put the knife down in amidst the mushrooms and turned to leave the kitchen, but Tanya grabbed her arm.

"Just tell me this," Tanya said. "What makes me a fool for having loved Johnny, but not you?"

"I don't love him. I don't even *like* him."

"But you were just saying how you were attracted to him."

Zeffy sighed. "Okay. For a moment there this afternoon, yes, I was attracted to him."

"So why's it different for you than for me?"

"He sucked me in," Zeffy told her. "Okay? Is that what you wanted me to say? If you'd been listening, you would have heard me saying the same thing half an hour ago, but you've been too busy playing that weird game you like to play where you hang on to a guy long after it's over, hanging on to him even when you're in another relationship."

"Is that how you see it?"

Tanya looked so devastated that Zeffy quickly shook her head.

"No," she said. "Of course not. I don't know why that came out the way it did. You're just driving me crazy with this whole jealousy business."

"I'm not jealous."

"Okay. So jealous isn't the right word. Let's say – oh, I don't know. Possessive after the fact."

"You really don't get it," Tanya said. "The thing that hurts so much is that you think I'm stupid when I fall for someone like Johnny, but when it happens to you it's just a natural mistake."

"I have not fallen for Johnny Devlin."

"Then why did you have stars in your eyes when you were talking about him?"

Zeffy felt like screaming. Instead, she took a deep breath and slowly let it out.

"The Johnny I was talking to," she said, trying to stay calm, "seemed like somebody else entirely. He *told* me he was someone else entirely. This guy was nice, vulnerable, everything Johnny's not. Okay? He worked his charm on me and I almost bought into the line he was giving me. But I didn't. End of story."

The look Tanya gave her was pitying.

"You are so hypocritical," she said. "And the sad thing is, you don't even realize it."

"*I'm* hypocritical?"

Tanya raised a hand between them before Zeffy could go on.

"No more," she said, pushing past Zeffy. "I don't want to hear any more of this."

Tanya's abrupt departure took on a surreal quality that left Zeffy momentarily speechless. As though in a daze, she watched her roommate walk into the living room, pick up her purse and a jacket, then leave the apartment. It was the slamming of the front door that finally brought Zeffy back. She shook her head as though coming out of a daydream.

I guess I deserved that, she thought. Not all of it, but enough. And really, hadn't she known it would upset Tanya? Her roommate might be seeing somebody new, but she still hadn't let go of Johnny yet. And Tanya was right about the trusting business, too. But what had seemed so patently impossible yesterday morning in Johnny's building had taken on a fairy-tale character this afternoon in the park, a kind of doomed swan-prince-in-peril, frog-under-a-spell quality to which – for whatever reason – Zeffy hadn't been able to remain immune. Reason had prevailed, only not soon enough for Tanya. Fair enough.

But by the same token, Zeffy knew she hadn't done anything wrong. She hadn't tried to hide anything from her roommate. She'd admitted up front that she'd made a fool of herself, much good it had done.

Zeffy sighed. She surveyed the kitchen, then slowly went about gathering the makings for dinner and putting them away, rebagging the vegetables, draining the half-cooked pasta and dumping it in the trash. She doubted Tanya would be back and the fight had stolen her own appetite.

When she was finally done in the kitchen, she made her way into the living room. The Trader guitar lay in its open case by the stereo, Johnny's carving on the coffee table, holding court in the middle of a scattering of magazines and paperbacks. She wanted to smash the carving – actually had it in her hand and was about to throw it against the wall, before she gently set the little figure back down on the table. Breaking it would solve nothing.

Turning her back on the carving, she knelt down on the floor beside the guitar and ran her finger across its strings. She'd had such a great time playing it before Tanya had got home. The action was so perfect the instrument almost seemed to play itself. She couldn't believe the richness of its tone, highs through midrange to bass, the amazing sustain, how every note resonated in perfect tune and harmony to the others. The simplest arpeggio sounded like a small orchestra of guitars. Running through a sequence of bar chords with a pick almost had her double-checking that it wasn't somehow plugged into an amplifier. It wasn't simply the volume, but that the chords had such individual and distinctive presence.

Not knowing when – if ever – she'd actually be able to buy an instrument this good for herself, she was determined to get as much playing on it as she could while she had it. Next Wednesday, when she had to take it back, was going to come all too soon.

She let her fingers trail across the strings again. She'd been so looking forward to getting back to it after dinner. But now . . . She closed the case and went to sit in the bay window, staring down at the street below.

Mrs. Grambs, from two doors down, passed by, walking her odd little dog Maggie. It looked like a cross between a dachshund and a beagle with the latter's features and ears, a dachshund's length and markings. The combination, along with Maggie's sweet personality, always made Zeffy laugh and want to cuddle her, but tonight the sight of the dog couldn't even call up a smile. She watched them until they turned at the end of the block, then stared morosely at the empty street directly in front of the apartment once more.

She was going to have to make it up to Tanya. Apologize, but not bother to explain it any more because that, it was obvious from this evening's fiasco, would only make it worse again. But it was so frustrating. It wasn't like Tanya and Johnny were still going out together and she was trying to steal him away.

God, like she'd want anything to do with him again. Just the thought of him made her feel crazy angry. No, if she saw him in the park tomorrow, the only question was, what was she going to hit him with?

XIV • LISA

Lisa hung up the phone, almost regretting that she'd taken the receiver from Julie earlier. Her mental equilibrium was all unbalanced, her emotions in an uproar. Worry was the constant, with relief and anger banging up against each other, guilt underlying them all. It was hard to make sense of anything with that tumult going on inside her. The only thing she was really sure of was that her headache had returned, lodged right behind her eyes once more, two bright shafts of pain that were impossible to ignore.

She put her arms on the table and leaned her head on them, not sitting up again until she heard the toilet flush and Julie came back into the kitchen. Lisa tried to smile, but could only muster a grimace.

"Got your headache back?" Julie asked.

When Lisa nodded, Julie ran some water at the sink and filled a glass. Returning to the table, she offered Lisa the water and a couple of painkillers that she'd taken from the medicine cabinet in the bathroom.

"I thought it might have," she said. "Hopefully these will help."

"Thanks." Lisa took the pills, draining the glass before setting it down on the table. "That was my ex," she added.

"I kind of figured that. But he had good news, right?"

Lisa nodded. "Nia called him and she's okay. She told him she'd run away and wanted to know if he'd take her in."

"Well, thank God for that," Julie said. "You must be feeling such a sense of relief."

"I'm happy that Nia's okay – he'd just gotten off the phone with her, so I know that – but . . ."

Lisa pinched the bridge of her nose, pushing her thumb and forefinger up against the headache. The relief was only momentary and it was still too soon for the pills to have started working. Why couldn't they develop a headache pill that did its magic immediately?

"The thing is," she went on, "he never even asked her where she was. All he did was tell her no, she couldn't stay with him, and for her not to call him anymore."

"I can't believe that."

"With Dan, believe it." She shook her head. "I could just kill him. All he kept going on about was how we had a deal." Looking across the table, she saw Julie's confusion. "It's kind of a long and not very interesting story," she explained. "What it basically boils down to is when we split up, Dan assumed all our debts on the condition that both Nia and I had no more contact with him. He wanted to 'close the chapter on that part of his life.' Frankly, I was only too happy to oblige."

"Let me guess – they were all debts he'd run up himself anyway."

"No," Lisa said. "I wasn't blameless. I was just as happy to spend money we didn't have as he was. The difference was, I finally came to see the hole we were digging ourselves into and he couldn't." She gave Julie a wan smile. "Let me tell you, it was tough, making do on one salary and not allowing myself to use my credit cards."

"But you did it."

"That's right. I did do it. Plus I kept my side of the bargain, and that was hard, too. Nia was so curious about her father and just couldn't understand why she couldn't just meet him." Lisa sighed. "A perfectly reasonable reaction. I'd tried to erase every trace of him from our lives, but you know how kids are. They want to know. Happily, by the time she finally started asking seriously, I didn't even know where he lived, what he was doing anymore . . ."

Her voice trailed off. The headache was subsiding a little, but the worry and hurt had swollen to take its place.

"What am I going to do, Julie? She's only sixteen. She can't make it out there on her own."

"We're a little better off than we were," Julie replied. "We can now rule out foul play. We know she's not hurt or in the hospital. All that's left is for us to try to track her down."

"The city's so big. She could be anywhere."

Julie nodded. "But kids tend to gravitate to the same hangouts they always have."

"Not Nia. I told you, I don't think she even has any real friends her own age. She just never hung out with anyone on a regular basis."

"But kids on the run do," Julie said. "Protection in numbers and all of that. Your daughter's bright, isn't she? She'll know to find people her own age, kids in the same situation as she is."

"I suppose. But Nia can be so contrary when it comes to what the other kids are doing." A faint smile twitched on her lips. "Gets it from her mother, I'm afraid. I was never much of a joiner either – especially not as a teenager."

Julie returned her smile. "I can imagine." She paused a moment, then added, "Unless you've got a better idea, I think we should start looking now. We can check in with your answering machine if you're afraid she might call while we're out."

"You're right," Lisa said, but then the immensity of the task returned to her all over again. "God, where can we possibly start?"

"I've got a niece who turned seventeen recently," Julie

told her. "Why don't I give her a call and see if she can't give us a list of a few places."

"And if we find Nia," Lisa began.

"Not if – when. Let's think positive."

"Okay. So when we do – how do we get her to come back? I don't even know why she ran away in the first place. I know we had an argument yesterday morning, but we've had them before and this has never happened."

"You said she was getting distant."

Lisa nodded. "I guess we both were."

"You'll have to talk it out," Julie said. "That's what I did with my parents. It wasn't easy, but we worked it out."

"And if we can't?" Lisa asked. Because that was her real worry. That even if they found Nia, her daughter was still lost to her.

"I don't know," Julie said.

Her voice was soft. She hesitated for a moment, then slowly reached a hand across the table. Lisa looked at her hand, then raised her gaze to Julie's face.

"About what happened earlier," Lisa said. "I was over-reacting, I guess. I didn't . . . I don't know . . ."

Julie shook her head. "Let's deal with one thing at a time."

Lisa gave her a grateful look, then reached her own hand across the table to take Julie's, accepting the present comfort. Her whole future felt uncertain – not simply the uncertainty of what was going to happen with Nia, but this whole other strange and somewhat frightening relationship that was developing with Julie. But she knew Julie was right. Trying to fit what was happening between them into the equation only made everything that much more confusing.

"Thanks," she said. "For . . . you know, everything."

Julie smiled. She gave Lisa's fingers a squeeze, then said, "I should call my niece . . ."

Lisa held on for a heartbeat longer before letting go.

XV • MAX

I FEEL sorry for Buddy, but it's all I can do not to laugh. I waited until we could have the place to ourselves, then took him into one of the park's public washrooms and gave him a scrub down, getting as much water on myself as on him in the process. Lord knows we both needed it. But he's looking at me now like I've betrayed his trust – bedraggled and wet, big eyes looking up at me like they're welling with tears, if I want to anthropomorphize. But at least he's cleaner than he was – almost respectable, the more his fur dries.

"The only reason you weren't smelling so rank to me anymore," I tell him, "is because I got used to the stink. Got used to my own, too."

He makes a querulous sound in the back of his throat.

"So what? We may be bums, but that doesn't mean we've got to look or smell like them."

I ruffle the wet fur on his head and that starts him into another vigorous bout of shaking, water spraying everywhere. I jump back from him and catch movement in the corner of my eye, but it's only my reflection in the mirror.

My reflection.

I step closer to the mirror and look at the stranger the glass throws back at me. I'm never going to get used to this. Every time I see Devlin's face I get this ache inside me for my own body that won't let go. But I know I can't run with it. I have to stand firm, play the hand I've been dealt. No matter how much it hurts.

I lift a hand to the stubble on my cheek. Next stop, a drugstore. Maybe I can get a collar and leash for Buddy while I pick up a razor and some deodorant. What else do we need? I start to think of toiletries and a change of clothes but that leads me to where I don't want to go, to what we really need: A home. A life.

Buddy pushes his muzzle against my leg. Perfect timing. It lets me step away from getting all maudlin and feeling sorry for myself.

"That's right," I tell him. "I promised you a decent meal, didn't I?"

I swear he understands everything I'm saying. His tail starts to wagging and he gets this eager look on his face as though I've already lifted the cover of the platter and I'm now offering him the steak.

"We're not rich," I tell him, "so don't get your hopes up."

I made around thirty-five bucks today. It's not going to take us far, but we're better off than we were this morning.

I turn to the mirror once more, slick my wet hair back with my hand. The stranger doesn't look any more familiar. I start to wondering if I shouldn't go for some facial hair, something to make me look less like Johnny Devlin, even if I can't be myself, but Buddy bumps my leg again.

"Okay, okay. I get the hint already."

We go looking for something to eat.

I've always been one to watch my money. Not exactly a tightwad, but I've always paid attention to how much I'm spending and what I'm spending it on. At least I thought I did. I realize now that I took a lot for granted. If I got hungry while I was out running some errands, I'd grab a takeout sandwich and a coffee and not even think about it. If the cover of a book or a magazine caught my eye, I'd pick it up.

Those days, I realize now, are long gone. My thirty-four dollars and change disappears so fast, it's like I never had it. In a discount store I buy some underwear and a T-shirt, deodorant, a collar, a leash, and a seriously cheap knapsack – lime green, which has to be why it was so cheap. In the Korean grocery next door: a few cans of dog food, stew and spaghetti, a lighter, a loaf of bread, a carton of milk, a jar of instant coffee, forget the sugar, some beef jerky. And that's it. I'm down to a couple of bucks, so we're sleeping in the open again tonight, but I'd already been planning on that.

I load everything into my knapsack, then go collect Buddy, who's tied to a light post outside. The poor guy's totally disoriented by all the people, the traffic going by on the street. Too much movement and noise. He cringes from me when I bend down to give him a hug and my heart feels like breaking. But what can I do? I can't let him run loose in the street.

I hold his head in my hands, look down into his big browns.

"Did you think I wasn't coming back?" I ask.

His tail thumps once on the pavement.

"No way," I tell him. "It's you and me. But there's things we've got to do if we want to get along with the rest of the world. I can't walk around naked and neither can you."

He squirms a bit when I put the collar on him, paws at it a couple of times while I'm uncoiling the leash, but he doesn't try to run away. I snap the lead on and he stops fidgeting to give me the big-eyed look again.

"Soon as we get back to the park, I'll take it off. Okay?"

I guess I'm really losing it, talking away to a dog the way

I am, but it helps to ground me. Makes me feel a bit more real. Because the weirdness is always there, lying underneath the so-called normality. I'm never far from completely losing it. The longer I'm in this situation, the more it feels like my previous life was a dream. I'll think of the crazy street people I've seen, mumbling away to themselves, and start to wonder if the truth is that I'm just like them. This is what I am and the rest is something I've just made up. Some people are hiding from aliens. Me, I used to have another normal life until I woke up in somebody else's body.

It's easier to believe that this is who I am. That this is who I've always been. Then I have to remind myself that, impossible as it seems, the other life was real. I'm not crazy. But I understand better than ever what Bones meant about getting too comfortable in this skin. It'd be so easy to simply go with the flow, make what I can out of this life instead of trying to deal with the impossible.

Buddy starts to sniff at the knapsack and brings me back. I coil up the rope that Bones gave me and stow it away. Slipping on the knapsack, I pick up Buddy's lead and we head back to the park, Buddy walking so close to my leg that I start to feel like we've become surgically attached. I don't push him away, though. I've got my problems, but he's had his, too. Maybe I can't help myself, but I can at least give him a better life.

I've been thinking lately about how we define ourselves. Part of who we are is dependent on our memories, on where we've been and what we've done with our lives, how the past has shaped us. But part of it depends on how others see us, too. If everybody treats you like a loser, it's hard not to be a loser. Buddy treats me like the one good thing that's ever been in his life and I find myself responding to that responsibility. Even if I could have my old life back, snap my fingers, here it is, right now, I wouldn't go without bringing Buddy with me. You can't turn your back on your friends, four-legged or otherwise.

And it's not just because he needs me. I need him, too. More than anything, he's what's keeping me sane.

Buddy starts to perk up when we get near the park, walks a few steps ahead of me, tugging on the leash. He smells the green. I can't smell it yet, but I can see it, dark and welcoming, the detail of individual trees lost in the failing light, but the forest of them rising skyward on the far side of the park's wall is impossible to ignore. My heart lifts the same as his does.

We stand on the curb at the corner of Palm Street and Lakeside Drive, waiting for the light to change. It's only been a couple of hours, but I feel we've been gone too long in the city. The park's our home and it's never looked more magical than it does right now. We're in that space between day and night, the long summer twilight that makes the days seem so long. The sky's a shimmery grey above us. Behind us, the sunset plays hide-and-seek between the office towers, a light show that ranges from blood red through orange to a mix of pinks and mauves. The traffic's sparse and we have the sidewalk to ourselves. When the light changes, I'm as eager as Buddy to cross.

I let Buddy off the leash once we're on the other side of the street. He does a little dance step, happy to be unencumbered by the lead, wants to run, but doesn't want to leave me behind. We walk along the wall toward the southwest gate, past a couple of phone booths. Buddy pauses at one of them, suddenly nervous, whining. At first I don't see what's got him upset, but then I see that what I took for shadows pooled on the floor of the booth, is actually a kid. A girl. Huddled up and crying.

I look up and down the street, hesitating, not sure I should – or even want – to get involved. Who'm I kidding? I can't just walk on by – especially when there's no one else around to help her.

I work the folding door open so that it doesn't bang into her, then go down on one knee beside her. I touch her shoulder.

"Hey," I say. "What's wrong?"

She turns and I can't believe what I'm seeing. Her name pulls free of my lips before I even realize I'm saying it.

"Nia?"

She looks at me, nervous, eyes so full of tears she probably can't even see straight. I can't figure out what she's doing here, what's got her so upset. This makes no sense. I feel my carefully propped up equilibrium unbalancing.

"You . . ." she begins, clears her throat. "You're that guy . . . are you really Max?"

I find myself nodding. "How can you know that?"

"I . . . I saw you . . . back at the apartment when you were . . . you were talking to the monster . . ."

That's as good a description of Devlin as any I've heard.

"Oh, Max!" she cries.

She pushes away from the side of the booth and totters on her knees. I grab her before she falls and she wraps her arms around my neck. The tears have started again. I pat her awkwardly on the back, but I don't know what to say. I can't tell her that everything'll be all right because I don't even know what's wrong. I feel Buddy pressed in close beside me, working on getting a smell of her. Nia's trying to say something through her tears, but it takes me a moment to work it out. When I do, it's like my heart stops cold in my chest.

"They got my mom, too," she's saying.

XVI • TANYA

As soon as she left the apartment, Tanya stopped at the corner store to buy a package of cigarettes. She lit one outside and smoked it to the filter in quick, nervous drags, then lit another. Stuffing the package in the pocket of her jacket, she set off, walking aimlessly, trailing smoke.

It was that time of day she liked the least, not quite night, but no longer day, the definition between buildings and street indistinct, the shadows all disjointed and swallowing detail, everything so grey and washed-out. She saw the dusk as a gloomy, unhappy pall, a cat lying on the chest of the day and stealing all the life from its lungs. A time when unpleasant things happened – or were remembered. This evening it suited her mood perfectly.

She and Zeffy rarely had arguments and she wasn't all that sure what this one had really been about. The anger that had come over her earlier made no real sense now. It wasn't that she'd been wrong. Zeffy *had* been unfair, the way she'd taken Johnny seriously enough to check out his story but pretty much laughed off Tanya's own feelings. And then there'd been that goofy look in Zeffy's eye when she'd started out talking about this Johnny who maybe wasn't really Johnny. It proved she was just as susceptible to his charms as Tanya had been. Tanya understood that. What she didn't understand was why she'd let it get under her skin, why she'd overreacted the way she had.

The whole thing had left her with a headache – especially this business with Johnny. Whatever Zeffy might think she'd proved one way or another, Tanya knew what she'd seen yesterday morning. She couldn't explain it, she couldn't tell who was there inside Johnny's head, but she knew it wasn't

Johnny. If it wasn't this Max Trader, then it was someone else, because it hadn't been the Johnny she knew. The differences were too many – the way he'd spoken, his body language, the fact that he really hadn't known them. There hadn't been any pretence in that. She knew Johnny better than Zeffy and those were all things that couldn't be faked. Not unless Johnny was a very good actor. Which he wasn't. That was something she knew as well.

Tanya sighed. The evening held a bit of a breeze now and she had to step closer to a store window to get yet another cigarette lit. Stamp albums, their pages open, filled the display in the window. Track lighting centered on the pages, leaving the draped cloth under the books in dark shadows. She leaned against the glass, gaze drifting from the colorful stamps on one page to those on another. Thinking of acting, seeing the stamps, reminded her of Kenny Brown, the key grip on the two-week shoot for *Sisters of the Knife*. Except for Kenny, that had not been a happy point in her life.

Considering her history with men, it was surprising that she hadn't slept with him, or even thought about it. It certainly hadn't been because he was unattractive. Kenny had probably been the best-looking guy on the shoot, including the leading man, Alan Clark, who by the end of the two weeks, had slept with every woman on the set, herself included – *not* a particular source of pride for her, even thinking back on it now. Clark was oblivious, of course, to any possible shortcomings on his part. He was always on center stage, whether the camera was running or not, while Kenny, good looks notwithstanding, preferred the background, which explained, perhaps, why one was an actor and the other a technician.

Kenny had figured out what she was getting into before

she herself even had. How, she still didn't know. She'd been shooting up between her toes so it wasn't like there'd been track marks or anything. But he'd known and taken her aside one day to talk to her about it.

"I know it's none of my business," he began, "but Clark's—"

"You don't have to tell me," she said. "I figured out pretty quickly that he'll sleep with anything that stands still for longer than a couple of minutes. Being one more notch on his bedpost isn't exactly a high point of pride for me."

"I wasn't talking about sex, Tanya. I was talking about the drugs."

"Oh, you don't have to worry about that. I'm not like a regular user or anything. I just need a little something to get me through this shoot, that's all."

"Some things are easier to get into than out of – trust me on this. I don't want to sound like a little Nancy Reagan voice in the back of your head, telling you to just say no, but if you don't give it up now, you're going to make it that much harder on yourself later. If you even have a later."

"Oh, come on," Tanya had said. "You make it sound like I'm already a junkie. So I've shot up a couple of times. It's no big deal. Really."

Kenny shook his head. "You've got a compulsive personality. I know, because I'm the same way."

"What's that supposed to mean?"

"That it's really easy for us to get addicted. Maybe it's shopping, or smoking—"

"Or boyfriends," Tanya broke in, a wry tone in her voice.

Kenny shrugged. "Or boyfriends. They're all things we do, inadvertently or not, that make it harder for us to get on with our lives. Smack's the worst."

"I'm being careful," she said. "Really I am."

"Do yourself a favor and be more than careful. Get out of it now, while it's still easy."

"There's only another week on the shoot," Tanya told him. "I need *something* to get through all this shit Castledore's putting us through. After that, no more."

Kenny could only sigh. "Whatever," he said, and went back to planning the camera tracking for the next scene.

If she hadn't liked him, she would never have listened to him. As it was, she'd listened, then gone ahead and taken the road to hell anyway. Kenny was still in the business – she saw his name roll up on the credits from time to time, A-list movies now instead of the low-budget cheapies he'd been working on when they met. She wondered if he was still as disappointed in her as he'd been at the end of the shoot, wondered if he even thought of her anymore.

"Let me tell you something," he'd said the day they were all packing up to go home. "You work on the tech side and no one cares how crappy the product is, you're just doing your job. It's the talent that takes the flak – the talent and the directors. The more of this shit you do, Tanya, the more you'll be typecast and the harder it's going to be to get work on a decent picture. You've got to believe in yourself. If you don't, who's going to do it for you? You'll look back in twenty years and realize you've never had a good part. I've seen it all too often."

And it was true. She'd dropped out of the business, but Alan Clark was still playing the lead in knockoff quickies, most of them for the direct-to-video market now, shooting budgets of a couple of hundred thousand tops, forget an ad campaign. It was harder still for a woman. Once the body started to go, there were a hundred fresh new ones to take its place. She didn't know how Clark could keep at it, year in, year out, with nothing to show for it but a series of bad films, each one a little more pathetic than the one before. She knew he was still a womanizer, but sometimes she wondered if he still had a habit, and if he did, how he fed it. You didn't get rich making B-movies – unless you were a producer.

She didn't know where she'd be if she hadn't got out when she had. The drugs hadn't come with the territory; they'd only made it more bearable. But she'd taken the habit back home with her, ran through her bank account and was starting to sell off her belongings when Zeffy finally twigged to what was going on and moved in with her, made her go cold turkey and stayed right there with her, through all the shit.

Zeffy.

Tanya sighed. Zeffy was always there for her, wasn't she, and maybe that was what the argument had really been about. Not so much that Zeffy was always there, but that she needed Zeffy to be there.

She took a last drag from her cigarette and ground the butt under her heel. Turning from the window, she continued down the street, stopping this time in front of a video-store window. What the hell? she thought and went in, heading straight for the "Action Films" section. She browsed through the titles until she found it, *Sisters of the Knife*, still available. The woman on the cover painting didn't look much like her – amazing how under that tiny little T-shirt, her breasts defied gravity the way that they did – but when she turned it over, there she was on the back photo, third bimbo on the left.

"Reliving old glories?"

Tanya started at the voice. Looking up, she found herself face-to-face with Jilly, who was standing on the other side of the rack of films.

"Hardly," she said. "I was just thinking what a good decision it was to get out when I did."

Jilly came around to her side of the rack.

"Yeah, well, it wasn't that great a film," she said, "but it wasn't your fault. You were good, it was just the script that sucked."

Tanya held up the video package. "You've actually seen this?"

"Sure. Gotta support our friends, don't we?" She smiled. "I'm even going to buy some of those greeting cards that Wendy's writing, though don't tell her I said that."

"She's showed me a few of them," Tanya said. "I think they're pretty good."

"Of course they're good. But I have to tease her about something. So what do you think of this?" Jilly held up the film package she was holding, Kieslowski's *Rouge*, with a profile of Irène Jacob on the cover set off by a swirl of surrealistic reds in the background. "I'm taking it over to Sophie's. We loved *Bleu*, but neither of us liked *Blanc* – at least not the ending. It seemed so misogynist."

"I didn't like it either."

Jilly nodded. "So we never did get around to seeing the third film, but everybody keeps saying that *Rouge* is as good as the first one, so I don't know. I thought we could give it a try."

"Well, it's better than this," Tanya said, tapping the cover of the film box she was holding. "Actually, it's wonderful. If I could have worked with directors like Kieslowski, I'd probably still be doing films."

"So what made you give it up?"

"Remember Susanna Moore?"

Jilly nodded. "She was in all those B-movies. What about her?"

"I didn't want to end up like her, in my forties and still playing those kinds of roles."

"But there's no reason you'd have to. I wasn't just saymg it, Tanya. You were the best thing in that movie. I didn't believe in any of the other characters, but I believed in yours and it really creeped me out at the end when it was just you and that horrible man in the building."

"Alan Clark."

"I've *never* liked him."

"That's because you've got taste."

"But I did like your work," Jilly said. "Why didn't you go on? I mean, seriously. I'm sure you could've gotten into better films."

Tanya shook her head. "I developed too many bad habits." She hesitated, then added, "Or maybe I should say, one bad habit and that was enough."

Jilly nodded. "Tell me about it. Been there, done that. I wish now I'd been a little smarter, but nobody was going to tell me what to do about anything." She gave Tanya a rueful smile. "It's amazing the stuff we'll do to ourselves, isn't it? I'm surprised any of us survived adolescence."

"How could you know—"

"Nobody had to tell me," Jilly told her. "All I had to hear was the way you said habit and I knew what you were talking about."

"But you . . . you're so . . ."

Jilly laughed. "What? Perfect?"

"Something like that."

"Hardly," Jilly said. "I survived by the skin of my teeth. It was pure luck that I ran into some people who cared enough to help me through some really bad times."

"Like Zeffy helped me."

"Did she? I'm not surprised. She's good people."

Tanya nodded, feeling worse than ever about their argument.

"You look like you need someone to talk to," Jilly said. "Do you want to go for a coffee?"

"What about your movie with Sophie?"

Jilly smiled. "She was painting when I left to get it. She'll never notice if I'm late getting back. So what do you say?"

"I'd like that."

"Let me go pay for this and we'll see if we can't find a place that's not too crowded."

XVII • NIA

FINDING THE real Max didn't solve anything, Nia realized. If anything, it made her feel more confused. It was so strange looking at him, listening to him speak, the familiar mixed with the alien, the way his really being here in another body made the world feel out of kilter, the ground no longer sure, or even safe, underfoot. The stranger with his dog didn't look at all like Max, but he spoke like Max, sat like Max, even knew things that only Max would know. She believed he was Max, so she let him comfort her, grateful for the human contact, but still felt unbalanced because he *didn't* look like Max and the voice murmuring awkwardly in her ear was all wrong.

Finally she pulled away from him. Leaning back against

the glass of the phone booth, she stared at him, trying to find something, anything, one known landmark in those unfamiliar features, but there was nothing she could anchor on.

"It . . . it's *really* you . . . isn't it?" she asked again.

Her voice echoed in the booth. It sounded distant, as though she were speaking down a long tunnel.

"I know," he said. "It's too weird to seem real, isn't it?"

She nodded. "Really weird."

"I'd offer you a Kleenex or something, but I don't have either."

"'Sokay."

She made do with the sleeve of her shirt until she remembered she still had a napkin left over from when she'd bought her sandwich. Pulling it out of her pocket, she blew her nose, then let him help her to her feet. Slipping his arm under hers, he started toward the park, the dog following at their heels. They walked in silence, Nia needing the support of his arm more than she'd thought she would.

"I . . . I guess this is sort of like a date," she said after a while.

She tried to make a joke of it because she felt that if she didn't laugh, she'd start crying again.

Max glanced at her. "I hope you've had better."

"Not really."

It was true. And that made her want to cry all over again. Shit, Nia, she told herself. Grow up already.

"Where are we going?" she asked before the flood of tears pushing up against the back of her eyes broke free.

"Down by the lake. Buddy and I sort of have a little campsite there."

This was better, she thought, having something to talk

about that didn't deal with either of their problems. She could concentrate on the conversation, use it to keep from breaking down again.

"Buddy being the dog?" she asked.

When she spoke his name, Buddy's ears perked up. She leaned over to pat him, but he cringed away from her.

"He's not really used to people being nice to him," Max told her. "Give him a little time to get to know you."

"Where did you find him?"

"He found me." Max hesitated, then asked, "What were you saying about your mother?"

Wrong question, Nia thought as her chest clenched up tight. She swallowed thickly.

"Tell . . ." She cleared her throat. "Tell me about what happened to you first."

"Okay."

They were down by the lake now. Nia clambered up the rocks behind Max and Buddy until they came to a flat granite outcrop, backed by a dense cedar thicket, the lake spread out before them on the far side of one of the park's paths and a stretch of stony beach. Sitting down on the rock with Max, she watched while he fed Buddy and had his own supper, telling him she'd just eaten when he offered her some. She grimaced as she watched him eating cold spaghetti out of a can. She'd have to be a lot hungrier before she'd eat that, she thought.

While he was eating, the last of the day leaked out of the sky, blurring their features. It was easier to talk to him then, the indistinct shadow shape sitting across from her who could be anybody. And she was getting used to the voice now.

She listened to him describe what it had been like, waking up in somebody else's body, about what a lousy guy this

Johnny Devlin was, how he'd been evicted from Devlin's apartment, how he'd slept in the park last night, here on this same outcrop, and this was where Buddy found him.

"I think he's what's been keeping me sane," Max said. "Knowing that I'm looking out for him, having him to talk to. Just his company. It kind of takes a bit of the edge off of what's been a truly bizarre experience."

"I know," Nia said. "I've been wanting someone to talk to ever since I took off from home yesterday afternoon."

Max shook his head. "I don't get it. How did things get to this?"

"It's hard to explain."

She shrugged, but the movement was lost in the dark.

"I know you and your mother have been arguing a lot lately," Max said, "but it's not like you to run away from your problems."

"I guess. It's just . . ."

So she told him about overhearing his conversation with Devlin in the hall outside his apartment, her own confrontation with the imposter Max, how she'd spent the day wandering the city because she was too scared to stay at home by herself, how she'd run away for real when she'd seen her mom kissing this woman.

Max seemed to hesitate before he finally said, "You know, just because you saw your mother kissing another woman doesn't mean that—"

"They weren't just kissing," Nia told him. "They were necking."

"But it still doesn't mean she's not your mother."

"Oh, I get it. It's real when it happens to you, but not to anybody else."

"I'm not saying that. It's just . . . what's so wrong with her, you know, dating a woman?"

"She's my *mom*, that's what's wrong. How would I even be here if she didn't like men?"

"People change," Max said.

"Exactly. Or rather, they're being changed. I don't know who's doing it – aliens or some weird government experiment or what – but they've already got two people in our apartment. And how many more has it happened to?"

"If that's the case, why didn't it happen to you?"

"I don't know. Maybe I'm too young. All I know is that my mom – my real mom – is wandering around somewhere in the city in another person's body. Just like you. And I have to find her."

A long moment went by before Max said, "Okay. We'll look for her."

"But you don't believe me."

That woke a humorless laugh from him.

"I don't think I have much of a right to say that anything's impossible right now," he told her.

"But you don't."

Max sighed. "I tell you how I'm handling this: *wu-sei*."

"Woo what?"

"*Wu-sei*. It was the way Janossy used to approach a new experience. It's a Chinese thing from the *Tao Te Ching* – the principle of noninterference."

"What? Like you don't do anything and everything magically gets better?"

The shadow shape of his head moved slowly back and forth. "Not even close. It doesn't imply not acting, but acting appropriately – only when, where and to the least degree necessary to guide rather than force events to their natural conclusion." Max laughed. "He even built instruments that way."

"So looking for my mom is inappropriate?"

"No. Looking's fine. It's jumping to conclusions, or trying to force things to happen, that's a problem."

"I don't get it," Nia said. "How're we going to get anything done any other way?"

"Well, jumping to conclusions doesn't help because it closes the door on other possibilities. For instance, if we're not absolutely certain that the same thing's happened to your mother, then—"

"I *told* you what I saw."

She saw Buddy start nervously as she raised her voice. Max reached out and soothed the dog, quieting him with an absent, natural gesture that Nia found herself envying. If only there were something that could make her feel better that easily.

"But you haven't talked to her," Max said. "You don't *know* – you can only assume from having seen one incident that you perceive to be out of character."

Nia took a steadying breath before replying. "Okay," she said. "I'll try to keep an open mind. So then what?"

"We could try calling her in the morning."

"No way."

"Why not?"

'Because, because . . ." Nia's voice trailed off. "Because I'm too scared," she finally said.

"If there is somebody else inside her, I won't let her hurt you," Max said. "We'll call from a phone booth and you can ask her something that only the two of you would know . . ." She sensed his smile more than she could see it. "You know, the way you were testing me earlier."

"I had to know."

"Of course you did," Max said. "And tomorrow we'll do the same with your mother."

"And if I'm right?"

265

"Then we'll deal with it. But let's not—"

"I know," Nia said. "Jump to conclusions."

"Now you've got it."

"I'll try."

"That's all I can ask for," Max said. He yawned. "Now let's try to get some sleep. I don't know about you, but I've had too long and weird a day and I'm beat. You can use this knapsack for a pillow if you like."

"It's okay. I've got my own."

Last night Max had slept on the rock, but tonight they moved back under the cedars, making rough mattresses for themselves by pushing together heaps of the leaves. It wasn't home, Nia thought, but it sure beat the way she'd spent last night.

"Max?" she said when they were both lying down, Buddy snuggled up beside him.

"Umm?"

"I'm glad I found you."

"Me, too."

She lay there for a long time, listening to the sound of the lake and the wind in the trees above. Max's breathing evened out quickly – long before she was finally able to fall asleep herself.

XVIII • LISA

LISA LOOKED out the passenger window of Julie's car, unable to take her gaze from the face of the girl sauntering by on the sidewalk. While she couldn't have been much older than Nia, the girl already had a world-weary, hard look about her. She sneered at Lisa as she went by, but Lisa barely noticed. Her attention wasn't taken so much by the girl's clothing – all evening she'd seen variations on the girl's short jean skirt and combat boots, the bustier with a frayed jean vest overtop – as by her multitude of earrings. There were at least six to each ear, but then she had a pierced lip as well, another ring through her nose, a stud and a plain ring in her left eyebrow, another stud in her right.

"I guess I should consider myself lucky," she said when the girl had passed the car. She resisted the urge to turn in her seat, though she did continue to watch through the sideview mirror.

"How so?" Julie asked.

"The worst Nia's come up with so far is to try and relive the old Beat days. Late-night coffee and bebop jazz are a lot easier to take than the way that girl's mutilated her face. My God, what must her parents think?"

Julie gave her an amused look. "Probably the same thing our parents did when we were teenagers."

"But that girl looked like a freak. I was never that bad."

"Not from your perspective."

"Be serious," Lisa said.

"I am being serious."

"But . . ."

Lisa let her voice trail off. She glanced in the side mirror again, watching the girl continue down the block.

"I suppose you're right," she said. "It's just . . . it seems so extreme."

"I saw a girl with 'Nine Inch Nails' tattooed on her cheek the other day," Julie told her. "Now, that's extreme."

Lisa nodded in agreement. She'd been very lucky with Nia, she realized. At least up until now.

After Julie had spoken to her niece Anna-Leigh, they'd set out on a tour of hangouts where they might find Nia, working from a list of Anna-Leigh's suggestions. To look more inconspicuous, they'd both changed into casual clothes – jeans and T-shirts, Lisa at home, Julie at her own apartment when they went by to get her car. They were glad they did, for while they didn't fit in much better, dressed-down and driving Julie's old beat-up Honda, at least they didn't look like they were worth mugging.

Their search took them into some of the rougher parts of the city, areas where neither of them would have gone alone, clubs on unfamiliar backstreets, abandoned buildings where runaways squatted. Most of the time they didn't even leave the car, cruising slowly by congregations of hostile teenagers, most of whom returned their scrutiny with unfriendly expressions. Often the promise of violence lay thick in the air, directed at each other as much as at Lisa and Julie. Twice they'd seen minor scuffles, once a serious fight.

Many of them were still children, Lisa found herself thinking, but not any kind of children she'd ever known. They gave off a very real sense of danger – like once-domesticated animals gone feral. It was as though the punk scene had returned, but more menacing, its nihilism less a fashion statement, more a way of life. The longer they drove by their various hangouts, the less Lisa expected to find Nia among them. She didn't know why Nia had run away, but she couldn't believe that overnight her daughter had turned into such a stranger that she'd suddenly seek out the company of people such as this.

"What's next?" Julie asked.

"Maybe we should call it a night," Lisa said.

"How many places do we have left?"

"One. But it's way up in Lower Foxville."

Julie nodded. "That's right. Your Second Home." She smiled. "How could I forget?"

"What's so funny?" Lisa asked.

"I used to hang out there when I was a teenager. They had the best bands."

"According to your niece, I guess they still do."

"I always thought the kid had taste."

"So is it in the Tombs?" Lisa asked.

"Right on the borderland between civilization and the wilds," Julie said. She shot Lisa a look. "Don't feel nervous. It'll be perfectly safe."

She took the next street heading west, then worked her way across town until they reached Lee Street, which would take them north, all the way up to where the club was situated on the corner of Lee and Gracie Street. The sign on the marquee read TONITE! LIVE! BLOODFRUIT! Lisa guessed they were a metal band from the small pool of black leather, chains and jeans that was waiting to get in. The age of the crowd seemed to vary between high school and college, though from the extreme clothing and hairstyles an exact reckoning of years was hard to figure and she couldn't tell which might be which. The threat of violence lay in the air here as well, but it didn't seem as strong. Or at least it wasn't so strongly focused on them. Lisa still wouldn't have described the place as safe.

"Boy, this brings back some memories," Julie said as she pulled up to the curb.

Lisa scanned the crowd for Nia, but with this band playing at the club tonight, and the audience it had drawn, she was only going through the motions. This really wasn't Nia's scene.

"I don't see her," she said.

"I'm not surprised. It's hard to see anything from this vantage."

She opened the driver's-side door as she spoke and got

out before Lisa could tell her there was no point in looking closer. Then she realized that Julie probably wanted to get a closer look at an old stomping ground, drawn by the same curiosity that brought people back to houses they'd once lived in or high-school reunions. Lisa joined her on the sidewalk. Julie turned and smiled at her.

"I can't believe it hasn't been condemned yet," she said. "It looks exactly the way it did in the seventies when I used to hang out here."

"You're right," Lisa said. "It doesn't look like much."

"But the music was great. Punk and rock bands at night, a place for unemployed blue-collar workers to drink away their welfare checks during the day, and weirdly enough, everybody pretty much got along. I'll bet it looks exactly the same inside."

Lisa felt nervous enough out here on the pavement – they were already drawing more attention than she cared for. She couldn't imagine actually venturing inside.

"You're not going in," she said.

Julie laughed. "No – though I won't say I'm not tempted. Any sign of Nia?"

"It's not really her kind of crowd," Lisa said.

"And if I remember what it was like when I was a kid, half of the attraction of going to see a band in a place like this was who you'd be seen with. Or by."

"Exactly."

"Well, we tried," Julie said. "All we can do now is go back to—"

She broke off when a young man detached himself from the general crowd and blocked their way back to the car. Half his head was shaven, revealing a snake's head tattoo; on the other side, long black hair, dyed so often it had taken on the texture of straw, hung to his shoulders. He wore motorcycle boots, jeans that were stiff with grease and dirt, and a black leather vest to show off the gallery of other tattoos on his chest and arms. He seemed a little older than the rest of the crowd – mid-twenties, perhaps – but still young enough that either of them could have been his mother.

"Hey, ladies," he said, his voice a slur. "Wassup?" He gave them a grin that seemed to say that even he couldn't believe his own charm and wit. "Not leaving, are you?"

Oh shit, Lisa thought. This was exactly what she'd been afraid of. She shot a quick glance toward the crowd to find no help there. This was merely entertainment for them, something to pass the time until they could get into the club.

"Actually, that's precisely what we're doing," Julie calmly told him.

"That's hard, man. Dissing us before you even know us."

"Please," Lisa began.

"Please?" he repeated in a high pitched voice, mocking her. "Please what?" He cupped his hand around his crotch. "Please can you suck my cock?"

"Okay," Julie said. "That's enough of this crap."

She stepped forward, moving to one side to go around him. Lisa quickly followed suit, but he shifted his position, blocking them once more.

"We haven't started nothing yet," he said.

When Julie started forward again, he lifted a tattooed arm, grabbed her by the shoulder.

"Relax," he told her. "We're just having ourselves some fun."

"I'm not having fun," Julie told him.

Lisa didn't know how Julie could stay so calm.

"That's because you're not trying," he said, the grin never leaving his face.

Behind them the crowd made appreciative noises.

"Yo. Tell 'em, Taxman," someone called.

"Tell 'em you got this urge to breed."

The comment woke a general laugh.

"Taxman?" Julie asked.

He shrugged. "I'm the Taxman. People know, they got to pay me what's due."

Julie tried to shake off his hand, but he wouldn't budge and Lisa was really starting to get scared now. The Taxman caught Julie's jaw with his free hand and pulled his face in close.

"So you ready to pay?" he asked. "You ready for some fun?"

Julie smiled sweetly. "How's this for fun?"

She jerked her knee up into his crotch with so much force that he dropped his hands and stumbled back, bent over, good humor evaporating into pain.

"Let's *go!*" Julie cried.

Lisa didn't need to be told twice. She bolted for the car. Behind her, she heard someone in the crowd yell.

"Taxman, no!"

Lisa couldn't help herself. She turned to look, saw the Taxman straightening up, pain written across his face, anger blazing in his eyes. The knife in his hand didn't register at first, didn't register at all until she saw him lunge forward and stab Julie in the back with it. A horrible wheezing cry escaped Julie's lips, her eyes opening bird-wide from the shock of the sudden pain.

Lisa's mind seemed to close down, refusing to accept what she had just seen. Everything went still – her own breathing and heartbeat, the crowd around the theater, Julie and her assailant. The awful tableau held for an eternity;

then the Taxman pulled the knife free and Julie began to fall to the pavement.

"Oh, shit," Lisa heard someone say.

Her own stasis evaporated and she stepped forward to break Julie's fall, buckling under the sudden load. She sank slowly to the pavement, supporting Julie's limp weight. Her hands grew slick with Julie's blood and panic quickened her heartbeat into overdrive. Looking up over Julie's head, she saw the Taxman staring at the knife in his hand as though he was as surprised as anyone else at what he'd done. His gaze lifted to meet hers and he took a step forward – whether to help or continue his attack, Lisa didn't know.

"I-touch her again and I'll kill you," she heard herself say, barely recognizing her own voice.

She held Julie protectively against her chest and knew she looked about as capable of hurting him as a puppy, all bluster and no real bite. But something stopped him all the same. He hesitated for a moment, then turned and ran down the street, turning in to the blocks of abandoned buildings that made up the Tombs. In the far distance a police siren could be heard. It was too soon for someone to have phoned the police, too soon for a cruiser to be on its way here, but the crowd broke up at the sound all the same, bolting in all directions until there was only a boy left, no older than seventeen, but as rough-looking as the Taxman, all leather jacket and jeans, dirty blond hair, black T-shirt, a small mandala tattooed on one cheek.

"Put your hand on the wound," he said.

Lisa looked blankly at him.

"She's losing too much blood. You've got to stanch the flow until help gets here. I'll get them to call for an ambulance."

Lisa did as he said, wincing at how Julie moaned and stiffened in her arms when she pressed against the wound. The boy hammered on the door of the club, yelling through the glass to the man summoned by the disturbance for him to call 911. Then he ran off as well.

The police cruiser arrived first, with the ambulance a close second, but they still took forever to come. Julie was so still in her arms by then that Lisa feared the worst. When the paramedics crouched beside her she was reluctant to let go. Scared now, so scared. Even more than she'd been during the attack.

"Is . . . is she going to die?" she asked as the medics took over.

One of the men shot her a sympathetic look. "Not if I've got anything to say about it, lady."

The police wanted to question her, but all she could do was shake her head. She followed the stretcher into the ambulance and crouched beside Julie, clutching her hand as they sped toward the hospital.

XIX • TANYA

JILLY WAS so easy to talk to that Tanya found herself telling her everything, from how she was feeling about Johnny and the stupid argument she'd had with Zeffy to the growing dissatisfaction she had for how her own life was going. They sat at a window table in The Black Bean Dream on Lee Street, nursing café lattes and sharing one of the café's famous huge chocolate-chip cookies, while it all spilled out. She was sure that she sounded like the most hopeless, whining loser anybody'd ever heard, but once started, she couldn't seem to stop, and Jilly gave no indication that she thought the same.

"So you don't agree with Zeffy, then?" Jilly asked when Tanya circled back to start in again on Zeffy's visit to Max Trader.

"What, about this guitar guy? I've no idea. I've never met him and I don't know a thing about him except for what Zeffy's told me. I just know there's something seriously wrong with Johnny."

"And you're mad at Zeffy because she won't take you seriously?"

"I suppose. That, and for not telling me how she's been feeling about Johnny herself."

"This is going to sound like I'm taking Zeffy's side," Jilly said, "but she hadn't seen you all day. Telling you when she did was the first opportunity she had."

"I know. But it's like, when I was with him it was always, what're you doing with that loser?, but now she's interested in him and everything's different. I've got bad judgment, but she's been tricked."

"Do you still care about him?"

Tanya shrugged. "I guess. I don't know. Not like before." She sighed "How do you do it, Jilly?"

"Do what?"

"Live by yourself. Go through life without a regular boyfriend."

Jilly gave her a rueful smile. "It's not exactly out of choice. I'm just not really good with relationships. I get along really well with people, but whenever I'm with a guy and things become intimate, he either turns out to be married, or a jerk, or I get all screwed up and closed up inside and tend to blow it."

"Really? You?"

"Really, me. Now you know my secret side. I'm actually Jilly, the Amazing Messed-Up Lady."

"But how do you stand being alone?"

"Well, I've got my friends . . ."

"You know what I mean."

Jilly nodded. She broke the last piece of the cookie in two and dipped the half she took in her coffee.

"It's so unfair, when you think about it," she said around a mouthful of cookie. "I mean, the warped way society looks at us. Single guys are called bachelors and there's this whole mystique about them – you know, the older they get, the better they get and all that crap. We, on the other hand, get called spinsters or old maids and if we're not married off, or at least a part of a couple before we're thirty, it's like we're losers or something. We have no *meaning*, we're defined only by the guy we're with. Or not with."

"But I *like* being with a guy," Tanya said. "I like being in love."

"Well, sure. Who doesn't? But the point is, you're still a worthwhile person if you're not. What gets to me is the perception that's pushed at us from the minute we're born: that we need a man to give our lives meaning. Never mind the women's-rights movement. Never mind plain common sense. The perception's still there. The propaganda's waiting for us wherever we turn."

"So how do you deal with it?"

Jilly shrugged. "I learned to be happy with myself. I figure if I can't be happy with who I am, with my own company, then how can I expect anybody else to like me? Or maybe more to the point, how could I respect them?"

"You make it sound so easy."

"It's not. And if I didn't have the support of my friends, I probably wouldn't be able to keep it up, because let's face it. We're social animals, right? We need people to talk to, to confide in, to be close to."

Tanya nodded. "Zeffy's like that, too. Except I think she uses her music as a substitute."

"I can understand that. It's like a kind of therapy. I use my art the same way." She smiled. "Mind you, I don't really get much of a choice. I have to paint. If I don't, I go crazy."

"I just thought you guys were so . . . you know, focused."

"I can't answer for Zeffy, but I know art's something I have to do. It's what keeps me sane. Truth is, it saved my life. When I was a kid growing up, drawing was the only thing that let me escape from all the horrible things going on around me. I wasn't any good, mind you. I made the same mistakes over and over again – screwing up my perspectives, everything coming out flat – but it didn't matter. The hours I spent drawing took me into a safe place where no one could hurt me. It was only later I learned to do it properly – learned the language of what I was doing, how to put down on paper what was in my heart. I doodled as a kid, now I do art, but the impulse and need to capture the images hasn't changed."

"I guess that's my real problem," Tanya said. "I don't do anything. I *can't* do anything."

Jilly shook her head. "Everybody carries the gift of the creative impulse. Some people just find it easier to access, that's all. Or can access it in ways that are more traditionally recognizable."

"I don't know if I believe that. I mean, I know I can do

things. I *have* done things. My problem is that I don't have this burning need to do anything – not the way you and Zeffy have to paint or play music."

"Passion doesn't have to come from creating art. You can be just as passionate in your appreciation of it."

"That's what Geordie said."

"Well, he was right. I can't write stories, but I love to read. I couldn't play an instrument for the life of me, but I don't think I could live without music."

"But it's not the same."

"No," Jilly agreed. "But that doesn't make it bad. Personally, the thing I admire the most in a person is their goodness and decency, not whether or not they can paint or carry a tune."

"I suppose. But I want that passion. It's like I have this hole in me and since I can't fill it up with something creative the way you or Zeffy do, I fill it up with men. I leave Johnny, so right away I want to hook up with Geordie."

"Do you care for him?"

"Yes. I guess." Tanya sighed. "I don't know. I thought he was interested in me, but now I'm not so sure. I think he just wants to be friends."

Jilly smiled. "I don't know which of the Riddells is worse when it comes to relationships, Geordie or Christy. You'd never guess they were so deathly shy about meeting women from the way they are the rest of the time."

"Well, that's hopeful."

"*If* it's what you want," Jilly said.

"I guess that's the thing I have to work out first," Tanya said. She sighed again. "You think what I should do is get comfortable with myself first, don't you?"

Jilly shook her head. "I think you should do whatever feels right for you."

"I feel so whiny. So needy."

"Everybody feels like that sometimes."

"Nobody else seems to. To me, everybody else seems so together. They're all creative and productive."

"You shouldn't compare yourself to other people," Jilly said. "All that does is get in the way of being yourself."

She fished around in her pocket and came up with a few bills and some change. She laid the money on the table and then stood up.

"What you need right now is to get away from it all," she said. "Give yourself a break from thinking about Zeffy and Johnny and Geordie and everything else that's cluttering up your life."

"Easier said than done."

"Why don't you come back to Sophie's with me and watch this movie?"

Tanya shook her head. "I don't want to intrude."

"Oh, please. Sophie'll probably stay in her studio all night and I'd have to watch it on my own anyway. Talk about focused – sometimes that woman gives a whole new meaning to having a one-track mind."

"Has she got a show coming up?"

"Um-hmm." Jilly smiled down at her. "So what do you say?"

Tanya stood up to join her. "I'd like that," she said.

The film was better than Tanya remembered it. Of course, the first time she'd seen it she'd been with Johnny and he'd hated it. The only thing worse than a foreign film, he liked to say, was a foreign film with subtitles. Watching it with Jilly was a whole different experience. She sat beside Tanya on the sofa in Sophie's living room utterly engrossed from start to finish and then wanted to immediately watch the whole thing all over again when it ended.

True to Jilly's prediction, Sophie had been impossible to pry from her studio. She looked up from the painting on her easel when they came into the high-ceilinged room she used for a studio, and gave them a quick grin before returning her attention to the canvas to add a dab of paint here, another there.

"We have the film," Jilly said, holding the video up in her hand. "We have the machine, waiting in the living room, and we have the time."

Sophie stepped back from the easel. She pushed an errant lock of curly hair from her forehead and sighed.

"I feel so rude," she said, "but I really need another hour or so on this."

Jilly turned to Tanya. "What did I tell you?"

"Like you were never running late on a show," Sophie said.

"This is true. But woman can't live by work alone."

Sophie laughed. "This one has to – at least until I get this finicky bit done. Why don't you guys go ahead and watch the film? I'll join you when I'm done."

Jilly started to nod, but Sophie was already focused on her painting again.

"No problem," she said. "But first we'll do a little tour for Tanya since she's never been up here before. Don't worry," she added when Sophie looked up. "We'll be quiet as mice."

"Quieter," Tanya said.

"Mmm," Sophie murmured, head bent, hair falling back across her brow as she started to mix a new color on her palette.

"That means yes," Jilly translated.

Tanya was entranced with the paintings that lined the walls – bright, vibrant oils on canvas that, while plainly cityscapes and character studies, were all larger than life, more imbued with Sophie's personal vision than being faithful renditions of their source material. Colors pulsed, outlines ran into each other, perspectives seemed to owe as much to a child's view of the world as an adult's. But there was still a maturity in the work that was impossible to deny, a sense of spirit and a connection to the real world and its concerns for all the liberties she'd taken in her depictions.

More surprising to Tanya was how tidy both Sophie and her studio were, especially in consideration of the apparent looseness and abandon of her approach in the finished works. There was some paint on her smock where she wiped her hands, and a little on the drop cloth under her easel, but otherwise everything was remarkably under control. Tanya had been to Jilly's studio when Jilly was working and there seemed to be paint everywhere – from Jilly's hair, face and hands, to every surface, likely and unlikely, within a six-foot radius of her easel. Ironically, Jilly's paintings were incredibly precise, high-realism for all their fantastic content, while Sophie's were almost Impressionistic, capturing the essence of her subjects rather than their details.

But their opposite takes on art became a real strength when they collaborated on a piece, creating a fascinating tension between their disparate styles. In the same way as their different ways of thinking, Sophie's tidiness set against Jilly's casual scruffiness, seemed to draw them closer as friends, the one complementing the other. It was something like her own relationship with Zeffy, Tanya realized, the dissimilar focus of their personalities adding a spark of extra interest to those things that they did hold in common, except unlike the rest of them, she didn't bring a creative element to her relationship with Zeffy. No, she just complained, while Zeffy soldiered on with her songs and her music and still found time for Tanya's problems.

She really did owe Zeffy an apology, she realized.

Sophie joined them for the second viewing of the film, becoming as engrossed as Jilly had been from the first few frames, shushing Jilly every time she started to effuse over a camera angle or the soundtrack. Tanya wanted to stay awake, but her eyelids kept drooping, the long day finally catching up on her. She meant to get up and go home a half-dozen times, but ended up falling asleep in her corner of the couch, waking stretched out on it and covered with a blanket the next morning with no time to go home and change before she had to go in to work.

XX • LISA

THE REMAINDER of Lisa's night dissolved into a confusing blur of half-remembered images that she could only put in a vague semblance of order. Punchy from being up for almost forty-eight hours now with next to no sleep, she sat on an uncomfortable hospital chair, elbows on her knees, clutching a Styrofoam cup of cold coffee and staring down at the linoleum between her feet. It was almost dawn and quiet now – far quieter than it had been in the ER when she'd arrived at the hospital, doggedly following the paramedics as they wheeled Julie into the crash room.

A nurse had stopped her and steered her toward a chair before she could join the trauma physicians that convened around Julie's gurney. He knelt in front of her, asking her questions that she couldn't focus on. All around them was chaos – a constant bustle of movement and noise that made her feel dizzy.

"Can you hear me? Where were you hurt? Can you . . ."

She strained to see what was happening in the crash room, but the door closed, cutting off her view. The nurse touched her knee.

"Miss?" he tried again. "Can you tell me where you were hurt?"

Finally she understood what he was saying. It was the blood, Julie's blood that was all over her hands and arms and jeans. He thought she'd been hurt, too.

"I – I'm okay," she said. "This . . ." She couldn't say the word. "It's not mine."

The nurse stood up and called a female colleague who took Lisa into a washroom so that she could clean up. When she returned to the ER, they wanted to treat her for shock, but she refused, insisting instead on seeing Julie, on knowing how she was, what were they doing to her. Before she could get any answers, the door to the ER opened again and the emergency unit was suddenly so busy again that she was left alone. Paramedics had brought in two gunned-down teenagers, flanked by the policemen who had shot them. One of the boys was in a wheelchair, the other lashed to a backboard in a high neck brace and black traces, incongruously reminding Lisa of Frankenstein movies and Egyptian pharaohs.

Later.

She filled out forms for Julie, putting herself down as next-of-kin, shivering at the reminder of how critical Julie's condition was.

Later.

Someone brought her a coffee. She sipped from the Styrofoam cup, not even noticing how hot it was, how bad it tasted.

Later.

Detectives spoke to her, took down her description of the Taxman, asked her to come down to the station to go through the mug books. She promised she'd go in the morning, though she couldn't understand how they would need any more than she'd already given them. How many people looked the way the Taxman had in this city?

"You'd be surprised," one of the detectives told her.

"Okay. I'll be down first chance I get."

She would have promised them anything, just so that they'd leave her alone for now.

Later.

Julie was wheeled out of the crash room, on her way to the surgical theater, and Lisa followed, was stopped, argued until she was allowed to wait in a hallway outside, alone now, everything seeming so hushed after the ER. Trying to stay awake, dozing.

Later:

"Miss?"

She jerked awake. A young doctor stood in front of her, the right sleeve of her jacket spotted with blood.

"Your friend's been taken to intensive care," the doctor told her.

Julie was alive. She was going to live.

"We're still listing her as critical," the doctor went on, "but she has a very good chance of pulling through."

"Can – can I see her?"

"I'm afraid not. Only the immediate family are allowed."

"But . . ." Lisa hesitated, then plunged on. "I am family. We're . . . a couple."

284

The doctor nodded sympathetically. "I see," she said, and gave Lisa the necessary directions.

Later.

She was only allowed in the room for a few minutes, but it was enough to give her hope. She watched the rise and fall of Julie's chest, touched her cheek with fingers like feathers, leaned forward and whispered, "Don't die on me now." Kissed her gently on the brow.

She didn't argue when the nurse came to tell her she had to leave, but went without protest to sit in another hall. And waited some more. Dozed. Couldn't sleep, because she kept seeing the Taxman's face, the knife plunging into Julie's back, and would start awake, a fine sheath of perspiration on her brow, her shirt clinging to her chest and back.

After a while, she went in search of another coffee, found a machine and fed it change. Returned to her vigil, sipping at the coffee until she forgot about it and it went cold. The dawn found her there, staring at the floor, her mind a numbed blur until suddenly she sat up.

Nia, she thought.

She'd forgotten she even had a daughter, little say that Nia was still missing. Setting the cold coffee on the floor, she went looking for a phone and called home. She let it ring four times. When the answering machine answered, she returned the receiver to its cradle and slowly made her way back to the hall outside Julie's room.

She couldn't deal with Nia, why she'd run away, why she wouldn't come home. Not now. Not when Julie needed her.

XXI • MAX

DESPITE THE raucous birds' chorus and the constant squabbling of the gulls by the lake, we all sleep in late this morning – even Buddy. Making beds under the cedars was a much better choice than dozing off on the rock the way I did the other night. I don't feel nearly as stiff today. I let Nia sleep while Buddy and I make our way down to the lake. I wash up and he has a drink. By the time we get back to our campsite, Nia's up and we talk about breakfast, settling on getting something from the food carts at the entrance of the park.

I feed Buddy before we go, then stash away most of my stuff so that I don't have to carry it around all day. The food gets wrapped up in a plastic shopping bag and I hang it from a tree with the rope Bones gave me, out of sight. All I'm taking with me is Bones' knife and the knapsack to carry my finished carvings and raw materials to make more. I turn the knapsack over in my hands. Damn thing looks even more garish in the daylight, but what do you do? I don't even try to defend it when Nia makes some crack about it.

We get coffees and muffins with the last of the money I made yesterday and have breakfast on one of the benches before following Palm Street south to the phone booth where I found Nia last night. I can tell she's tense – she doesn't want to be doing this, that's obvious – but she puts on a good front, drops in her quarter, dials her mother's work number. After the buildup, it's kind of anti-climactic when the receptionist tells her that her mother isn't there. All she gets is an answering machine at their apartment. She doesn't leave a message.

"So now what do we do?" Nia asks.

It's going on eleven. I touch the knapsack hanging from one shoulder.

"I'm going to stake out a spot where the craftspeople are selling their stuff," I tell her. "This woman said she'd lend me a cloth, help me make things look a bit more attractive." I pause when I see Nia's only half-listening. Still thinking about her mom and I can't blame her for that. "You're welcome to come along."

She shakes her head. "I think I'll find a place to wash up and then walk around for a while. I need to think a little. Maybe I'll try my . . . my mom again."

"Are you going to be okay?"

She gives me a brave smile that doesn't do more than twitch on her lips. "Sure. I'm fine."

"Well, you know where to find me," I tell her.

So we leave her there and head back to the park. Buddy's being real good about his collar and the leash. He's even got a bit of a bounce in his step except when someone passes us. Then he gets a little schizophrenic – fear swallows the happy puppy – and Velcros himself to the side of my leg. I tell him it's okay, and I can see he wants to believe me, but I guess old habits are hard to break.

I glance back once to see Nia still standing beside the phone booth. I feel bad for her and wonder if I've been entirely fair with her. Who's to say what happened to me couldn't have happened to her mother? It's not so much that I think it's impossible. Like I told Nia last night, after what's happened to me, I'm the last guy to say anything's impossible anymore. But if this is more than a singular phenomenon, then the rules have changed again and that scares me. Right now, all I have to do is figure out how Devlin worked his voodoo and either force him to fix the problem, or come up with a way to reverse it on my own. But if this is happening to other people, too, if it's some kind of random event – an act of nature, albeit a supernatural one, instead of the deliberate act of someone's will – then how will I ever get my life back again?

I look for Bones when I get past the food carts, but see he's already busy with some businessman, shaking those tiny bones of his onto the deerskin, reading something in the way they fall. I decide to see if Jenna remembered to bring me that cloth. I'll connect with Bones later. But then I see a familiar tangle of red hair. I start to smile, but my good humor only lasts until I get close to where Zeffy's standing. I see the guitar she's tuning and I go a little crazy.

XXII • ZEFFY

IT WAS going to be a bad day, Zeffy realized as soon as she got up and discovered that Tanya had never come home last night. She stood in the doorway of Tanya's bedroom and stared at the bed that so obviously hadn't been slept in. Silence clung to the apartment, an unhappy film of dusty stillness, as though the rooms had been untenanted for years. The empty feeling seemed to promise more trouble to come when Tanya did come home – the need for soul-searching and long talks and everything else that accompanied one of Tanya's downturns. The weight of it, the expectation of the long hours it would take to work everything through, bore down on Zeffy.

She didn't want to be unsupportive. It seemed so selfish. She felt guilty just for thinking of Tanya the way she was, but she didn't think she could face another round of it today. Because nothing was ever solved. The whole sorry mess would simply rear its head again – if not next week, then in two weeks. A month. It was hard for Zeffy to remind herself of Tanya's many positive qualities when the bad times rolled in, to remember the kind and generous spirit when it got swallowed by a dark cloud of depression. This morning she could feel a mood settling in on her, a malaise that was set to taint her whole day.

No, she thought. Screw this. I'm not going to buy into another one of Tanya's dramas. Not today.

She returned to her own bedroom, determined to put on a cheerful face to the world. Maybe if she pretended she was in a good mood, some of it would actually rub off on her. Rummaging through her clothes closet and dresser, she found a pair of blue-and-white striped cotton pants, baggy enough to be comfortable but not too clownish, a white T-shirt and a denim vest that she'd bought for two dollars at a rummage sale. She added her favorite high-tops and a touch of lipstick and headed out the door with Max Trader's guitar, determined to be on her way before Tanya should return to the apartment.

Once outside, she immediately felt better. It was another perfect day, and instead of taking the subway, she caught a crosstown streetcar so that she could enjoy the weather. Because it was midmorning, she had almost the whole car to herself, sharing it with a young mother and her infant and a pair of old men carrying a thermos and a chessboard who probably had the same destination in mind as she did. She felt sorry for anyone stuck working inside, but then they'd made their choice. She might not have acquired the accoutrements considered necessary for the modern life, but then she didn't have to work the long hours to pay for them either. Of course to have a guitar like this one she'd borrowed from Max Trader . . .

Zeffy sighed. Maybe there was something to be said about having some discretionary funds.

She held the case between her legs, arms wrapped around its neck in a loose embrace, and stared out the window as the city blocks went by. How many years would it take for her to save up and buy an instrument of this quality? She still couldn't believe that Trader had just up and lent it to her with only her old guitar for collateral. It was going to be such a treat to play it today. Then she had to smile. Anyone who knew anything about instruments wasn't likely to toss any change at her case this afternoon. They'd figure if she could afford a Trader, well, she didn't need the money, did she?

New passengers came, went or stayed, an ever-changing array as the streetcar stopped and started its way across town, from mailmen, high-school kids and street punks to older women going shopping, young mothers with toddlers in tow and Scandinavian and Filipino nannies with their infant charges. Two schoolgirls settled in the seat behind Zeffy, giggling about what someone named Cheryl had said to her boyfriend. In the seat ahead, two punky-looking girls of the same age, but with half-shaved heads and multiple earrings, gossiped about a knifing they'd witnessed in front of a club in Foxville the night before. When the streetcar stopped at the north gate of Fitzhenry Park, she and the two old men with the chessboard disembarked amidst a bustle of women, strollers, and infants. The punky girls got off as well, still talking about the knifing, except now they were commiserating over the fact that they hadn't got back to the club in time to see the band that had been slated to play that night.

Zeffy could only shake her head. Neither of the girls could have been much more than seventeen. Not many years separated her from them, and she'd been just as dedicated in making outlandish fashion statements at that age herself, but she couldn't imagine a time that she would ever have had such disregard for the victim of an attack as they'd witnessed last night. Had neither of them thought to stay and help the poor woman?

The whole situation just depressed her and she quickened her pace so that she wouldn't have to listen to them. Now, if it had been Johnny who'd gotten stabbed . . .

Catty, she told herself. Don't think about him or Tanya any more today.

But when she got to the area around the War Memorial, she couldn't stop herself from looking for him. She wasn't sure how she felt when he didn't seem to be around. She wanted to give him a piece of her mind – the *nerve* of him stringing her along the way he had with that stupid story of his – but some part of her also wanted to see him again.

This is so stupid, she thought.

There was no one in the spot where she'd played yesterday, so she decided to claim it again today. It had certainly proved lucky for her so far.

Except for meeting Johnny, she amended, and felt irritated all over again that she couldn't get him out of her head.

Tanya had been right about one thing last night: he'd got his hooks into her, no question. Charmed her in the same way he seemed to mesmerize everybody else. She didn't know how he did it. Even someone like Tanya, who knew he was stringing her along, still seemed so ready to forgive and forget. And as for herself . . . Zeffy sighed. She'd been immune to him before, so what had changed?

Taking the Trader out of her case helped her focus on something more pleasurable. She'd never played an instrument as good as this before. It was like the wood had a soul of its own and they were collaborating on the music, instead of it all having to come from her. She wondered if he'd lend it to her again some time so that she could use it to record a demo.

It was so easy to tune it, so easy to call up the music from its strings. Remembering the conversation of the two punky girls, she started off playing Richard Thompson's ironic "The World Is a Wonderful Place," knowing that half the people who stopped to listen wouldn't get it, but she didn't care. She sang it anyway. By the time she was through the song, the sheer pleasure of playing the guitar had swallowed her melancholy. She played a couple of more cheerful songs, then switched to an open tuning for an instrumental that she'd written years ago and hadn't played in months.

It was either the guitar, or she was simply on today, but the tune had never sounded so good. The crowd she'd drawn seemed to appreciate it as well. Gaze on her fingerboard, she was startled at the end of the piece when she looked up and saw the size of it. The crowd gave her a round of applause and she felt a hot flush rise up her neck to color her cheeks. It was still hard to get used to people liking her music.

Remembering Geordie's warning yesterday, she played one more song in the same open tuning, then took a break. Coins clattered in the case, along with a handful of one-dollar bills. She smiled her thanks and sat down on the grass to put the instrument back into a standard tuning. By the time she was done, most of the people had drifted away. She stood up and was about to start playing again when her heartbeat did a little flip.

Here came Johnny Devlin and his dog. They were both still fairly scruffy, but at least the dog appeared to have had a bath. She knew she should blast him for how he'd taken her in with his oh-so-earnest delivery of that outrageous story of his, but she was in too good a mood to spoil it with an argument. So she smiled at him and was completely unprepared for the blast of venom that came out of him.

"Where the hell did you get that?" he demanded.

"I beg your pardon?"

"Don't give me that crap."

He started to reach for the guitar, but she pulled it out of his reach, swinging it on its strap so that it hung at her back. Her good mood fled and she glared at him, every bad thing she remembered about him rising up in her mind.

"I don't know what the hell's the matter with you today," she began, "but don't even think of touching this guitar."

Johnny let his hand drop, but the anger stayed in his eyes, a smoldering fury that might have scared Zeffy if she wasn't so angry herself. Beside him, the dog stood trembling, picking up on his mood. Zeffy's heart went out to the animal, but not so much that she wasn't ready to stand her ground.

"Do you have any idea how much this instrument is worth?" she asked.

"Do you have any idea what it means to me?" he replied.

"I don't see how it can mean a bloody thing. I doubt you ever saw it before this moment."

"So he just gave it to you."

Zeffy shook her head. "Not that it's any of your business, but he lent it to me until he could do a fret job on my guitar."

"Until he does a fret job for you?" Johnny repeated. He shook his head and gave a mirthless laugh. "So I guess that means you can have it forever."

"You are so pathetic."

"At least I know how to repair a guitar. I'd love to see your boyfriend manage."

"First of all, Max isn't my boyfriend – I only met him yesterday."

"When he, out of the blue, lent you this priceless guitar."

Zeffy glared at him. "And second of all, he was inlaying this guy's name on a mandolin neck when I got to his shop."

"This guy."

"Some guy named Frank," Zeffy said. "What's the difference?"

"And he told you Frank was a guy?"

Zeffy nodded. "We were talking about the inlay. I thought it was kind of neat, having your name on the neck of your instrument, but he thought it was a bit of a joke."

"I would never laugh at someone wanting their name on one of my instruments."

"What's that supposed to mean?" Zeffy asked.

"A person wants their name on an instrument I make for them tells me just how much they respect my work. That it's not just some monetary investment for them, but something they're planning to keep and play for the rest of their life. Who'd laugh at something like that?"

"It wasn't like that," Zeffy told him. "I mean, it wasn't like he was mocking this Frank guy. We were just ... talking."

"Right. While he was doing the inlay on 'Frank's' mandolin. You saw him actually working on it, of course."

"What difference does it make?"

"And then you made such a wonderful impression on him that he just gives you my guitar."

"Not your guitar," Zeffy said. "*His* guitar. And he only lent it to me."

"I would never lend that guitar," Johnny told her. "Not to anybody."

Zeffy rolled her eyes. "Oh right. Mr. I-Switched-Brains-With-Max-Trader. How could I forget? Of course it'd be *your* guitar, wouldn't it?"

"You've played it," Johnny said. "Would you just lend it out to a stranger?"

"That's not the point. The point is Max made the guitar, not you. He decided to lend it to me, not you. This has got nothing to do with you except for this delusion you're dragging around with you to explain how screwed up your life is."

"You're right," Johnny said. "I didn't make that guitar – just the neck, and I still haven't got it right either, though I've gotten pretty close. Janossy made the body before he died. The perfect guitar body. I'm hoping that, before I die, I'll be able to fit it with the neck it deserves – the one he'd have made for it, if he'd been given the time."

"Janossy . . .?" Zeffy began, but then it clicked and she knew who he was talking about.

Sandor Janossy was to guitars what Antonio Stradivarius or Niccolo Amati were to violins. You were about as likely to find an old Janossy guitar at a rummage sale as you were a Strad – and for the same reason. What most people didn't realize about Stradivarius violins was that they were never lost in the first place. They were bought by the aristocracy in the 1700s and remained in the hands of people who understood what they had ever since. All those violins that could be found at swap meets and the like, with "Antonio Stradivarius, 1720" plainly visible when one looked in through the F-hole, dated back to the days of patent medicines when advertisers could put whatever they liked as a label on their product, make any outrageous claim at all.

Janossy guitars were all accounted for and changed hands with price tickets that made even a Trader seem cheap. Zeffy remembered that Max Trader had studied under Janossy for almost a decade – right up until the time Janossy died. All of which only meant that Johnny had done his research well. He had the information and the facts; unfortunately, his basic premise was unsound because no matter what he tried to get people to believe, Max Trader was still the luthier, and he was still the loser.

"Yeah, well, it's all really interesting," she told him, "but it doesn't make a whole lot of difference, does it? I'll admit, you were so convincing yesterday, you had me half-believing you, but you only get to jerk my chain once."

"I'll jerk more than your chain," Johnny said.

He took a step toward her and started to reach for the guitar again. Zeffy backed away.

Oh shit, she thought. If the guitar got broken . . .

"This guy giving you a hard time?"

She felt so grateful for interruption, more so when she saw that the man who'd spoken had been in the crowd listening to her yesterday – one of the people that had seemed particularly appreciative. Clean-cut and clean-shaven, he was a tall, broad-shouldered man in his early twenties with a wide face and honest eyes. He wore chinos and a short-sleeved shirt with a nametag sewn above the pocket that read HANK.

"He's trying to take my guitar," she told him.

"It's *my* guitar," Johnny said.

Hank stepped in between them, making Johnny back away from her. Johnny's dog pressed tight against his leg, shivering and shaking and looking more miserable than any animal should have to feel. That just made Zeffy even more angry.

"Look, fella," Hank told Johnny. "Why don't you take your problems away and then nobody'll get hurt."

"Why don't you mind your own fucking business," Johnny said.

He tried to step around Hank, but Hank would have nothing of it. He stiff-armed Johnny in the chest, making him stumble back. Every time Johnny tried to get his balance, Hank pushed him again until the dog got in Johnny's way and Johnny stepped on its paw. The dog squealed and Johnny fell down, tripping over the animal's back. He lost his grip of its leash and the dog scurried a few yards away where it cowered, chest against the ground. Johnny came up swinging.

He didn't get a chance to connect with Hank. In all the excitement, neither Zeffy nor either of the combatants had noticed the approach of a pair of policemen. The taller of the two grabbed Johnny's arm and gave him a push that knocked him back down onto the grass again. The other stepped in front of Hank, who held up his hands.

"I was just trying to help the lady," he said.

"Let's see some ID," the policeman told him.

"You, too," his partner said to Johnny. "Let's go. On your feet."

Hank took his wallet out and passed over his driver's license. Johnny got up and made a show of checking his pockets.

"I—" He cleared his throat. "It looks like I left my wallet at home."

"Somebody want to explain what this is all about?" the officer holding Hank's driver's license asked.

They all started to talk at once until one of the policemen made everybody stop. He got the story from them one at a time. Hank started, explaining how he'd seen Zeffy and

Johnny arguing. Before Zeffy could say anything, Johnny told the policemen that the reason they'd been arguing was because of this song she'd played, it was stupid, he knew, but it always drove him nuts and she went ahead and played it anyway. All Zeffy could do was look at him, wondering where this was going. But then she realized that Johnny wasn't about to get into the ownership of the guitar – maybe even he was beginning to realize that no one was going to believe his crazy story. She was tempted to tell the truth, to tell the cops he was crazy and just let them haul him away, but she relented. It wouldn't cost her anything to go along with him and more to the point, he was going to owe her one now, big time.

"That's pretty much what happened," she said. "It was supposed to be a joke, but it got out of hand. I didn't think he hated it *that* much."

"Uh-huh." The policeman turned back to Johnny. "So where do you live?"

"I . . ."

In for a penny, in for a pound, Zeffy thought.

"He's been staying with my roommate and me," she said, coming to Johnny's rescue again. She gave the policeman her address. "Just until he gets a job."

"Aw, Jesus," Hank said. "Isn't this typical? And here I thought she really needed a hand." He looked at the policemen. "Can I go?"

The officer with his license nodded and handed his ID back to him.

"I understand what you were doing, stepping in the way you did," he told Hank, "but next time, call an officer to deal with the situation."

"You got it," Hank said, and beat a quick retreat, fading

into the crowd that had gathered to watch the entertainment.

The officer who'd knocked Johnny down turned to Zeffy. "Can I see your busker's license?" he asked.

"I . . ."

Zeffy's heart went still. Now it was her turn to hesitate, but there was no one to step in and give her a hand. Then the other cop gave her a break.

"Forget about it, Tom," he said. "It's too nice a day." His gaze moved from Johnny to Zeffy. "Put it down to my being in a good mood and liking your music, lady. But I'm warning you. Either of you start something up again and we'll run the pair of you in. Understand? I'm not that nice a guy."

"Yes, sir," Zeffy said. "Thank you."

Johnny nodded and the policemen continued on their beat. Turning his back on Zeffy, Johnny went over to where his dog was still cowering in the grass and soothed it, stroking its fur and talking softly until it stopped shaking. He collected his end of the leash and stood up, walking back to where Zeffy was standing. The crowd around them had broken up and drifted off.

"You owe me for this," Zeffy told him.

"I *owe* you?"

"I saved your ass."

Johnny shook his head. "I don't think so. I think you're just feeling a little guilty about what you and your friends are doing to me – that's all."

"I can't believe you're saying this."

"Believe it." He sighed. "Christ, we both know what's going on here. What else is part of the deal for you – besides my guitar, I mean?"

"Johnny, this is getting way out of hand. I'll admit you've never been my favorite person, but you're acting seriously crazy and I really think you need some help."

"You're right about my needing help. You're just wrong about what kind I need. And my name's not Johnny."

"Have it your way," Zeffy said.

Maybe keeping the cops from dragging him off hadn't been such a good idea, she found herself thinking. Not when he was this out of it.

"Nothing's going my way," Johnny told her. "But that's going to change."

Oh-oh, she thought. "What are you going to do now?"

"If you're not involved with what's happening to me," he said, "then you've got nothing to be afraid of. It won't concern you. But if you are, you'd better warn your boyfriend that I'm coming for him."

"All I've done is borrowed a guitar and listened to your wild stories."

"Okay. So here's something else you can add to those stories: This 'guy' Frank whose mandolin your friend is supposedly working on is actually a woman named Frankie Beale. She plays in a bluegrass band called the Oak Mountain Girls. I just hadn't gotten around to finishing her whole name on the neck. Her number's in the book and you can ask her."

"I'm not going to call up some stranger just because you're trying to convince me that—"

"And the other thing," he went, not letting her finish, "is take a look inside that guitar you're holding and see what it says on the maker's label."

He started to walk away then.

"Johnny!" she called after him.

He turned and she took a step back when she saw the fury in his face.

"My name's Max. Got it?"

Zeffy swallowed thickly, but she forced herself to go on. "Okay. Whatever you want to call yourself. Fine. But you've got to get some help. If you go on like this . . ."

"Fuck you. Is that clear enough? Just stay out of my way or the same thing that happens to your boyfriend is going to happen to you."

He walked away again and this time she didn't call him back. She watched him stalk off down the path, the dog trailing mournfully behind him. People gave way to him, and no wonder. Everything about him exuded anger and the promise of violence.

She watched a young girl dressed all in black come up to him. He paused as she started talking excitedly to him, but he didn't give her much of his time, brushing her off with a few harsh words. She looked as much hurt as surprised. She began to say something else to him, but he handed her the leash and left her standing with the dog as he walked away. The girl stared at his receding back, obviously unhappy from what he'd said to her. Then a young Native American man, one of the fortune-tellers, approached him. They, too, had words, before Johnny snarled something at him and walked off once more.

Zeffy shivered. Johnny'd lost it, she realized. Totally. She *really* should have let the cops take him away. But it was too late for that now. What she had to do was call Max – warn him that Johnny was on his way and he was acting way crazy, capable of anything.

Max.

Zeffy hesitated a moment, then brought the guitar around

so that she could look through the sound hole and see inside the body. There was a small piece of off-white parchment glued where the neck joined the body. It read:

BODY FASHIONED BY SANDOR JANOSSY,
SUMMER 1984.
NECK BY MAX TRADER,
FALL 1989.

How could he have *known*?

Hold on a moment, she told herself. It didn't mean anything. It was just more of his research. He'd seen the guitar before, looked inside. But she remembered Max bringing it down from his apartment yesterday, the casual way he'd handled it. Like it was nothing. Just some old guitar. While Johnny . . . Johnny spoke of it with reverence, the kind of reverence she remembered Max expressing for his old mentor in the articles she'd read.

An eerie feeling settled in her. She looked across the park, but Johnny appeared to be gone now. Or at least she couldn't see him anymore. But she could still see the young dark-haired girl he'd left his dog with. She was standing where he'd deserted her, shoulders shaking.

Zeffy gathered the change in her guitar case and stuffed it into her knapsack. The guitar went back into its case and she closed the snaps. Hoisting it and her knapsack, she went to talk to the girl. As she closed the distance between them, she thought about Max yesterday, him telling her about the future owner of that mandolin he was making, the way he'd referred to him as a man. She compared that to what Johnny told her. She'd heard of the Oak Mountain Girls, of course – they were a popular, all-female bluegrass band based just north of the city – but she didn't know the name of their mandolin player. Maybe she would call this Frankie Beale – if there even was a listing for her. But first she'd talk to the girl with Johnny's dog. Then she'd . . .

She didn't know what she'd do. It was all so crazy. Except, crazy or not, Johnny was about to do something she couldn't let him do.

XXIII • MAX

ZEFFY'S RIGHT. I am crazy – but not the way she thinks. It's more as if I'm becoming Johnny Devlin, as though pieces of him that got left behind are trying to change me, Devlin antibodies trying to expel or at least neutralize the virus that's me. I can't imagine being Devlin, but I can feel the impulses. That's the kind of crazy I am and it scares me.

I could've hit her – that's just the kind of thing I can imagine Devlin doing. I could feel it building up in me. If that guy hadn't shown up, I don't know what might have happened. It wasn't simply Janossy's guitar. But seeing her with it, just casual as you please, out busking with it, like there was nothing special about it . . .

It reminded me too much of all that's gone wrong – how everything in my life is subject to Devlin's whims. My instruments, my tools, my wood. My life. If it had been him standing there instead of Zeffy, I think I would've tried to kill him. And I don't think this Hank would have been able to stop me.

Hank.

I almost want to smile, thinking of that nice little nametag sewn to his shirt. Once I would have done the same thing as him – stepped in to help instead of being the cause. But I told him to fuck off. Just as I told Zeffy fuck off. I don't think I've ever told anyone to fuck off before. Thought it, sure. But I've never said it like I meant it – with so much anger.

I have all these mood fluctuations. The depression and the hostility, especially – they're not me. Nor is this strange complacency I keep falling into, as though it's simply not worth the trouble to confront Devlin and take back what's mine, so why make the effort?

But right now it's the anger that's got hold of me. I've got so much anger in me at the moment that someone's going to get hurt. I can feel it building and I can't seem to control it. That's why I've decided to go after Devlin. If someone's got to be hurt, then let it be him. Not people I like. And speaking of people I like . . .

I wish there were some way to avoid seeing Nia right now, but she's already running up to me, looking so pleased with herself. I hope to God she got through to her mother and worked stuff out.

"Look at these," she says when she reaches us.

Buddy's still a little skittish around her, but he seems interested in what she's holding out. He moves a bit closer, body still pressed tight against my leg, neck stretched out, nostrils quivering. Nia's showing me a handful of flat, rounded pebbles with animals and designs drawn on them. Wolf, crow, what might be an otter, turtle. The borders are simple knotwork or reminiscent of Southwestern sand paintings.

"I got this permanent black marker at the art shop," she's saying, "and then I collected these stones down by our camp and drew on them. Aren't they neat?"

I don't want to bring her down, but I can't be around her right now.

"I thought we could sell them with your carvings," she adds.

"We'll talk about it," I tell her. "Later."

She gives me a questioning look. "What's happened? You look so mad."

"Now's not a good time for us to be together," I say.

"But—"

I don't let her finish. "Look, there's something I've got to do and it's better if I do it on my own."

"I don't understand. What do you have to do?"

What am I going to tell her? That I'm going to go beat on Devlin's head until he gives me back my life? That I think I'm turning *into* Devlin, another scummy loser who just drifts through life, using people, never caring about how they feel?

"I don't want to talk about it," I say.

"But maybe I can help you."

"I don't want your help."

I regret the words as soon as they come out of my mouth and I see the hurt they wake in her. But it's too late to call them back and I *can't* have her tagging along.

"Here." I hand her Buddy's leash. "Take care of him for me. He needs a friend as much as you do."

She takes the end of the leash automatically and I leave her standing there with the dog, Buddy whining, straining to follow, while she's only just managing to hold back her tears.

"But . . . but, Max . . ."

I don't turn, I don't even look back. I can't. I have to get out of here. I need to hit something so bad I can taste it and I want it to be Devlin's face. There's a smoldering burn deep in my chest and I mean to use it to give me the courage I need to confront him. I won't back down this time. He can threaten to call the cops, but I won't let him. I won't give him the time.

I walk fast so that Nia won't be able to catch up with me, but it's Bones who stops me before I leave the park. He's got this inscrutable expression on his face, but I know he's going to get on my case. I try to be polite.

"I'm in kind of a hurry," I tell him.

"I can see that." That scary look drifts into his eyes again, part clown, part wise man, the one that makes it seem as though he can see right into my head and read what I'm thinking. "I just want to collect my knife before you go."

I shake my head. "I think I'm going to need it for a little longer."

Could I use it on Devlin? I don't know. But I can threaten him with it.

"I'm not asking for it," Bones says. "I'm telling you. I didn't lend it to you for what you're thinking of doing with it."

I shake my head again. "You'll get it back."

He sighs. "I know that. It's you I'm worried about."

"Thought you told me that all you do is let people know where they stand. If they don't take your advice, then you're finished with them."

He nods. "So here's where you stand: You're carrying a shaman's knife and you're thinking of spilling blood with it. I'm telling you, don't. You piss the spirits off and they're going to want payback – big time – and blooding that knife is going to seriously piss them off."

I can't believe this line he's taking.

"Hey, save it for your customers," I tell him. "Maybe they buy into your mumbo jumbo, but I sure don't."

He doesn't say anything for a long moment, just looks at

me, studies me, as though he wants to remember my face. I'll give him this: he's good at what he does. I can't shake the eerie feeling that comes creeping up my spine, but I'm not letting him stop me either.

"If you blood that knife," he says finally, "I don't want you coming around me with it later – understand? I've got enough problems with my own without dealing with the spirits that'll be looking for you."

"Let it go," I tell him. "The only spirits in this park are what the winos are brown-bagging."

"If it's all such bullshit," he asks, "then what're you doing in that skin?"

He knows. I don't know why I'm surprised. My situation is right up his alley. Or maybe Nia's right. Maybe what's happened to me has happened to other people. Maybe it happens all the time and we just don't know it. Doesn't make the regular papers, but you can read all about it in the tabloids, just saying you actually get past the headlines in the supermarket and pick one up to read. Or you can talk to the self-proclaimed mystics like Bones here.

Doesn't change what I have to do.

"You told me to take my life back," I say. "Remember?"

"But I didn't tell you to take somebody else's in the process."

He thinks he's helping, like he's going to talk me out of this, wave his hand, throw those bones, declaim a little mojo and everything'll be better, but all he's doing is fanning the anger that's smoldering away inside my chest.

"All Devlin's got to do is give me back what's mine."

"And if he doesn't?" Bones asks. "If he can't?"

Like he knows everything. He doesn't know who Devlin is.

"Are you saying this is my fault?"

"How satisfied could you have been with your life," he says, "if someone else could step in and take it away so easily? This guy who's living your life – he wanted a change. But you've got to have wanted one, too."

"What the hell do you know about any of this?"

"I've seen it before," Bones says.

So Nia was right. I'm not the only one to lose my life.

"So who's behind it?" I ask. "Aliens? The government? Your spirits? Maybe you?"

"Nobody's behind it," Bones says. "Not the way you're thinking. It's more like you're in the wrong place at the wrong time. Someone's got a jones for a new life and you get caught in the cross fire. Or maybe you've both got a need and a kind of magic takes over, something connects. These things happen."

"These things happen? Christ, could we touch base with reality here."

"What's happened to you *is* part of reality – it's just a part of it that most of us don't understand yet."

"Happens all the time, does it?" I want to laugh, but all I can do is shake my head. "What? When the stars are aligned just right?"

"No. Mostly it's when the need is great enough."

"Get this," I tell him. "I had a good life. I didn't give it up. Someone took it from me."

He gives me the look you give a child when you think you're talking about something they couldn't possibly understand.

"Just leave the knife," he says. "You don't want to hurt anybody."

"Fuck you," I tell him. "You don't know what I want."

I leave him then, leave him and Nia and Zeffy and the park all behind, because I've got nothing else to say and I don't want to listen to any of them anymore. I don't have the patience left. All I've got is this anger and I don't care where it comes from – me, or some residual piece of Devlin that he didn't take with him when he discarded this body and assumed my life. It doesn't really matter, so long as it does the job and keeps me primed.

I look down at my clenched hands as I stalk across town. They're funny tools, these. They can create and heal, but not so easily as they can hurt and destroy. It's not the kind of thing I ever think about much. But Janossy did. Janossy thought about everything. The way he looked at it, everything has a philosophy, every little forgotten piece of the world and what's in it has its own gossip and history, stories big and small that connect it to the rest of the world. Understand that connectedness and balance, and a piece of wood can explain the secrets of the universe to you. You just have to be patient. You just don't force it, but let it come to you instead and then act appropriately.

Wu-sei.

That's what Bones doesn't understand. Right now, I *am* acting appropriately, doing what I should have done the first time I saw Devlin looking out at me from my own face. And I'll use whatever tool that comes to hand to do it.

XXIV • TANYA

TANYA AND Jilly had a busy time of it in the café that morning. With both Wendy and Anita calling in sick Wednesday, they had to work twice as hard covering the extra tables, but Tanya didn't mind. She liked it when it was busy. It made the day go quicker and besides, sharing a shift with Jilly was always entertaining. She was the most efficient waitress Tanya had ever worked with, but never seemed to be too busy to share a joke or a bit of gossip. One of her favorite pastimes was constructing elaborate life stories for the customers she didn't know, dropping a new outrageous tidbit Tanya's way whenever they were together behind the counter, or passing each other between the tables.

This morning she'd been convinced – or at least had tried to convince Tanya – that the man sitting by himself at table seven was a spy.

"Watch him reading the classifieds," she said when they were both getting fresh pots of coffee. "I swear he's using a decoder ring as he goes down the columns, reading secret messages in between the lines or something."

Tanya had glanced at the slightly overweight, balding man and had to smile. He leaned forward over his paper, his attention equally divided between the personal classifieds and this large ring on his right hand that he kept twisting, back and forth, back and forth. He couldn't seem to stop blinking either, though whether it was because of what he was reading or simply the early-morning sunlight, Tanya couldn't have said.

"Spies always eat a continental breakfast," Jilly confided. "It's like it's in their contract or something."

"He's not exactly James Bond material," Tanya said.

Jilly pretended to look carefully around her before she leaned close and whispered, "Have you ever heard the term 'mole'?"

Tanya had to stifle a giggle. With the shape of his body and the way he sat there blinking, he looked exactly like one – the small mammal, that is, not a double agent.

The spy was gone now, his table taken by a pair of morose young women obviously nursing hangovers – "The one on the left writes a humor column," Jilly informed her, "while the other's a stand-up comic."

"Okay," Tanya said. "I'll play straight man. What gives them away?"

"Sad clown syndrome. Professionally funny people are almost always glum when they're offstage, as it were."

She left Tanya smiling over that nugget of questionable wisdom to take her break. Tanya cleaned the table of her last customer, pocketing the meager twenty-five-cent tip, then went to put on another pot of coffee. She was wiping down the counter when a new customer came in and took a table across the café from where the two women were sitting. He was lanky, just this side of thin, light brown hair tied back in a ponytail, not exactly handsome, but friendly looking. Casually dressed – jeans, plain shirt, a cotton sports jacket.

Tanya tried to make up a story about him as she went to bring him a menu, but she didn't have Jilly's knack.

"Hi," she said when she reached his table. "Can I get you a coffee?"

"Sure."

She left the menu and fetched the coffeepot, returning to fill his cup.

"I'll let you look over the menu for a few minutes," she said, "then I'll be back to take your order."

"Actually," he said. "I'm here to see you, Tanya."

Tanya sighed. It didn't happen very often, but every once in a while some guy who'd seen one or more of those awful films she'd been in managed to track her down. Video stores were to blame. In the old days, B-films headed straight out to the drive-ins and then thankfully disappeared into the limbo realm of late, late, late movies. But no more. Now every bozo with a VCR could rent your career mistakes and watch them over and over again, ad nauseam. And then, of course, they knew you, didn't they? There was a connection between you – they could always feel it.

"Whatever movie you saw me in," she said, "I'm not that person. Okay?"

She'd never met him before, of that she was sure. But when he smiled, there was something about that smile, the slight smirk that dropped one corner of his mouth, the accompanying look in his eyes, that seemed oddly familiar.

"Feeling a little touchy this morning, are we?" he asked.

Why do I have to get them? she asked herself.

"Look, mister. I just work here, okay? If you want to order something, fine. Otherwise—"

He didn't let her finish. "Relax," he told her. "You should be happy to see me. I brought you a present."

She stiffened as he reached into the inside pocket of his sports jacket, but all he took out was an envelope. When he laid it on the table she made no move to pick it up.

"It's the money I owe you."

"You can't owe me anything. I've never seen you before in my life."

"Not looking like this, maybe. But you know me."

An eerie feeling came whispering up her spine. He was a complete stranger, yes, but at the same time she couldn't shake the sense that she did know him.

"Who . . . who are you?" she asked.

"That hurts, sweetheart. I know I look a little different, but are you telling me you really don't recognize your old lover Johnny Devlin?"

"J-Johnny . . . ?"

He leaned back in his chair, hooked an arm over the back. The body language was so impossibly familiar.

Tanya had to sit down. She put the coffeepot down on the table beside his envelope and pulled out a chair. Sat. Couldn't take her gaze from him. It was the other morning, all over again, except in reverse. Then it had been a stranger with Johnny's face. Now it was Johnny, wearing a stranger's features as casually as if he'd put on a new set of clothes.

"Hey," he said, leaning forward. "Are you okay?"

Tanya took a steadying breath and slowly let it out. "What do you think?"

"I know. It's weird, isn't it? Creepy weird. I've been walking around, looking like this, for a couple of days now and I still can't get used to it."

"It's not possible . . ."

"Two days ago, I'd've been agreeing with you, babe. But now . . ." He spread his hands between them, palms up. "Hey, I know who I am and this is definitely me – no matter who I look like."

"But . . . how?" The "how" came out in a kind of a squeak.

"That's the funny thing. I've been working on that – kinda hard not to. I mean, something like this happens and how can you stop thinking about it?"

Tanya didn't trust her voice anymore so she simply nodded.

"The way I see it," he said, "I just wanted out so bad, that something happened and I got out. I mean, I'd pretty much screwed up my life. No decent job and no real chance of getting one. I was about to lose my apartment. No real friends. And then there was you."

"Me?"

"Well, I screwed that up, too, didn't I? Treated you like shit when really, it was the last thing I'd ever want to do. But I couldn't seem to stop myself. It's like, when things are going bad and you start to brooding on them, they just seem to get worse, you know? All I ever wanted was to have something to offer the world that was different – something that could only come from me. I didn't want to be one more drone. I wanted to be something special. Because you deserve something special."

Tanya had been nodding along with what he was saying, because she understood all too well that need to leave one's mark, but he lost her at the end.

"What . . ." She cleared her throat and tried again. "What've I got to do with what's happened to you?"

"I think it happened because of you. I knew it was over between us, but I couldn't help but feel if things were different, if I was different, we could make a go of it."

"But—"

"So I fall asleep," he continued, cutting her off, "and all of that's floating around in my head – that *need* – and when I wake up, I *am* somebody different."

Tanya was coming to accept that this really was Johnny sitting across the table from her, but at the same time the rational part of her mind couldn't believe it.

"This isn't possible," she said.

It all came back to that. No matter what her senses told her, no matter what she'd experienced the other morning.

"I agree," he said.

"But—"

He smiled. "But here I am all the same. It's like God, or whoever's in charge, gave me that second chance, Tanya."

"What about the guy whose body you've taken?" she asked. "What about him?"

"I feel bad," Johnny said. "And that's the truth. I mean, it's not right – I get the new life and he gets stuck with the mess of mine. But I tell you, I've been trying my damnedest to set things right – I mean, it's only fair, right? Except the deal only seems to work one way. I can't get back to my body." He paused for a long moment. "Or maybe he just won't let me back in."

Tanya was starting to feel dizzy. She knew that if she tried to stand up, she'd probably fall flat on her face. So she gripped the edges of the table.

"Just tell me why you're here," she finally said. "What do you want from me?"

"I want to know if you'll give me another chance."

"What are you talking about?"

"You and me, babe," Johnny said. "This is the way I see it: We have to liquidate all of this guy's assets and the best way to do that is if we turn them into joint accounts – you know, we'll tell the bank that we're engaged or something. We wait a few weeks, then you can withdraw the money – see, your signature's going to stand up to the kind of scrutiny they'd give it like mine wouldn't because it'll be real. I don't have the knack of faking a signature and believe me, I've tried."

Tanya shook her head.

"I know what you're thinking," Johnny said, "but we're not cutting the other guy out. We divvie it up, give him a chunk of cash and take the rest to make a new start of it somewhere else."

This was giving her a headache.

"Why would anyone settle for part of what already belongs to them?" she asked.

"But it doesn't – not anymore. *I'm* Max Trader now and everything's in my name."

"Because you took it from him."

He shook his head. "I didn't *plan* this. How could anybody plan something like this? But the way I see it, he can't have been very happy with the way his life was going, or why would he buy into the switch?"

"Maybe he didn't have a choice."

"I swear," Johnny said. "I didn't run roughshod over anybody. And I tried to put things right. Now either it only works one way, or *he's* blocking it. I've been trying to find him, but it's like he took a hike. Just vanished."

Tanya shook her head. "Zeffy's met him. In fact, just last night she told me about going to your, I mean, to this Max guy's shop to check things out. She came back convinced he was who he was and Johnny was Johnny and it was all a scam."

She paused then, thinking. No wonder Zeffy had been so taken in. It really *hadn't* been Johnny she'd been talking to. Now she felt even worse about last night.

"Yeah," Johnny was saying. "I got a little freaked when she came in."

Tanya brought the jumble of her thoughts back to the conversation at hand.

"So why didn't you say something to her?" she asked.

"I don't think Zeffy should know." Johnny gave her one of his trademarked people-always-do-me-wrong looks and sighed. "You know how she feels about me. Even when things were good between you and me, she was always cutting me down."

Tanya nodded, remembering. Except Zeffy hadn't been very far off the mark, had she? Johnny *had* treated her badly.

"Now all I want to do is make things right," Johnny said. "We'll give the guy a decent cut, and then we'll go make our own start someplace else. I know we can do it, Tanya."

He looked so sincere it was hard not to believe him. People could change, couldn't they? She wasn't attracted to him anymore, but she was willing to hear him out. Only now she didn't know what to think. Maybe he was right about Max Trader. Maybe, for whatever reason, he didn't want his old life back either. Except ... She sighed. She couldn't believe she'd been having this conversation. Couldn't believe she was really buying into it – *and* thinking of helping him.

"I need a smoke," she said.

She got up before he could say anything, collected the coffeepot and headed back to the counter. Leaving the pot on the counter, she went into the kitchen and fished a package of cigarettes from the pocket of her jacket. But then, instead of taking them back out into the café, she sat down on a wooden fruit crate and lit one up. She took a couple of long drags, tapping off the ash into her palm for later disposal.

She started when the screen door at the back of the kitchen opened, but it was only Jilly returning from her break with Frank the cook in tow. Frank went to check on his soup of the day – an organic vegetable broth – while Jilly joined Tanya, pulling up another crate.

"Kitty's going to kill you for smoking in here," she said.

Tanya sighed. "Only if she finds out," she said, then she gave Jilly an exaggerated look of fake panic.

Jilly laughed. "I won't tell her."

Tanya smiled with her, but then the momentary good humor ran away again. She sighed and took another drag of her cigarette.

"So what's the matter?" Jilly asked. "And don't say 'nothing,' because you wouldn't be sitting here smoking if it was nothing."

"It's Johnny."

"What about him?"

Tanya jerked her thumb back toward the café. "He's in there."

"Well, we'll just get rid of him," Jilly said. She stood up and peeked through the small oval window in the door separating the kitchen from the rest of the restaurant. "You're okay. He's gone."

Tanya shook her head. "He . . . he doesn't really look like himself anymore."

Jilly turned her back on the door and sat down on the crate again. She leaned forward, eyes shining with excitement.

"You mean all that stuff about Johnny switching brains with somebody else is true?" she asked.

"Seems like it."

Tanya filled her in on the very weird conversation she'd just had with Johnny. As she spoke, she began to have her doubts again.

"Maybe he's trying to drive me crazy," she said. "He could've just gotten this guy to go along with it."

"That makes no sense. Why would he bother?"

"Don't forget," Tanya said. "This is Johnny. Do things ever make sense around him? Here's a guy who let his whole life go down the tubes because he couldn't be bothered to get it together enough to take care of regular business – the stuff everybody else has no problem dealing with."

"So test him," Jilly said. "Make him tell you something that only Johnny could know."

Tanya smiled. Of course. Why couldn't *she* have thought of that?

She took a last couple of drags from her cigarette and threw it out the back door, then returned to the café to sit back down at Johnny's table.

"I thought you'd deserted me," he said.

She made no response to that. "Tell me something that only you and I could know," she said.

"A test," he said, nodding. "That makes sense. Except I think you should ask me something that only I should know. I mean, if this is all faked. I would've prepped the guy, right?"

"Um, right."

Ask him what? she thought, her mind suddenly blank.

"Well?" he asked after a moment.

"What's my mother's maiden name?" she asked, saying the first thing that came to mind.

Johnny frowned. "Aw, come on. How am I supposed to know that? The only time I ever met the woman, she had this huge mad on, like who was I to be hanging around with her perfect daughter. So I was supposed to ask her her maiden name?"

That was actually a better response, Tanya realized, than if he'd been able to answer her question. Her mother had *not* been impressed with Johnny that day. But then her mother was never impressed with any of her friends.

"Okay," she said, "then how about . . ."

But before she came up with something else to ask him, the front door of the café opened and Geordie came sauntering in, fiddle case under his arm. He looked around the café and waved a greeting to Jilly behind the counter. When he spied Tanya, he smiled and came over to the table to join them.

"You're Max Trader, right?" he said to Johnny as he sat down beside Tanya. "It's nice to meet you."

Johnny frowned. "How'd you know my name?"

Geordie looked from him to Tanya, then back again.

"I just saw that piece on you," he said. "The one in *The Daily Journal*, and everybody knows your guitars."

When Johnny made no reply, Geordie turned to Tanya.

"So," he said. "Are you getting off soon?"

"This is a private conversation," Johnny said before Tanya could reply.

Geordie turned to him, his confusion obvious.

"I'm sorry?" he said.

Johnny gave an exaggerated sigh. "Do I have to spell it out for you? Take a hike, pal. We're talking."

"Johnny!" Tanya cried, mortified at his rudeness.

"Johnny?" Geordie said.

"Work it out someplace else," Johnny told him.

Geordie looked from her to Johnny, still confused, but flushed now. He looked a little angry, Tanya saw, but a little disappointed, too. Disappointed in her. She couldn't blame him.

"Maybe this is a bad time," he said.

"Now you've got it," Johnny said. "Go hit on somebody else's woman already."

"Will you just shut up," Tanya told him.

Johnny feigned being hurt, laying the palm of his right hand over his heart. How could she ever have been attracted to him?

"What's going on here?" Geordie asked.

"Yeah, what's going on?" Johnny repeated. He spoke in a whiny, mocking voice that deepened the flush on Geordie's cheeks.

Geordie stood up. "Okay," he said. "I can tell when I'm not wanted. Seems like I've stumbled into the middle of some old business and it's definitely not mine. See you round, Tanya."

"No, wait," Tanya said, but Johnny grabbed her arm before she could follow Geordie out the door.

The shock on Johnny's face when she slapped him almost

made the whole awful mess of the past few minutes worthwhile. He let her go and sat back in his chair. This time she was able to get up from the table. She shot a glance at Jilly.

"Go on," Jilly told her. "I'll hold the fort."

Smiling her thanks, Tanya hurried out the door. She saw Geordie down the block and called after him. At first she thought he wouldn't stop, that he wasn't going to let her explain. But she waited for a bus to go by, then called after him again in the relative quiet that followed in its wake. This time Geordie paused. When he turned to look back at her, she jogged down the street to where he was waiting.

"I'm really sorry about what happened back there," she said. "He can be such a pain."

"That's okay. You don't have to explain."

"But I want to. It's just . . ." Tanya sighed. "It's all so weird, I don't know where to start and you're *never* going to believe me."

"Try me," Geordie said.

He took her hand and led her off between a couple of stores to the grass verge that ran in back of the café and the other buildings fronting Battersfield Road. There they sat on a low stone wall overlooking the river and Tanya talked. She thought it'd be hard, but Geordie gave her his undivided attention, encouraging her whenever she began to falter, and the whole story came out. And strangely, considering all the stress of the past hour or so, she didn't even find herself wanting a cigarette.

XXV • JOHNNY DEVLIN

BACK AT his table in the café, Johnny gingerly touched his cheek where a red welt was forming. He stared at the envelope of money he'd laid on the table earlier.

"Fuck," he said.

Picking it up, he stuffed it into his pocket, then lifted his head. The two women sitting at a table across the café quickly looked away when his gaze went to them. Then he saw Jilly leaning on a nearby table, arms folded across her chest.

"Yup," she said. "You really are Johnny Devlin. Or as close to an asshole as he ever was to make no difference."

Johnny's eyes narrowed. "What's it to you?" he asked.

"Nothing," Jilly said, smiling. "I'm just going to stand back and watch you make a mess of this life, too – that's all."

"You don't know what the hell you're talking about."

Jilly shrugged. "So it doesn't matter, does it?"

"Christ save us from flakes and do-gooders," Johnny muttered.

"What was that?" Jilly asked.

He didn't bother answering. Instead he got up from the table and headed for the door.

"That's a buck fifty for the coffee," Jilly called after him.

He turned, some choice retort sitting there on the tip of his tongue, until he caught sight of the café's cook leaning against the wall by the kitchen door, watching him. He pulled a handful of change from his pocket and dropped it on the nearest tabletop.

"Happy now?" he asked.

"I'm always happy," Jilly said. "It's like this gift I have."

"Yeah, well, fuck you, too," Johnny told her, but he couldn't muster much conviction in the sentiment.

He turned and left her to collect the change he'd tossed on the table. Once outside, he looked up and down the street, but there was no sign of either Tanya or the guy with the fiddle.

Okay, he thought. Fine. I can do this without her help. It would've been easier, putting her name on Trader's accounts and having her withdraw the money. Would've been nice having someone help him sell off all this crap Trader owned, too. But he could do it on his own. No problem.

He gave the front of the café a frown, then started walking back to Trader's apartment.

Some people, he thought, remembering the way Jilly had treated him, were just so full of themselves.

XXVI • NIA

NIA STOOD there with her fetish pebbles fisted tightly in her hand, all the joy she'd found in making them now drained away. Holding Buddy's leash in her other hand, she stared at Max's receding back. She managed to not cry and that was about it. Her legs trembled and her throat felt thick, too thick to breathe properly. Behind her eyes, the pressure of tears threatened to blur her vision. There was a sudden hollow place deep in her chest because she realized that she was completely alone now. There was no one left to turn to. First her mother had been stolen from her, now some kind of new craziness had rooted itself in the man she'd come to accept as Max and she couldn't trust him anymore either.

She watched him have an argument with one of the

fortune-tellers, and then he was stalking off through the thinning park crowd, out onto the sidewalk paralleling Palm Street, and gone. Still fighting tears, she turned away. He hadn't said it in so many words, but she knew where he was going: to kill the guy who'd stolen his body. She couldn't suppress a shiver.

Maybe she'd been wrong. Maybe he hadn't really been Max – or only part of Max, the rest a stranger. The rest, a piece of darkness with a silver tongue to make you trust him. To let him draw you in before he hurt you, too. Maybe he'd been there all along, sitting in his own head pretending to be Max, but he was in Max's and her mother's as well, riding them like they were puppets, taking what he needed out of their memories to get people like her to accept him.

She shivered again.

Only why? What was the point of it all?

Because things just happened, she realized. She remembered asking her mother once – her *real* mother – about why bad things happened to people. How did it get decided, who died in a fire or who got hit by a car?

"I guess that's the difference between believing in God or not," her mother had replied. "If you believe in God, you have to say it's His will, even if you don't understand why. If you don't believe in God, then it's all random, no more than the luck of the draw." She'd regarded Nia unhappily, as though disappointed in herself for not being able to do more than answer one question with others. "I don't know which is worse," she'd added after a few moments.

Nia didn't either. Because you couldn't feel safe no matter which you believed in. You didn't feel safe, thinking about it, and you especially didn't feel safe when whoever it was, God or chance, had turned its attention on you.

She swallowed thickly. Stuffing her fetish pebbles into her

pocket, she bent down to give Buddy a pat, needing the comfort as much as giving it, but the dog cringed away from her.

"Don't be like that," she whispered to him. "I'm not a bad person. I'd never hurt you."

But Buddy crouched, backing away from her, belly to the ground, ears twitching. He had an unhappy look in his eyes. He knew Max had abandoned him, she thought. Just as Max had abandoned her.

"He looks scared," someone said. A woman's voice.

Nia looked up to see that one of the park's buskers had stopped beside her, a red-haired woman carrying a guitar case. It took her a moment to remember that she'd seen Max talking to her, just before he'd left Buddy with her and stalked off. She felt a little nervous – anything to do with Max made her feel nervous now – but the woman gave off such a sense of warmth and caring that it was hard to maintain her jumpiness.

"I guess someone wasn't very nice to him at some point in his life," Nia said.

The woman crouched down and put out her hand, but Buddy backed away from her as well, belly still low to the ground, tail between his legs now. The only thing that was keeping him from bolting, Nia thought, was the leash. She held her end a bit tighter. The woman raised her gaze to Nia and shrugged.

"He doesn't seem to want to make friends with me, either," she said.

"I sort of just got him."

"I know," the woman said. "My name's Zeffy. Do you feel like talking to me for a couple of minutes?"

"What about?"

"Johnny Devlin."

"I don't know any—" Nia broke off. "Oh, you mean Max."

Zeffy moved off the path and sat down on the grass. After hesitating a moment, Nia joined her. She had to give Buddy's leash a tug before he reluctantly followed.

"So he's laid this Max business on you as well," Zeffy said.

"Well, he is Max," Nia said. "I mean, I know Max and . . ." She sighed. "This is so confusing."

"You're telling me. I take it you believe this business about them switching brains or whatever?"

Nia sighed. "I guess it sounds pretty stupid when you say it like that. But . . ."

"He's convincing."

Nia nodded. She looked down at her jeans and picked at a loose thread.

"Do you want to talk about it?" Zeffy asked.

"What for?"

When Zeffy didn't answer, Nia looked up, searched her face. Zeffy regarded her sympathetically, but Nia wasn't sure she bought the sympathy. It felt too much like she was setting herself up to be hurt again. She wished Buddy trusted her, wished he would press up against her leg the way he did with Max. She'd feel braver then.

"I bought it, too," Zeffy said finally. "Not once, but twice. I know it's all bullshit, but even now I find myself more willing to believe him than not and it's making me crazy."

"I know that feeling," Nia said.

"So how do you know him?" Zeffy asked.

Nia hesitated, then said, "Depends which him you're talking about. Max moved into the apartment downstairs about six months ago. I've never met this Johnny Devlin."

Unless he really was sitting there in behind those stranger's eyes, assuming what he needed of Max's personality to convince her.

"And you're convinced it's your friend Max in Johnny's body?" Zeffy asked.

"I was – until he just blew me off."

Zeffy's eyebrows rose questioningly.

"But it's not just Max," Nia said. "It's my mom, too."

She found herself describing what she'd heard that morning outside of Max's apartment, then seeing her mother kissing the other woman, running away, meeting up with Max again.

"But he's acting different now," she said. "I think he's going after the other guy. I think he's going to kill him and that's something Max'd never do – not the Max I know."

"You know him that well?"

Nia nodded. She'd spent too much time downstairs in his workshop to not feel that she knew him.

"I don't know," Zeffy said. "It's all so improbable. Why Johnny? Why Max?"

"But it's not just them."

Zeffy gave her another of those sympathetic looks. "I know you feel weird about your mother," she began, "but—"

"You're just as bad as Max," Nia said. "Why's it so impossible when it comes to my mom? Why's it possible for Max and Johnny, but not her? Even he didn't believe me and he knows how it can really and truly happen firsthand."

"But if Johnny's running some scam," Zeffy said, "then where does that leave you?"

Nia shook her head. "It's not like that."

"Look. Your mom must know you're homophobic, so

it's not like she's going to come out and tell you that she's gay."

"I'm *not* homophobic!"

"Then why are you taking it the way you are?"

"You don't get it. You don't know her. This is my *mom* we're talking about."

Zeffy sighed. She looked away across the park for a long moment, before turning back to Nia.

"You're right," she said. "I don't know her. But what if it's a new thing for her, too? The media might be romanticizing gays at the moment, but most people grew up thinking there was a stigma attached to it. That kind of thinking doesn't change easily – not even in the present social climate." She paused a moment, then added, "How old is your mother?"

"Thirty-eight. But what does that have to do with anything?"

"It just puts her in the right generation to still feel ashamed and embarrassed of her feelings. She's probably as confused about it as you are."

Nia thought about that, about how strained their relationship had been lately, how everything had seemed off-kilter and weird.

"Why wouldn't she just tell me?" she said.

She wasn't asking a question, thinking aloud really, but Zeffy reached out and covered her hand, giving her fingers a squeeze.

"Maybe she was trying to find a way to get around to it," she said. "It wouldn't be the easiest thing to bring up with your daughter."

Nia nodded glumly. Especially not with the way things had been between them lately.

"You should try talking to her about it," Zeffy said.

"Have someone else there with you when you do, so you'll feel safe – you know, in case she's really not herself – but . . ." She shrugged.

"But you don't believe it."

Zeffy shook her head. "Not about your mom and not about Johnny and Max. I don't know what's going on with them, but switching brains can't be part of the answer. It's just not possible."

"But what if it is?" Nia said, remembering the look in Max's face when he'd left her with Buddy. Max, Johnny, whoever it was. "Somebody's going to get hurt."

"People have already been hurt," Zeffy said. "My room-mate Tanya for one. This whole business has really messed her up. She used to go out with this guy and now he acts like they've never met."

"I don't mean that kind of hurt."

Zeffy nodded. "I know what you mean." She sat up a little straighter, looking over to where the fortune-tellers were working the crowd. "Maybe that guy he was talking to after he left you knows something."

Nia remembered. "The Indian," she said, turning to look herself.

But the man was gone.

"Well, there's one other person we can talk to," Zeffy said. "It's this friend of mine named Jilly. If anybody's going to be able to make sense of this, she will. Are you up to seeing her?"

Nia's nervousness returned. She didn't know anything about this woman or her friend.

"Is it . . . far?" she asked.

"No, she's working at the café today – Kathryn's, over on Battersfield Road. We could walk." Her gaze traveled to Buddy. "Actually, with him in tow, we'll have to walk."

Nia knew the restaurant, though she'd never been inside. At least it was a public place.

"You'll like her," Zeffy said when she saw Nia hesitating. "She's really sweet."

Yeah, but who's she got living in *her* head? Nia wanted to ask. Who've you got living in *yours*? Instead, she rose to her feet. They both had to coax Buddy into coming with them. Nia felt awful the way he slunk along beside them, flinching at every person passing by.

This was really mean of you, Max, she thought, just deserting Buddy like this. Really mean.

And it made her all the more uncertain as to who it had been wearing that stranger's body in her company last night and this morning, because the Max she'd known hadn't had a mean bone in his body.

XXVII • MAX

CLIMBING THE stairs to the hallway outside my apartment, I realize I'm not nervous this time. I've got too much of a burn on, an unfamiliar smoldering anger that's sitting deep in my chest and fuels my courage. I ring the buzzer, give the door a couple of bangs with the heel of my hand. No answer. Either Devlin's not in, or he's not answering. I don't really much care which it's going to turn out to be. I want a showdown, but there are things I need here as well.

I go back downstairs and circle around to the rear of the building. It's quiet in the lane, no one paying any attention to me except for a couple of sparrows sitting on the edge of the garbage bin that I startle as I come around the corner. I make my way up the metal stairs of the fire escape to my kitchen window and pause there on the landing to study it for a moment. The screen pops off easily and with the window open a crack, I have no problem fitting my fingers under the bottom rail and lifting it up. I listen for any sound from inside. Nothing. I poke my head in to look around. Everything's still quiet.

Maybe he did the world a favor, I think as I climb in, and died in his sleep or something.

It feels different inside. Nothing looks right. Then I realize what it is. Not Devlin's presence – he hasn't been here long enough to put a mark on the place. It's more like wearing a pair of high-heeled boots in a room where you've never worn them before. The perspective's off. Not by a lot, just enough to make things seem a little askew. That's the way it feels standing here in Devlin's body. It brings home my situation all over again and stokes the burn in my chest. I'm wishing now he *were* here so that we could have it out, here and now, winner take all.

I move from the window into the center of the kitchen and look at the mess. Maybe I'm wrong about Devlin not having had time to make his mark. Dirty dishes everywhere. Empty soup cans on the counter. A couple of cupboard doors ajar. Box of cereal on the table, a half-finished package of soda crackers beside it. A sour smell comes from the garbage – chicken gone bad. Lovely.

Most of the reason I'm here is to confront Devlin and I feel let down. But at least I can grab a few things to make my life a little easier. I start with my old canvas knapsack, pulling it off the top shelf in the hall closet. Haven't used it in years and it smells a bit musty, but it beats the plastic job I bought last night. The spare key for the shop catches my eye, hanging there just inside the closet door. I fish it off its hook and head downstairs, leaving the door of the apartment open behind me.

There's less of Devlin's presence in the shop. He's been through all my papers and the desk's awash with them, but otherwise things are pretty much the way I left them. I go to the cash register, turn it on and hit No Sale. The cash drawer slides open. He's taken all the large bills, but there's still almost forty dollars in ones and twos. I stuff the money in my pocket, then look around.

What else do I want?

I settle on some carving tools – the palm-handled set that Janossy left me and the long-handled detail carving tools that had been my father's, the tips protected with pieces of wine cork. I wrap them in cloth and put them in the bottom of my knapsack, adding a handful of antique chisels and gouging tools that I've collected over the years, a sharpening stone and a pair of opinel knives, the high-carbon blades folded into their hardwood handles. Neither of the latter are as good as the one Bones lent me, but they'll do.

I look around a little more, hesitating beside Frankie's mandolin. I feel bad, leaving it unfinished, knowing how much she's been counting on it, but I can't overburden myself.

Back upstairs, I add a few more things to the knapsack – a photo of my father and mother, taken on their honeymoon. Janossy's leather-bound journal, filled with his spidery handwriting and sketches. A pair of flannel shirts, some socks, underwear, my traveling toilet kit. I wish I could take my hiking boots, but they wouldn't fit Devlin's feet. My feet. Whatever.

On the way back to the kitchen, I spy my wallet lying on the sideboard. Devlin's taken all the cash, but my credit cards are still in it. And my bank card. I smile for the first time since I got here and pocket the lot of them and leave his wallet and address book in exchange. I didn't want to use Devlin's ID when the police asked me because that felt too much like buying into the lie. I feel better with my own wallet, even if the photo on my driver's license doesn't match the face I'm wearing. Funny how a few pieces of paper can make you feel better.

What else?

The momentary good humor fades as I realize how little I really need to take with me. There are books, instruments, recorded music, a chair my father and I built, but nothing I can't live without. When I study my belongings, I realize that, yes, they make a statement. They say who I am. But beyond my obvious profession, that person is a cipher. And the people he knows? How do they see him?

I remember that first morning I woke in Devlin's body. It seems like a hundred years ago now. But what I'm thinking about is how I needed to contact someone, needed a connection to who I knew I really was, and there was no one. There is no one. The closest thing I've got to a friend is Nia and she's just a kid. A good kid, but it's not like having a common history with someone. I've only know her for six months, since I first moved here.

How do you get to a point in your life like this, I find myself wondering. How can you get to my age and have nobody important in your life? Lots of acquaintances, but no friends. I might as well really be a street person – no one to turn to, nowhere to go.

I'm veering into the maudlin and get depressed just thinking about it. Depressed and angry, though my anger's not really directed at Devlin anymore. If I could aim it at something and let it loose, I would. But I can't. I'm not even sure I know why I'm so angry. All I know is that Bones was right. There was so little to hold me to this life that it's no wonder Devlin was able to take it away and claim it for his own. I certainly wasn't doing very much with it.

I lived in a routine, my only real outlet the instruments I built, and what the hell does that say about me as a person?

I can't get out of there quick enough. Shouldering my knapsack, I step out into the hall, close the door behind me. I hesitate for a moment, thinking of Nia again. Maybe I left myself open to a future that puts me on the street, but there's no reason for her to be there. I should never have let her hang around in the shop as much as I did. I should have encouraged her to get out more, meet people her own age, live.

The smile I feel twitching on my lip has no humor in it. Right. Get out and meet people. Live a little. Advice I could have used for myself, when you come right down to it. But just because my life's a mess doesn't mean hers has to be, too.

I start up the stairs to her apartment and knock on the door, but there's no answer there, either. I wish I'd taken a pen and some paper from my own place so that I could leave a message. I hesitate, trying to decide if it's worthwhile to go around by the fire escape and in through the kitchen window again to get one. But then, from below, I hear footsteps on the stairs.

Devlin, I think. But I'm not so ready to meet him now. I've got some things to work through first. It's not just getting my life back anymore, but what would I do with it if I did? There has to be some point to the way we live, doesn't there? But the anger's back, smoldering in my chest. I want to hit something again – preferably Devlin. I clench my hands into fists, then force them open. Force myself to steady my breathing.

Where's this anger coming from?

Same place as the sudden depressions – I'm sure of it now. Residues of Devlin bleeding through into my own personality. Does that mean he's getting more easygoing? More boring? Falling into routines?

I decide to wait here on this landing until he goes into my apartment. A confrontation's due, but now's not the right time. I need to think. I need to talk to Bones, I guess. He's the only one who seems to know what's going on.

But the footsteps don't stop at my apartment. A momentary panic hits me. I want to hide, but there's no place to go. Then I see it's Nia's mother coming up the stairs. She looks terrible, like she hasn't slept in days. Worn down with worry. I knew Nia was wrong. I knew nobody'd stepped into her mother's head the way Devlin stepped into mine.

She notices me and gets a wary look that confuses me until I realize she's not looking at her neighbor, standing here outside her door, but a stranger.

"Ms. Fisher?" I say, pitching my voice low. Calming.

She makes a decision and comes up the rest of the way. Or maybe she's simply too tired to be afraid.

"Whatever you're selling," she tells me, "I'm not interested."

I step aside so that she can get by me. She pauses in front of her door and leans against the wall, but makes no move to fish out her keys and unlock the door. I don't blame her.

"I'm not selling anything," I tell her.

She's dead on her feet. Dark shadows raccooning her eyes, shoulders, her whole body, sagging.

"Whatever you want," she says, "this is not a good time.

I've just spent the night sitting in the hospital, waiting to hear if a friend's going to make it through the night, on top of which my daughter's suddenly taken it into her head to readjust her life so that I'm not in it."

"I understand. That's part of the reason why—"

She doesn't give me a chance to say my piece. "So could you please just go," she says. She's not making a question of it.

"I'm here because of Nia," I say.

She studies me for a long moment, looking more carefully this time – trying to figure out where I fit into her daughter's life. I don't know what she sees, but at least she's listening now.

"I just wanted to let you know that she's okay."

"Who are you?"

"Nobody. Just a friend. I ran into her in Fitzhenry Park." She doesn't say anything, so I go on. "She's convinced that you're not really her mother anymore – that there's someone else in your head."

Now it's my turn to study her, but her only reaction is one of tired disbelief.

"Do you realize how ridiculous that sounds?" she says finally.

You don't know the half of it, I think, but all I do is nod.

"I know," I say. "I told her the same thing myself. But she . . ." I hesitate. "I know none of this is my business. I'm just telling you what she thinks."

"And what does she think?"

"Well, she saw you with a woman . . . kissing her . . . and . . ."

My voice trails off.

"Is that what this is all about?" she says. She shakes her

336

head, the weariness settling over again. "Well, it's my own fault, I suppose." It's like she's forgotten I'm here. She's looking past me, into the stairwell, thinking aloud. "I should have talked to her. I should have told her. But where do you even start with something like this?"

I hold my peace, wait for her to finish. Her gaze finally focuses back on me.

"Will you be seeing her again?" she asks.

"It's likely. She's taking care of my dog for me."

That pulls a vague smile from her. "She always did want a dog. I just didn't think it would be fair, living in an apartment the way we do."

"I used to feel the same."

She nods. "Well, could you tell her to come home? Or at least ask her to call me? I know we have things to work out, but her running away isn't the answer."

"I'll tell her." I hesitate a moment, then add, "I'm sorry about your friend."

"My friend . . .?"

"The one you said was in the hospital. I hope everything works out."

She nods again. "Me, too." The tiredness leaves her eyes for a moment. They flash with an anger I recognize. "We were just out looking for Nia and this guy stabbed her." Her gaze pins me. "What kind of a world are we living in where this kind of thing can just happen? Casual, random violence. Julie gets stabbed and it doesn't mean anything to anyone except to me – trying to make sense of it – and Julie lying there in intensive care, fighting for her life."

"I'm sorry."

"He wasn't," she says. "The guy that stabbed her. He just took off and ran, but he wasn't sorry. What does that say about the way we live?"

"I don't know."

I really don't. Except it reminds me that no matter how bad you've got it, somebody else has always got it worse. It's not exactly a comforting sentiment.

"You should get some rest," I tell her. "I'll give Nia your message."

"Thank you."

The fire's gone from her eyes and she's using the wall to keep herself upright again. I'd like to give her a hand, help her inside and put her to bed, but I know the best thing I can do right now is give her some space and leave. So I do. I don't hear her door open until I'm almost on the ground floor.

It's brighter outside than I feel it should be – like coming out of a matinée and the afternoon sun surprises you. I stand there blinking, adjusting to the light as the foyer door closes behind me. It's not just the relatively poor light from inside the hallway. I'm carrying a piece of Lisa Fisher's darkness with me now as well.

What kind of a world are we living in where this kind of thing can just happen?

I wonder if the world's getting worse, or if we're just paying more attention to the shadows.

There's no answer for me, out here on the cobblestoned street. No answer to my own dilemma either. So I start walking back to Fitzhenry Park, hoping I'll be able to find an answer there. Wondering if Bones will even talk to me after the way I laid into him earlier. I have bridges to mend with Nia, too. And Buddy. I promised him I'd never walk out on him and look what I've done. Dumped him on Nia and just took off, ready to commit some of that violence that Lisa Fisher was railing against. If I'd had Devlin in front of me at that moment, I'd've been just like

338

the guy that stabbed her friend. I wouldn't have felt sorry either.

What does that say about the way we live?

I feel tired then, soul-tired, as though I've taken some of Lisa Fisher's weariness as well as her darkness out into the street with me. I want my life back. I want to negotiate my freedom. But I'm not even sure what any of that means anymore.

I pay no attention to my surroundings as I make my way out of the Market and walk downtown. The crowded sidewalks could belong to another city entirely. Some strange alchemy allows me safety as I navigate streets against the light, walk unaware into oncoming traffic, oblivious of the car horns and angry cries of the drivers. I'm so busy looking inside that I see nothing of my walk back to the park, not the store windows, not the cabs and buses and cars, not the passersby, not the presence of the man who stole my life as he follows me.

You'd think I'd at least be aware of him. But I'm not. Not until it's too late.

XXVIII • TANYA

WHEN TANYA finally ran out of words, she turned from her view of the river to look at her companion. She didn't see the disbelief she'd expected. Didn't even get the sense that Geordie was simply humoring her. Instead, he smiled, then leaned closer so he could put his arm around her shoulders. An unfamiliar self-consciousness swept over Tanya. She felt like a teenager again. It was like one of those rare times that she'd finally managed to escape her parents' attention for long enough to sneak off with a boy. Those liaisons never lasted very long – in retrospect, why should they have, they were all so young, both she and the teenaged boys who paid court to her.

She felt the same awkwardness with Geordie, but she hoped this would be different. It already felt different and not simply because Geordie was so shy and everything was moving at a far slower pace than she was used to in a relationship.

"If somebody told me the kind of story I just told you," she said, "I'd be having real serious thoughts about getting cozy with them."

"Why's that?" Geordie asked, his voice slightly muffled. His cheek rested against her head and he spoke through her hair.

"Because it's so crazy."

Geordie drew back so that he could look at her. "Crazy weird, or crazy impossible?"

"Both. I mean, really. How can you take it all so matter-of-factly?"

"I'll tell you the truth," he said. "I've never been that comfortable with the wild and wonderful side of life that most people don't even think about, little say see. But if you hang around with someone like Jilly as much as I do, you end up having to accept it. When you're with her, the thing waiting for you around the corner is never what you expect it to be."

"Really?"

Geordie nodded. "And if Jilly wasn't enough, there's my brother Christy. I've been denying their more fanciful notions for most of my life, but there comes a time when the weight of their convictions gets to be too much and you have to give in."

340

Tanya gave him a considering look. She'd only ever browsed through one of Christy's collections of urban folklore – and that was for the giggle it gave her, not because she took any of it seriously.

"And besides," Geordie went on. "Once or twice I've seen an odd thing myself. Nothing that couldn't be explained away if you really worked at it, I suppose, but when you start to put them all together . . ."

"But flower fairies and talking pigs and – what was that one with the crocodiles?"

Geordie smiled. "I think it was a subway conductor."

"Isn't it all pretty far-fetched?"

"Very much so. But people swapping brains isn't?"

Tanya sighed. "Okay. But still . . ."

"I'll admit it," Geordie said. "Both Christy and Jilly tend to mix up strange occurrences with things they've only imagined. But that doesn't mean that some of what they talk about isn't true."

"Such as?"

Geordie shrugged. "I don't know. I think the whole thing boils down to the idea of conceptual reality that they both hold."

Tanya gave him a blank look.

"It's the idea that things are the way they are only because enough people have agreed that's the way they are. Their reality might be far different – it's only our consensus that gives them their current appearance."

"Do you believe that?" Tanya asked.

"Well, on some levels it makes a certain amount of sense – mostly late at night, I'll admit, when everything feels different anyway. Or at twilight, when things shift around simply because of the light."

Tanya shivered. "I've never liked that time of day."

"Really? I've always felt it was magical. Comes from having read too many fairy tales and folk stories, I suppose."

"If it's magical," Tanya said, "then it comes from the darkest part of the wood."

"Sometimes you have to go through the wood – if you want to get to the other side, that is."

"Face your fears."

Geordie nodded. "Something like that. If you want to view it as metaphor instead of literally. But to get back to this idea of consensual reality, to take it the step further, if you have someone who – for whatever reason – can see beyond, or happens to stumble out of that agreement we all have, then who knows what they'll experience?"

"Except is it real?" Tanya wanted to know.

Geordie shrugged. "Who knows? To them it is. And when it comes to matters of the mind and heart, sometimes that's more important: not what a thing actually is, but what a person perceives it to be."

"So this business with Johnny and Max . . . where does it fit in?"

"That's something you'll have to ask them." He smiled. "Or Jilly."

Tanya remembered Jilly's excitement when she'd told her about all of this back at the café. Tanya had been so relieved at the time to have someone to talk to about it that she hadn't even thought to question Jilly's easy acceptance.

"Maybe a better question," Geordie said, "would be, what do you think?"

"I don't know. I just wish it would all go away. And I *really* wish I hadn't had that fight with Zeffy last night. I feel just terrible about it."

"She's a good person," Geordie said. "She'll understand."

"I don't know that I deserve a friend like her. It must be so hard living with someone like me who gets so easily depressed."

Geordie laughed. "That's funny. She said the same thing about you to me once."

"When?"

"We were talking about finding time to practice and she was telling me how when she's playing in her bedroom, she loses all track of time and you end up doing most of the cleaning and cooking and stuff around the apartment." He smiled. "Which is when she said, 'I don't know what I ever did to deserve a friend as patient as her.'"

Tanya returned his smile. "I guess we suit each other."

"I guess you do." Geordie hesitated a moment, then added, "So what are you going to do?"

"Apologize to her the first chance I get."

"No, I meant about this other business."

Tanya leaned back against him, snuggling close.

"I don't want to think right now," she said. "Not about that – not about anything. I just want it to all go away."

His arm was comforting around her shoulders, the light weight of his cheek against her head something she felt she could hold up forever.

"Problems never go away by themselves," he said. Before she could comment, he added, "But that doesn't mean you can't take a break from them."

"That's what I need. A little breather."

"Take as long as you like," he said.

What she'd like, Tanya thought, was for him to kiss her. Not a big production, but she wanted that closer contact. And if he was too shy . . .

She drew back a little, and turned her face to his. Only inches separated them. He blinked at her, making her smile, then they both moved forward at the same time, noses bumping, lips meeting. This was another familiar awkwardness for Tanya, something she felt she'd experienced maybe too many times in the past, but right now it felt like the first time and that had never happened before.

"Mmm," she murmured. "You're a good kisser."

He smiled. "You're just saying that."

There was no way to answer that except to simply kiss him again.

XXIX • ZEFFY

"Thank God, you're here," Jilly said when Zeffy and Nia came into the café with Buddy in tow. "Susan's on her way in, but we are seriously understaffed today."

"But I didn't come in to . . ." Zeffy's voice trailed off when she realized that Jilly was here all alone on a lunchtime shift. "Where *is* everybody?"

"Sick. Putting together their love lives," Jilly said. Her smile wasn't able to hide her weariness. "Who knows? But I could sure use some help."

"You've got it," Zeffy told her.

As she went to put her guitar behind the counter, Nia and Buddy trailed along behind her. Jilly joined them briefly to exchange an empty water pitcher for a full one. Her gaze touched the dog, then rose to Zeffy's face.

"What's with you guys today?" she asked. "First Tanya's smoking in the kitchen, now you're bringing a dog in. Kitty'll have a fit if any of this gets back to her."

Zeffy nodded. "We'll tie him up outside," she said, but she was already speaking to Jilly's back.

Half the tables in the café had customers, many still waiting to be served, and the front door opened on a group of four. Jilly was handling it with her usual good humor and charm, but while the customers probably didn't notice, Zeffy could tell she was feeling a little frazzled. The foursome seated themselves.

"Would you mind taking Buddy out back?" she asked Nia. "We'll talk to Jilly about this other stuff after the lunch rush."

"But what about Max?"

Zeffy hesitated. The front door opened again and a couple walked in. They looked around, then chose a table along the far wall, craning their necks to read the specials board hanging above the table once they were seated. The soup of the day was "Chicken Hurry" – obviously Tanya's handiwork. Zeffy smiled briefly before turning back to Nia.

"I can't leave Jilly to deal with all of this on her own," she said. "Johnny, Max, whoever he wants us to think he is – he'll keep for a couple of hours."

Nia didn't look at all convinced. Zeffy felt sorry for her – for both her and Buddy, who was so obviously a walking bundle of nerves – but what could she do?

"I really think something bad's going to happen," Nia said.

Zeffy shook her head. "I know Johnny. He's a lot of things I don't much care for, but violent isn't one of them. He's into mind games and we can't afford to get caught up in them any more than we already are."

"But—"

"Honestly. We'll deal with it all as soon as lunch is over. Meanwhile, why don't you see if Frank's got something for Buddy. Are you hungry?"

Nia shook her head.

"Well, if you want a pop or anything, just help yourself. I'll put it on my tab."

"You don't just get your food and stuff free?" Nia asked, obviously surprised.

"Nothing's free in this world," Zeffy told her, "except leftovers and friendship and even friendship costs. The difference is, usually we don't mind paying the coin it requires."

"I like the way that sounds," Nia said, smiling. "Did you come up with it?"

Zeffy nodded. "I guess I did. Maybe I'll put it in a song." Her gaze went out to the restaurant again, then returned to Nia. "I've really got to help out."

She showed Nia through the kitchen door and introduced her to Frank, then hurried back out into the main room to help Jilly. Susan arrived fifteen minutes later, full of apologies at having missed her bus, with a flushed but happy-looking Tanya coming in a few minutes after her. The first thing Tanya did was come up to Zeffy.

"About last night," she began.

"I was out of line," Zeffy said.

"No, I was. I'm so sorry."

"No, I'm the one who's sorry."

Jilly came up to them and gave them a quick smile. "The both of you are sorry already and we've got customers waiting."

Zeffy and Tanya grinned and gave each other a hug before getting back to work. With the four of them on the job, they finally managed to get customers seated, orders taken and filled, and everything back to a working semblance of order, but it wasn't until after two o'clock that Jilly, Tanya and Zeffy were able to take a break and join

Nia down by the riverbank where she was still trying to coax Buddy to relax without much success.

"Hey, there, big boy," Jilly said.

She knelt down on one knee and opened her arms. Buddy didn't hesitate. He went right up to her, almost pulling Nia off balance as the leash stretched tight. He pushed his muzzle up under Jilly's arm, his tail wagging for the first time that Zeffy had seen all day. When Nia looked up at her, Zeffy couldn't stifle a giggle that had as much to do with the adrenaline rush of the past couple of hours as it did with Nia's look of surprise.

"Animals just like her," Zeffy explained.

"Everybody likes her," Tanya added.

Jilly gave them a quick smile. She sat down on the grass and Buddy settled close beside her, putting his head on her lap. She ruffled the fur around his ears and looked over at Nia.

"It's just a — "

"Gift she has," Zeffy and Tanya chimed in before Jilly could finish.

Jilly laughed. "Or something. It's a reciprocal sort of a thing. If you put out good feelings, usually you get them back. Or to put it another way, I always see the cup as half-full instead of half-empty. Most people have something good about them."

"And those that don't?" Nia asked.

"I ignore. Unless they get in my face." Jilly glanced at Tanya. "Like Johnny Devlin today."

Tanya got a worried look. "What happened after I left?"

"Nothing much, really. He just swore a bit and swaggered out. I'm more interested in what happened when you caught up with Geordie."

Tanya blushed. "Oh, we worked stuff out."

"Time out," Zeffy said. "I'm missing something here and Nia's not going to know what we're talking about. How about we start at the beginning? What happened with Johnny and Geordie?"

As Tanya started to explain, Jilly leaned over to Nia and told her who Geordie was. They all seemed to talk at once, but their stories got told, the narratives crisscrossing each other as one series of events had their effect upon another. When they were done, they sat quietly for a while, thinking. Zeffy stared across the river to where the buildings of Butler University could be seen on the far side of the common. From this far away, the ivy-covered old stone structures were merely a grey blur against the green of the common's trees and lawn.

"I'm sorry," she said finally. "But I still don't believe it. Johnny's got to be pulling some kind of scam. I mean, it just doesn't make sense otherwise. How can this kind of thing make sense?"

"I believe it's real," Jilly said. "I've never met Max Trader and I don't know Johnny all that well, but the guy in Trader's body who came into the café today had all of Johnny's mannerisms and icky vibes."

"Oh please," Zeffy said, smiling to take the sting out of her words. "Not mumbo jumbo *and* tired sixties expressions."

Jilly shrugged. "Whatever. But I do believe it. Just because something's not generally known or seen, doesn't mean it's not real."

"That's what Geordie said," Tanya put in.

"And I can't tell you how long it's taken Christy and me to get him to admit to it," Jilly said.

Nia seemed a little smitten by Jilly, Zeffy thought. But

then Jilly got that sort of a reaction from most people who came within the sphere of her good humor and kindnesses.

"You really believe in magic?" Nia asked.

Jilly nodded. "Though everything strange isn't necessarily magic. Sometimes it's just stuff we don't know yet, or have never seen before."

"Jilly's Believe It Or Not," Zeffy joked.

"Exactly," Jilly said, taking her seriously. "Those things exist whether we accept them or not."

"But *how* can you believe in that sort of stuff?" Zeffy had to ask.

"Because I've seen it. Not once or twice, but many times. Bits and pieces of things that shouldn't exist in this world, but do."

"Like what?"

Jilly's ready smile returned. "Oh, I don't know. It all seems so preposterous when you start to talk about it, doesn't it? But this business with Johnny and Max is a perfectly good example."

"Of a successful delusion," Zeffy couldn't help but mutter. She gave Jilly a guilty look when she realized she'd spoken aloud. "I'm sorry," she went on. "I just find it so hard to accept."

"There comes a point," Jilly said, "when not accepting is simply being stubborn. I understand why you feel the way you do: it changes things. It's like a kind of vertigo takes hold of you and you don't know where to step because stone might be quicksand and vice versa. Suddenly, everything you see or hear is suspect. But I'll tell you from experience that you quickly learn to figure out what's truly magic and what only seems to be."

"I believe it," Tanya said. "I can't not believe it after Johnny's visit to the café today."

Nia nodded. "I believe it, too. And I think if we don't do something soon, things are going to get worse. Even if . . . if my mom's okay, there's still something wrong with Max."

Zeffy shivered, remembering Nia's theory that maybe Johnny hadn't exactly switched brains with Max, but had a finger in his head instead, controlling him and taking what he needed out of Max's memories to lend credence to this convoluted scam he was trying to pull off. She didn't believe – not in her head because it made no sense, and not in her heart where perhaps it mattered more. But she could imagine it and the thought of someone being in her head, little say pushing her right out of her body, made her feel queasy. Because if it was true for Max, then it could happen to any of them.

"But what can we do?" Tanya asked.

No one knew – not even Jilly.

"There was that Indian he was talking to in the park," Zeffy said finally. She glanced at Nia. "You remember – the guy he was having that argument with? He might know something."

"Handsome guy with spooky eyes?" Jilly asked. "Reads fortunes in the park?"

Zeffy nodded. "I guess that's what he does. He does something with, I don't know, chicken bones, I guess. Some kind of small bones anyway. Nia and I were going to talk to him, but he was gone by the time we went to look for him."

"I know him," Jilly said.

Zeffy smiled. "Why didn't I just know that?"

"His name's Joseph Crazy Dog," Jilly said.

"Crazy Dog?"

Jilly nodded. "I don't know if it's really his family name or something he just acquired along the way, but it suits him. He's kind of like all those stories about Coyote – a good man, but things always seem to go a little off-kilter around him."

Off-kilter, Zeffy thought. That certainly fit the bill for how the last few days had been for her.

"Anyway," Jilly said. "Most people call him Bones because of what he uses to tell his fortunes."

"Do you think he could have something to do with all of this?" Zeffy asked.

"Ah-ha!" Jilly said, loud enough to startle Buddy. He lifted his head nervously until she calmed him. "Listen to the unbeliever now," she added in a quieter voice and then scratched the fur around Buddy's ears.

"I'm willing to keep an open mind," Zeffy said. "I just don't want my brain to be mistaken for Swiss cheese, that's all."

Buddy settled his head back on Jilly's lap and gave a contented sigh as she continued her ministrations.

"Could he be involved?" Tanya asked.

Jilly shrugged. "He might know what's going on. The only way to find out is to ask him."

"Do you know his address?"

"He lives somewhere in the Tombs, but I don't know exactly where. He's got squats in a bunch of different buildings."

"Great," Zeffy said. "That makes it easy."

"Well, you're going to hate me for saying this," Jilly went on, "but he's actually pretty easy to find. He just kind of shows up whenever you're looking for him – like you'd made plans to get together or something. It's this—"

"Gift he has," Tanya said.

"Exactly."

Zeffy sighed. "You're right. I do hate you. I was hoping for something practical, like a phone number or an actual address – you know, the way you get in touch with normal people."

"Normal people aren't going to be much help to you right now," Jilly said.

"I *really* wish you hadn't said that," Zeffy told her.

"Why don't we just go to Max's apartment?" Nia asked.

Jilly shook her head. "I don't think that's such a good idea – not until you know what's going on with him. Otherwise you could make things worse."

"So we go wandering about," Zeffy said, "hoping to run into this guy, and he's going to show up?"

"Something like that." Jilly looked at her watch. "Some of us should head back and help Susan."

"I'll go back with you," Tanya said.

Zeffy glanced at Nia. "That leaves it up to you and me. Are you game?"

"I guess."

Jilly shifted Buddy's head so that she could stand up.

"You be good now," she told him. "Do what Nia tells you. She's your friend, too, you know."

Buddy gave her a quizzical look. When the rest of them stood up, he scrambled to his feet and went to Nia. She gave him a tentative pat, smiling when he didn't shrink away.

"How did you do that?" Nia wanted to know, then added before anyone could speak, "Never mind. It's a gift, right?"

Jilly laughed. But as they headed back toward the café, she held Zeffy back, letting the other two walk ahead of them.

"What's up?" Zeffy asked.

"I don't want to make you nervous or anything," Jilly said, "but there's something I should tell you about Bones."

"I'm not going to like this, am I?"

"Depends on how open you're keeping that mind of yours."

Zeffy sighed. "Okay. I'm in this far, I might as well go all the way. What do we have to be careful about?"

"Two things," Jilly told her. "If he decides to help you, make sure you find out what kind of a bargain you're getting into."

"He's going to charge us?"

"Not money. Think of it along the lines of those old fairy tales. You know, don't promise to give him the first thing you see when you get home or something."

Lovely, Zeffy thought. "And the other thing?"

"Don't give him your full name."

Even Zeffy knew enough folklore to understand why.

"You're kidding, right?" she asked.

Jilly shook her head. "It's not so much that I think Bones would do anything himself. But like I said, spirits seem to crowd around him, good and bad or just plain mischievous. You don't necessarily want them to know your true name."

"Or what? They'll change us into newts or something?"

"I'm just asking you to be careful," Jilly said. "Humor me. You don't have to believe."

She looked so serious that Zeffy couldn't joke about it. Instead she found herself nodding, promising to be careful on both counts, but it made her uncomfortable. Unaccountably jumpy. She couldn't help but feel that by doing so, she was buying into Jilly's world of make-believe. Buying into it and making it real.

"Are you okay?" Nia asked after they'd left Jilly and Tanya at the café and continued on to the park with Buddy. "You look kind of pale all of a sudden."

Zeffy managed to find a smile, though she had to rummage through her sudden nervousness to do so.

"I'm fine," she said. "It's just . . ."

She repeated what Jilly had told her, the unfamiliar anxiety growing as she watched Nia's eyes widen. Nia believed. Tanya did. And Jilly. Everybody believed in magic except for her. Then she glanced at Buddy, padding along so docilely beside Nia since Jilly had told him to be good. That was a kind of magic, too, wasn't it?

"Do you think it's going to be dangerous?" Nia asked. "Talking to this Crazy Bones guy, I mean?"

"Crazy Dog," Zeffy said, correcting her without even thinking about it. Then she fell silent again.

"But do you?" Nia wanted to know.

"I hope not," Zeffy finally said. "But I'll tell you the truth, I have no idea what we're getting into anymore and that scares me."

They walked along in silence for a while, following Lakeside Drive on their way back to the park. This time Buddy was the only one of the three of them who didn't appear to be feeling skittish.

"Jilly wouldn't have sent us looking for him if it was too dangerous," Nia said, obviously trying to convince herself as much as Zeffy. "Would she?"

"No. I suppose not."

Certainly not on purpose, Zeffy thought, but she kept that to herself.

"One way or another we'll get to the bottom of all of this," she added aloud. "*And* we'll stay in one piece."

It sounded good and it seemed to make Nia feel better. Zeffy only hoped she could keep that promise.

XXX • LISA

LONG AFTER the stranger had gone, Lisa lay on her bed, staring up at the cracks in the plaster of her ceiling, unable to relax. She'd been too tired to undress, or even take off her shoes, little say get under the covers, but once she'd lain down, sleep eluded her. All she could do was think about what the stranger had said regarding Nia, about what his relationship really was to her daughter, about the distance that had crept into her relationship with Nia, and a hundred other things that only a mother could find to worry about. The more she tried to relax, to find the sleep she so desperately needed, the more she worried. The focus of her anxiety alternated from Nia to Julie – lying there now in intensive care and how did she *really* feel about their relationship? – before returning full circle to her daughter again.

Turning her head into the pillow, she thought she could still smell Julie's presence on the slipcase – a faint whiff of perfume that couldn't quite mask the scent that was uniquely Julie. She grew flushed, remembering the two of them, bodies entwined on this same bed, how soft and slippery it had all felt. But the heat died in her when she also remembered afterward, how weird it had seemed, how she'd thought that what they'd done was right, but wrong somehow, too, and she couldn't decide if she really thought it was wrong, or if it was something she'd been conditioned to think because of the way she'd been brought up.

Finally she sat up.

How can my life have become such a mess? she asked herself.

Any hope of sleep was long vanished now. Between

worrying over Julie and Nia, there was no point in pretending she could rest. There was nothing she could do for Julie at the moment, but the same couldn't be said about Nia. She might be making a mess of her love life, but she didn't have to lose her daughter at the same time. Things were really bad when some stranger knew more about Nia than she did.

That stranger, she thought as she made her way into the bathroom.

It was true she'd never seen him before, but there'd been a certain familiarity about him all the same. Nothing in the way he looked, but something in how he carried himself, the cadence of his voice. It nagged at her and made her feel uneasy for no reason that made sense, except perhaps that he knew something about Nia that she didn't. Nia had confided in him, where she couldn't with her own mother.

How had he become part of her daughter's life? Nia never seemed to have any real friends except for Max Trader, who, after talking to him yesterday, *definitely* gave Lisa the creeps now. If Julie hadn't been with her, she didn't know what she would have done.

That reminded her of Julie's plight all over again. The rock in the pit of her stomach grew heavier, her chest tightening.

She splashed water on her face. It helped a little – not so much to wake her up as for something to do. Something to prove that she was still functioning, still capable of dealing with her problems instead of simply folding up the way she wanted to. She washed her face, dried it, brushed her teeth, went through the mechanics of the actions without really thinking about what she was doing. She didn't bother with makeup. A pale face looked back at her from the mirror as she gave her hair a cursory brushing. The washed-out features reminded her of Nia.

Back in the bedroom, she exchanged her dirty T-shirt for a clean one, then put her jacket back on. When she left the apartment, the only thing she took with her that she hadn't had when she'd been out with Julie the night before was a small canister of pepper spray. She'd bought it a year ago when she'd had to work overtime more often than not over a period of a few weeks. The walk home from the bus stop through the Market at night had made her nervous.

She hadn't had to use it then and she hoped that wouldn't change. But when she thought of the boy who'd stabbed Julie last night, she knew she wouldn't freeze up again. She couldn't afford to be a victim. Not with Julie and Nia depending on her. They were both going to need nurturing and she was determined to be there for both of them.

Dropping the canister into the pocket of her jacket, she checked to make sure she had both her wallet and keys, then left the apartment. She held the pepper-spray canister tightly as she passed the door to Max Trader's apartment, half-expecting a confrontation with the creep, but the door remained closed and she made her way safely downstairs and out onto the street.

Nothing seemed quite the same as she looked around her neighborhood. Everything seemed to have an edge – both a stridency and a sense of foreboding.

Don't let something have happened to Nia, too, she thought as she walked toward Lee Street.

She had more to go on now than she'd had last night when she'd been out looking with Julie – little enough though it was. Fitzhenry Park, the stranger had said. He'd met Nia in the park. He could have been lying. There was no reason for her to trust him. And he'd said nothing about Nia still being there. But it was the only lead Lisa had and she meant to see it through.

When she reached Lee Street, she was too impatient to wait for public transport. She flagged down a cab.

"Fitzhenry Park," she told the driver as she settled into the backseat.

She met his gaze in the rearview mirror.

"No problem," he said. "Which entrance do you want?"

Lisa remembered her own teenage years, hanging around by the War Memorial with the other disaffected youth of the seventies. Her mother had been so embarrassed the day *The Newford Star* had run an op-ed piece on the hippies in the park and their be-ins and love-ins. A staff photographer had taken a candid group shot of a bunch of them, just hanging out, and there Lisa had been, in between a couple of guys, the one looking like Davy Crockett, the other with so much hair he might as well have been Grok from the comic strip "B.C."

"The main entrance," she told the cabbie. "Where the kids hang out."

XXXI • MAX

OF COURSE when I get to the park, there's nobody here. Not Bones, not Nia and Buddy, not even Zeffy, though I'm sure *she'd* really be happy to see me again. I take a stroll through the area where the vendors and fortune-tellers are set up and can't spy Jenna either. I wonder if she remembered to bring me that cloth and what she thought when I didn't stop by to get it. Not much, probably. I get the feeling that there's only a small core of real regulars working here; everybody else is transitory. Like me.

I see a guy playing an octave mandolin where Zeffy had been earlier with my guitar and that reminds me of my show with Zeffy and the cops and all. I don't know why I snapped the way I did. It's not like it was her fault Devlin lent her my guitar.

Devlin. Everywhere I turn, he's waiting for me. All I have to do is look in the mirror.

I didn't like him, almost right from the start, and I still don't. But I find I don't much like myself either. And for good reason. Truth is, I don't know who I am anymore. It's not only the moodiness. It's this sense of having no roots, no commonality that I can tie into, no connections like everybody else has. Family, friends, job. Switching bodies with Devlin isn't the cause of it. I was like this before any of this started. It took the switch to show me.

But I want my own skin back. I feel like yelling to whoever's in charge. Okay, I get the point. Let me have my own body back now. But there's nobody listening. No way back.

I recognize the sense of depression that's coming over me, but can't seem to do anything about it. Can't seem to be bothered. Intellectually, I know it's an echo of Devlin's personality. I never had a lot of high good times, but I never had a lot of lows, either. I just coasted. But Devlin, he's mildly manic, I suspect. Up or down and no in between. Now it's my problem. But recognizing it's easier than dealing with it. It's so much easier to coast, to stop fighting it and simply go with it.

I buy myself a cup of coffee from a cappuccino cart and take it back to the free end of a bench. Welcome to your new living room, I tell myself. I drop my knapsack to the ground and sit down. Holding the coffee gives me something to do with my hands. There's a couple of guys at the other end of the bench, one standing, looks like he's in the middle of a run with his sweats and Airwalks, the other sitting, his back to me, one arm hanging over the back of the bench. I try not to pay any attention to them, but it's easier to eavesdrop than it is to deal with my own problems.

They're talking about sports scores and dance clubs. One of them's going to a new gym tonight. The other guy thinks he might be losing his job, but he doesn't much care because he never liked it anyway.

After a few more minutes of this, the runner leaves, heading deeper into the park on one of the trails. He's got good form, looks like he knows what he's doing, like the last thing he needs is more exercise. The guy on the bench turns so that he's facing forward, smiling at nothing in particular. Must be nice. But then he notices me and he loses the smile.

"You," he says.

I hadn't really been looking at him, so we recognize each other at about the same time. He's Zeffy's knight-in-shining-armor. Hank. He's not wearing the shirt with the nametag anymore, but I don't need it to remind me. I'm about as happy to see him as he is to see me. More trouble I don't need, so I look away from him. He doesn't take the hint.

"The thing I can't figure out," he says, "is why do they put up with you?"

I sigh and shift so that I'm facing him. "Why does who put up with me?"

"It's not just you in particular, but all the guys like you. You treat women like shit and all they do is come back for more."

"I don't treat women like shit."

His eyes are cold. "Hey, pal. I was there. Bullshit your girlfriend if you want to, but don't try it on me."

I take a sip of my coffee and look away again, trying to ignore him.

"It's a simple question," he says.

I don't say anything. I'm not going to give him the satisfaction of arguing.

"Hey, I'm talking to you, pal."

Trouble is, it seems like he's not about to back down.

"Doesn't mean I have to answer," I tell him.

I keep my tone reasonable, but I can feel the anger rising in me. Devlin's legacy. No wonder nobody likes him. I glance at Hank. He's smiling now – the kind of smile you see on a barroom brawler when he's looking for a fight.

"Let's not get into anything," I add.

"Who's getting into anything? I'm just talking."

"You're bothering me."

His eyes narrow. "The way you bother your girlfriend?"

"She's not my girlfriend. I don't know her. I don't live with her. All that was going on was we were having an argument because someone lent her my guitar. End of story."

"That's not the way she had it," he says.

"Well, then go talk to her about it."

He shakes his head. "You don't get it, do you? I'm holding *you* accountable."

"Accountable for what? Having an argument with someone? You might as well take on the whole world."

"Maybe I will – a piece at a time and starting with you. Because I'll tell you, pal, I'm sick of hearing about people like you. I'm sick of seeing the way you treat people."

It's all I can do to stay reasonable now. I know if it had

been Devlin sitting here, the two of them would already have been at it.

"You don't even know me," I say. "You know nothing about how I treat people."

He stands up. "I know how you treat your girlfriend. Christ, do you think I'm stupid? I've seen this kind of crap going on since I was kid. You're like my old man. Happy to smack around those that can't hit back, but you turn into a pussy the minute you run into someone who won't back down from you."

He's starting to get on my nerves now – my nerves, not Devlin's.

"If you've got a problem with your father take it to him," I say. "Same goes for Zeffy – the woman with the guitar."

He stands there looking at me and all I can do is feel sorry for him. He's obviously got a lot of old problems he hasn't worked through yet. But that doesn't give him the right to take them out on me.

"Get up," he says. Voice cold, hard. Mr. Tough Guy.

My sympathy leaves and I feel like throwing my coffee in his face. But I don't move. Don't say anything, don't move, hoping my passiveness will undermine his need for a confrontation. Doesn't work.

"I'm only going to tell you one more time," he says.

I try one more argument, though I already know this has gone too far for it to have any impact. "What you're doing now is no different from what you're accusing me of."

"There's a big difference," he tells me. "You can fight back."

He starts to reach for me to haul me to my feet, so I let instinct take over and throw the coffee in his face. It's not hot enough to do any real damage, but I know it's got to hurt. He cries out and stumbles back, out of my way. I grab my knapsack and rise off the bench. I mean to make a run for it. I've got no real fight with this guy and can't see any point in sticking around. All I need right now is for the cops to come by again because this time I don't have Zeffy around to bail me out – not that she even would, considering how well we got on the last time I saw her.

But I don't get the chance to run. Someone grabs me from behind. A voice shouts, loud in my ear.

"Here, I've got him!"

Hank comes at me, swinging. I jerk my head back and it rams the face of the guy holding me. And then . . .

I don't quite know what happens. I have this fleeting thought that I must have given myself a concussion, because a severe vertigo hits me. My eyes are open, but there's nothing to see. It's as though someone's erased the world, deleting everything in it except for me and the stranger holding me.

But he's not a stranger, I realize. It comes to me that I recognized his voice. His voice? My voice. It's Devlin that grabbed me. Devlin that's with me here, wherever here is.

And then I lose it. The ground comes rushing up to hit me. I'm pulling Devlin down with me. But there's no impact. We just keep falling, falling. I hear someone yelling something, but I can't tell if it's Devlin or me. Can't tell up from down. There's a pulling in my head, as though my mind is being sucked into a funnel, squeezed into an ever-narrowing conduit that it simply won't fit through and—

Everything goes black.

Owning Your Own Shadow

For every evil under the sun,
There is a remedy, or there is none.
If there be one, seek till you find it;
If there be none, never mind it.
    – from Mother Goose

I • NIA

THE MORE time she spent in Zeffy's company, the better Nia liked her. She'd liked the whole group of them – Zeffy, Tanya and especially Jilly. They were so *interesting*. The fact that they were all probably twice her age didn't strike her in the least bit odd. She'd always gotten along better with adults than kids her own age. That wasn't something that had started with Max; it was just the way it was. If she thought about it at all, it was probably because her mother had always treated her as a friend instead of a child.

Used to treat her that way, Nia corrected herself. Before the walls went up. Before her mother decided she liked women better than men. Before the aliens came and set up house in her head. Whatever.

She sighed heavily which made Zeffy turn to look at her.

"We're almost there," Zeffy said.

"I'm not tired," Nia assured her. "I was just thinking."

Zeffy's features took on a worried look that Nia already knew didn't fit in at all with her new friend's usual good humor.

"You and me both," Zeffy said. "I'm still trying to figure out why I'm even letting myself get mixed up in all of this."

At Nia's side, Buddy seemed to have taken Jilly's advice

to heart. He'd been relaxed ever since they'd left the restaurant, actually butting his head against Nia's leg and wagging his tail whenever she reached down to give him a pat.

"Is it Max you like?" she asked Zeffy. "I mean, the person he is, or is it the way he looks?"

"What makes you think I like him?"

Nia smiled. "Because I figure that must be why you're here. If you hated him, you wouldn't be helping out."

"If I buy into it – which I haven't completely . . ." Zeffy's voice trailed off. She glanced at Nia. "Well," she tried again. "He looks like Johnny Devlin, but that's not necessarily a good thing."

"I think he's handsome."

"Handsome's perhaps too strong a word. I'd say attractive instead, except Johnny – the Johnny *I've* always known before the last few days – has always been so full of himself and there's nothing worse than a good-looking man who's too aware of his good looks, you know? There's something in their eyes, or in the way they smile, that just gives me the creeps."

"But Max isn't like that."

Zeffy gave her a tired smile. "Max. Who's supposedly living in Johnny's head now."

Nia hadn't lost her own confusion in dealing with it all, either. Last night, she'd have had no doubt. But after he'd jumped all over her earlier today and been so mean, she wasn't so sure anymore.

"Except for the two big fights we've had," Zeffy went on, "and even they weren't anything like arguing with Johnny, I have to admit he's been really sweet. He wasn't all full of himself like usual, his gaze stayed on my face instead of my boobs and he just generally seemed like another

368

person." She shot Nia a glance. "And yes, he was someone I could like."

Nia didn't say anything.

"Okay," Zeffy said. "I could like him a lot."

"How do you think you'll feel when they're both back in their own bodies again? Do you think you'll still like him?"

"What are you now – a matchmaker?"

Nia shrugged. "I just like Max and I like you and I think it would be really cool if you guys were together. Who knows?" she added, teasing now. "Maybe he'd make you a guitar."

"Oh, please. Like that's a good reason to get into a relationship? Though when I think of what it's like to play one of his instruments, maybe that's not such a bad idea."

Nia gave her a quick worried look.

"Now *I'm* teasing," Zeffy assured her.

"I knew that." Beat. "So? Would you still like him as much?"

"I really don't know," Zeffy said. Then she smiled. "Who knows? Maybe I'd like him more because then he wouldn't be carrying around the baggage of Johnny's face."

Nia gave her a puzzled look.

"You know," Zeffy explained. "Looking at him, I wouldn't keep thinking of everything that went down before."

"I guess there's that."

"What about you?" Zeffy asked. "Do you have a boyfriend?"

Nia shook her head. "I only ever seem to meet dorks."

"Well, thank you very much."

Nia laughed. They waited for a last light. Across the street, they could see the entrance of the park ahead. Buddy pushed his face against Nia's thigh, the way he did every time they stopped for a moment, and she gave the wiry fur around his ears an affectionate ruffle.

"You know what I mean," she said. "I never seem to attract the kind of guy I'd like to hang out with."

"Welcome to the real world," Zeffy told her.

The light changed and they crossed over.

"So Max isn't really your type?" Nia asked as they approached the park's entrance.

"I don't know," Zeffy said. "I'd have to get to know him first." She gave Nia a wry look. "I will tell you that there were sparks when I met him in Johnny's body – and that was when I was still entirely sure he was Johnny and had absolutely no inclination to like him, little say think about getting into anything more intimate with him. But looking back, I know those sparks came from who he was inside because Johnny never appealed to me in the looks department."

"I wish—" Nia began.

But then Buddy tugged on her leash at the same time as Zeffy said, "There they are!"

Nia looked in the direction Zeffy was pointing and spied Max sitting on a bench, arguing with a man she didn't recognize. Behind, out of Max's line of vision, Johnny was making his way toward the bench. There was something about his body language that told Nia he meant Max harm, though she couldn't have explained exactly what she thought he was going to do. It was just a warning tingle that went racing up her spine, but before she could shout a warning, the opportunity was gone. She watched Max hurl a coffee in the stranger's face, Johnny grab him from behind, Max whip his head back as the stranger took a swing at him and then the world went surreal.

One moment there were three men jostling about beside

the bench, the next there was only the stranger, staggering back from where Max and Johnny had simply disappeared. The stranger backed away slowly. He glanced in their direction, eyes widening slightly, then he took off, running in the opposite direction.

"He . . . they . . ."

Nia couldn't get the words out. For all that she'd come to accept that it was possible, if not probable, for people to switch minds with one another, the abrupt disappearance of Max and Johnny simply wouldn't register as real. Buddy, tugging at the leash a moment ago, now crouched beside her, whining, his head and shoulders stuck to her leg like glue. She turned slowly to see Zeffy staring at the bench with a look on her face that would have been comical in other circumstances.

"I . . . I don't believe it," Zeffy said.

She started walking toward the bench, one hand stretched out in front of her as though she were feeling her way through a dark room. Nia followed with a reluctant Buddy in tow, her own nervousness mirroring his. As they drew nearer, she looked around and realized that except for the man who'd been fighting with Max, no one else seemed to be paying any attention to what had happened, no one except for . . .

She stepped up her pace and caught Zeffy's arm. "Over there," she said, her voice sounding far more composed than she was feeling. "By that tree."

Zeffy paused, then looked in the direction Nia was indicating.

"That's him," Nia added needlessly. "The Bones guy."

He was sitting cross-legged under the spreading boughs of a tall oak, wearing an old khaki army jacket over a T-shirt and jeans, black hair pulled back into a braid. Zeffy gave the bench a last uncomprehending look, then proceeded in his direction. He watched their approach with interest.

"I guess you've been looking for me," he said when they drew near.

'How do you know that?" Zeffy asked.

He shrugged. "You wouldn't be able to see me otherwise." While Nia was still working that out, he jerked a thumb toward the bench and added, "Some show, don't you think?"

Buddy stepped away from Nia's side to push his muzzle toward Bones. Bones smiled and gave the dog a scratch under the chin.

"Why wouldn't we be able to see you?" Nia asked.

"I tend to blend in when I don't want to be noticed," he replied. There was something about his eyes that made Nia feel he was both pulling a joke on them and deadly serious. "It's like being invisible, except it's just people not paying attention."

Zeffy sat down on the grass across from him with Nia happy to follow suit. Nia's knees had been feeling rubbery and she hadn't trusted her legs to hold her up much longer. She gave Bones a long studying look. There was something way too surreal about all of this and she couldn't quite figure out how she felt about it. Not scared, exactly, but not comfortable either.

"How'd you get this dog to put a damper on his nerves?" Bones asked.

"Jilly asked him to be good," Nia found herself answering. "And he has been."

"Ah, Jilly," Bones said, as if that explained everything.

"She's the one who told us to come look for you," Nia added.

"Then I guess you're okay. Never met a woman with as good a bullshit detector as Jilly."

"What . . ." Zeffy paused. She had to clear her throat and try again. "What just happened over there?"

Bones smiled. "Well, that's kind of complicated – depending on what you know, it'll get either more or less complicated."

"Those two guys," Nia said, "that . . . that disappeared. We know they kind of switched brains or something."

Bones looked from Nia to Zeffy. "But you're not entirely sure it's true."

"Well, I mean, really," Zeffy said. "It's just so . . . so . . ."

Her voice trailed off and she glanced back at the bench. An old woman was sitting there now, feeding pigeons birdseed from a brown paper bag she held on her lap. It was such a prosaic scene that Nia started to wonder if what they'd seen had even been real.

"It was just so weird," Zeffy said.

"But it happens all the time," Bones told them. "Or at least it used to. Where do you think all the stories about the animal people came from? Bears and wolves that can talk like men. Buffalo women and snake girls. Coyote and raven and hare. It's not always the little manitou talking to us, maybe making mischief. Sometimes it's people getting mixed up with animal spirits."

Zeffy remained silent, but Nia leaned closer. "You mean, like, for *real*?"

Bones nodded, strange lights dancing deep in his dark eyes. "What happens is, they trade spirits and the medicine gets strange. Sometimes they only trade partway; most times they trade for good, one spirit swapped for the other. They get their dreams mixed up and they lose their way back to where they're supposed to be.

"Human to human – that's not so common. Harder to fix, too. You end up with two stubborn human minds and one of them almost always wants to leave things the way they are because they usually had a good reason for wanting to escape whatever kind of mess they've made of their own life. It's easier when one of them's an animal spirit. Animals always want to get back. The trouble in that kind of situation is getting them together. But once you do, you can usually work it out."

Zeffy shook her head. "This is so . . ."

"Unfamiliar?"

She nodded.

"Doesn't make it any less true," Bones said. "Anyway, that's what happened with your friends. They dreamed too close and now they can't get back to where they belong. Maybe they don't even want to get back. You'd have to make them dream together again, for starters, and they'd have to want to get back into their own skins. Both of them."

"What if we can't?" Nia asked.

Bones shrugged and leaned back against the trunk of the oak. "Too late to worry about that now. The whole thing's out of our hands anyway."

"I don't understand," Zeffy said.

Neither did Nia. "Where did they go?" she asked.

Bones took the time to fish a package of cigarette tobacco out of the pocket of his jacket and rolled a cigarette. Nia watched the economic movement of his fingers with interest. When he was done, he offered it to her, but she shook her head.

374

"No, thanks," Zeffy said when he then offered it to her as well.

He lit the cigarette and blew a wreath of blue-grey smoke up into the droop of the oak's low-hanging boughs.

"Here's where it gets complicated again," he said finally.

Beside Nia, Zeffy gave a short humorless laugh. "Maybe a better word would be improbable."

"Depends," Bones told her.

"On what?"

"On how married you are to everything being only one way." He paused and took another drag. "Your way."

"Please," Nia said to Zeffy. "Let's just hear what he's got to say."

Bones smiled. "They say we get born wise, but we have that wisdom studied and bullied out of us when we're growing up and it takes us a lifetime to get back to being wise once more."

Nia returned his smile uncertainly, not quite sure what he was getting at.

"He means the younger you are, the more gullible you are," Zeffy said.

"Or the more clearly you can see," Bones put in. "Take your pick."

Zeffy looked like she was about to add something to that, but she glanced at Nia and then said, "Sorry." She returned her attention to Bones. "You were going to tell us where they went."

"The spiritworld." Bones waited a moment for that to sink in. When neither of them spoke, he went on. "It's the place where the manitou live. We're not meant to go there in our bodies, you see."

"Why not?" Nia wanted to know.

"It's the place where our spirits travel to when we're looking for knowledge or wisdom or to speak to ghosts and spirits. You might go there to find a totem. Maybe you just stray into it when you're dreaming and there's no harm done. Fact is, there's people go there on a regular basis when they're dreaming."

"Like Sophie," Zeffy murmured.

Bones raised his eyebrows.

"She's just a friend," Zeffy explained. "Of Jilly's. She's always talking about how she goes somewhere else when she dreams – lives a life there that's as real as the one she lives here."

Bones nodded. "Lots of people do that." He smiled. "Most of them just don't know it."

"So why's it so dangerous to go there in your body?" Nia asked.

Bones took a last drag from his cigarette and butted it out on the ground. Buddy lifted his muzzle and regarded the butt as though hoping it might be edible, but Bones simply stowed it away in another pocket of his jacket.

"It changes things," he said. "In you, in the land, in the spirits that inhabit it. It's like the stories you Europeans have about fairyland, how people stray into it and come back either crazy or poets." He grinned, looking so loopy for a moment that Nia decided he had to have been there himself and not come back a poet. "Same place, different name, that's all. Spirits come to you looking like you expect them to. You want little elves, that's what you'll see. Totems? Got them, too. Little green men from Mars in spaceships. Whatever."

"But *why's* it so dangerous?" Nia asked.

"Don't know exactly," Bones said. "That's just the way

it is. Everything's different there. Time's different. You can be there for years and maybe a minute's passed when you get back. Or you can be there for a moment and a hundred years have gone by."

Nia and Zeffy turned to each other. It was hard for Nia to figure out exactly how her companion was taking this, but she knew she believed.

"And that's where Max and Johnny went?" she asked.

"Touched skin to skin," Bones said. "Set up a kind of backlash, I'm guessing, and it sucked them right into the spiritworld, because that's the first place dreams go." His dark eyes grew thoughtful. "But a simple thing like that can get messy when the two of them are carrying pieces of each other around the way they were."

"Pieces of each other?"

Bones nodded. "The spirit's not a plain and simple separate thing. Bits of it are all mixed up with our bodies, tied to various parts." That loopy smile returned. "Why do you think things like acupuncture work the way they do? But the personality's mostly by itself and that's what goes traveling."

"So that's why Max was acting so weird," Nia said.

"What were the two of you arguing about?" Zeffy asked Bones.

"I thought he was going off to kill the other fellow and I didn't want him to use my knife to do it."

"You didn't try to stop him?"

Bones shrugged. "Except for the knife, it wasn't my business."

"But—"

"Look," Bones said. "Who's the one person nobody likes? The one giving advice."

"But you tell fortunes," Zeffy said.

"Only when people come to me. Hell. I'll give anybody a hand if they ask. But they've got to ask."

"And what does it cost?"

Nia nodded, wanting to know the answer as well because hadn't Jilly warned them to ask?

"Depends," Bones said, "on what they're willing to pay." He fished out his tobacco again and started rolling another cigarette. "And before you go all sanctimonious on me, remember this: Nobody puts much value on anything anymore unless they have to pay something for it. When you get to the kind of mojo we're talking about now, believing in it's a whole part of what makes it work." He touched a match to the end of his finished cigarette. "People nowadays only believe in what they've paid for."

"Not everybody's like that," Nia said.

"That's true," Bones agreed. "And that's why there's a sliding scale. What a person gives me all depends on what they want, and how much it'll take them to believe that I can deliver the goods."

"So what would you charge us?" Nia asked.

"To do what?"

Nia glanced at Zeffy before replying. "To show us how to go after Max – into the spiritworld."

"Not a good idea," Bones said.

"Definitely not a good idea," Zeffy agreed. "You heard what he said about the place. We'd probably never even be able to find them."

"I could," Nia said. "And Buddy'd help."

"Nia, I know you want to—"

"Max is my *friend*. Maybe the only one I have. I'm not going to leave him there without trying to help."

"But—"

"Look, this is my business, okay? What do you even care, anyway?"

"I'm just worried about what might happen to you."

"Well, don't," Nia said. "We only just met so you don't have to act like my mother."

"I'm not—"

"You don't even believe in any of this," Nia went on. "But I do and I'm going to help Max." She turned away from Zeffy. "What'll you charge to show me how to get there?" she asked Bones.

He gave her a long studying look.

"You can't be thinking of helping her," Zeffy said.

"Well, now," Bones said, ignoring Zeffy. "My wife Cassie's always telling me how she'd love to have a totem painting on a pebble – you know the kind of thing I'm talking about?"

Nia nodded slowly. How could he *know*? He must have seen her making them – walking around invisible the way he claimed he could.

"What kind?" she asked.

"A crow'd be nice, considering the way she's always collecting things. Sometimes I think she and some crow got to dreaming too close one night."

Nia reached into her pocket and took out her stones, sorting through them until she found the one she'd done of a crow.

"How's this?" she asked, handing it over to him.

Bones gave her that grin that made his eye go clown-bright. "Beauty."

"And me?" Zeffy asked. "What would you charge me?"

Nia turned in surprise.

"Well, I'm in this far," Zeffy said. "You don't think I'd really back out at this point, do you?"

"You're tougher," Bones said. "Have to get you looking past the end of your nose and really *seeing* for a change."

"Don't mince words, do you?"

"No point."

Bones finished his cigarette, thinking. When the butt was ground out in the dirt and stowed away in his pocket with the other one, he finally nodded.

"I'm going to need a song from you," he said.

"What? You want me to sing you a song?"

"No. Write me one."

"I don't know if we have that kind of time."

"Not now," Bones said. "When you get back."

When, Nia thought, holding on to the word. Not if, but when. Maybe everything he'd been saying was just to scare them, make them cautious.

"What about the dangers?" Zeffy said. "What if I come back crazy?"

She was bringing that up, Nia decided, in a last-ditch hope to dissuade Nia from seeing this through, but it wasn't going to work. Nia had already made up her mind.

"Then I guess I won't get my song," Bones said. "Or if I do, it won't make much sense."

Zeffy sighed. She put a hand on Nia's knee.

"You're sure about this?" she asked.

Nia nodded. "What do we have to do?" she asked Bones.

"Nothing. Just think hard about your friend and sit there. I'll do the work."

He reached into another pocket of his jacket and pulled out what looked like a packet of grass, tightly wound with string, or maybe jute. One end looked as if it had been burned. It took Nia a moment to recognize if for what it was. A smudge-stick. She'd seen them at a powwow up on the Kickaha reservation that her mother had taken her to last summer.

"What can I call you?" he asked.

Not what were their names, Nia noted. She looked around a little nervously. Maybe there really *were* spirits hanging around, watching, like Jilly had said there'd be. Then she had to laugh at herself. She was worried about that when she was planning to head off into the place they came from?

"Nia," she said, thinking that'd be safe enough since it wasn't her whole name, just a part of it.

"Zeffy."

"Nia and Zeffy," Bones repeated, his voice low, chanting their names more than speaking them. "*Oh-na, oh-nya-na,*" he went on. "*Hey-canta, nowa-canta . . .*"

He lit the smudge-stick and the smoke that rose up from it seemed far out of proportion to what should come from such a small source.

"*Oh-na, hey, oh-nya-na . . .*"

The smoke was sweet, billowing rapidly around them making it impossible to see much farther than a few feet in any direction. Buddy stirred uneasily by Nia's leg and she stroked his fur to comfort him. Her ears popped and the quiet murmur of Bones' voice began to fade.

"*Hey-canta . . .*"

She kept one hand on Buddy's back, tangling her fingers under his collar so that they wouldn't be separated. Along her knee, she felt Zeffy's hand, searching, and she reached for it with her free hand, holding Zeffy's fingers in a tight grip. She thought she heard her name being called – it was her mother's voice, rising above the almost inaudible sound of Bones' chanting.

That's so weird, she thought as the billowing smoke from the smudge-stick finally stole away her ability to see anything. For a moment it was as though she was sitting on nothing, floating, a part of the smoke, then there was something soft and gritty under her, loose sand of some sort, and she felt so light-headed, she thought she might faint.

Think of Max, she told herself. Concentrate on him or who knew where they'd end up.

But then another thought rose, unbidden and worrying.

They'd never asked Bones how they'd get back.

II • MAX

I'M LITERALLY dumbfounded when I crawl back out of whatever black space swallowed me up. I sit up slowly, feeling the whole time as though I'm moving through a lucid dream, lucid only because I know I'm dreaming, have to be, the whole simple procedure of sitting up taking forever, nothing making sense, not any sense at all, because I can't be where my eyes are telling me I am

Hank ... Fitzhenry Park – Newford itself, for God's sake. They're all gone. All that's left of them is my knapsack, and an ache in the back of my head where I cracked skulls with Devlin. And in their place ...

I must have been out cold for a while, I realize, because it's at least a three-hour drive from downtown Newford to here – here being Janossy's old farm, nestled in the foothills of the Kickaha Mountains. But at the same time that's going through my head, I know it can't be true, because the farm's been deserted since Janossy died, half the outbuildings fallen in on themselves, the fields all overgrown, herb and vegetable beds gone wild. This farm looks the way it did when I lived here. When Janossy was still alive.

And that's not possible.

Even if someone's bought the place and fixed it up, it couldn't look like this. How would they know to trim back the rosebushes just so far? How could they duplicate Janossy's peculiar pattern for the cedar shingles on the roof of the workshop so that it looked like the Japanese ideograph for autumn, floating in a sea of clouds? How could they have found another old sleigh and positioned it so exactly at the side of the house, just the way Janossy had? I can still remember breaking that sleigh up when it finally rotted through one winter, burning the wood in the fire pit behind the barn. And the barn's back, too. The last time I was here, the roof had finally collapsed and all that had been left was the stone foundation and two of the wooden walls.

It's like that wherever I look, everything that time wore down over the years returned to its original state. A feeling of such dislocation comes over me that I'm afraid to stand up. It's like climbing the stairs of a stopped escalator – it's too disorienting. All I can do is stay seated on this low rise where I've found myself and try to quiet the thunder of my pulse.

I have to look away from the farm, so I turn to trace the long laneway that leads out of the farmyard and joins the highway, except the highway isn't there anymore. The lane peters out into an overgrown field, raspberry bushes pressed close and hanging over it, tall weeds growing up between the ruts. A hawk floats high above the field, hunting. It all registers, but only in my peripheral vision. All my attention is now focused on Johnny Devlin, sitting there on the ground a half-dozen yards away from me. There's blood all over the front of his shirt, streaks of it under his nose and chin and smeared across one hand where he's been trying to stanch the flow.

I must've broken his nose when I whipped my head back and hit him in the park. His nose. My nose.

The park. A buzz starts up in the back of my head. Where the hell is the park? How did I get from—

I stop that train of thought because I know if I ride it any further, the panic I'm trying to keep down is going to swallow me whole and the next place I'll wake up is in the Zeb, strapped to a bed and pumped full of tranquilizers. I focus on Devlin, instead. The new bend in his nose makes those familiar features of mine less familiar. It's easier to look at him and deal with the fact that we're still inhabiting each other's body.

When he sees me looking at him, he starts nervously. For a minute I think he's going to bolt, but then his shoulders sag. What did he think I was going to do – give him another head-butt?

"What'd you do to me?" he asks.

I can't believe he's blaming me for this. The flow of the blood has stopped, leaving his nose discolored and swollen, black smudges around his eyes. It's got to hurt, but I don't feel much sympathy for him. The swelling gives his voice a nasal quality, like he's got a bad cold.

"What did *I* do to you?"

"I didn't bring us here," he says.

I shake my head. "You're the one who got us into all of this in the first place."

"I saw the look on your face when you sat up," he says. "You know this place. You've been here before."

"I *knew* this place," I tell him.

He looks at me, absently dabbing the sleeve of his jacket against the bottom of his nose, and waits.

"It was like this years ago," I explain, "but it doesn't look like this anymore."

"So what're you telling me? You've dragged us back into the past?"

I feel like giving him another head-butt, but I manage to keep my – his? – temper in check. Fighting's not my style. I hardly ever argue either – though you'd never know that from the past few days.

"I'm telling you," I say, "I had nothing to do with bringing us here."

He gives me a yeah-sure look.

"Why'd you grab me in the park?" I ask, deciding to put him on the defensive for a change.

For a moment I don't think he's going to answer. When he does, his answer makes no sense.

"You ripped me off," he says.

It's my turn to look blank.

"Don't play innocent," he says. "I saw you coming out of my apartment building with that knapsack you're carrying. What'd you take?"

I can't believe this guy.

"*Your* apartment building?"

"It's mine now. And so's whatever you took. I was waiting for a chance to get it back when you started arguing with that guy." He touches his nose gingerly. "Christ, this hurts. Why'd you have to hit me so hard?"

"Well, excuse me."

He points to the knapsack. "What've you got in there, anyway."

"I don't believe you," I say. "No wonder your life's such

a mess. You don't think of anybody but yourself and even then you're too screwed up to get it right."

He gives me a sullen look. "Easy for you to say. You've had all the breaks."

His logic is so skewed I can't help wanting to hear him out. It's that, or slap him silly.

"All what breaks?" I ask.

"You know." He shrugs. "Things just went your way. I've been through your stuff. You've got a good business, a nice apartment, money in the bank – all the things I've never had. Can you blame me for wanting a piece of it?"

"So you just step into my life and take it?"

"Hey, I had nothing to do with what happened to us. But the deal's done, so I might as well take advantage of it, right?"

For the first time since we switched, I'm not so keen to get my own body back. There's something about the way he's wearing it that's giving me the creeps – like he's soiled it, just by inhabiting it for the past few days. Which doesn't make sense, considering I'm sitting here in his skin and who knows what he's put this body through. I've got God knows how many residual pieces of him floating around inside me, but this skin still feels more like my own at the moment. The temper, the depression . . . I don't know what else he's left behind for me to deal with. But the thing is, I feel as though I can work it all out. What I'm not so sure I can handle is being back in my own skin – even if we could figure out how to make the switch – because this body feels like my own now.

We're funny creatures, we human beings. My father was right. It seems as though we can adjust to anything.

"What're you looking at me like that for?" he asks.

"I'm just thinking about how anything you touch seems to go bad."

That wakes a spark of anger in his eyes, but his body language tells me he's too scared to do anything about it. Scared of what? Me? Because I managed to break his nose when all I was doing was panicking and trying to get away from him and Hank? I guess it's the classic bully syndrome. Once someone stands up to them, once they get hurt, it lets out all the air and bluster. Or maybe it's the pieces of me left behind in him that stop him.

"What would you know?" he says.

"As it stands," I tell him, "I already know too much."

"Yeah, well I just never got—"

"The breaks. I know. We've already played that side of the record. Did you ever think of making your own breaks instead of stealing them from other people?"

"I never—"

I don't want to hear it. "Look at what you did with your life: no money, no job, lost your apartment, treated your girlfriend like shit. That's not bad breaks. That's just you being a loser."

"I was going to pay Tanya back," he says. "I even went by the café today to give her the money, but she wouldn't take it."

"And where'd you get the money? From my till."

"This is bullshit. The money's mine now. Your life is mine."

I think back to that first morning when I saw him in the doorway of my apartment, standing in my skin, and how I just fell apart. Backed down. Took off. Panicked. All I'd had to do was stand up to him.

And what? Everything would have been better?

No, but different. It's too late to know now. But it's not too late to deal with him.

"You better start walking," I tell him. "I don't want to hear you, I don't want to see you, I don't even want to remember that you're taking up any space in this world."

"Hey, you can't just—"

I point to where the laneway trails off onto the field. "There used to be a highway over there. Head south, it'll take you into the city. North, you'll be entering Kickaha land. I don't care which direction you pick, just get going."

He gives the forest beyond the field an uncertain look. The hawk's still floating above the field, the sun's pouring down like liquid gold, but it's dark under the trees, the thick upper canopy casting a deep shadow on the forest floor. He's got a city boy's nervousness about heading off into the bush on his own. I know the feeling. Without the gridwork of streets and city blocks laid out for you, it seems like it would be so easy to get lost. And it is. I dealt with it the first summer I came to stay up here with Janossy, so I do understand what's going through his mind. Thing is, I don't care. I just want him out of here.

"I don't think the city's there anymore," he says slowly.

He's got a point. I'd already come to a similar conclusion, but I've been trying to ignore it.

He looks back at me. "I don't think we're anywhere *real* anymore."

"Then you'll fit right in," I tell him with more bravado than I'm feeling.

"You can't do this," he says.

"Try me."

"We've got to stick together."

I look at my watch, but it's stopped. So I check the height of the sun.

"You've got about five, maybe six hours, before sunset," I say. "You better put them to use and make tracks because I can't guarantee what I'm going to do to you if you stick around."

I may be bluffing when it comes to acting calm about where we are and how we got here, but I'm more than half-serious about threatening him. Every time I look at him, all I want to do is hit him. I know it's residual pieces of his own bad temper that's making me feel this way, but I'm too unbalanced at the moment to deal with both the current situation and the crap he left behind when he quit this body. The main priority for me right now is to figure out where I am, how I can be back here with the farm unchanged. Dealing with him on top of that is too much.

I don't know what he sees in my face, but it gets him to his feet.

"You'll be sorry," he says.

"That I ever heard of you? I already am."

He staggers a bit, vertigo making him unsteady on his feet. I make a note to be careful when I get up myself. He looks as though he's trying to think of something to say, a withering comment of some sort that'll let him get the last word in, but he finally turns and shuffles away. I watch him go down the lane. He looks like an old man, shoulders sagging, head bowed, and I almost feel sorry for him.

It's probably not entirely his fault that he is the way he is. And he's not a truly bad person; I don't think he's evil. He's just so caught up in himself – the whole world revolves around Johnny Devlin – and that selfishness blinds him to what he's doing to the people around him. And himself. We're all born self-centered. Babies only have one thing on their minds – themselves. Feed me, warm me, soothe me. They learn to expand their world as they grow older, learn to take other people into account, learn to share. Devlin was just never taught that, or he didn't absorb it when he was.

Or maybe he's the way he is because he wants to be. At this point, it doesn't make much difference. Just so long as he's gone.

I turn back to look at the farm, trying to center myself. The sun is drenching the fields with a golden glow, all the greens leaning into the yellow end of the spectrum. The skin of my face and hands soaks in the warmth. My clothes feel heavy, confining. I close my eyes and listen to the hum of the bees, distant birdsong, crickets and June bugs.

When I open my eyes, the farm's still there, unchanged, as though the years never went by. I wonder if there are ghosts waiting for me down there, and I'm not sure if I like the idea, or dread it. I can't shake the feeling that this is a dream, that it has to be, or the farm wouldn't be down there, the lane would connect to a highway that appears to have disappeared, but the experience has none of the qualities I associate with dreaming. Unless I've been dreaming since I woke up in Devlin's body.

Devlin. I glance back in the direction he took. He's out of sight now, but the weird thing is, I know exactly where he is, how far into the forest he's gone. There's a connection between us that I'd never noticed before, a thin invisible line of something attached from me to him, or rather from me to my old body, as though I'm still linked to the pieces of myself I left behind in it, the way Devlin left pieces in me.

I try to ignore it.

Standing, the vertigo hits me the way it did Devlin, but I'm expecting it. I sway for a few moments, close my eyes until my equilibrium settles, then pick up my knapsack and walk down the hill toward the farm. I know there'll be ghosts down there – there can't not be. If they're not waiting for me, then I'm carrying them down with me.

III • LISA

L ISA HAD the cabbie let her off at the main entrance of Fitzhenry Park. He stopped in a no-parking bus zone and leaned over the front seat to tell her the fare. When the #74 pulled in behind them and the driver leaned on the horn, he simply ignored it, but the unexpected sound made Lisa almost drop the bills she'd pulled out to pay the cabbie. She was on edge and only half-aware of her surroundings, worry clinging to her thoughts like unwanted autumn burrs. How was Julie? Should she call the hospital? What if she couldn't find Nia? What if she found her, but Nia wouldn't come home?

"You have a good day now," the cabbie told her.

She felt like laughing. Did people even have good days anymore?

Murmuring a rote response without being quite sure what she'd said, she got out of the cab and watched it pull away into the traffic. A little boy ran headlong into her, but she barely noticed either him or heard his mother's apologies. When she did realize that the woman was saying something to her, she had no idea what had been said. It took her a long moment to sift some meaning from the words.

"I'm fine," she said at last, and turned away.

At the entrance to the park, she paused beside one of the stone lions, shading her eyes as she studied the crowd. Her heart sank. All the vendors and street musicians gathered near this entrance made it one of the busiest areas of the park, drawing as many tourists as locals. The weather was so perfect today, it seemed as though half the city had taken the afternoon off and come down. Where would she even begin to look?

Don't panic, she told herself, but her breath quickened with anxiety all the same.

She took a few steps into the park and paused once more. This time her gaze was more focused as it swept the crowd, panning slowly from left to right. The War Memorial, with its usual crowd of street people and teenagers. The vendors, shoppers, musicians, joggers, bicyclists, in-line skaters. Clusters of older women gossiping, nannies and new mothers pushing baby carriages, old men playing checkers and chess on small folding tables. People walking, reading, tanning, exercising. People with their dogs, their friends, their lovers, their children.

Her gaze searched all the way around to her far right where one of the park's enormous oaks lifted its boughs to dizzying heights. It froze there on the figures gathered under the wide sweep of the tree's branches: an Indian, sitting cross-legged, holding a burning smudge-stick. A red-haired woman. A dog.

And Nia.

The smoke from the man's smudge-stick grew impossibly thick, billowing about them. She could smell it from where she stood. Sweetgrass and sage, with a hint of cedar. She cried her daughter's name and ran forward, but it was like breaking a spell. Her voice, her sudden movement, *something* made the whole scene evaporate as if it had been nothing more than a desert mirage. There was no one under the tree now. No people, no smoke, nothing.

She came to an abrupt halt and someone bumped her

from behind. She stepped aside, nodding at the jogger's quick remark until she realized that he hadn't been apologizing, but telling her off. Anger was impossible to muster. All she could do was turn away to stare at the empty stretch of lawn under the tree.

She was losing it, she realized. All the lack of sleep and worrying. It had her hallucinating now. But they had seemed so real – Nia and her two companions. The dog. She remembered the man in her hallway telling her that Nia was looking after his dog – was that why she'd imagined the animal as well?

She made a slow circle around the oak, studying every square foot of the lawn under its boughs. Logic told her that she had to have imagined what she'd seen, but she couldn't help wonder, what had the Indian been doing? There had been something almost ceremonial about what she'd seen, as though she'd intruded into some secret tribal ritual.

None of it real, of course, she reminded herself.

He'd been very striking, the man. Dressed like some war vet in a khaki jacket, T-shirt and jeans, though he could just as easily have been a hobo. No, that didn't seem right. There'd been something about him that gave off a sense of ... what? She wasn't quite sure. Confidence, certainly. Maybe ... enchantment?

Ludicrous, but she knew why the idea of it had popped into her mind. It was because of the smudge-stick and the smoke and the way they'd all been here, under the tree, and then simply vanished as though she'd stumbled into a fairy tale with the last few pages torn out. As though the story went on, but the ending was now hidden from her.

"Where did you go?" she asked, unaware for a moment that she was speaking aloud.

The sound of her own voice startled her.

If I'm going to start talking to myself in public, she thought, I should at least carry around a cellular phone so that people will think I'm talking to someone.

But she had been talking to someone. She'd been talking to her daughter and the red-haired woman and the Indian with the too-deep eyes who she was sure, just before he'd vanished, had been looking right at her as though . . .

For an instant she thought she'd closed her eyes and called up a memory of the Indian when he suddenly appeared almost at her feet. Then she realized he was really there. She jumped back, heartbeat drumming in her chest.

"You—" she began. "Where did . . .?"

The man regarded her with a clownish gaze, but there was something dark behind the mocking humor, a sense that he could see into whole worlds that she couldn't, places hidden and strange.

"I guess this is just one of those days," he said. "Did Jilly send you, too?"

What he was saying made no sense, so Lisa ignored it, concentrating instead on what was foremost in her mind.

"My daughter," she said. "Where did my daughter go?"

The Indian regarded her steadily for a long moment.

"Am I supposed to know what you're talking about?" he asked finally.

Lisa didn't know what to think. *Had* she seen Nia sitting with this man and another woman, a dog lying by her daughter's knee? Had they all disappeared? Or had she imagined it? Had the Indian been sitting here all along and she simply hadn't seen him? But he was still holding the smudge-stick in his hand. While it was no longer burning, the scent of the smoke still hung in the air, faint, but unmistakable.

She sank slowly to the ground and sat facing him, legs tucked under her.

"No," she said. "Of course not."

"So are you here to have your fortune told?"

Lisa glanced at where the other fortune-tellers were set up near the War Memorial.

"Is that what you do?" she asked.

"It's one of the things I do."

And was one of the others making people vanish? she wondered. Did it also include appearing and disappearing out of nowhere like a Cheshire cat, with those spooky clownish eyes in place of the cat's long-lasting grin?

"I'm looking for my daughter," she said. "She's run away from home." She hesitated, then added, "I thought I saw her here, sitting with you and a red-haired woman. There was a dog, too. And smoke." She pointed at his smudge-stick. "The smoke was coming from that – lots of it. More than should be possible, really."

"You saw all that?"

Lisa sighed and nodded. "You all vanished and I was sure I'd imagined everything. But then you came back, except you must've been sitting there all the time and I just didn't see you for some reason."

"I must've been," he agreed.

"I'm sorry. I shouldn't be telling you all of this. It's just that I haven't had much sleep in the last few days and it seems like one bad thing after another has been happening and I guess I can't seem to shut up."

She started to rise, but he put out a hand to stop her.

"You don't know Jilly." It was more a statement than a question.

"No. I'm sorry."

Why was she apologizing? she wondered.

She started to get up again, and again he put out his hand. He didn't touch her. Instead he seemed to simply press the air above her knee in such a way that it was too much of an effort to rise.

"Look, I really shouldn't be taking up your time, Mr., uh . . .?"

"People call me Bones."

She blinked for a moment at the odd name, but then thought for a moment about what he'd said. Not his name was Bones – people just called him that.

"I'm Lisa," she said and automatically put out her hand.

He smiled, mostly with his eyes, then gravely reached over and shook.

God, Lisa thought. What am I doing? She had to be really screwed up if she was now going around introducing herself to street people.

"So why'd your daughter run away?" he asked.

"You don't really want to hear my problems . . ."

"Normally I'd agree," he said. "But this seems to be turning into a helping people kind of a day and if that's the way the wheel's turning, who am I to try to stop it or get off?"

The more he said, the less Lisa understood. It was as though they were having two separate conversations.

"So she ran away," Bones prompted her.

"And I've no idea why. No, that's not entirely true. Just before I came to the park today, a man I'd never seen before met me in the hallway of my building with a message from her. He said Nia was upset because I'm . . . um, dating a woman."

"I see."

Lisa was glad that someone did. She felt more as if she'd

stumbled back into that fairy tale, because here she was telling a complete stranger things that she'd never spoken of to anyone before.

"I should've talked to her about it first, I guess," she found herself saying.

"Or," Bones said, "if it was troubling her that much, she could have brought it up."

"This guy also said she thinks that I'm not me anymore – that there's someone else living in my head."

She gave him an apologetic look, knowing how ridiculous that sounded. But he merely regarded her seriously.

"Because of your dating women?" he asked.

"Just one woman," Lisa replied. "And it was only our first date. And now she's in the hospital and she might even die." She rubbed her face with her hands. "Oh God, how can everything be so messed up?"

"Why don't you start at the beginning of your story," Bones said.

It made no sense – unless she really *had* been enchanted – but she found herself telling him about Julie and Nia, her ex's phone call and the stabbing last night, the whole sorry mess of her life. Bones never interrupted her. He smoked hand-rolled cigarettes while she spoke, nodding encouragingly whenever she seemed to hesitate, but let her dictate how much she told him and in what order.

"This is so weird," Lisa said when she'd finally run out of words.

Bones lifted his eyebrows questioningly.

"Talking to you like this. I mean, no offense, but I don't usually run on at the mouth with strangers."

"How does it make you feel?"

"Confused."

Bones smiled. "Good answer."

He paused to grind out a cigarette in the dirt, carefully stowing the butt away with the others he'd smoked while she was talking. Lisa waited, wondering, what came next? She should be going through the park, looking for Nia. Or she should return to the hospital. Sitting here was doing nothing to solve her problems.

Bones fixed her with that dark, troubling gaze of his. "You did see Nia here," he said.

Whatever she'd been expecting him to say, this hadn't been it.

"But that . . . that's impossible . . ."

"That she was here," he asked, "or that she appeared to vanish?"

Lisa clung to one word. Appeared. Her own gaze seemed to get swallowed by those dark eyes of his.

"She only appeared to vanish?" she asked.

She looked around, hoping to discover that Nia had been sitting with them all along – the same way Bones had, remaining unnoticed by her for some reason until she suddenly realized he was there. But except for a black squirrel, busily digging up something a few yards away, the two of them were alone under the oak's spreading canopy.

"So to speak," Bones said. "She's stepped away into another place."

"Stepped away . . ."

"But she'll be back soon. You can wait with me if you like."

"What do you mean by stepped away?" Lisa asked.

"She's in the spiritworld," Bones explained. "Chasing after a friend of hers who got himself lost."

Lisa was sure he was making fun of her, but while the

mocking humor was still there in his eyes, he seemed completely serious about this.

"Maybe I'm just stupid," she said, "or perhaps I didn't hear you right, but I have no idea what you're talking about."

Actually, when you came right down to it, she realized that had been the story of this whole conversation so far.

"Do you believe in heaven?" Bones asked. "You know, with all the angels and seraphim?"

"I guess."

"Well, the spiritworld's like that, but a bit more personal. You can't see it from here, but unlike heaven, you can visit it some times. When you're dreaming, say, or on a vision quest. It's harder to get there from here in your physical body, but that's not to say it can't be done." He smiled, but Lisa didn't find it particularly comforting. "Case in point: your daughter and her friend."

He was trying to tell her that she was in a fairy tale, Lisa realized. So who did that make him? The kind stranger, offering help, or the big bad wolf?

"You're saying Nia's in another world."

Bones nodded

"That's right beside this one, only we can't see it.'

He nodded again.

"And she was . . . following someone there."

"That pretty well sums it up," Bones told her.

Lisa had to struggle with this. It made more sense that she'd only imagined Nia and the red-haired woman disappearing. But then she thought she'd imagined Bones disappearing, too, and he'd come back. And if it was true . . .

"Can you send me, too?" she asked. "To go find Nia?"

"I don't think so."

Not, he couldn't, Lisa noted.

"Why not?" she asked.

He hesitated. "The spiritworld's a big place – not an easy place to find somebody."

"But that's what you're saying Nia's done."

The worry burrs were clinging all over her thoughts again. Without even thinking about it, she'd gone from disbelief to acceptance – with all the uncomfortable anxieties that called into play.

"Is she in some sort of danger?" she asked.

Bones hesitated again. "Not if you don't follow her," he said finally, seeming to choose his words with care. "Wait with me. It shouldn't be long. Time doesn't move the same there as it does here. She could be there a month and be back here only a few minutes after she left."

Just like in the fairy tales.

"And she won't be hurt?" Lisa asked. "She'll come back okay?"

For a third time Bones was slow to respond.

"So long as she doesn't do something stupid," he said.

"Stupid? Like what?"

Bones sighed. "Like listen to her head instead of her heart. The spiritworld's more of an intuitive place. Things happen because you expect them to happen. You meet who you expect to meet. But if you think about it too much, it throws the equation off." He tapped the ground beside his knee. "This is the logical world, for all that it doesn't seem to make sense half the time. You can't bring the perceptions you use here and expect them to work there."

"But she . . . she knows all that, right?"

"Oh, sure. Got herself a guide and everything."

"You mean the red-haired woman," Lisa said.

"Her name's Zeffy."

"And she's the guide."

Bones shook his head. "No. I was talking about Buddy – the dog."

Lisa put her face in her hands. She felt like Alice, falling down the rabbit hole. Why was she even listening to this nonsense? She lifted her head to look at Bones. He smiled at her, then licked the gum on the paper of the cigarette he was rolling. Twisting off the ends, he dropped the excess tobacco into his pouch and stowed it away. Lit a match with a thumbnail and got the cigarette going, blue-grey smoke wreathing his head for a moment until a breeze took it away.

"You want one?" he asked.

Lisa shook her head. His cigarette didn't smell like plain tobacco. There was a hint of something else in the smoke.

"Is that just tobacco?" she asked.

God, had he been sitting here smoking joints and spinning this bizarre story all along? But then she recognized the smell at the same time as he replied.

"Mostly tobacco," he said, "with just a pinch of sweetgrass to keep the manitou smiling."

"The manitou."

"The little mysteries," he explained. "Spirits."

"And they're, what? Watching us now?"

"They're always watching," he said. "And full of mischief. That's why I offer them the sweetgrass and tobacco – to keep them from pulling tricks on me."

Lisa swallowed. Either she was more tired and out of it than she thought, or everything was actually beginning to make some sense. The problem was, when you started to accept any of it, it all began to clamor for belief.

"Maybe I will have one of those cigarettes," she said. "Just while we're waiting."

Bones pulled out his tobacco pouch and began to roll her a cigarette. He gave her another one of those smiles of his that almost seemed to be mocking, but not quite. The worry burrs clung thick to Lisa's mind, clumps of them, brambled and prickly.

I hope I'm not going to regret this, she thought.

IV • ZEFFY

"THIS IS a joke, right?" Zeffy said as they took in their surroundings. "I mean what kind of a spiritworld is this?"

Beside her Nia shook her head, obviously as confused as Zeffy was feeling herself.

They were sitting on a sandy public beach – Pacific Ocean, Zeffy decided, because the sun was making its way down toward the distant horizon. So they were somewhere in California. Unless the sun was just rising, but that didn't feel right at all. She'd always been good with directions and the horizon, where the ocean and sky blended together into a hazy line, definitely felt westish.

All around them, tanned people were lying on towels or in beach chairs, sunbathing, reading, dozing, listening to portable radios and Walkmans. A volleyball game was under way over to their right, close to where a long concrete and wood pier thrust out into the ocean. There appeared to be a restaurant at the end of it, a one-story structure with a flat roof and mostly windows for its walls. Skateboarders and in-line skaters were practicing their moves where the pier descended at a mild incline into a parking lot filled with cars, the westering sun dazzling on their windshields and chrome. Beyond the lot were a small town's worth of buildings stretching as far as she could see down either end of the beach. Mostly adobe or wood-frame, some brick, none taller than three stories. Some were obviously store-fronts, others private homes.

So they were in some Southern Californian beach town. Only which one? And why? How had they ended up here instead of this spiritworld that Bones was supposedly sending them to?

"It's still pretty amazing," Nia said.

Zeffy turned back to her. Nia was stroking a nervous Buddy and obviously trying to project a nonchalance she couldn't be feeling. Zeffy knew the feeling. You wanted to pretend everything was normal, even when you knew the world had gone completely off-kilter.

"What is?" she asked.

"Well, that he could send us all the way here, just like that." Nia snapped her fingers. "This is like one of those places where the old Beats used to hang out, back in the fifties – don't you think?"

Being reminded of how they'd gotten to this place didn't make Zeffy feel any better. It just confirmed the sense that nothing was as it seemed any more and brought the queasiness in her stomach to the forefront.

Don't think about it, she told herself. Soldier on.

"Yeah," she said. "I suppose it does. But we were *supposed* to be going after Johnny and Max."

"Maybe this is where they went?"

Zeffy sighed. "I don't know." She scanned the beach again before returning her attention to her companion. "We were supposed to keep them in mind when he sent us," she said, "but I didn't do a very good job of it. I started to, but then I got to thinking about Max's guitars. More than Max himself. And I didn't think of Johnny at all."

"Me either," Nia admitted. "I tried to, but then I got worried about how we were going to get back."

"What do you mean?"

Nia put her arm around Buddy's neck and stared out at the ocean. "We never asked Bones how we're going to get back."

Zeffy's heart sank. How could they have been so dumb?

"No," she said slowly. "We never did."

"So what do we do now?" Nia asked.

"I guess finding out *where* we are would be a good start."

Sitting close to them on an incredibly garish towel – all Kelly greens and yellows – was the proverbial Californian from a hundred beach movies: a young man with long blond hair and a deep tan wearing shades and a pair of brightly patterned cotton shorts. He was reading a paperback, his thumb across the title, but if the cover art that Zeffy could see was anything to go by, it had something to do with dwarves and large-breasted women in metal bikinis.

"Excuse me," she said.

He looked over to them, finger holding his place in the book.

"Could you tell me where we are?" Zeffy asked.

He shook his head. "The beach, man – where'd you think?"

"No, I meant what town?"

"Santa Feliz." Smiling, he added, "You got any more of whatever it is you're on?"

"We're not *on* anything."

"Whatever you say."

Zeffy sighed. Of course it did sound ridiculous, asking where they were like this. But what else could they do?

"In California?" she asked, bracing herself for yet one more incredulous look.

"You got it. South of L.A. You need some help?"

"No we're fine."

"Cool."

At least her sense of direction was still good, Zeffy thought as the man returned to his book.

"Why don't we have a look around?" she said to Nia. "Maybe we'll see something that'll make sense of why Bones sent us here."

Just don't think of how he did it, she told herself. Don't get into the fact that none of this should be possible in the first place.

"Okay," Nia said.

She stood up, dusting the sand from her jeans, and gave Buddy's leash a little shake.

"C'mon, boy," she told him. "We're going exploring."

The dog scrambled to his feet, muzzle raised to give her a quizzical look. Either he really had taken Jilly's advice to heart or, somewhere in his doggy brain, he'd come to the conclusion that Nia equaled safety, because ever since they'd left the café – and don't start thinking about how far away *it* is, Zeffy reminded herself – the dog had become inseparable from Nia.

Rising, Zeffy brushed the sand from her own clothes. "That looks like the main drag," she said, indicating the street that joined the parking lot directly across from the end of the pier.

They stepped over a low stone retaining wall and followed the concrete path that lay between the beach and the tiny walled-in yards of the properties facing it until they reached the parking lot, dodging in-line skaters as they whizzed past. Cutting a zigzagging diagonal path through the parked cars, they made their way to the street and walked down its four-block length of restaurants and galleries, stores specializing in sports gear and souvenir shops. Among the more popular items – they had to be, since almost every store seemed to carry them – were T-shirts with the legend LIFE'S A BEACH and seashells that, Zeffy thought cattily, had probably been imported from Hawaii. Grudging space appeared to have been given over to a grocery store for the locals – or perhaps it was a holdover from a time predating the tourist boom.

The last few blocks after the core of shops were shaded with tall palm trees, the spiky trunks thrusting out of small front yards, their enormous dark green fronds crisscrossing where they met above to cast sharply patterned shadows on the pavement below. The very last house was a Spanish-styled adobe painted a faded pink with a thick hedge of jade plants running along the front of the property. Zeffy took it in with wide eyes and fingered one of the thick shiny leaves.

"This is so weird," she said. "I've got one of these growing in a tiny pot in my bathroom. But this is huge. I never knew they could grow so big."

Beyond the last house, the sidewalk ran out and the street became a narrow highway. There were fields of dried brown grass on either side of it and a sign indicating how far it was to the freeway. In the middle of one of the fields was an old wooden water tower with enough slats missing that they knew it was no longer in working order. Zeffy shaded her eyes, but there wasn't much more to see. Just the fields and the highway running off into the distance where a dull blue smear on the horizon looked like mountains of some sort. She had to take the existence of the freeway on faith.

"So," she said. "Do we try to get a ride to L.A., or do we go back and look around some more?"

Nia shrugged. "Look around, I guess. There has to be some reason we ended up here."

"Beyond a certain individual's perversity?" Zeffy asked as they started back.

"Oh, come on," Nia said. "You two just got off on the wrong foot."

"He had a right one?"

"At the end of his other leg," Nia said, grinning.

Zeffy had to smile with her. "Okay. We'll give him the benefit of the doubt and check around a little more. But don't blame me if we don't find anything."

Halfway down the block, Zeffy paused to remove a stone that had got stuck in the tread of her shoe and was making an irritating clicking sound whenever she took a step. Standing again, she looked down the street toward the ocean and arched her back, working the kinks out of it. Santa Feliz was larger than it seemed at first. The town hugged the oceanfront, but when she remembered how far it had stretched along the shore, it was obviously far longer than it was wide.

Beside her, Nia knelt down to give Buddy a bit of reassurance. She looked up at Zeffy over the dog's head, her features serious.

"Are you scared?" she asked.

Zeffy nodded. "But I'm pretending I'm not. And I'm working really hard at not thinking about how we ended up here in the first place."

"What if we can't get back?"

"Can't get back to where?" a voice said.

Zeffy and Nia stared at each other; then they both looked at Buddy. The voice had appeared to have come from him – a gruff, rumbly sort of a dog's voice, or at least the kind of voice Zeffy had always imagined a dog would have if it could talk.

"Did he—" Nia began.

"I could swear—" Zeffy said at the same time.

Nia stood up and gave Buddy an uncertain look. Buddy immediately picked up on their nervous surprise and swung his gaze back and forth between them. They waited for him to speak again, holding their breath, but all he did was loll his tongue, his tail banging against Nia's leg.

"Pretty good, huh?" the same voice said, but this time it came from the yard they were standing beside.

They turned to find a bizarre figure sitting on the browned grass, back leaning against the trunk of a palm tree, a goofy grin on his face. He was in his late forties, a white man with a deep tan, his brown hair hennaed in places and hanging in matted dreadlocks down his back. His face was painted – blue lines under his eyes, a jagged red lightning bolt on his right cheek, a yellow circle filled with dots on the other. Or maybe they were tattoos – Zeffy couldn't tell. His ears were adorned with silver earrings, hoops of all sizes from which hung dozens of small silver milagros – virgins, crosses, saints, various arms and legs.

His clothes were a combination of rags and sewn-together affairs – plaid sleeves attached to a white T-shirt with a multitude of ribbons and brightly patterned strips of cloth hanging from the shoulders to form a raggedy vest. The baggy pants had once been army-issue green, but they were now so faded as to be almost colorless. Each leg had an extra half-dozen pockets sewn onto it, none of which matched the others. He wore one red hightop and one very scuffed and worn leather workboot. Beside him on the grass was a water container with the blue-skinned genie from *Aladdin* on the front.

Eucalyptus trees by the house behind him filled the air with a heady, pungent scent that, for the first time since they'd arrived, took the salty smell of the ocean out of the air. Zeffy decided she liked the ocean smell better. And she wasn't at all sure she wanted anything to do with the man grinning at them from under the palm. His eyes were the intense pale blue that, perhaps unfairly, always reminded her of psychos.

"I'll bet you never even saw my lips move," he added.

Now Zeffy understood. Of course Buddy hadn't spoken; dogs couldn't speak. The man had thrown his voice.

"We weren't even *looking* at you," she said.

"You're looking at me now," he said.

There was only the faintest tremor in his lips, and his voice now seemed to come from Zeffy's shoes.

Nia laughed. "He's good."

"So now we're stuck in the middle of a variety show," Zeffy said, though she had to agree with Nia. He was good. Crazy and a little scary, but good. And probably harmless. But then she thought of Bones. Look where trusting crazy, probably harmless but still scary guys had got them so far.

"So where you trying to get back to?" the man asked.

"Home," Nia said.

"Well, that's simple enough. Just wake up."

Zeffy gave him a withering look. "Oh, right. That really helps."

She backed up a step as the man lumbered to his feet. He was taller than she thought he'd be – maybe six-five – and towered over them, a swaying, tattered scarecrow figure who suddenly seemed to be made of debris more than flesh and bone. His pale gaze studied them carefully, moving from Zeffy's face to Nia's, then back again.

"Well, shit my drawers," he said. "You're really here."

Zeffy frowned with distaste, mostly because it was all too easy to imagine him doing just that.

"What a lovely turn of a phrase," she said.

"And la-di-da yourself, little missy."

"What do you mean we're really here?" Nia asked.

"I mean you're not dreaming yourself here, you really *are* here."

That vague sense of vertigo returned in a rush. Zeffy had been afraid of something like this, of finding out that Bones hadn't magically transported them to the West Coast – disconcerting enough on its own – but that they really were in some other world.

"This . . . this guy on the beach," she said. "He told us we're just south of L.A."

The man nodded. "Yeah, but it's *this* L.A. – not the one we know. You really don't want to head up there, uh-uh. It's a dark and dreadful place."

"So is it bad – being here like we are?" Nia asked. "I mean, not dreaming, but really being here?"

He held up his water container. "Starts the water talking. Next thing you know, everybody's in on it."

The confusion that spread over Nia's features mirrored how Zeffy was feeling herself.

"What are you talking about?" she asked.

The man gave her a suspicious look. "You one of those vampires from Jupiter, huh? Walking around with a box of mad?"

This conversation, Zeffy realized, was rapidly degenerating. She touched Nia's shoulder, indicating that they should start walking.

"Nice talking to you," she said.

"You don't think the water's listening?" Nia's knapsack seemed to say. "Think it's too busy, huh?"

Nia looked over her shoulder. "He's opening that water bottle of his," she said.

"Ignore him," Zeffy said.

410

"Don't you start rummaging around behind my eyes!"

Now the voice seemed to come from Buddy again. The dog shook his head, as though trying to dislodge a fly that had landed on his muzzle.

"How'd you find me anyway, huh? Who told you you could carry my cross? Fucking parasites! You keep your cannibals away from my dick – you hear me? Huh? Huh?"

He was following along behind them, weaving back and forth on the sidewalk, waving his water container above his head. There was a sudden slap of footsteps against the pavement. Zeffy turned, putting herself between the man and Nia, but he wasn't attacking them as she'd feared. He was only catching up to them.

"Had you fooled, huh?" he said.

"Look, we're not really interested in anything you've got—"

"The name's Gregory," he said, breaking in. "Like the saintly pope they named the chanting after. Course no one's going to canonize me. Been there, done that, haven't got an ounce of innocence left in me."

He stuck out his hand, but Zeffy studiously ignored it. Her snub didn't appear to register.

"See, I act crazy," he told them, "but it's all a front – so they can't get to me."

"Who can't?" Nia asked.

"You know. Them. The ones that are out to screw us all. I'm as normal as you, except I know they're out there, waiting for us to let down our guard. Act like a poet or a crazy and they don't touch you and since I can't rhyme worth a shit, I put on this act, get it?"

"Not really."

Zeffy started walking again, but Gregory fell in step beside them.

411

"Three kinds of people you'll meet here," he told them and counted them off on his fingers. "First you've got your dreamers – people sleeping, maybe meditated themselves here, whatever. Lots more dream questers now, too – white folks, you know? Not just the indigenous and Buddhist kind. Second there's the people that aren't really here. They're more like backdrop – get too close to them and they kind of fade away. I guess the only reason they're around is to fill out the picture or something."

"And the third?" Zeffy found herself asking.

"They're native to this place. Spirit-types. And they're the ones you've got to watch out for because they all want a piece of you. More real you are, the bigger piece they want."

"So what're you trying to tell us?"

"Get with the program. Start rhyming, or act crazy. Or get your pretty asses out of here, unless you don't mind going home missing a piece or two of who you are." He lowered his voice. "If you ever get home at all."

"Oh, give it a rest," Zeffy told him.

She wanted to laugh it off, for Nia's sake if not her own. Nia was staring wide-eyed at Gregory, a scared look in her eyes. But the trouble was, Zeffy couldn't. She'd tried hard, from the moment they'd found themselves on the beach, but she was long past the point now of pretending that none of this was unusual. And if it was possible to end up in some parallel world, peopled by crazies and who knew what else, then maybe Gregory's warnings weren't implausible either. Even Bones had warned them about the poetry and madness bit. And the spirits. And so had Jilly, she now recalled uncomfortably, before they'd ever tracked down Bones. Jilly had talked about the spirits, too, and warned Zeffy not to let them hear her true name. Or what? They'd get a piece of her the way Gregory claimed?

412

"What do you mean by a piece of us?" she asked him.

But he was no longer paying attention to them. He came to an abrupt halt and stared down at his water container.

"Now we're in trouble," he said. "Deep, bad, dreadful trouble."

"What're you talking about?"

He held up the container and turned it upside down, but that didn't make anything clearer for Zeffy.

"The . . . the genie's gone," Nia said.

Zeffy looked again. So it was. There was no longer a blue-skinned *Aladdin* genie on the side of the water container.

"Run!" Gregory cried. "Run for your lives!"

He flung the container onto the street where it bounced on the pavement until it finally rolled up against the curb. But he was long gone before it lay still, dashing off between the houses, a comical scarecrow come to life, dreadlocks and ribbons streaming behind him as he ran. Panic went skittering through Zeffy and she almost bolted herself, but she forced herself to stay calm as she scanned their surroundings. She gave Nia a reassuring smile that didn't come close to how she was actually feeling, but at least it seemed to help Nia deal with her own panic.

"It's okay," Zeffy said. "Look around. There's nothing to be afraid of."

The street was quiet on their block. Over where the shops began, tourists were going about their aimless business. Across the street a matronly woman with a dark Spanish complexion was watering the plants on her porch. She smiled at them and waved. Nervously, Zeffy lifted a hand in response. But already her panic was ebbing.

"He was just nuts," she told Nia. "That's all. I mean, think of some of the stuff he was saying."

"But he said he was only pretending . . ."

"Pretending so well it was real, I'd say." She started walking again. "Come on. Let's finish having a look around, then we'll grab something to eat – you like Mexican?"

"Sure."

Zeffy nodded at a restaurant across the street. The sign above the door read CANTINA ROSA.

"We'll eat there later," she went on, "but for now, why don't we look around a little more."

Think calm thoughts, Zeffy was telling herself. Think positive. And it worked, too, at least for a while. They spent the afternoon wandering around the small beach town, ate at the Mexican restaurant, stopped in at an instrument shop on a little backstreet where they found a couple of Trader guitars hanging in amongst the store's other merchandise.

"See?" Zeffy said. "I guess that's what brought us here."

Nia nodded. "That and this place. It's just like the kind of little bohemian towns I've always wanted to go to. There's probably some really cool café around here where people are reciting their poetry against bebop jazz."

Once outside the shop, they made their way back to the main street and sat on a wooden bench outside of one of the souvenir shops. Buddy plunked himself comfortably at Nia's feet and immediately went to sleep.

"So now we have to figure out how to get back home," Zeffy said.

"Or find Max."

Zeffy nodded, but she didn't hold out much hope for that.

"You notice how people keep looking at us?" Nia said. "It's been like that all afternoon and it's starting to give me the creeps."

Buddy lifted his head, obviously catching the nervousness in Nia's voice.

"Maybe we're overdressed or something," Zeffy said, trying to keep her tone light. "Everybody else is wearing shorts or bathing suits."

Nia shook her head. "I don't think it's that. I think it's like what that crazy guy was saying. They know we're here for real, not dreaming."

And they're all looking to see how they can get a piece of us, Zeffy thought, finishing what Nia left unsaid. She wanted to laugh it off, but she couldn't shake the feeling that Nia had hit too close to home.

"Makes me wish we could run into Bones," she said. "Get him to whisk us back home. I'd happily trade him another song."

"You haven't even written the first one yet."

"Not true," Zeffy said. "I've already got the – " She smiled. " – *bones* of it running around in my head. It works like that sometimes," she added when Nia gave her a curious look. "You start to think about it and then you end up with a melody and some words sticking around like a commercial jingle that won't go away. Which is good, if you don't happen to be someplace where you can get it down on tape."

"Like here."

"Exactly." Zeffy looked around and sighed. "This place is nothing like what I expected. As things stand. I'd trade Bones a couple more songs just to get back home."

Nia nodded. "Me, too. But not home. I want to go to where Max is. I mean that's the whole reason we— "

She broke off when a fat woman in polyester shorts and a halter top that could only barely deal with the pull of

415

gravity on her massive chest suddenly stepped up close to her.

"Hey!" Nia cried as the woman pinched her.

"Real as real can be," the woman said, her voice a happy drawl.

"Leave her alone," Zeffy said, standing up.

The woman turned to look at her. "Don't get your panties all in a twist, honey. I'm just making nice."

She reached for Nia again and Zeffy slapped her hand away. Nia stood up, looking as scared as Zeffy felt. Because the woman wasn't alone. A half-dozen other ordinary-enough-looking people were standing nearby now – tourist types, all of them, except for the hungry look in their eyes. Zeffy felt a strange pressure at the back of her head that moved into her eyes, giving her double vision, and all her hard-won composure dissolved. One moment she was look-ing at beach-town tourists, the next they had various animal parts and heads superimposed over their own in a nightmare collage. Nia stood closer to her and took her hand. Buddy whined at their feet and sidled in behind them.

"Oh shit," Zeffy said.

Maybe crazy Gregory hadn't been so crazy after all. The fat woman seemed to have the head of a boar now, all tusks and coarse bristles. Tiny pig eyes regarded them with undisguised spite.

"Don't be scared," she said, sugar-coating her voice. "It won't hurt."

A fox-tailed man nodded in agreement. "We're not greedy. We only want a taste."

Think of a rhyme, Zeffy told herself. Start talking crazy. But she couldn't think of a thing to say, her throat seemed to have filled with dust, and she was sure it was way too late to pretend to be a poet or crazy anyway.

V • MAX

T HE GHOSTS are here, but only in my head.
I can't face the workshop at all – the memories are
too strong. But as I walk down into the farmyard the
memories are strong whichever way I turn. I keep expecting
Pitter and Hoo to come tearing across the yard from around
back of one of the outbuildings, barking shrilly and launch-
ing themselves at me in their excitement. Thinking of them
reminds me of Buddy and I wish now I hadn't left him with
Nia. He'd love it here. Nothing to be scared of. He could
chase rabbits and groundhogs and squirrels to his heart's
content. Play with Janossy's dogs . . .

The happy images trail off.

Pitter and Hoo are only here in my mind. The same way
Janossy is.

I cross the farmyard to the house, hesitate for a moment
on the porch when I see the oil lamp I rescued from the
dump hanging where it's supposed to from the big iron nail
by the door, then open the door and step inside. It takes
my eyes a moment to adjust. I realize I'm holding my breath,
listening. Listening for Janossy. But the house is empty. I
can *feel* its emptiness, the same way I can feel Devlin
stumbling through the bush. He's circling around to where
he can watch the farm, but not be seen. Guess he doesn't
feel the connection the way I do, doesn't *know* where I am
the way I could step back out the door and walk right to
where he's crouched in a stand of cedar at the end of the
apple orchard, hiding there in the no-man's-land of new
growth that blurs the distinction between forest and
orchard.

I return my attention to my surroundings. The inside of

the farmhouse is exactly the way I remember it. No one's renovated this place – they can't have, not and duplicate it so perfectly. I've stepped back into time. I can imagine Janossy at the kitchen counter, chopping vegetables for a stir fry. Or reading in the rocking chair beside the old cast-iron stove. Sitting at the pine kitchen table in the center of the room, tuning that odd eight-stringed guitar of his. We might have slept in the bedrooms upstairs, but the only room that saw any real use the whole time I lived here with him was the kitchen.

I can't seem to walk into the room. All I can do is stand there in the doorway and stare at its familiar confines. I don't remember seeing powerlines outside, but my hand reaches up and tries the light switch anyway. The overhead comes on, the bare hundred-watt bulb that we always used – not that the overhead was on very often. More often than not we lit our evenings with candles or oil lamps.

My fingers are still on the switch. I turn the light off and step back out onto the porch, look across the yard to the workshop. I remember my dreams, then, the ones I had of Janossy before my world turned upside down. Janossy working on that unfinished guitar of his, Nia sitting in the corner, watching, listening.

I have to be dreaming. How else could this place exist the way it does, every detail so faithfully reclaimed from the past? How could there be electricity without powerlines? No highway beyond the lane. This eerie sixth sense in the back of my head that lets me know where Devlin is. None of this fits the world as it should be. It's the stuff of dreams.

I have to laugh. But then how do I explain this body I'm walking around in?

Dreams don't go on this long, with this much detail.

I'd like to put it off longer, but I'm through being easy on myself. I cross the farmyard, walk briskly right up to the door of the workshop and open it up, step in. It's so perfectly the room I remember, it can't be possible. The past few hours should have prepared me for this, but the unchanged, physical presence of the shop hits me like a punch in the chest. I have to grab the doorjamb to keep from stumbling. For one moment Janossy is there, looking up from the other side of the workbench to see who's come in. I blink, and he's gone. But the guitar he was working on is still there. Only the body, no neck. The way it was when he died.

I back slowly out and shut the door. The click of the latch lets me breathe again.

Returning to the past – even this ghostly, uninhabited version of it – is proving harder than I thought it would be. I go back to the farmhouse and make myself a cup of tea, no longer marveling that the stove works, the water runs, there's milk in the fridge. I take the tea out onto the porch and sit on the steps, drinking it while it's too hot, scalding the back of my throat, but somehow that helps make it all more bearable.

When I've finished the tea, I go back inside, set the empty cup on the counter and go up the back stairs to my room. It's unchanged as well. I remember the quilt on my bed – my father and I bought it at a church rummage sale a couple of years before I first apprenticed with Janossy. The books on the table by the window are old friends: naturalists' diaries, travelogues, an antique violin maker's handbook, a few novels. I still have some of them. My parents' wedding picture is in a place of prominence on the wall behind my head. Elsewhere hang reproductions of old photos and paintings taken from magazines, a pencil schematic design of Janossy's for a flat-back bouzouki and a small watercolor by an old girlfriend of mine from my high-school days. Cathy Galloway. I haven't thought of her in years. I wonder whatever happened to her.

What holds my gaze longest after the first cursory glance is the guitar in its stand, set up beside a straight-backed chair in the corner of the room. It's the first steel-string I made entirely on my own. I've still got it, back at my shop in the Market, hanging on the wall beside the door that leads into my spray booth – a claustrophobic little room at the back of the shop where the instruments I build have their lacquered finish applied. Janossy had nothing so fancy, just one of the horse stalls in the barn that he'd sealed with sheets of plastic. We'd use an old, if workable, army gas mask to protect us from the fumes while we worked, looking like alien bugs when we emerged from behind the plastic.

I walk across the room and sit down, pick up the guitar. Every one I've made since this has been better built, has a better sound, but as I hold my first guitar on my lap, the warm glow of how I felt when I finally finished it returns to me in a rush. I go to play a C chord, but my fingers feel all wrong and fumble the simple shape. My clumsiness reminds me of a discussion I had with Janossy once about memory – whether what the body remembers is as important as what the mind remembers.

"They remember differently," he said. "The mind remembers logistically, the body instinctively. Our *präna* lives in our flesh and bones, not the place where we calculate equations."

Präna. The Hindu term for both breathing and spirit. That was another of those words he took for his own. Like *wu-sei* and *feng shui*, they acquired their own resonance in his conversations.

Devlin's body doesn't remember how to shape chords on

the guitar. But it didn't remember simple carving either, back in Fitzhenry Park, and it took to that with alacrity after a first few awkward cuts. Playing the guitar takes more time either because it requires more complex motor skills, or because the bits of himself Devlin left behind in this body are becoming stronger. Some certainly are. The depression. The anger. The impatience.

That starts me off on another train of thought. I remember having heard somewhere that, after a certain number of years, every cell in the human body is replaced. So how long will it take before this body is entirely mine, until it no longer remembers anything of Devlin?

I practice chords and simple scales until the room grows dark and the uncallused tips of my – Devlin's – fingers get sore. Setting the guitar back into its stand, I stretch and look out the window. The sun's almost behind the hills, casting ever-lengthening shadows. Bats are out, shadow shapes that dart and swoop across the lawn, chasing moths and mosquitoes. The sound of the frogs from the marsh is suddenly loud. I can still sense Devlin; he's fallen asleep under those cedars.

Turning from the window, I make my way back downstairs. I don't question the leftover vegetable stew I find in the fridge, or the half loaf of bread in the breadbox, any more than I do the electricity or the other incongruities about this place. I help myself to both, wash them down with a bottle of Janossy's homemade cider and go back up to my room to bed. Sleep comes almost instantaneously and without dreams.

When I wake in the morning, the bird's chorus is loud outside my window, an oriole's sweet warbling cutting strongly across the rest. I lie there for a few moments, unwilling to open my eyes, afraid of where I'll find myself when I wake. I want to be on the farm, to embrace the strange return to the past that it offers, to find safety in being myself, instead of having to deal with the residue Devlin left behind. It's easier to do that on the farm. I don't want to be back in Newford. Not just yet.

I get what I want for a change.

The fresh air coming in through the window tastes better than I remember it did when I lived here. There's a thickness to it, a presence, a . . . vitality. I almost feel as if I could survive on it alone, but my rumbling stomach tells me otherwise.

I shave and take a shower. My old clothes in the closet fit Devlin's body better than they'd fit my own. I've gained weight over the years. I put on fresh socks and underwear, jeans and a cotton shirt, Devlin's shoes, and head downstairs to the kitchen to brew some coffee. I search for Devlin as I wait for the coffee to be ready and find him crouched on the far side of the barn, out of sight.

I think he slept in the barn last night. I'm probably lucky he didn't feel brave enough to come into the farmhouse while I was sleeping, though what could he do? He's more afraid of me than I am of him at the moment. I don't know what my hitting him did to bring us here any more than he does, but I'm not complaining. I feel alive for the first time in far too long.

I take my coffee out onto the porch along with a toasted cheese-and-honey sandwich. Devlin's probably hungry, but I don't much care. Today I'm going to face up to the workshop and I'm more concerned about that. I keep thinking of that unfinished guitar of Janossy's. I made a new neck for it once, but I was never happy with it. I've got some other ideas now, as though the *feng shui* of this place will allow me to perfect what I couldn't do on my own.

I clean up the dishes and set them to dry in the drainer. Starting for the door, I hesitate. Maybe I don't care for Devlin, but I'm not as hard-hearted as I'd like to pretend. I make up a couple of sandwiches for him and take them and a big mug of coffee out on a tray to where he was hiding in back of the barn. He's gone now, of course. I can sense him in the tall grass at the edge of the field, but I pretend I don't know exactly where he is. I leave the tray where he can find it and return to the farmyard.

The workshop doesn't rattle me so much today. I can step inside and walk around without dizziness, fingering the various tools and woods. For a long time I sit at the workbench with my hands on the body of Janossy's unfinished guitar, trying to absorb its essence the way he would, mapping its energy patterns in my mind, breathing in the smell of the wood.

There's a bin at the back of the workshop with a stack of various lengths of softer hardwoods, the kind needed for an ideal neck, wood that's not too heavy and not too dense, strong for its weight and generally stable. Tropical mahogany, local maple, some beautiful bird's-eye. But none of it's quite right. After sorting through it all a second time, I make my way to the outbuilding where we stored the rest of our seasoned wood and spend most of the afternoon choosing a piece of curly maple that resonates perfectly with the pattern of the guitar body I'm holding in my mind.

I wouldn't normally have chosen it for a steel-string guitar. The metal truss rod and heavy, geared machine heads will already add greatly to the weight of the neck. With the inherent nature of the steel-string wire, there would be good sustain right from the start so there's no need to enhance it.

If I were building a more sensitive classical guitar, I wouldn't have hesitated with the maple. Here it's not necessary, but the resonance is right.

I take it back to the workshop and make a few rough cuts with a handsaw. Although it's becoming almost old-fashioned, I'm planning to use a dovetail neck joint to attach the neck to the body. I have nothing against the bolt-on neck that Leo Fender first came up with in the sixties – most of the steel-string guitars I build now have them. It's easier to attach them and I can service them better. The bolt-on was a great idea, but the acoustic guitars Fender was making at the time sounded bad, so the technique got a bad reputation, even though the bolts have little to do with the sound. The only reason I'm going with the dovetail joint is that, as in choosing the wood, it feels right. More of Janossy's mystic approach. The pattern points that way.

By the time I'm ready to rough out the neck, my stomach reminds me that I never stopped for lunch. I always shape out my necks by hand – I probably enjoy that aspect of building the guitar more than any other, but it's a long job and one I'd rather start after I've eaten. I put together a pasta dish – tomatoes, black olives, pesto and spiral pasta – making enough for two. Half I eat by myself in the kitchen, the other half I take out behind the barn and leave for Devlin.

He's still hanging around, just off the main property at the moment, skulking in the woods. I've no idea what he's up to or how he spent his day – I was too busy to pay much attention to him.

After dinner, I clean up and put on a pot of tea. I decide to go back to work on the guitar in the morning. When the tea's ready, I sit down in the straight-backed chair by the window with my guitar and practice, smoothing more of the kinks out of my fingers, getting some of my speed back, until the clock over the sink tells me it's going on nine. My fingertips are aching. I want to get an early start in the morning – I still have to finish the neck, cut and fit the fretboard, install the frets; it'll take me most of the day. So I turn in early.

I don't know if it's the good air, or a return to a kind of routine, but I fall asleep immediately again tonight. And don't dream.

By late afternoon I've got the neck finished, oiled, fretboard attached. I spend the next few hours installing the frets, then glue the neck to the body. Tightbond dries in about thirty minutes, so I won't have long to wait. All that's left now is gluing the bridge and saddle that Janossy had already made to the top and doing the final setup – installing the tuning machines, making the nut, that kind of thing.

I take a break for dinner and work into the evening. By sunset, I've got the guitar loosely strung. I just have to wait for bridge glue to dry and I can tune it. I find myself thinking of Zeffy as I'm tidying up the shop. Seeing her with the other version of this instrument in Fitzhenry Park that day made me go crazy. I'm not sure how much I can blame on the bits of Devlin still left floating in me and how much on my simply having been a jerk, but I do know she didn't deserve my snapping at her the way I did.

She can't help disbelieving that Devlin and I've switched bodies – who would, outside of a movie? And it certainly wasn't her fault that Devlin lent her the guitar. I owe her an apology, big-time. I glance at the guitar and smile. Hell, if I can bring this back with me, the way I brought my backpack here, I'll have two of these guitars. Maybe I'll just give her one of them. It's not like I could ever sell either one of them – wouldn't feel right – and I don't need two.

I think the thing I regret the most about this business – beyond the obvious, of course – is that I didn't get to meet Zeffy under better circumstances. That strong attraction I felt toward her is a very rare occurrence for me. Last time it happened was with Donna and that was more years ago now than I care to remember.

But any chance of making something good with Zeffy is long gone now. There were a few times when I was talking to her in the park when she seemed interested in me – even though she was still convinced that I was Devlin. But after that incident with the guitar, and the way I lit into her when I left the park, I doubt she'll even listen long enough for me to apologize, never mind my trying to express anything beyond that.

I've got a bunch of apologies to make. To Nia. To Bones. To Buddy. Maybe I'm turning more into Devlin than I'd like – but at least there's this difference: I'm willing to admit I've made a mistake and I'll do what I can to straighten things out. I may look like Devlin, I may have pieces of him still floating around inside me, cellular memories and patterns of behavior, but I'll be damned if I'll let myself be like him, too.

When I'm done cleaning up the workshop, I take the guitar back into the farmhouse with me and lay it down on the table, eager to give the instrument its first proper workout. I light a candle and the finish seems to turn into honeyed gold, holding the light and drawing it deep into the wood's grain. There's a magic in completing an instrument, a high that can't be matched by artificial mood enhancers such as drugs or alcohol. This is the time I always understand that touch of mysticism that Janossy brought to his craft, a moment of satori that's both humbling and enlightening, akin to bringing a child into the world.

For an instrument is a child, innocent, yet wise beyond its years, its wisdom inherent and pure, unlike the rough experience that we accumulate and piece together during the time we spend in the world, colored as it is by the limitation of our attention spans and the general confusion through which we process what we learn.

Like a child, an instrument requires our input to fulfill its potential. How well or badly we satisfy our responsibilities is what makes the difference.

This guitar isn't entirely my work, but that isn't relevant to what grips me at the moment. Self-possession isn't the point. It's not that I made this, or helped in its making, but the wonder that it exists at all. The transformation of natural elements, the raw wood and tempered metal, into a perfect instrument is an alchemy as potent as lead into gold and as rare to attain. But I believe we've come close, Janossy and I, with this posthumous collaboration. I only wish Janossy were here to share the moment with me. He'd fill the room with his exuberant delight.

Finally I turn from my contemplation of the instrument to get a glass of water from the tap, but as I cross the kitchen, the outside world intrudes once more. A buzz starts up where the sixth sense keeping track of Devlin seems to sit and I realize that my few days here have only been a hiatus from the strangeness that's become my life – or at least a calming oddity in amongst all the less pleasant aspects.

I start to follow the connection to see what Devlin's up to when the buzz flares in the back of my head. The jolt it gives me is like putting my finger in a socket and all the calm

I've managed to store up in the past few days is washed away. I lean over the sink to keep my balance and another fierce jab of pain throbs in the back of my head. This time the pain is so bad I have to press my face against my hands, thumbs pushed tight against my temples as though to keep them in place.

It's a long time before I can straighten up. My face is wet with a fevered sweat, shirt sticking to my chest and back. The immediacy of the pain has faded into a dull ache that settles in behind my eyes and I realize something's changed in my connection to Devlin, but I can't tell what.

He's up on the ridge behind the farm, running back and forth across a small clearing with something – I flash on confusing, stuttered images of wings, a sharp beak, talons – battering at him, keeping him in motion. He's so panicked there isn't a coherent thought left in his mind.

I push slowly away from the sink and step outside – a little unsteady on my feet, but that goes away by the time I'm off the porch. There's a full moon tonight, the farm-yard almost as brightly lit as day. That'll make it easier to reach Devlin. I stop long enough to pick up the hickory-handled axe from beside the woodpile and start for the ridge.

Devlin's panic is ebbing, but his thoughts are no more coherent. The sense I get is that he's tiring, as though whatever's sent him into this frenzy is wearing him down.

I want to hurry, but I force myself to go slow. The moonlight might be bright out in the open, but once I'm under the trees visibility drops considerably and the footing can be treacherous. Breaking my own neck isn't going to help Devlin.

Why this sudden impulse to help him? Self-preservation, for one thing. That's my body he's wearing, broken nose and all. I don't want something worse to happen to it. But there's another reason, too. The same reason I couldn't let him starve: he's another human being. It's that basic. I might've wanted to thump him at one point, but I've managed to get past that. And while he's not particularly likable, I can't quite think of him as evil either. He's just not the sort of person I want to spend any time with. Neither's a good enough reason to stand back and not lend a hand if he's in trouble.

If?

There's no question he's in trouble. Serious trouble.

It's gone so quiet in the back of my head that I wonder for a moment if the connection's been broken. I stop for a moment, concentrating. The sound of my passage has made the forest go still. The first thing I hear is my own pulse, drumming in my ears. Wind, up in the higher boughs. A mosquito, whining by my ear.

It occurs to me that I should have reached the top of the ridge by now. The old game trail I'm following up cuts a pretty straight path from the farm and I've walked it hundreds of times. But it feels different tonight. Longer, and twistier. And the incline is much steeper. The birch and cedar around me seem older – though that's hard to tell for sure in the vague light. What I do know is that, in the forest I remember, the granite backbone of the hill never pushed out of the dirt and tree roots as dramatically as it does here.

Finally I get a sense of Devlin again, but it's only a vague presence now, as though he's worn right out and barely conscious. I don't know what he's gotten himself mixed up in this time, but it can't be good.

I begin climbing once more, following the trail as it winds in between massive granite outcrops and thick stands of old cedar. It's another ten minutes before I finally push through young birch and raspberry bushes into the clearing at the top of the ridge. The moonlight's bright here and I can see more easily now.

I don't know where I am, but it's not on the ridge behind Janossy's farm – at least not any ridge around it that I remember. But I do recognize the ancient pine standing alone at the very edge of the drop, growing out of the wide fissure that has pushed apart the massive granite slab that makes up most of the ridge. It's the same one as on the ridge behind Janossy's that I thought was my destination. And then I spot Devlin, lying on the open stone to the right of the tree, limbs twitching, eyes rolling so that I can see their whites reflected in the moonlight.

The sight of him puts a sudden tension in my chest and makes me grip the axe more tightly. I make a quick study of the other parts of the ridge, listen carefully to the forest around me, but I can't spy what's left him in this state, don't hear anything except the harsh sound of my own breathing. Even the mosquitoes haven't followed me up here. Finally, with a last nervous look around myself, I start toward him.

Careful, a disembodied voice says. *Don't get him going again.*

I stop dead in my tracks and slowly look around again. Then it slowly registers. Nobody spoke aloud. I heard the voice inside my head.

I'm up in the tree, the voice adds.

"What . . .?" I begin.

Christ, Trader. Will you keep it down?

I know who the voice belongs to now. It's Devlin talking to me in my head. But if he's in the tree like he said, then who's in the body lying there on the rock?

430

I know, Devlin goes on. *Big shock. I sure as hell wasn't expecting it either.*

I sidle along the left side of the ridge, making my way toward the pine as quietly as I can so as not to startle whoever it is that's lying on the rock. I still can't see anyone in the branches of the pine, but then I make the mistake of looking over the side of the ridge and I freeze. The drop I remember was maybe twenty, thirty feet. This one's over a hundred. I'm not normally bothered by heights, but there's something about the way it looks in the moonlight, or perhaps simply the unexpectedness of it, that wakes a sudden vertigo in me.

I look quickly away. Bending down in a half-crouch, I scrabble the rest of the way to the pine. The boughs still appear empty, except for a large bird perched about fifteen feet up on one of the first branches. I can't quite make out what it is. A crow, maybe. Or a raven.

"Where the hell are you, Devlin?" I whisper.

Right above you. Before I can say anything, he adds, *That's right. I'm in the bird.*

"Give me a break, would you?"

Give you a break? If it wasn't for you, I wouldn't be in this mess.

"What are you talking about?"

Being here, wherever the hell "here" is. You hogging that farm to yourself leaving me to try and make do in the bush. And now this.

I'm past arguing about how we got here and whose fault it was. As for why I don't want him hanging around me, if he hasn't been able to figure it out by now, nothing's going to explain it to him. The thing I don't get is what he means about being in the bird. And how did he suddenly learn to project his voice inside of people's heads like this?

"Are you going to bother explaining any of this to me?" I ask him. "Because if not, I'm going right back down to the farm and—"

Oh, no, you don't. Not till you give me my body back.

This voice inside my head is really creeping me out, but I'm determined not to show it. I'm through with letting Devlin intimidate me. I want my body back, but there's something not right here.

"You're the one with the monopoly on switching bodies," I say.

I look up into the tree at the bird again, then over to where Devlin is lying. He's not moving now, but I can see the rapid rise and fall of his chest. I think of what I've just said, but then I shake my head. No. There's no way.

I hear a sigh in my head. *Okay,* the voice says. *Here's how it went down: Thought I'd do a little exploring – I mean, you were such good company frigging around in that workshop, weren't you? So I spent the day hiking around in that out-of-shape body of yours and when I got tired, I thought I'd take a nap. Fell asleep and the next thing I know, some bird's taken over your body and I'm stuck in the bird's.*

I shake my head. No. I won't accept this.

Look up, the voice tells me.

I don't want to, but I can't not do it. I look up.

I'm going to lift my left wing.

The bird does it – unfolds its left wing to full length, then tucks it back along its side.

Now I'm going to hop down to the next branch.

It does that as well.

Need any more convincing? the voice asks.

"How could you do this?" I ask.

You think it was on purpose?

"Did you go to sleep wishing you were somebody else again?"

Man, I'm always wishing after what I haven't got. So what? Everybody does it.

"But everybody can't make it happen."

I didn't make it happen. Do I look like some clown in a wizard's hat? It just happened.

I shake my head. "You were the catalyst."

So what? What's done is done. We can worry about who's to blame later, okay? Right now I want my body back and you should be looking after your own before that bird gets some strength back and tries to take another leap off the edge of the cliff.

"What?"

Hey, what do you think I've been doing up here for the past hour? Saving your ass, buddy. I just about wore myself out beating that stupid bird back from the edge. I didn't have to do it. I could've just let it do a high dive and then where'd you be?

Safe in this body, I think. I'm shocked at the thought. Have I gotten so comfortable in this skin that I can have such disregard for my old body?

Man, you don't think things are going to stay this way, do you? I'll tell you right now, when we shift back to normal, you'd better hope your body's still habitable, because otherwise you'll be up the proverbial creek without a paddle.

I know he's right. The idea of reinhabiting my body after its been used by both Devlin and some bird is even less appealing than if it had just been Devlin using it, but I probably won't get a choice. If the balance does shift back again, I'll want a place to go.

"So what do you suggest I do?"

Go tie that sucker down before he gets perky again.

"Tie him down with what?"

How should I know? Use your belt. Or give him a whack on the side of the head with that axe.

Now there's a sensible solution. Give my original body a concussion.

"People just don't realize how caring you are, do they?" I tell Devlin.

What's that supposed to mean?

"Nothing."

I look at where my body's lying. The eyes are open now, watching me, but I get no sense that the bird inhabiting the body has any understanding of the situation. Truth is, I don't have much either. Remembering what happened when Devlin attacked me in Fitzhenry Park, I worry about what'll happen if I grab hold of that body. Will we switch, me to my own body, the bird into Devlin's? Or will we end up in yet some other place, leaving Devlin stranded here in the bird's body?

What're you waiting for? Devlin asks.

"I have to think this through," I tell him. "We have no idea what'll happen if I grab him. It could just make things worse."

Bullshit. You just want to hang on to my bod'.

"Use your head."

My head? Christ. Look at this head. It's probably got a brain the size of a pea in it.

Which would make it right about the size you need, I think.

"I meant you should think things through first for a change," I say.

You're stalling.

"I'm not. I just think we have to be careful how we—"

Screw this. I don't have to wait for you to make up your mind – not when I can make it up for you.

The bird suddenly launches itself from the tree, coming straight for me. I drop to the ground and it skims by over my head. By the time it comes circling back, I'm ready for it. I've got the axe lifted so that I can take a whack at him with the handle.

"Don't be so stupid!" I shout at him.

He doesn't listen, veering away only when I take a swing at him. He circles a second time, screaming audibly now, a raw, ragged cawing sound that sends a shiver up my spine. And then, like a kind of dissonant harmony cutting across the noise he's making, the bird in my body answers with its own loud, inarticulate cry. The pain wakes in the back of my head again, drops me to my knees.

Devlin banks away from me and I turn to look at the bird, hardly able to focus because of the screaming pain in my head. It's got my body standing up, head bent back, still howling. I drop the axe and stumble to my feet.

"Easy now," I say. It's all I can do to voice the words. My brain feels like it's on fire, but I have to do this, have to try to keep my voice gentle but still audible over the horrible sound the bird's making, have to try to calm it down. "No one's going to hurt you."

I start to take off my shirt, thinking maybe I can get it over its head, blind it, calm it, the way people throw a cover over a budgie cage. The bird looks at me, but then Devlin comes winging down from the sky. I don't know what he's hoping to do – scare it back from the edge, maybe startle it, take its attention away from me so that I can tackle it? It doesn't matter. All he accomplishes is to panic it more.

The back of my head feels as if it's exploding. My knees

buckle under me and I drop to the ground again. I see the bird in my body, moving toward the edge of the cliff. Devlin comes down at it once more, but the bird isn't putting up with his trying to make it back off anymore. Or maybe it's just getting more used to my body. Right at the edge of the cliff, one of its flailing arms catches Devlin a stunning blow; then it launches itself off the side of the cliff.

I have this frozen image that locks in my head: I'm on my knees, buckled over in agony, one hand supporting my body, the other reaching out toward the two of them. Devlin's dropping off the cliff, dazed, unable to use his wings. The bird hasn't got any wings, but it's flailing its arms as though trying to fly. Then the two of them are gone.

Pain flares white hot between my temples. The whiteness starts to spin, like the funnel of a tornado, and I feel as though I'm falling into it, falling through a spinning white corridor with a flare of light at the end that's even brighter still, grabbing handfuls of air as I fall, until my limbs go weak and I can't fight it anymore.

I just let myself go.

VI • TANYA

I T WAS like attending a funeral, Tanya thought.

Boxing up Zeffy's belongings had been hard enough, but actually driving with Geordie out to the warehouse where she'd rented some cheap storage space made her feel as though a part of her had died. But she couldn't afford to keep the apartment, and the landlord's charity would only go so far.

It had been almost three months since Zeffy had disappeared and Tanya had borrowed enough money from friends, begged enough with the landlord. It couldn't go on. Life had to go on. That's what everybody said – like they did when someone died. Life had to go on.

Where are you, Zeffy?

The question ran through her head, as it had a thousand times since that day in June. She and Geordie stacked the boxes filled with Zeffy's clothes, books and knickknacks, as well as a lot of Tanya's own stuff that she didn't have room for in the tiny bachelor apartment she'd rented in Upper Foxville. As though working on a three-dimensional jigsaw puzzle, they fit pieces of furniture in wherever there was room. The sofa standing on its end. End tables, bookcases, chairs. Zeffy's futon and her bed frame, broken down into its component parts. All too soon the space was full, the back of the pickup truck Geordie'd borrowed from a friend was empty, and their job was done.

The only thing of Zeffy's that Tanya hadn't put in storage was the guitar Zeffy had borrowed from Max Trader, the one she'd left behind at the restaurant the afternoon she and Nia disappeared. It wasn't that Tanya wanted easy access to it in case Trader showed up to reclaim the instrument so much as to have something in her new apartment to remind her of her missing friend. The guitar, for all that it was a borrowed one, summed Zeffy up for Tanya, the perfect metaphor for what had been most important in Zeffy's life. It stood in its case now, in a corner of her one-room apartment under a poster advertising Zeffy's opening slot for the Glory Mad Dog gig. The gig she never got to play because . . . because she'd gotten swallowed up in some weirdness that neither of them would have become involved in if it hadn't been for Tanya's dating Johnny Devlin in the first place.

No matter what anybody said, she knew it was her fault,

the guilt eating away at her as much as her grief. Neither allowed her much respite, but the worst was not knowing. Where was Zeffy? Tanya was no closer to understanding now than she'd been the evening the Indian had come into Kathryn's to talk to Jilly. All this mumbo jumbo about spiritworlds and getting lost in them made no sense. But then what had happened with Johnny and this Max Trader made no sense either. Overnight, the rules of the world had changed and she didn't have a handbook to see her through. All Tanya knew for certain was that the catalyst to Zeffy's disappearance had come out of her own stupid need to have a boyfriend. Beyond that, everything was confusion.

"I guess that's it," Geordie said as they locked up the storage space.

Tanya lit up a cigarette and nodded. "Thanks for your help. I don't know what I'd've done otherwise."

"Listen. About us . . ."

"It's not you, Geordie. Honestly. It's me. I'm really shitty company and I can't deal with the extra pressure of knowing I'm bringing somebody else down as well."

He looked as if he was going to say something, but then only nodded and went around to the driver's side of the pickup. They'd been through it all a hundred times before. She hadn't expected to see him today. She'd asked Jilly if she knew someone who could help her and the next thing she knew, Geordie was on her doorstep, the borrowed truck parked at the curb, and what was she going to do? Turn him away? She still liked him – liked him a lot – but she had to make some changes in her life and one of them was trying to make a go of it on her own. If someone was going to get hurt in her life, let it be herself. Except it didn't work that way, did it? Geordie was hurt because she wouldn't let him into her life now. But she had to make a start of it somewhere. She had to learn to like herself, to trust in herself, before she could be part of a couple again.

So she was moving. She'd quit her job at Kathryn's and started working for a temp agency. Office work, and she hated office work, but it paid better than waitressing and who was she fooling? She was never going to be a waitress-slash-anything. She didn't have aspirations like everybody else she knew. Oh, she wanted to do more with her life, but she didn't have it in her. Didn't have the drive. Didn't have the *need* to be painting, or writing, or playing music, or anything. But she wasn't going to simply be the appendage in a relationship anymore either. She wasn't going to define herself by who she was sleeping with or hanging out with. She had to be something more. And until she could figure out what that something was, she might as well try to make the day-to-day aspects of life easier to deal with. Might as well learn how to make it on her own for a change.

"You want to go back to your new place?" Geordie asked when she slipped into the passenger seat beside him.

"If it's not out of your way."

"No problem."

Jilly had been trying to do her a favor. Tanya knew that. But why couldn't she have played matchmaker some other time? Why did she have to send Geordie to help her?

"It's not like you don't mean a lot to me," she said as Geordie started up the truck.

"I know. But you just want to be friends."

Tanya sighed. She butted out her cigarette in the ashtray and lit another.

"I hate the way that sounds," she said. "It's like saying somebody's got a great personality, but you know that just means they're not all that good-looking."

"I understand," Geordie told her. "Really, I do."

No, he didn't, she thought. Nobody did. How could they? *She* didn't understand what she wanted, what she was feeling, so how could anybody else? All she knew for sure was that she had to make a go of it on her own. For once she had to not lean on just whoever happened to be handy.

She wanted to pay back the money she'd borrowed. She wanted to save some. Maybe by the time she had a couple of thousand dollars put away in a savings account, she'd have a better idea of what she wanted to do with her life.

Maybe Zeffy would come back.

No, she told herself. Don't think about that. You're just going to make yourself crazy.

"How do you like your new job?" Geordie asked.

"Well, you know me. If WordPerfect didn't have a spellchecker program, they'd probably have fired me on my first day. But it's okay. I got four days last week, three at a shipping company and one with an accounting firm."

"I couldn't work in an office."

Tanya gave him a half-hearted smile. "I know the feeling. I think what I hate the most is all the packaging. You know, the right clothes, the right makeup, the right attitude."

"My point exactly. Some people just aren't cut out for that kind of thing and I'm one of them."

Me, too, Tanya thought, but she didn't seem to be cut out for anything else either, so she had to make do.

"Monday I'm filling in at a talent agency," she said. "Two weeks while the regular secretary gets to go to Hawaii."

"Hawaii's not all it's made out to be."

"You've been there?"

Geordie shook his head. "No. But if it was that great, then everybody'd be living there, wouldn't they?"

"With that kind of logic—"

"I'm joking," Geordie said. "I'd love to go there someday."

Tanya lit another cigarette from the butt of the one she'd only half-finished. I remember jokes, she thought. They were part of the world before everything went horrible. She didn't know how people could appreciate them now. She didn't know how people could all just carry on as though nothing was different when in reality, *everything* was different and showed no signs of getting any better.

It was only a few minutes' drive from the warehouse where she'd rented the storage space to her new apartment, but it seemed to take forever. She knew Geordie meant well. She knew he was sweet and kind and all the things she liked in a man, but any kind of intimacy, even something so simple as sharing the cab of a pickup truck for a short drive such as this, made her uncomfortable these days.

When they reached the end of her street and Geordie had to stop because the light was against them, she unfastened her seat belt.

"I can just get off here," she said.

Geordie glanced down her street and she knew what he was seeing. Run-down tenements, litter collecting against the curbs, beat-up vehicles parked along the street, including one near the corner that was up on cinder blocks, its wheels missing. A handful of tough-looking boys were gathered in front of the corner store, pushing each other around and joking. On the step of the building next to them, an unsmiling man in chinos and a white sleeveless undershirt was smoking a cigarette and staring blankly across the street. There was nothing to see there, only a couple of boarded-up storefronts.

"Are you sure?" he asked. "It looks kind of rough."

Tanya nodded. "I guess. But it's my neighborhood now, so I'm going to have to get used to it."

Before he could protest further, she had the door open and stepped down onto the pavement.

"Thanks for the ride, Geordie," she said. "And for all the help moving everything."

"No problem. Listen, if you decide you want to—"

"I'll keep in touch," she told him, and closed the door.

She started walking briskly down the block, not looking back, half expecting him to follow anyway, part of her *wanting* him to follow, but when the light changed she heard him put the truck in gear and continue on up Lee Street. She slowed down, but not much. She was nervous walking up the street by herself, even now, in the middle of the day. At night it seemed like a war zone and most of the time she flagged down a cab at the bus stop on Lee and had it drive her the two blocks down to her apartment.

Nothing's going to happen in broad daylight, she told herself, but when she walked past the pawnshop and a thin, dark-haired man rose up from the weeds in the lot beyond it, she wasn't so sure anymore. He had a haunted look in his eye that she recognized from her own junkie days – the jones was fed, but it didn't seem to be enough.

"Crack?" he said. "Smack?"

She wasn't sure if he was selling or looking to score. All she could think was – and it wasn't the first time since Zeffy had disappeared this came to mind – how a couple hits would be the way to take the pain away, to forget everything, just for a while. But then she remembered all those hours hidden away in bathrooms, jabbing away at her welted arms, stashing needles in Tampax boxes, suffering

442

mild convulsions because she'd done a little too much, eyes rolling, staggering into the shower to stay alive . . .

And she didn't want to forget. Not Zeffy. Not why she was making this break from her old life. Drugs weren't going to solve anything.

"No, thanks," she told him.

"'Scool."

But she was tempted. Even looking at him, so wasted he could barely stand upright, shuffling back to his nest in the weeds and trash, dirty clothes and dirty skin, back prematurely stooped, arms below the sleeves of his T-shirt covered with small scabs . . . she was still tempted and that probably scared her more than the idea of what she'd have to suffer going through cold turkey again. If she didn't OD and kill herself first.

But it didn't have to be like that, a part of her reasoned. This time she'd know how much she could handle before the jones threatened to take over her life again. She could give herself small snatches of oblivion – just enough to let her deal with the emptiness that was swallowing her from the inside, to give herself some breathing space from the crying jags and the loneliness that filled up the long hours that stretched between coming home from work and going back in the next morning.

Yeah, right, she thought. Like that wasn't every junkie's rationale before they let the monkey climb up on their shoulders and ride them back down into wasteland. She knew that this time, it'd be a one-way trip.

"No, thanks," she repeated.

The junkie wasn't listening, but that didn't matter. She wasn't talking to him anyway. She gave him a last look, trying to impress the pathetic image of him on her mind so that she could call it up again when she needed a reminder, then hurried on down the block to her apartment.

VII • LISA

LISA ANSWERED the doorbell with the same nervous apprehension she felt whenever the phone rang or there was a knock on the door. Her heart would lift and she'd think, finally, it's Nia, but at the same time she dreaded the intrusion, believing that, after all this time, it could only be bad news. She could no more stop herself from feeling this way than she could stop herself from picking up the phone, or rushing to the door. This time it was a postal delivery man and the usual mix of relief and disappointment washed through her.

"Sorry to bother you, ma'am," the man said. "But your neighbor downstairs isn't in. Would you mind signing for his package?"

"No."

The man smiled. "Thanks. If you'll sign here."

"I meant, no, I won't sign for it."

"But—"

"He can rot in hell for all I care," Lisa said.

The police had established that Max Trader had disappeared around the same time that Nia had, while "Bones" hadn't pulled his own vanishing act until the police started to look for him. Lisa wasn't sure what the connection between her neighbor, her daughter and the strange fortune-teller she'd met in the park had been, but she did know that the two men had something to do with Nia's disappearance. They'd had to. Why else would Bones have plied her with whatever drug it had been in that cigarette, making her

444

think that she'd seen Nia disappear into some vague spirit land? Why else would a man such as Trader, twice Nia's age, ingratiate himself to her daughter?

What especially irked her was that because Trader had arranged for direct payments from his bank to cover his rent and utilities, the apartment and store on the ground floor remained waiting for him, as though he could step right back into his life whenever he'd finished with Nia. The landlord collected his mail for him.

"Look, Mrs. Fisher," he'd told her. "In this country, a man's innocent until proven guilty. Mr. Trader has seen that his bills are paid and until he stops, or he's convicted of a crime, I have no intention of evicting him."

"But he *kidnapped* my daughter."

"You don't know that."

"What? You think they eloped and ran away together?"

"I'm very sorry about what's happened with Nia," the landlord had said, obviously uncomfortable with the way the conversation was going. "But you don't know that Mr. Trader had anything to do with her disappearance. It's far more likely that she simply ran away at the same time Mr. Trader left on his trip."

Which was what the police said as well, though at least they were willing to look further into it.

"Nia wouldn't run away," Lisa told her landlord.

Except hadn't her ex told her that, in fact, that was exactly what Nia had done? And hadn't Trader still been in his apartment after Nia had disappeared?

"I'm sorry to have bothered you, ma'am."

Lisa blinked, memories brought up short when she realized that the delivery man was still standing in front of her.

"You have a nice day now," he said.

She didn't bother replying. Closing the door, she leaned against the inside wooden panels and fought to regain her composure.

"Who was that?" Julie called from the kitchen.

"Nothing," Lisa said. "Just somebody else trying to deliver a package to the monster who used to live downstairs."

She pushed away from the door and returned to help Julie prepare dinner, hoping she looked more composed than she was feeling. Julie was sitting at the kitchen table, chopping vegetables for a salad. She looked up as Lisa came in, the worry plain in her features.

"I know, I know," Lisa said. "Just because he's a creep, it doesn't mean he had anything to do with Nia's disappearance. But I still feel he's involved and I'll be damned if I'll do him any favors."

"I wasn't going to say anything," Julie said, her voice mild.

"But you were thinking it. I could tell the minute I walked in here."

Julie shook her head. "I'm just worried about you. You're taking this all so—"

"Badly? You try having your daughter kidnapped and see how you feel."

Julie made no reply. Lisa knew she should let it go, but she couldn't seem to stop herself from going on. She never could these days.

"And I know what you're going to say next: There's no proof that Nia was kidnapped. In fact, everything points to her having run away, but I *know* my daughter and running away isn't her style."

Julie laid the knife she was using down on the cutting board.

"You've got to stop blaming yourself," she said.

"Then who should I blame?"

"I don't think blame's the issue unless you make it that way. Everything you feel is understandable – from reproaching yourself to the worry and hurt you're feeling. But none of it's going to bring Nia back and you're only turning yourself into a nervous wreck. The simple fact of the matter is she *did* run away – we know that because of your ex's phone call."

Lisa shook her head. "You don't know him. Dan would say anything if he knew it'd get me going."

"How would he even know that Nia was missing in the first place?"

Lisa shrugged.

"What we're waiting for," Julie went on, her voice patient, "isn't to hear from kidnappers, but for Nia to either change her mind and come back home, or at least call."

"I can't just wait," Lisa said. "It's driving me crazy. I know this is all my fault. If I hadn't . . ."

Her voice trailed off at the pained expression that now touched Julie's features. She had never meant to tell Julie what the stranger in the hall had told her, how Nia had left because she'd seen her mother necking with another woman. It had just come out on a bad night, blurted out in a confused jumble in between bouts of tears. As soon as she'd told Julie, she'd regretted it and been determined not to bring it up again. But it did come up. Not once or twice, but a half-dozen times.

"I don't mean that," she said. "I mean, I wasn't getting into all of that again."

But Julie only sighed. She stood up, still moving slowly. The knife wound had healed, but she was far from being fully recovered. Lisa moved aside as Julie walked by her to go into the hall, then trailed along behind her lover.

"Where . . . where are you going?" she asked.

Julie put on her coat. "I don't think we should see each other anymore."

"Julie, please . . ."

"Please what? You're blaming our relationship for Nia's running away – that is, when you aren't constructing elaborate conspiracy theories. I'm really and truly sorry for how you're feeling – it makes me realize what I put my own parents through when I ran away – but this guilt you've got over our relationship isn't something I can live with any longer. It's just not healthy."

"I didn't mean it. I won't bring it up again."

Julie shook her head. "No, but you'll still be thinking it. And, God help us, somewhere inside you, I think you agree with it as well."

"It's just . . . I feel so crazy . . ."

"I know. And that's why I think this is better for both of us. With me out of the way, you won't have to constantly be reminded of how your unnatural desires drove your daughter away."

"I've never said that."

"No, you just think it. I'm sorry, Lisa, but I can't stay in a relationship like this."

"But . . ."

"I wish you the best, truly I do. I hope Nia comes back or calls you soon. And I hope you figure out just what you want and don't drive it out of your life when you finally get it."

"You're not being fair."

Julie sighed. "No. I suppose, I'm not being fair. But then you haven't been playing fair either, have you?"

"I'm just so confused."

Such an empathic look touched Julie's features that Lisa was sure she was changing her mind, sure that they'd work this out again. Instead, Julie simply nodded and said, "I know," then left the apartment.

Lisa stared numbly at the door as it closed. The faint click as the lock engaged echoed like thunder in her ears. She waited, unable to breathe, waited for Julie to come back in once more, but all she could hear was the other woman's slow descent down the stairs and she knew that she was being abandoned.

Again.

She found it hard to stand and had to walk carefully from the hall to the living room, each step deliberate to maintain her shaky equilibrium. When she reached the sofa, she had to hold on to an arm and slowly lower herself down. She stared numbly at the floor between her feet. There was an incredible pressure behind her eyes, but the tears wouldn't come. All she could think was that she hated the person who had done this to her – driven Nia away, made her life such a confused mess, now driven Julie away. She wanted to hurt that person, she hated that person, she . . .

Finally the tears came.

She fell to the side and buried her face against the arm of the sofa, her shoulders shaking.

When had she become this stranger that she now hated so much? How could she have become her?

She had no answer and that only made the pain worse, the tears come faster.

VIII • JILLY COPPERCORN

CLOSE ON midnight, Jilly left her second-floor studio on Yoors Street and walked down Kelly Street into the Rosses. She paused outside the open door of The Harp, listening for a moment to the music of the Celtic band playing on the small stage inside, then made her way around back of the pub. An orange tomcat skittered out of her way, startled by her unexpected presence, and frowned down at her from the metal stairs of the fire escape where it took refuge.

"Oh, don't look so cross," Jilly told him, looking up. "It's not like you own the alley."

The cat's response was to lick its shoulder and studiously ignore her.

Jilly smiled and continued down to the waterfront, then turned toward the Kelly Street Bridge. Ducking her head, she pushed through a loose board and stood for a moment in the darkness on the far side of the fence. She could hear the traffic going by on the bridge above, the sound of the Kickaha as its waters slapped against the wooden pilings and stonework of the abandoned dock on its way down to the lake.

"Guess you think I'm hiding on you," a voice said from the deeper darkness under the bridge.

"Course not," Jilly said. "But you know me. I'm just good at finding things, even when they're not lost. It's like—"

"This gift you have," Bones finished.

Jilly's eyes hadn't adjusted to the poor light yet, so she felt more than saw his smile.

"Something like that," she said.

450

She shuffled her way over to where his voice was coming from, feeling her way with her feet until her outstretched hand touched a stone wall. She followed it for a few steps, trailing her fingers along the damp stones, until Bones spoke again.

"Another step and you'll be treading on my lap."

Jilly looked down. Bones was a vague shape now; mostly she could make out his white T-shirt.

"I'm really not hiding from you," he went on.

Jilly slid down until she was sitting beside him. "I know."

"It's that damn woman – sicced the cops on me. I can't turn around for stumbling over one of them. They're all over my face. I'm lucky to be sitting here instead of in some holding cell."

"Can't blame her, though. Nia's only sixteen. And it looks bad."

"I don't blame her. I blame myself." Jilly heard something in his voice that she hadn't heard before. "I've never been much of a one for hanging on to regret," he added after a moment, "but I can't believe I just let them go. Helped them cross over and everything. What the hell was I thinking?"

Jilly touched his shoulder and he reached up to hold her hand.

"You were just trying to help out," she said.

Bones laughed humorlessly. "Yeah, that's me. Always ready to lend a hand. You'd think I'd learn."

"You wouldn't be who you are if you didn't."

"I suppose. And Cassie sure does like that stone crow Nia traded me."

"I'm not used to hearing you feeling sorry for yourself," Jilly said.

"I'm not used to feeling sorry for myself either. It was a little thing to do, but it messed up a lot of lives. Spiritworld's like that, but you forget. You get so used to making your own way through it that you forget just how dangerous a place it can be for anybody else."

"How's Cassie taking all of this?" Jilly asked.

"Getting pretty tired of not seeing me . . . and of having to hide out when she does. Not that we had all that much on our social calendar anyway, but it wears on you."

They fell silent then, listening to the river flow, the traffic overhead. Jilly's eyes had adjusted enough to the poor lighting that she could make out her companion's features. He'd lost weight. His face was thinner, with new worry lines.

"I know what you're thinking," Bones said. "I look like shit."

He took his hand from Jilly's, rolled himself a cigarette, lit it. When he offered it to Jilly, she shook her head.

"Take a small hit for the grandfather thunders," he said. "Tell them you're here. Offer them a prayer for your friends."

"Like they're going to listen to a white girl?"

"The manitou aren't about color – you know that. It's all spirit. Mix your breath with the smoke, it makes a prayer. They see the smoke, it gets their attention and then they see the spirit in your breath, listen to you, help you maybe, or show you how you can help yourself."

So Jilly took a drag, coughed when she drew too much into her lungs. Eyes watering, she passed the cigarette back to Bones. He held it up in front of his face and blew the smoke out across the water, making the end brighten like a small red eye in the dark, then took a drag himself.

"So are you going back soon?" Jilly asked.

"Heading out again tonight."

He reached into his pocket and pulled out the pebble that

Nia had given him. It was too dark for Jilly to see the crow drawn on it with a magic marker, but she knew it was there. Bones had shown it to her before.

"Trouble is," Bones went on, "Nia didn't have this long enough for it to get a real taste of her and I can't get a handle at all on your friend Zeffy. Makes tracking them hard – hit and miss and I'm coming up miss every time. I think maybe they're on a different time line – you know, things are rushing like usual for us, but they're on snail-time. It's usually the other way around, but it happens sometimes. I've put the word out about them, but it's a big place and I've got to be careful who I start in on looking for them. Don't want to set any hungry spirits on their trail."

"What about Max and Johnny?" Jilly asked.

"Can't find jack on them either, but they're not my responsibility."

"Wouldn't they all be together?"

"Maybe. But I can't count on it and Zeffy and Nia *are* my responsibility. Finding them comes first. If they're together, fine. But I'm not losing sleep over Max and the other guy. I can't afford to spread myself that thinly."

"Take me with you," Jilly said. "I could . . ."

Bones started to shake his head before she could finish.

"You know I can't do that," he said. "It's too dangerous."

"But not for you."

"It's dangerous for anybody, walking there in their own skin, but especially for someone like you. You're like a magnet for the spirits, Jilly. Got a light inside you that shines too bright. I've told you, I can teach you how to navigate that place, but you've got to give me a few years so you can study it properly."

"We don't have years."

Bones nodded. "And like I said, time's relative there. From their point of view, they might have only just arrived. Hard to tell. Takes a lot of study to get it right, find the right path that keeps you moving at the same pace or faster than time's moving here."

"But Sophie just goes there."

"Sure she does," Bones said. "But she doesn't go in her skin. She dreams her way across – she'd have to, seeing how she shines about as bright as you – and that's the only way you can go, too, until you learn more."

"I don't have those kind of dreams."

Bones smiled. "Maybe you just don't remember them. That light you carry's got to have come from somewhere. I don't know many people shine so bright without having touched a spirit or two along the way."

"I guess," Jilly said. "I only wish I could be the one to decide when it happens. You know, if when I want a piece of magic, I could just step across into it the way you do."

"You've got to accept your blessings as they come. Most people don't even get one, and when they do, they ignore it, or explain it away."

"I suppose."

They fell silent again. Jilly stared across the river, absorbed the slow flow of its current. The traffic overhead was so sporadic that for long moments it was as though the city didn't exist anymore, as though they'd been displaced into another place where the shadows gathered close around them held spirits, watching.

"Wish you could come, though," Bones said suddenly. He ground out his cigarette on the stone beside him and dropped the butt into his pocket. "What with that gift you have for finding things and all."

"No way I can hide this too-bright light I'm supposed to be carrying around inside me?"

"None that I know of. Or at least nothing that doesn't take time we don't have."

Jilly sighed. "That figures."

"Talk to Sophie," Bones told her. "Practice holding on to your dreams when you wake and deciding where you want to go in them before you sleep. It'll give you a start and it's only dangerous if you let it be."

"What's that supposed to mean?"

"Everything's got a risk attached to it," Bones said. "You know that, same as me. People forget, think that cross-world dreaming gives them a license to do anything they want, to anyone they want. They think there's no payback. But the things you do when you're over there mean as much as what you do here. Say you kill somebody in a cross-world dream. You're going to carry that with you into the here and now. It changes you, turns you into someone you weren't before you did it. And it calls down things you don't want to know about – hungry things."

"That's what Sophie says."

Bones nodded. "Then there's plain common sense. You know how they say if you die in a dream, you die for real?"

"But that's not really true, is it? I mean, not in the spiritworld."

"Let's just say it's not worth testing."

The way he said it made the shadows seem to draw closer and Jilly was glad she wasn't alone.

"I've dreamed that I was dead," she said.

"That's not the same thing."

"I guess you're right. I'd already be dead when the dream started." She shivered, remembering one such dream, ghosting through what she'd left behind of her life and no one able to see or hear her. "It was seriously creepy."

"But you don't want to focus on that kind of thing," Bones told her. "It's like inviting the hungry spirits to dinner."

"You keep calling them hungry."

"That's because they are."

"But what are they hungry for?"

"Pieces of what they can't have," Bones said. "Pieces of this world. They hunger for it the same way we hunger for the spiritworld. You know, the way people chase after ghosts, or gods, or anything that can explain why they're in this world in the first place."

"So the spirits aren't necessarily bad."

Bones shook his head. "They're not good or bad, most of them. They just want a taste of what they think they can't have – same as us."

"And what they can't have is living here?"

"Sort of. They can't have skin – they've got to borrow it and most people, they don't want to give it up. But the spirits visit. They're around all the time, looking for answers they think we're hiding from them. It's just we don't usually pay attention to them. Focus on them and they get secretive, most of them, and shy away."

Jilly felt a shift in the air as he spoke, that sense of being watched from the shadows around them lessening. She glanced at Bones and his teeth flashed with a grin. She couldn't see those startling eyes of his, but she could imagine them.

"So," Bones said. "Anything you can tell me about Zeffy that might make it easier for me to get a handle on her?"

"You could try offering her a gig. I've seen her go right across town for an open stage."

"She already owes me a song," Bones said.

"Maybe you should use that."

He nodded slowly. "Never thought of that. It's a connection we've got, all right. Don't know if it's strong enough, but it's worth a try "

"What'll you do when you find them?" Jilly asked.

"Bring 'em back."

"But what if they haven't found Max yet and they don't want to come back?"

Bones shrugged. "Cross that bridge when I get to it, I suppose."

He stood up and brushed off his jeans, then offered Jilly a hand up.

"Time I was going," he said.

"You won't change your mind?"

He shook his head. "Not about taking you now, but not about teaching you either. You find the time, I'll match it with my own."

"Okay."

"Careful now," he said. "Better step back a little. You don't want to get pulled in after me."

Jilly moved away from him, trailing her hand along the stone support of the bridge.

"You don't need to chant or something?" she asked.

"Naw. I only use the chanting and smudge-sticks to help other people focus."

Jilly smiled. "And you're always focused?"

He returned her smile. "It's this gift I have," he said.

He took a step into the darker shadows beyond and just like that, he was gone.

"Good luck," Jilly said, even though she knew he couldn't hear her.

She stood quietly, listening to the river. But when the

shadows seemed to thicken with watching presences again, she made her way back through the fence and into the alley behind The Harp. The orange tom was waiting for her, perched on the lid of a garbage can.

"Hey, big fella," she said.

He turned his back on her, pretending a sudden interest in the stone wall of the pub. A car went by on the bridge above. She regarded the fence through which she'd just come, felt the shadows quicken on the other side of it, sidling toward her from under the bridge, so she walked to the end of the alleyway. Pausing there, she looked back once more, then went into the pub for a beer before heading home, letting the noise and music dispel the queer mood that had overtaken her.

She found Geordie sitting in a corner, his fiddle still in its case by his feet as he nursed a draft. Ordering a Guinness at the bar, she took it over to his table and sat down across from him.

"Hey, fiddle-boy," she said. "How come you're not sitting in with the band?"

Geordie shrugged. "Oh, you know. Don't really feel like it, I guess."

Jilly knew all right. For Geordie it was Tanya, but it was all part and parcel of the same sorry business that had the police looking for Bones, Bones looking for Zeffy and Nia, Tanya withdrawing from life in general and Geordie in particular . . .

"It's that serious?" she asked.

"Not for Tanya."

"But it is for you." Jilly didn't make a question of it.

"She's got a big spirit, sitting there inside of her," he said. "I don't even have to look at her, just be with her, and it comes slipping over me like a warm, golden glow. The thing is, she doesn't know it. She's gotten this bum rap for too long where everybody makes her focus on how she looks instead of who she is." He paused and such a sad look touched his features that Jilly's heart went out to him. "I'm proud of her for doing what she's doing now – getting to know herself instead of accepting the image other people have of her. It's something she should have done a long time ago, and I guess it's something she feels she has to do on her own. But I miss her."

"I know you do," Jilly told him. "But she'll come around."

"Maybe. Maybe not."

Jilly sighed. She took a sip of her Guinness, then struck a pose, hands on hips, foam collected on her upper lip like a mustache.

"Look at me," she said. "I'm Charlie Chaplin."

"I appreciate what you're trying to do," Geordie told her, "but I'm not much in the mood to be cheered up."

Jilly pulled a pencil and small sketchbook from her pocket.

"Who's trying to cheer you up?" she said, not looking at him now, head bent over the sketchbook, curly hair falling in her face as she furiously scribbled on the paper. "I'm just here to get some sketches for a new series of paintings I'm doing. I plan to call it *Grumpy Young Men*. Here." She held up the rough caricature she'd done of him, his jaw drooping Dalíesquely down and across the table, where it served as coaster for his beer mug. "See? What do you think?"

Geordie couldn't help but crack a small smile. "Okay. You win. I feel all cheered up."

"No, you don't. But if you played a few tunes you might feel a little better."

"I suppose."

Jilly put her hand on his forearm. "I'm not trying to get you to forget her. I just don't want you to forget yourself in the process."

"It's hard."

"I know. And it must be harder with everybody around you here having such a good time. Why don't you come back to the studio with me? I've got a commission I need to finish and I could use a soundtrack while I'm working. I don't have *any* decent tapes anymore."

"You're just saying that."

Jilly smiled. "Of course I'm just saying it. But that doesn't mean it's not true at the same time. So, are you up for it?"

"I don't know . . ."

"Come on. When was the last time we did this?"

"Last week."

"Oh please. That's like forever ago."

"I'll probably only be able to play laments and dreary old airs."

"That's perfect," Jilly told him. "This is a really sad painting I'm working on."

"Okay. I give up. I'll come."

"Good." Jilly gave a furtive look around the pub. "Do you think Tommy would notice if I snuck out with my glass of Guinness?"

"God," Geordie said, and he had to laugh. "You're incorrigible, aren't you?"

Jilly gave him an innocent look. "I'm very corrigible. Everyone says so. It's this—"

"Gift you have," Geordie finished for her. He stood up. "Can you fit the glass under your jacket?"

"Not without spilling it."

"Okay. Then I'll cover for you. Wait now. Wait. Okay.

Tommy's looking away ... he's ... yes, he's serving somebody ..."

With Geordie providing a screen, the two of them made their way outside with Jilly's Guinness and not a drop spilled. They started up Kelly Street, walking arm in arm, sharing sips of the beer as they went.

"You know," Geordie said. "I am feeling better."

"Me, too. We should do this more often."

"What? Drink alcohol illegally on the street?"

Jilly punched him in the arm. "You know what I mean."

"I do," Geordie told her. "And thanks."

It was good to see a real smile on his face, Jilly thought. Bullying Geordie into a better mood was easy for her; they'd been friends for so long she knew all the right buttons to push. If only it could be as easy to fix everything else that had gone wrong over the past few months, but that was out of her hands.

It was up to Bones now. If he found Zeffy and Nia it would start to put a lot of things right. But she didn't think he'd have any more luck tonight than he'd had any other time he'd gone. She couldn't say how she knew, but she had the feeling that those hungry spirits he'd been talking about had taken matters into their own hands.

IX • ZEFFY

WHEN THE boar-headed woman moved forward again, Zeffy gave her a sudden, stiff-armed shove that made her stumble off-balance, arms and legs quaking like shaken Jell-O. She would have fallen if not for her companions, three or four of them lurching as they took the brunt of her weight. The spite deepened in the boar-woman's eyes when she regained her equilibrium. Zeffy glared right back at her, putting on a fierce look that was completely at odds with the thundering drumbeat of her pulse. But they didn't have to know that, she thought.

"You shouldn't have done that," the woman said.

"Done what?" a voice asked.

None of them had heard the pickup truck pull over to the curb. Zeffy glanced hopefully toward the speaker, but her hopes were dashed when she realized he was only more of the same. He had human enough arms, the hand at the end of one grasping the steering wheel, the other hanging out the window, its fingers drumming a rhythm on the metal door. Human chest in a white T-shirt and jean vest, on his head a tan-colored flat-brimmed hat with a beaded sweat-band. But the head itself was that of a crow – human-sized, all black feathers, blacker eyes and a long, sharp bill.

"None of your business," the boar-woman said.

"Everything's my business," the crow-headed man told her. His voice carried a harsh rasp, like a crow's *caw*.

He dropped his gearshift into neutral, put on his hand brake and hopped down from the cab of the pickup. Below the waist, he was also human. Worn jeans, an old pair of cowboy boots, high-heeled and pointy-toed. The other animal people made way for him – all except for the boar-woman, who stood her ground. Zeffy and Nia did, too, mostly because the boar-woman's bulk was blocking their escape.

The weirdest thing about all of this, Zeffy realized in some tiny part of her mind that was still capable of rational observation, was how nobody else on the street gave any of this a second glance. Skateboarders, pedestrians, the old man sitting on a bench not two feet away who had just glanced up from his newspaper. Not one of them seemed to see anything out of the ordinary with a man that was part bird driving a pickup truck or the coterie of animal people that had been threatening Zeffy and Nia. Maybe they saw this kind of thing every day.

"So," the crow-headed man said in that same raspy voice of his. "Are we having a problem here?"

The boar-headed woman stood her ground for a few moments longer, then reluctantly gave way to him. She waddled off down the street, accompanied by the fox-tailed man. The other animal-people drifted off as well, leaving Zeffy and Nia alone with the crow-headed man. He regarded them for a long moment, as though waiting for something, but neither Zeffy nor Nia seemed able to find her voice. Where the other animal-people had been like strange double-images, the human and animal features both visible at the same time, the crow's head on his shoulders was as solid as the rest of him – beak, feathers, the deep dark eyes.

"Name's Joe," he said.

Come on, Zeffy told her voice. This guy seemed all right. Chased off the boar-woman and everything. So say something.

Yeah, but he had a crow's head on his shoulders.

Joe waited another beat, still expectant; then he shrugged.

"First visit, right?" he said.

Zeffy managed a slow nod.

"Don't worry, you'll get used to it. It's like moving from the city to the country – you've got to adjust to all that fresh air."

Zeffy wasn't sure she'd ever adjust to something like this.

"Well, let's get going," Joe said. "Hop in. You can put the dog in the back."

"I . . . I don't think so," Zeffy said.

It was hard to read expressions in those feathered features, but he seemed to be amused more than anything else.

"That's really not a mask, is it?" Nia said, speaking up for the first time since the animal-people had accosted them.

Joe turned to her, lifting a human hand to his feathered head.

"What do you see?" he asked.

"A . . . a bird's head."

Joe turned to Zeffy. "You, too?"

She nodded.

"Interesting," he said.

All Zeffy could do for a long moment was stare at him. Finally, she cleared her throat.

"So other people don't see you the way we do?" she asked.

"Hell, no. Got to keep some mystery, right? People come, they can't find their way around – can't see – so you can make a pretty good living as a guide."

"Is that what you do? Guide people around in the – this *is* the spiritworld?"

"It is," he said, "and guiding's one of the things I do. I'm kind of a Joe-of-all-trades, you know? Do what needs doing when it comes up. I don't usually make plans too far in advance."

"And people pay you?" Zeffy asked.

He looked slightly uncomfortable. "In a manner of speaking. Things change hands."

Zeffy could hear Gregory's voice, rising up from her memory, warning them. *Get your pretty asses out of here, unless you don't mind going home missing a piece or two of who you are.*

"What kind of things?" she asked.

He shrugged. "This and that. Nothing anybody would miss."

"And what are you hoping to . . . get from us?" she asked.

"Nothing – unless you're wanting a tour of the place." He looked up and down the street, dark gaze finally settling back on her. "But maybe we should discuss this somewhere else. You know, hit the road before those spirits get their courage back up and something bad happens for real."

He started for his truck, but neither Zeffy nor Nia followed. When he turned to look back at them, the enormity of that crow's head being where it was struck Zeffy all over again.

"Now what's your problem?" Joe asked.

Zeffy had to ask. "What kind of bad things are we talking about?"

Joe leaned back against the door of the truck, propped one booted foot up on the running board. A dangerous light flicked in the depths of the crow eyes.

"Well," he drawled. "How about those spirits coming back and thinking maybe they'll take you apart, just to see how you work? Or they could take a liking to some story you got locked away behind your eyes and decide to take it for their own – maybe suck your personality dry, just for the buzz it'll give them."

Zeffy glanced at Nia. Her companion had gone pale, any sense of calm drowning in her panicked gaze.

"Jesus," Zeffy said. "What kind of a place is this?"

"A dangerous place."

Joe fished a package of tobacco out of his vest pocket and started to roll a cigarette, the action reminding Zeffy of

Bones. It wasn't a comforting reminder. It was because of Bones that they were here, though – she had to admit – he'd only sent them because they'd insisted.

"It's not like it's all bad," Joe added. He got his cigarette lit and blew out a stream of smoke in their direction. The salty breeze, blowing up from the beach, took it away before it could reach them. "But it's not like it used to be either. There was always danger, sure, but it wasn't as hungry as it is now. It didn't used to come looking for you so much – you had to stumble into it."

"What happened?" Zeffy asked.

Joe shrugged. "There's too many connections between your world and this. Shit happens in your world, it crosses over and affects us. Last hundred years or so, you people have been propagating like flies. And the nasty business you get into." He shook his head. "You've got guys raping babies. You've got genocide because one bunch of people got themselves born on the wrong side of some genetic line. You've got meanness for meanness' sake. It's always been there, but now there's just so goddamn much of it, I'm always surprised there's anything decent left."

"And it's not like that here?"

"Oh, we've got the good, the bad and the ugly – same as you. Thing is, the good used to way outweigh the bad. But the balance is shifting."

"Making the spiritworld a dangerous place."

Joe gave a humorless laugh. "Well, yours isn't any great shakes anymore either, sweetheart."

"My name's Zeffy."

"Sorry. No offense meant."

He actually seemed sincere about it, Zeffy realized.

"This is Nia," she said. "And Buddy."

"Good names."

Zeffy shrugged. "It's just what people call us."

"Careful names, too." Joe smiled. "That's encouraging."

'So the way our worlds connect," Zeffy began, wanting to get as clear an understanding of how things worked as she could while she had the opportunity.

"I know where you're going with that," Joe said, "and the answer's no. They're not real reflections of each other. The spiritworld's a malleable kind of place. Get enough people dreaming strong dreams about something and it could exist here, but everything doesn't match up with something in your world. Not by a long shot. You need strong dreamers and a lot of them – and you need a piece of real estate on this side that's willing to go along for the ride."

"So many people dream of going to Hollywood and making it big," Nia said. "That's why you've got an L.A. here as well, right?"

Zeffy glanced at her. Nia didn't look quite so scared now. She still seemed a little nervous, but the color had returned to her cheeks.

"You've got it," Joe said. "And so many of those dreams don't pan out, or they turn bad, so our version's a lot darker and more dangerous than yours."

He took a final drag on his cigarette, then dropped it onto the asphalt and ground it out with the toe of his boot. Stooping, he retrieved the butt and stowed it away in his vest – again reminding Zeffy of Bones. Though Bones didn't have a crow's head sitting on his shoulders like Joe did.

"Look," Joe said. "I don't mind filling you in on whatever you want to know, but we should get moving."

"Where are you planning to take us?" Zeffy asked.

"Don't know for sure. We'll drive until a place feels right. Then you can tell me where you want to go and we'll see what we can do about it." He hesitated for a moment, then asked, "You talk to anybody else while you were here?"

"There was this guy reading a book on the beach," Zeffy said. "We asked him where we were but he just thought we were stoned."

"And then we met this really crazy guy named Gregory," Nia added.

"Crazy, how?"

Zeffy and Nia exchanged glances.

"He was a white guy in his forties with dreadlocks like a Rastaman. Had ribbons and pockets sewn all over his clothes. And he was seriously paranoid."

Nia nodded. "He was really good at throwing his voice – like a ventriloquist, you know? He made it seem like Buddy was talking to us. Or my knapsack."

"Good trick," Joe said.

"And he had this water container with the genie from *Aladdin* on it, except the genie disappeared."

"The decal probably just fell off," Zeffy said.

"Or maybe he had a good reason to be paranoid," Joe said. "Maybe there was a little spirit hiding in that genie image and it ran off to tell the fat lady and her friends that you were here. And maybe now they've gone off to tell something bigger and stronger." He paused a moment to let that sink in. "I'm telling you, we've got to get moving. Now."

He opened the door of his truck, but again neither of them moved forward.

"We still have a problem?" he asked.

Zeffy nodded. "Why are you helping us? What's it going to cost?"

"I'm helping you because I'm feeling benevolent and it's not going to cost you a damn thing if you don't want it to."

"What's *that* mean?"

"It means you want to give me something for my trouble if I get you out of this, I won't turn it down, but I'm not *asking* for anything. Now you've got a choice – either you come with me, or you wait here and see who's going to show up next. Maybe you'll luck out. Maybe they'll only take a memory or two and leave the rest of you pretty much intact."

He looked from one to the other.

"So," he asked. "Which is it going to be?"

X • NIA

MAYBE, NIA thought, they shouldn't have been so quick to accept Joe's offer of help, for no sooner had they left town, than she was already having regrets. It was nothing Joe did or said, but the trip itself.

He took the highway out of Santa Feliz, but when they reached the freeway, he cut under its six lanes, following the sandy bed of a dry wash on its way toward the distant mountains. A half-mile from the freeway, he steered the truck through an opening in the mesquite and scrub bordering the wash and drove straight out into the desert. Mirages flickered in the late-afternoon sun, vanishing moments before they were upon them, while the confined space of the cab was soon an oven, dust rising up from a hole in the floor and the open windows letting in far too much hot air.

They were positioned three across with Zeffy in the middle, banging back and forth against each other and the sides of the cab as Joe navigated their course across the rough, uneven terrain. Buddy sat on the floor between Nia's legs, his head on her lap when he wasn't mournfully peering up into her face. She kept giving him comforting pats and wishing there were someone to calm her down in the same way.

Her pulse went into overtime when Joe suddenly bent down to reach for something under the seat, not seeming to pay any attention to his driving. He came up with a bottle of water and passed it to Zeffy.

"Get some of that into you," he said. "You won't believe how fast you'll get dehydrated out here."

Zeffy accepted the bottle, but reluctantly it seemed to Nia.

"This place," Zeffy said. "It's like being in Faerie, isn't it?"

Joe gave her a sidelong glance with a dark crow's eye. "I suppose. But I don't see what difference – oh, I get it. You think you're not supposed to eat or drink anything while you're here or you'll be trapped for a hundred years or something."

"The thought crossed my mind."

"That's just in stories," Joe assured her.

"And you're not?" Zeffy asked.

"What does it matter? I'm one of the good guys. Any story I'm in always has a happy ending. Trust me."

Zeffy didn't say anything, but Nia knew what she was thinking: Why should they? Except they were already here with him, weren't they, bouncing their way across the desert on route to who knew where, so it was a little late for second thoughts. And he had chased off that horrible boar-headed woman and her friends.

"I'll have some," Nia said.

Zeffy shrugged and passed it over. The water was warm and flavorless, but Nia thought she'd never tasted anything half so good. She took a couple of long swigs, then handed the bottle back to Zeffy. Cupping her hands, she asked Zeffy to pour some into them for Buddy, who lapped it up gratefully when it wasn't tossed in his face by the truck hitting a bump. Nia rubbed the spilled water into his fur.

"I'll bet that feels good," she said.

Beside her, Zeffy sighed and had a drink herself, then passed the bottle back to Joe.

"So," he asked after having some himself. "Feel any different yet?"

"Are we supposed to?"

"I feel less thirsty," Nia said, wishing Zeffy wouldn't be quite so antagonistic.

Joe laughed. "I just thought maybe, what with the way you're thinking and all, you'd feel like it was making you smaller or bigger. Or maybe turning you into something."

"What kind of something?" Zeffy asked.

"Oh, I don't know. A crow?"

Zeffy finally cracked a smile. "Okay. I guess I deserved that. It's just—"

The rear wheel on the driver's side chose that moment to blow. Before Nia could register what the loud bang meant, the bed of the truck dropped and the whole vehicle slewed off course in a cloud of dust. She braced herself against the dashboard with her hands, and wrapped her legs around Buddy, everything going in slow motion as Joe fought the wheel. It seemed to take forever as they spun 360 degrees and then finally skidded to a halt.

"Shit!" Joe said. He thumped his fist against the steering wheel, then turned to look at his passengers. "Everybody okay?"

"I guess," Zeffy said slowly.

Nia gave him a numb nod.

"Okay. Good."

He opened his door and unfolded his lanky frame through the gap. Nia wanted out as well, but because of the angle of the truck, her door was too heavy for her to get open. She had to wait for Zeffy to follow Joe before she could slide across the seat herself.

"C'mon, Buddy," she said.

She had to work at convincing the dog it was safe. By the time she had coaxed him through the door, Joe and Zeffy were already standing by the back of the truck, surveying the damage.

"Okay," Joe said. "It's not so bad. We blew a tire, that's all." He shaded his eyes and looked to the west. "Getting on to nightfall anyway, so we might as well make camp here."

"Your face," Zeffy said when he turned back to them.

"What about it?"

"You've got one."

She was right, Nia realized. There was still a birdlike quality to the features under that flat-brimmed hat – beaklike nose, wide-set eyes so dark they seemed to be all pupil, the sharp plane of the cheekbones – but it was a human face now, tanned and weathered. Long black hair hung in a braid down his back.

Joe smiled. "I was wondering when it would kick in."

This was too weird, Nia thought.

"When *what* would kick in?" Zeffy asked.

"This," Joe said, lifting a hand to touch his cheek. "Means we're doing okay."

Zeffy looked as confused as Nia felt.

"Look," Joe explained. "You get a place with too many dreamers like Santa Feliz – you know, all that energy floating around, dreams banging into each other and stuff – and sometimes it's hard to hang on to a look. It's the same reason it's easier for the spirits to get a handle on you there

– they're drawn by all the traffic. But out here, the medicine's strong. A spirit could spend the rest of its life looking for you and never track you down."

Zeffy cleared her throat. "I'd think it'd be the other way around. That we'd stand out here."

Joe shook his head. "No. The mojo's so thick here, the only tracking you can do is by the eye and ear and nose. It's like we're in the middle of a slow soup, all the flavors kind of casually mixing into each other, so you can't tell where one begins and the other lets off."

"So we're going to camp here?" Nia asked.

"Don't sound so dubious. You two go look for some fuel – the wooden bones of some of the cacti burns well – and I'll set up camp. Oh, and ladies. Mind the critters – some are pretty nasty."

Zeffy gave him a look. "What kind of critters?"

"You know. Scorpions, spiders – that kind of thing. Just watch where you're putting your hands."

Nia couldn't help the "Yuck" that came out before she could stop it.

Joe laughed. "Don't worry. Most of them'll be more scared of you than you are of them. I just want you to be careful."

"What about the truck?" Zeffy asked. "Do you have a spare?"

"That depends."

"On what?"

"On how much we believe we've got one."

Nia and Zeffy exchanged worried looks. They were out in the middle of nowhere, Nia thought, with a broken truck and a man who sometimes had the head of a bird on his shoulders. And now he was telling them that fixing the truck depended on how much they believed there was a spare tire?

"Is this some kind of Zen thing?" she asked.

Joe grinned. "More along the lines of quantum physics. You know, like Schrödinger's cat, working out the probabilities and possibilities?"

Nia shook her head, but Zeffy picked up on what he was talking about.

"He means," she explained, "that until we actually look in the back of the truck for a tire, the possibility exists that it's either there or not there. It's a potential tire. Only the act of looking can force a resolution of the possibilities."

"Exactly," Joe said. "Except there's a little faith involved, too."

"That part I don't remember from physics classes," Zeffy said.

"It's like the bottle of water we shared earlier," Joe said. "I had to believe it was there first."

Nia got it now. "So if we haven't got enough faith . . ."

"We're walking from here on," Joe said.

Nia started for the side of the truck, meaning to look over the side, but Joe caught her arm.

"First we'll set up camp," he said. "We'll let the idea sink in a little, maybe sleep on it. Then we'll look."

"But . . ."

Nia looked to Zeffy for help, but all Zeffy could do was give her a helpless shrug.

"Let's get the wood," Zeffy said.

She had to give Joe this, Nia thought later. He made a seriously excellent cup of coffee. The flat bread and chili he'd cooked for them earlier had been good as well.

Now they sat around a small campfire, huddling close for warmth, hands cupped around tin coffee mugs filled to the brim with a rich, dark brew. The mesquite wood, mixed in with the cacti ribs and other wood they'd found, gave off a sweet, aromatic smell. Buddy, calmed down now, was sprawled along Nia's thigh, fast asleep. His body warmth helped – as did the tatty old blanket Joe had pulled from behind the seat of the cab that she was sharing with Zeffy. They needed all the warmth they could get. As soon as the sun had gone down, the temperature seemed to have immediately dropped into the low sixties.

"So what brought you guys here, anyway?" Joe asked.

Nia let Zeffy explain. She listened to the crackle of the fire and the desert night instead, all the rustling and mur-murings in the scrub around them, the wind that made the canvas sides of the shelter Joe had set up earlier flap against its poles. She'd heard coyotes while they were eating, but the far distance only held silence now.

She started paying attention again when Zeffy got to the part where the boar-woman had shown up. It was hard to tell because of the poor light, but she got the impression from what she could see of his face in the campfire flicker that Joe wasn't much surprised by their story. Well, why should he be? she thought. What was amazing to them was probably an everyday kind of thing over here.

"Focus is the big thing," Joe said when Zeffy was done. "Your friend should've told you that."

"He did. We just . . ." Zeffy shrugged. "We weren't very good at it, I guess."

He nodded and started to roll himself a cigarette. "So are you about ready to head back home now?"

"Not without Max," Nia said before Zeffy could reply.

Joe nodded again, as though he'd been expecting that. He thumbed a match and lit his cigarette, tossed the spent match into the fire.

"Okay," he said. "I guess we can work around that. Do you have something that belongs to the people you're looking for?"

"Like what?" Zeffy asked.

"Something to connect you to them."

"There's Buddy," Nia said. "He's Max's dog."

Joe gave the sleeping dog a look. "Maybe I could learn to hear him. Let me think on it for a while.'

Nia waited, but Zeffy didn't come out with the "You can't be serious?" she'd been expecting.

"You can teach him how to talk?" she asked.

"Everything already talks," Joe told her. "Plants, animals . . . even that old truck of mine. The trick is figuring out their language, learning to hear what they're saying so that it makes sense "

"Is it hard?"

Joe's grin flashed in the firelight. "Depends what you mean by hard. Takes focus, so for you two, yeah, I guess it'd be hard."

"Ha-ha," Zeffy said.

"No offense meant," Joe assured them.

He looked less human once more, features flickering confusingly from man to bird to other animals in the light of the fire. Nia remembered how when she'd heard the coyotes earlier, he'd seemed to have a kind of lupine cast to his features, just for a moment, a flicker of fur and muzzle, ears sticking up through the flat brim of his hat; then it was gone again.

"Are you real?" she asked.

The question popped out before Nia was even aware she was asking it and she immediately wanted to take it back.

"Define real," Joe said.

"I . . ."

She started to look to Zeffy for help, but Joe took pity on her.

"Looking like this, no," he said. "At least not in the sense you'd use the word. But here I'm about as real as it gets – pretty much native to the place by now."

"But you'd be a spirit in our world?" Zeffy asked.

Joe shrugged. "Not exactly. But most of us, we need to borrow a body to get by on your side. Sometimes we can make our own, make do with leaves and cast-offs and stuff, put together a pretty good semblance, you look at us in the right kind of light."

"But here . . ."

"This is the place the spirits come from," he said. "And no, it's not like this everywhere, and it's not necessarily like Santa Feliz or L.A. or Mabon or any other place that cross-world dreamers have brought into being. The spiritworld's like a jewel that goes on forever, with as many facets as everyone put together, spirits and dreamers, can imagine. Or expect to find."

"And you're a guide?" Zeffy asked.

"When somebody needs one and I'm in the mood."

"It seems so different from the way you hear about it," she went on. "You know, dream quests and all that sort of thing."

Joe smiled. "It's all those facets. Everything depends on what you expect to find."

"But we didn't expect to find you."

Nia nodded in agreement.

"Well, I can't say the same," Joe said. "When I got the smell of you in the air, it brought me right to you. Saw your trouble and I knew I had to help. Some of us, we've got bigger hearts than others."

Nia had to smile. He had such a good opinion of himself.

Normally, that kind of attitude really irritated her, but with him it was sort of simple and charming.

"More coffee?" he asked suddenly, holding up the pot.

"No thanks," Zeffy said. "I'll be up all night. And since I haven't convinced myself there's a washroom nearby, I don't feel like leaving myself a target for a snake or a scorpion or something when I'm making do with the great outdoors."

Joe smiled. "They won't bother you. Just make sure you shake out your shoes before you put them on in the morning."

Hearing that, Nia was determined to sleep with her shoes on.

"Why don't you two turn in," Joe said. "Me and Buddy here, we'll take a walk in the desert, see if we can't find ourselves some common ground."

Understanding their nervousness, he put a couple more pieces of wood on the fire, then called to Buddy and walked out into the darkness. Buddy lifted his head, but turned first to Nia.

"You can go," she said.

He scrambled to his feet then, bumped his head affectionately against her shoulder and padded off into the desert after Joe.

"Is he getting smarter or something?" Nia asked.

Zeffy shrugged. "I'll believe anything in this place. Are you sleepy?"

Nia shook her head. But she followed Zeffy into the shelter anyway and lay down beside her, sharing the blanket.

"Do you think we'll ever get home?" she asked after they'd been lying there for a while.

Zeffy's voice came back to her from the darkness. It seemed to be right in her ear and impossibly distant at the same time.

"I'd like to be reassuring," she said, "but I'll be damned if I know. I just keep hoping I'll wake up and this will all be a dream."

"I bet that's what Max's been thinking all along," Nia said.

There was a long silence before Zeffy finally replied. "I guess I owe him an apology, big time." She paused for a moment before adding, "Though he owes me one, too."

"I suppose. But imagine what it must have been like for him. I mean, this is weird, but at least we're still ourselves."

"Are we?"

Nia shivered. "What do you mean by that?"

"I'm sorry," Zeffy said. She put an arm around Nia's shoulders. "I didn't mean to spook you. It's just, going through something like this . . . how can anything ever be the same for us again?"

Nia remembered what the crazy man back in Santa Feliz had told them, about having to be poets or crazy like him to get by. Bones had said something along the same lines. But she didn't think Zeffy meant that. It was more like how, after all of this, it'd be hard to trust anything again. To know what was real and what wasn't. What could be and what couldn't.

She wanted to talk about it more, but Zeffy had been quiet for so long that Nia thought she'd fallen asleep.

"You know what I think about the most?" Zeffy said suddenly. "What if when we do get back, all we can think about is this place? All we're going to want is to find our way back?"

"That won't happen."

"But think of all the fairy tales, all those people straying into Fairyland, trying to get home, but when they do, nothing seems as vibrant or alive anymore. If the stories are real, maybe that part of them's real, too."

"I guess," Nia said. "But it won't happen to me. I already miss my mom too much. When I get back, I don't care who she wants to sleep with, I'm just going to tell her how sorry I am that I ran away and I won't ever do it again."

Zeffy's arm tightened around her shoulders. "You'll get your chance," she said. "I don't know how we'll work it, but I promise you that much."

Nia knew there was no way Zeffy could promise that, but she didn't care. It was what she needed to hear.

"We should try to get some sleep," Zeffy said. "God knows what this guy's going to have us doing tomorrow."

"Okay."

Nia didn't think she'd be able to sleep. The ground was so hard, it felt so alien lying out here in the desert, and even with Zeffy pressed up against her on one side, it was so cold. Besides, she thought, if this was the place dreamers went, how could you fall asleep here? So she lay there, listening to the desert again. When that just made her feel more awake, she started thinking about how long it had been since she'd heard some good music. She closed her eyes and called up one of the solos from Coltrane's "A Love Supreme," letting the music reduce the rough jangle of her nerves with its soulful calm. It was an album she knew front to back, she'd played it so often, but tonight the solos went in different directions from how she remembered them. They played against the desert, echoing through the scrub and cacti.

Lying there, listening to the soundscape in her mind of Coltrane's tenor sax, music he'd never played but so indisputably his, she finally fell asleep. All night long she heard that music in the distance and dreamed of Buddy running through the desert. Sometimes there was a crow flying in the air above him, sometimes a lean coyote ran at his side.

"Okay, ladies. Rise and shine."

Nia groaned at the sound of Joe's cheerful voice. She pressed her face more tightly against her knapsack, which was serving as a pillow, but it was no good. The light was far too bright and the heat was already creeping in under the shelter where she and Zeffy lay. She rolled over onto her back, eyes still closed, then yelped and sat up when Buddy licked her face.

Joe laughed. "Coffee's on and there's water in the basin for you to wash up in."

The coffee smelled wonderful, especially with the aroma of frying bacon added to it. Nia's stomach rumbled. Where did he get the food? Don't ask, she told herself. Just appreciate.

"So *do* we have a spare tire?" she asked later when they were eating and she was more awake.

"Well, I'd say Zeffy's the one to check."

Zeffy looked up and smiled. "Of course we have a spare, because there's no way I'm walking anywhere in this heat." She got up from where she was sitting and wandered over to the back of the pickup. "See?" she said. "There it is. Complete with a jack and a tire iron."

Buddy had already eaten twice as much as any of them, but he lay near Nia now, studiously watching the last few bites that went into her mouth. She gave him a piece of toast.

"I dreamed about Buddy last night," she told Joe. "So what does that mean? Was I seeing him somewhere else in the spiritworld, or does this place have *its* spiritworld?"

"Good question," Joe said.

Zeffy returned to finish her coffee. "Which means he doesn't know," she translated.

"I was considering the question," Joe said. "That's all."

Zeffy gave Nia a smile. "Doesn't matter where you go, does it? Guys never want to admit it when they don't know something." She turned back to Joe. "Okay, you're off the hook, because the big question we *do* want an answer to is this: What happens today?"

"Do you want to go home, or find your friends?"

Nia's pulse quickened. She could feel herself grinning.

"You know where Max is?" she asked.

"Not exactly. But Buddy's given me a good line on him and I think I can find him."

Nia turned to Zeffy. Part of her wanted to go home, right now, but having come this far already . . .

"So what are we waiting for?" Zeffy asked. "Let's replace that busted tire and start driving."

Joe kept to a more sedate pace this time. It was still hot and dusty in the cab of the truck, the terrain was still bumpy, bouncing them around on the seat, but it didn't seem so frantic, now that they were taking it at a slower speed.

"So can you really talk to Buddy?" Nia asked.

She had her hands in the dog's wiry fur, twirling it around her fingers while he slept contentedly with his head on her lap.

"Let's say we came to an understanding," Joe told her.

"Could I learn to talk to him?"

"First you have to learn to focus."

"And then you have to believe it'll happen," Zeffy said.

Joe shot her a quick grin. "Now you're getting it."

"I can focus," Nia said. "Just because I screwed up getting us here, doesn't mean I can't."

"I screwed up, too," Zeffy said.

Nia gave her a grateful look.

"So what's the problem then?" Joe asked her.

"I don't know if I can learn how to believe."

"It's not something you learn."

Nia sighed. "I know. Wanting and having's never the same thing."

"Unless you want it bad enough," Zeffy said. She put her hand on Nia's knee and gave it a quick squeeze. "Then maybe anything can happen."

Nia regarded her for a long moment.

"I know, I know," Zeffy said. "I'm the last person you'd think to come out with something like that. But I've been thinking a lot about this magic stuff and I'm starting to realize that maybe we had more of it in our lives back home than we realized."

"I don't get it."

"Didn't you ever know people who always seemed to have things go their way?"

"Sure."

"I think half the reason it works like that for them is because they expect things to go their way. They expect everything to work out. It's like Jilly. She puts out so much confidence and belief, that it's rare for something to go wrong in her life. And then when it does, she treats the experience as something she can learn something from, instead of getting all bummed out by it."

"I can see how she'd be like that," Nia said.

"But then there's my roommate Tanya. She always expects everything to go wrong for her, and it does." Zeffy shook her head. "So the thing is, if we can exert so much influence on our own lives simply through our wills, I'm starting to see it as not much more of a step to affect other things in a way that might seem to be magic."

"Good point," Joe said. "Except you're missing one part of the equation."

"What's that?"

He waved a hand out through the window of the cab to take in the landscape all around them.

"All of this exists whether you believe in it or not," he said.

Zeffy nodded slowly. "There's that," she agreed.

Nia turned her attention back to Buddy. So what are you thinking? she wondered as she ruffled his fur. He opened an eye and gave her a sleepy look, before shifting into a more comfortable position. Then sighing deeply, he went back to sleep. Nia smiled. She guessed he was thinking that they were all talking too much.

They reached the mountains in the late afternoon, having stopped only once for a lunch of tortillas and refried beans. Neither Zeffy nor Nia spent much time wondering where they'd come from, and Buddy, from the enthusiasm with which he devoured his share, obviously didn't think about it at all.

Joe parked the truck by a dry riverbed under some tall mesquite trees, their boughs spreading out from their twisted trunks to form a perfect shelter against the last of the day's sun. There was even grass, tall, the blades sharp, but it was browned and yellowed.

"We'll camp here," Joe said, "and head on into the mountains first thing in the morning."

"Why don't we keep driving for another hour or so?" Zeffy asked.

Joe was already out of the truck, stretching his lanky frame. He leaned back in to reply.

"Because we're running on fumes at the moment. You'll be wanting to concentrate on there being a nice big jerry can full of gas in the back of the truck come morning."

Nia got out, studiously not turning to look in the back of the truck in case, by looking too soon, she affected the potential of the gas can being there. Zeffy remained behind for a moment.

"I'll get dinner," she said.

She closed her eyes, brow wrinkling as she concentrated, and reached under the seat, her hand moving back and forth until she seemed to find something. Nia watched her with a puzzled look, then smiled when Zeffy pulled out a Tupperware container. Zeffy popped the lid and showed off the kabobs inside, skewers laden with chunks of tomato, onion, green pepper and beef.

"I could get seriously used to this," she said as she passed the container to Nia and hopped down from the cab.

Late that night, Nia awoke suddenly, her pulse drumming. She found Zeffy already sitting up beside her, Buddy standing just outside their shelter, whining softly, the fur all prickled along his back. Their campfire had long since died down, but there was enough moonlight for her to spy Joe out in the riverbed, his hat pushed back on his head as he stared up into the foothills.

"What . . . what is it?" she said.

Her throat was so dry her voice came out in a raspy whisper. Joe turned to look at them.

"Something's happening," he said. "Something bad. Can you sense it?"

Nia nodded.

"It's Max," Zeffy said.

Joe nodded. "I don't know what the hell he's gone and done, but if we're picking up the echoes of it, you can be damn sure others are as well."

Buddy whined again, such a plaintive sound that Nia quickly got up and knelt beside him. She put her arms around his neck.

"What are we going to do?" she asked.

Joe straightened his hat and joined them by the shelter. He crouched down, sitting on his heels.

"Depends," he said. "Try to get him out of whatever he's gotten into, I guess, and then out of the spiritworld quick as we can. Problem is, the echoes we're feeling could call up a pack of my cousins and they might not be so ready to let him go. Might want to give us a hard time, too. So you've got to ask yourself, how much are you willing to risk for these friends of yours?"

"For Johnny," Zeffy said, "not much. But Max?" She sighed. "God, why can't I stop thinking about him?"

Nia lifted her head from the warm comfort of Buddy's neck and swallowed hard.

"What happens if your cousins show up?" she asked.

"Depends on which ones they are," Joe said. "And how hungry they are. Truth is, we could all end up as their meal."

Nia gave him a startled look. "Even you?"

"Even me."

"But you're one of them."

Joe nodded. "I think so, but I don't know how many of them would agree. I'm a little too comfortable walking both

486

sides, your world and mine, for a lot of the cousins' tastes. Got things they don't have but want."

"Like what?" Zeffy asked.

Joe shrugged. "Like a skin that fits me on either side."

Nia looked from him to Zeffy. She was so scared now all she wanted to do was run. Send us home, she wanted to tell Joe. Right now. But Buddy whined again and she thought of Max.

"We can't not help him," Zeffy said.

"Your call," Joe told her. "But everybody's got to decide."

When he looked at Nia, she nodded quickly before her courage completely fled.

"Okay," Joe said. "Let's break camp. I'll fill the gas tank, you guys throw our gear in the back of the truck."

He stood up and started kicking dirt over the last coals of their fire.

"You don't have to do this," Zeffy said. "I mean, Max – he's not your friend."

Joe smiled. "But you are."

"Just like that?"

He turned to look at them. "You think I've got it wrong?"

Nia was happy when Zeffy didn't even hesitate.

"No," Zeffy said. "I guess I'm just not used to everything happening the way it has. It's all so quick."

"Things move fast here," he said. "That's all. It's dream-time, remember? Everything's intense like in a dream. And I promised I'd help you, didn't I?"

Zeffy nodded. "I just . . . Thanks, Joe."

He smiled. "Hey, can't have too many friends, right?"

You can't have too many friends, Nia thought, the words ringing in her mind the way Coltrane's sax had last night.

And all I've got is Max. Then she corrected herself. All she had *was* Max. All she'd allowed herself before this was first her mom, and then Max. Nobody else seemed to measure up. But now she found herself wondering, was that the real reason, or was it more that *she* didn't measure up? That *she* couldn't face up to the responsibility that having friends involved? But that wasn't entirely it, either. The thought of making friends scared her so much she didn't even bother to try anymore, because it was easier to stay aloof and not get hurt.

You can't have too many friends.

The thing she realized when Joe said that was how ever since all this craziness had begun, she'd actually made other friends – Zeffy, Jilly, Buddy, now Joe – and she liked the feeling, the sense of belonging to something other than herself. She even liked the responsibility.

"C'mon," Joe said, pulling her from her reverie. "Let's get a move on."

XI • MAX

I DON'T expect to ever see the morning light again, but there it is when I wake up on top of the ridge, the old pine towering over me, my body stiff and sore from lying on the rock all night. I guess I'm not a quick study because it takes me a while to realize I'm still alive. When I do, I don't feel relief so much as confusion. I sit up slowly and images flash through my head. The bird. Devlin. The two of them going over the side. I turn and study the spot from which they fell, but I can't seem to move, can't make it those few feet across the granite to look over and down. Instead, I let the spectacular view grab my gaze and hold it, try to lose myself in the jagged waves of forested mountains that blue off into the distance.

The birdsong coming from a half-dozen warblers in the big pine that shares the ridge with me seems incongruous, somehow. There's so much life in the racket they're making. The sky's so blue, not a cloud to be seen in its robin's-egg expanse. The light of the sun cascades through the boughs of the pine in a cathedraling effect. Everything, from what I see and hear, to the drumming heartbeat in my chest and breathing, tells me I'm alive. But I don't feel I should be. I remember falling into light last night, the tunnel with something welcoming me at the end, a classic near-death experience. That was *my* body that went over the cliff.

So how can I still be alive?

There's no sense to it. But then nothing's made sense since the morning I first woke up in Devlin's body, so why should it suddenly change now? And yet ... and yet ... there's what happened last night. I saw the bird and Devlin go over the edge. I feel firmly rooted to this body, but it still seems unimaginable that I could survive beyond the death of my own body – even if I'm not in it.

I steel myself and work my way toward the edge on my hands and knees. When I finally peer over, I'm expecting to see my body lying on a ledge a few feet down, maybe snagged in the branches of a tree – some innocent if improbable explanation. Vertigo takes my breath away and has me scrambling back. I forgot. It's at least a hundred feet, straight down, sheer rock. I close my eyes and see them going over again, Devlin in the bird's body, knocked unconscious, the bird in mine, flailing its arms with less preparation than Icarus put into that flight of his and about as much success.

Nothing could have survived that fall.

Nothing did. I know that. But as I work my way down the forested slope on the far side of the ridge, I'm hoping for a miracle. If the impossible can happen to me – the first switch of minds, being *here*, for God's sake – is one more miracle so much to ask for?

It takes me the better part of forty-five minutes to reach the valley floor, fighting the thick brush, holding on to branches and tree trunks whenever my feet slip out from under me on the steep slope. The angle of my descent takes me farther away from the ridge than I expected, so it's another ten minutes before I reach the foot of the cliff. The brush opens up here, kept clear by rocks falling from its face. Only weeds and small saplings grow up between the fallen stones. A sweep of raspberry bushes grows thick in the border between forest and clearing, their fruits just coming into season.

There's no sign of the bird anywhere, at least not that I can see, but it's hard to miss my body lying on the stones, neck and limbs bent at impossible angles. A sick feeling starts up in the pit of my stomach and I can't seem to breathe.

So much for miracles.

I go numb – not just my mind, but everything. I can't move, my limbs feel thick and prickly, like they've gone to sleep. There's an ache inside that won't go away. I know it won't ever go away.

I don't know how long I'm standing there, but finally the numbness gives a little and I can move again. I push through the raspberry bushes, ignoring the thorns that catch at the sleeves of my shirt and my jeans, and walk slowly over the uneven footing until I'm standing directly over my body. My body. I'm dead. I'm standing here, but I'm still dead.

Looking down at myself, I suddenly understand what

Janossy meant when he tried to describe *Nada Brahma* – the Great Tone of the Hindu tradition – to me, because as I stand here, I feel myself resonating against some impossible depth, touching the tone that rang out at the beginning of the world, a tone which, as he put it, "continues to sound at the bottom of creation, and which sounds through everything.

"You don't need an instrument to appreciate that sound," he added. "All you need is ears."

I've got ears. I hear it. It's the blood rushing in my ears. It's the panicked drum of my pulse. It's my ragged breathing. But it's also the sound from which life originated, a music reverberating from spirit to spirit, mine and the world's. It's what we came from and where we go to. Except I'm still standing here. Somebody else wore my body and went on. The bird? Devlin? I don't know.

I sink to my knees beside my body, but I don't touch it. I'm too afraid of what will happen if I do. Too afraid that contact with it will reverse the shift and I'll be trapped in a corpse. That the same power allowing me to live on in this body will deny me access to the journey that should have been mine when my body died, will leave me lying here on the rocks, staring blindly up into the sky until the body finally decomposes.

I feel like Tom Sawyer attending his own funeral, except there really is something to bury here and there's no one to mourn me. I wish I hadn't been so quick to alienate everyone around me – Nia, Zeffy, Bones. I need someone to hold me, to let me know that I still have a connection to the real world. I need someone to talk to – I'd even take Devlin with his bird voice ringing inside my head.

The bird.

A false hope rises up in me. I force myself to my feet to

make a careful survey of the rocks, starting near the body, then walking in widening circles across the uneven stones, but with no success. If the bird fell anywhere nearby, something's come along and carried it off. Or maybe it recovered in the air and flew away.

No. Not *it*. Devlin. Devlin sitting in the bird's head, steering its body the way I'm steering his.

I cup my hand and call his name, over and over again, until my voice goes hoarse, my throat starts to hurt. There's no reply.

Finally I return to where the corpse is lying on the stones behind me.

It doesn't seem quite real, I think as I kneel down beside it. By now, lying out in the sun for half the morning, it should be pretty ripe, but there's no smell, no change, not even a fly. It seems more like a mannequin, or a wax figure from museum diorama than a real corpse.

I can almost hear a voice in my head, the logical part of my brain asking me, What are you planning to do? I can tell by its tone that it thinks I'm making a serious mistake. But I can't not do it.

"I have to find out where I belong," I say aloud.

There's no one to hear me. Only the corpse.

I lay the palm of my hand against its cheek. I'm given enough time to register the cold, waxy feel of the skin; then the vertigo hits me hard, taking me by surprise. I'll be honest. For all my fears, deep down I didn't believe my old body had any more of a hold on me. Now I know, but it's way too late. Devlin's body sloughs off like an ill-fitting suit and I'm falling back into myself, back into the broken body lying on the stones. There's nobody home – until I'm in there.

Devlin's body collapses across me, but I'm only peripherally aware of it. I can't feel its weight. I can't feel anything. Can't move. Neck broken, limbs broken. Eyelids dried open, the sun burning my pupils. I can't even blink. But I can hear.

There's a sound, but it's so out of context I can't place it at first. Then I realize what it is. It's an engine, a motor. I don't know how far away the vehicle is. Sound carries in the bush, so it's hard to tell. I don't know if it's coming here, or just passing close by. Doesn't much matter anyway. Even if it is coming here, there's nothing anyone can do to help me now.

XII • TANYA

SNOW WAS falling thick on the street outside. Tanya sighed, watching it come down, the wind pushing the white blanket into drifts that buried the curbs, changing the contours of the street. It looked like they were going to have a white Christmas this year, after all. Better still, the snowfall hid the ugliness of her neighborhood, drove the pushers inside, covered the litter and abandoned cars, smoothed the rough edges. It almost looked pretty.

A soft *ding* coming from her oven told her that dinner was ready. With a last lingering look at the snow-covered street outside, she turned from the window and went into the kitchen to take it out. A TV dinner, turkey, mashed potatoes and all the trimmings – two days early, but she was in the mood and couldn't wait. If she wanted it again on Sunday, she could always pick up another of these culinary wonders tomorrow, before the stores closed.

Pouring herself a glass of white wine, she took her dinner

into the living room and sat down on the couch. She lifted her glass in a toast to the poster in the corner, guitar case still standing under it.

It had been six months now. Hard to imagine a Christmas without Zeffy. Hard to imagine that the door wouldn't burst open any moment and in she'd come, her arms laden with Christmas goodies and decorations. The only decoration Tanya had put up was a small plastic Christmas tree on top of the TV. Zeffy would have had the place positively glittering with Christmas cheer. Streamers, mistletoe, a real tree, lights, stockings by the heating grate, the whole works.

Tanya smiled, remembering the year that Zeffy had constructed a fake fireplace out of cardboard and set it up in front of the heating grate so that they could hang their stockings from it, the hot air coming out of the large hole she'd left for that purpose. Tanya had been afraid of it being a fire hazard, so Zeffy compromised, only setting it up Christmas Eve and turning the heat way down for the night. They'd woken to a frosty apartment and then huddled in front of the grate as though it were a real hearth, sitting close to it for warmth as they sipped coffee and opened the presents they'd gotten for each other.

There was a wrapped present under the tree on the TV – a small silver broach in the shape of a guitar – but Tanya didn't think it would be opened this year. Only she and Jilly ever expected to see Zeffy again. She, because she was too stubborn to give up hope; Jilly, because that was just the way Jilly was, full of optimism.

Cleaning up after the meal was easy. She had only a fork, knife and wineglass to wash; the TV dinner packaging went straight into the garbage container by the oven, calling up a twinge of environmental guilt before she closed the lid on it.

Making herself a cup of tea, she returned to the living room and found herself reaching for a cigarette before she realized what she was doing.

She hadn't had a cigarette in two months, but tonight she felt like smoking a whole pack. It wasn't so much that she was depressed as suffering from a seasonal malaise. There was so much relentless good cheer in the air that it was hard not to be reminded how so little of it was hers. Most of the time she did pretty well – missing Zeffy, but dealing with it. Getting on with her life. But with the snow making a Christmas card of her dingy street outside and carols still ringing in her ears – even after having finally turned the radio off after dinner – it was hard not to dwell on the mystery of Zeffy's disappearance and how much she missed her.

After a while, when she realized she was in danger of slipping into a serious bout of melancholy, she put on her coat and went walking through the snow. The fresh air cleared her mind and the snow was turning everything into such a fairyland that her spirits soon lifted. She had no particular destination in mind, but when she found herself on Yoors Street, a block or two away from Jilly's studio loft, she decided to drop in for a visit.

Jilly answered the door with a ready smile, a tangle of red and green ribbons looped around her neck like dangling ivy. Stuck to the back of her hand and all along her forearm were a half-dozen or so small pieces of cellophane tape. A Christmas carol was playing cheerfully from a tape deck behind her, but it didn't bother Tanya here. Cheerful things simply made sense in any proximity to Jilly.

"Hey, stranger," Jilly said. "It's good to see you. C'mon in."

"I'm not interrupting anything, am I?"

Jilly shook her head. "I'm just wrapping some presents to take by St. Vincent's. You can help if you like."

"Who do you know at St. Vincent's?"

"Everybody."

"No, really."

St. Vincent's Home for the Aged was a seniors' residence located in an old, greystone building downtown that catered to those who didn't have families, or whose families couldn't afford to put them in a regular retirement home. They were privately funded and run by volunteers. Only the medical staff received a salary.

"No, really," Jilly repeated, smiling. "I go there all the time and hang out with the old folks. They get so few visitors, you know?"

"And you're still volunteering at the Grasso Street soup kitchen?" Tanya asked.

Jilly nodded. "But that's only once every couple of weeks. We've already had our Christmas party, though there's going to be a special dinner on Sunday."

"I don't know where you find the time."

"Me, either," Jilly told her. "But we can't just forget about them. It could just as easily be you or me there, you know."

"You're right. I should be doing something like that."

"Whatever feels right."

Jilly led the way back through her cluttered loft to a section of floor she'd cleared to wrap the presents.

"There's eggnog in the fridge," she said. "And rum on the counter, if you want to spike it."

"What are you having?"

"Spiked, of course."

Tanya wandered over to the part of the loft that served as the kitchen, pausing on the way to admire a work-in-progress on Jilly's easel. At the moment it was simply a rough sketch of an old building, rendered in oil, burnt umber on a pale yellow ochre ground, the drawing done with a brush, but knowing Jilly's work, Tanya could easily imagine how it would turn out.

"That new piece is nice," she said as she helped herself to some of the eggnog and rum.

"Got a show coming up in January," Jilly said, "and three more pieces to finish for it. That's going to be the old train station."

"I thought I recognized it."

Tanya brought her drink back to where Jilly was and sat down to help her wrap. The presents reflected Jilly's whimsical nature: old toys, small porcelain vases, books, a few of her own paintings – small four-by-six pieces in used frames.

"Who's this for?" Tanya asked, holding up a plastic Cookie Monster figurine.

"Janet Avens. She's always telling me about how she used to watch *Sesame Street* with her grandchildren. I think it was the best time in her life."

"How come she's in St. Vincent's?"

Jilly shrugged. "No one to take care of her, I guess. She never talks about how she got there and it's not something I ever ask."

Of course not, Tanya thought, as she found a little box to stick the Cookie Monster figurine in and carefully wrapped it. She knew from experience that you didn't need anybody to remind you of the depressing things in your life – you could do that all too easily for yourself.

"So I hear you're back in the movie business," Jilly said.

Tanya laughed. "Who told you?"

"Mary Drake – she works in the copy shop under your office."

Tanya knew her. She'd met her because Eddie kept sending her down to get this copied, and that copied. They had lunch together sometimes at a coffee bar down the street, where Mary would fill her in on all the building's gossip.

"Is there anybody you don't know?" she asked.

Jilly assumed an exaggerated thinker's pose, elbow on her knee, chin cupped in her hand. "Let's see. I think a new family's moved in that apartment complex by the zoo . . ."

They both laughed.

"So tell me all about it," Jilly said when they caught their breath.

"It's no big deal really," Tanya began, then caught herself. "No, I'm lying. It is a big deal. Just a bit part – maybe three days' work, tops – but it's a Ron Howard film, set right here in the city, and if any of my scenes actually make the final cut, it could open a few doors. Eddie's ecstatic, naturally."

"And how's Tanya?"

Tanya smiled. "She feels good about it, too."

She could still remember how weird it had been that first morning three months ago when she'd walked into Eddie Flanagan's two-room office. The outer room had the secretary's desk, file cabinets, phone on the desk, computer on a small workstation to one side, a small waiting area with a couple of chairs. The walls were plastered with glossy eight-by-tens, all signed to Eddie, nobody Tanya knew except for a buxom model she'd seen on a recent series of stereo ads that seemed to be plastered all over the city.

Eddie came out of the inner office to greet her when she arrived, a short, dapper man in suit pants, white shirt, tie. He looked to be in his early forties, brown hair cut short and brushed back from a broad face, pronounced laugh lines around his dark eyes and mouth. He stopped abruptly in the doorway of his office and studied her for a long moment.

"I know you," he said.

"I'm from the temp agency," Tanya said.

"No, I mean I *know* you. What's your name?"

She told him.

"Tanya Burns, Tanya Burns," he repeated, then his face lit up. "*Sisters of the Knife*, Phil Castledore directing. Crap movie, but you were good in it – better than Castledore deserved."

Tanya's heart sank. Of all the people to work for, she had to run into some old fan. And she was stuck here for *two* weeks. The only good thing was that he wasn't liable to turn into Johnny on her. She hoped.

"What happened to you?" Eddie asked.

"What do you mean?"

"*Sisters of the Knife* did decent box office, considering. Still moves in rental. But you, you're in, you're good, then *nada*."

"I decided to be a waitress, instead."

Eddie laughed. "Hey, that's good. That's funny. But seriously. What've you been doing since? Theatre? Foreign stuff?"

"Just waitressing. Now I'm doing office work."

Though she might walk right out of here, if he got too weird. Trouble was, she really needed the money.

"Jesus," he said. "You're wasting your talent."

"What talent? Shower scenes? Getting cut up in slasher films?"

"No," he said, looking serious – genuinely serious, not phony show-biz solemnity. "I mean, acting talent. Everybody's got to go through some bullshit movies – crap like *Sisters*. But then you move on. Use your talent – why do you think you were given it? To piss it away?"

After that, he began a campaign to get her back into the business; nothing overtly pushy, he simply wouldn't let it go. Just before her two weeks were up, serendipitous fate intervened: his regular secretary phoned from Hawaii to quit and he offered Tanya a regular job. She accepted, mostly because she liked working for Eddie. He was funny, but he took his work seriously. Understood the difference between box office and art, but didn't feel you necessarily had to give up one for the other. He was a well-reasoned idealist, a pragmatic dreamer.

And he never gave up.

Finally she agreed to sign with him. A couple of modeling jobs. A walk-on in a low-budget art film that was shooting on location just outside of Newford.

"But if I don't like it," she said, "that's it. I keep my job, but you don't bug me anymore."

"Never do what you don't like," he told her. "But always weigh your options. Maybe you don't like six weeks on the set, or a forty-eight-hour glamour shoot. But how much do you like tapping on a keyboard and answering phones nine-to-five, five days a week? Everybody's got to make a buck – the trick is, either find something you like to do, or do something to pay the rent that doesn't take too much out of you. *Capisce?*"

"What about art?"

"I'll tell you about art. Do the best job you possibly can. Have something to say. And stop equating it only with what you find in libraries, galleries and foreign film festivals. The eye of the beholder, you see what I'm getting at?"

She still didn't like the modeling, and said no after three shoots. True to his word, Eddie didn't press her on it anymore. "It was just to get the face out there," he explained, "and put a little folding money in your pocket. You no like? No problemo." But the walk-on film role ended up as a two-day job and she even got a couple of lines that looked like they wouldn't end up on the cutting-room floor. More to the point, she'd loved it. On the set, something woke up inside her that had never been there her first time around, and she found herself yearning for a meatier role.

Eddie was good. Didn't say I told you so. But he smiled. A lot. And busted his ass to get her the small role in the Howard film. Went with her to the first cattle call and two subsequent callbacks. Yesterday afternoon, Thursday, he'd come out of his office, then leaned casually against the doorjamb, arms folded across his chest, ankles crossed, Mr. Casual. Tanya'd looked up, trying to figure out what was on his mind at first, but then knew.

"You heard back from them," she said.

Eddie nodded. "And I've got just two words for you: Hello Hollywood."

"The weird thing," Tanya told Jilly as they continued to wrap presents, "is that I never thought I'd find this . . . enthusiasm inside me. For anything, never mind acting."

"I'm happy for you," Jilly said.

"Thanks. I just wish I could share the news with Zeffy. It never mattered how screwed up I'd get, she was always there for me. I guess I'd just like her to see me happy about something that doesn't revolve around a boyfriend."

"Nothing wrong with boyfriends," Jilly said.

"Unless you base your life around them." Tanya shook her head. "No, thanks. This time I'm doing it on my own. I mean, look at you – or Zeffy. You don't need guys to be happy."

Jilly seemed about to say something, but then bent back to the book she was wrapping.

"Okay," Tanya said. "What were you thinking?"

Jilly shook her head. "Nothing. It's not really any of my business."

"But," Tanya prompted her.

"But nothing. Really."

"It's about Geordie, isn't it?" Tanya said.

She still thought about him, felt bad for the way she'd treated him, but knew she couldn't give in, couldn't simply become somebody else's appendage, no matter how nice they seemed.

"Let me put it this way," Jilly said. "Maybe if Zeffy or I had someone as nice as Geordie feeling about us the way he does about you, we'd have boyfriends, too."

"Oh, shit. I didn't want to hear that."

"I know. And I wasn't going to say anything." Jilly finished tying off a bow, then sat back. "You've got to do what's right for you," she added, "not what other people think is right. And if you don't care for him the way he does for you . . . well, it's nobody's fault, right? It's just the way it goes."

"But that's the whole problem," Tanya told her. She could feel tears welling up in her eyes, but she blinked them fiercely away. "I'm crazy about him. But I just don't want my life to get swallowed up by somebody else again."

Jilly was silent for a long moment.

"Did you ever tell a guy that?" she asked finally.

Tanya shook her head. "I didn't think they'd take it all that well."

"You're probably right."

"But not with how Geordie would take it – is that what you're saying?"

"I have no idea what Geordie'd say," Jilly told her. "That's something you'd have to ask him yourself."

XIII • LISA

THE LAST thing Lisa wanted to do was attend the office Christmas party, but there was no way out of it. It had nothing to do with disappointing her coworkers. She hadn't exactly been the most popular person in the office over these last few horrible months: off sick too much, barely able to find a smile when she did come in, other people always having to pick up her slack. How she'd managed to still hang on to the job, she had no idea, but if she wanted to keep working with these people, she knew she'd better try to reinforce some positive connections with them soon.

The depression she carried around with her couldn't be easy to take. Lord knows, she couldn't stand herself the way she was – so why should anybody else? But she had to work with these people, and if standing around smiling and making small talk with her coworkers and their spouses helped ease some of the inevitable tension her moods created in the office, then it would be worth it.

So she trudged through the deepening snow, head bent against the wind, the present everybody was supposed to bring cradled against her chest. The ploughs weren't out yet

– at least not in this part of town – and the sidewalks were always last to be dealt with, especially in her neighborhood, where vehicles couldn't fit anyway so the narrow streets were quickly blocked with drifts. Four blocks from Old Market and her calves were already aching; she was cold because her coat, while fashionable, wasn't exactly warm; and she'd already taken a couple of falls. But she was determined to get there and be cheerful tonight, even if it took getting tipsy to do so, and she wasn't going to let the bad weather undermine her resolve.

She gritted her teeth. Except, she thought, she'd like to have whoever'd had the nerve to design and sell a coat such as this as winter clothing in front of her at the moment so that she could give them a good slap in the head.

But it was her own fault, really, wasn't it, for going out and buying it, rather than something more sensible. Her fault for buying into the fashion industry's false promises that if she looked like this, if she bought that, she'd have a perfect life. Her fault. Just as everything that had gone wrong with her life was her fault. Maybe her mother was right. She was a screwup, and that's why her life was such a mess. And since that must be true, then why even bother to—

Neither she nor the woman she bumped into was watching where she was going. Heads bent, they banged into each other with enough impact for Lisa to lose her balance yet again. Her feet went out from under her and she fell backward, the snow breaking her fall.

"Oh, I'm so sorry," the woman said, quickly bending down to give her a hand up. "I was so busy looking at my own feet that I never . . ."

Her voice trailed off. They recognized each other at the same time and regarded each other for a long moment, Lisa lying in the snow, the woman crouched beside her. Lisa was first to find her voice.

"Julie?"

A brief smile touched Julie's lips as she finished helping Lisa to her feet.

"Hello, Lisa." Julie retrieved Lisa's present for her from a nearby snowdrift and passed it over. "Out delivering presents?"

"It's just an office party at The Rusty Lion. Everybody's supposed to bring something, then they hand them out at random."

"Ah."

"I . . . I've missed you," Lisa said. She couldn't believe how fast her pulse was racing. "I kept wanting to talk to you."

"I've got a phone."

Lisa nodded. "I know. I . . . I just didn't have the courage." And barely had it now, so she quickly plunged on before she lost the little she had. "I wanted to apologize for – for everything. You were right. I was blaming you and it wasn't fair, because it wasn't your fault. It was only the stupid way I was looking at things."

"And now you're all better?"

Neither Julie's expression nor tone of voice gave away what she was thinking. Serious or sarcastic? Lisa couldn't tell. It was hard to concentrate with the wind and the snow and Julie standing there in front of her looking as beautiful as ever. Maybe more so.

"No," she said. "I'm not better at all. But I'm working on it."

Julie sighed and seemed to relent. "I've missed you, too."

"Do you have time for a coffee or something?" Lisa asked.

"What about your party?"

"It's just for . . ."

The people in the office and their spouses, she was about to say, and what would that add to the office gossip if she showed up with Julie on her arm? Then she realized she didn't care what they'd think. If they had a problem with it, let them deal with it.

"Why don't you come with me?" she said. "Be my date."

Julie's eyebrows rose. "Just like that?"

"Please. I'm not asking for a commitment or assuming that you can forgive me or anything. But I'd really like to talk to you. I want to be with you and I don't care what anybody thinks about it. Except for you."

Julie shook her head. "I can't believe I'm doing this," she said as she took Lisa's arm and started walking with her.

Lisa was caught between the delight of being so close to Julie, walking with her like this, and knowing that it probably wouldn't last. There was no reason on earth for Julie to give her a second chance.

"I guess I'm kind of hopeless, aren't I?" she said.

Julie shot her a sidelong glance. "Hardly. You're messing up some, that's all. And you've had good reason to feel messed up."

Lisa's spirits lifted, hope fluttering in her chest.

"How are you feeling?" she asked. "I mean . . ."

"I know." Julie touched her side. "Physically, I'm all better. But I still get bad dreams. They caught the guy, but he's already out on bail and it doesn't look like he's going to do any real time."

"That's horrible."

"Tell me about it. And how about you? Have you heard from Nia?"

Lisa shook her head.

506

"How're you dealing with it?"

"Not well," Lisa admitted. "Anyone who says time heals all wounds is full of it."

Julie nodded sympathetically and gave her arm a squeeze.

"I guess the hardest thing," Lisa said, "is not knowing what happened to her. Where she is. Is she okay?"

"I don't know how you deal with it."

Lisa gave her a startled look.

"Don't look so surprised," Julie said. "What kind of a person would I be if I didn't understand your being so worried? If you want to know the truth, I've felt like a heel for walking out on you the way I did. I knew what you were going through. I *knew* it wasn't your fault you were all messed up." She sighed. "But it was hard to take all the same."

"I understand."

"No, you don't. Not completely. See, it wasn't just your fault. My last girlfriend was pretty young, fresh out of college. A sweet little LUG, though I didn't know it at the time and I guess she didn't either."

"LUG?"

"Lesbian Until Graduation. You know, bought into the lesbian chic while she was on campus, then changed her mind after being out in the real world for a few months. No harm done, right? – except I got left with the broken heart. I didn't have another serious relationship until we met."

Lisa caught and held the words "serious relationship" close to her chest, hope flaring.

"And then," Julie went on, "when you seemed to have second thoughts about the morality of it all, I just got scared. The only thing I could think to do was cut and run. I felt I had to call it off before I got hurt again."

"I didn't know."

507

Julie shrugged. "I never told you. But the funny thing is, I got hurt all the same."

She paused. Lisa looked up, surprised they were already at The Rusty Lion. The windows of the restaurant were steamed with condensation, but she could make out a few of her coworkers.

"You sure you want to go through with this?" Julie asked.

The snow whirled around them. Lisa heard a distant rumble and saw the flashing amber lights of the ploughs far down Lee Street, coming their way. Julie's face was damp, glistening with melted snow, and she wanted to lick the moisture away. Instead, she leaned forward and gave Julie a quick kiss that turned into one that was far longer and more intimate.

"I'd rather go back to your place or mine and be alone with you," Lisa told her when she stepped back and was able to catch her breath. "But, yes. I'm sure."

"Then let's do it."

XIV • ZEFFY

USING THE dry riverbed as a road, Joe drove them up into the foothills. It had to give out at some point, Zeffy thought, and then they'd be walking, but the riverbed simply led them deeper and deeper into the forested hills. It was as though Joe had determined they'd find a usable route, so the usable route was there – the same way they acquired food and gas and the spare tire. If that was the case – and really, Zeffy thought, what else could it be? – she put her own will to the task as well, *expecting* the route to continue as it did.

The riverbed remained usable, but it wasn't flat. Half the time she and Nia had to brace themselves, arms stiff against the dashboard. From the creak and rattle of the truck, Zeffy wasn't sure how long it would hold together. The headlights bounced across the landscape like a pair of flashlight beams held in an unsteady hand. Images flashed out of the darkness – sheer stone cliffs, tangles of vegetation, bone-dry roots that reached out for water that was no longer there. Occasionally the beams caught the eyes of some animal and reflected them back. Joe always slowed down then, allowing it to escape into the underbrush flanking either side of the riverbed, before returning to their previous speed.

Deer. Raccoons. Fat, waddling porcupines. Once a wolf or coyote, it was hard to tell, the lanky shape was gone so quickly. If it weren't for the urgency of their journey, Zeffy would have been delighted, but she rode instead with what seemed like a stone in the pit of her stomach, her nerves all stretched taut.

She kept thinking of Max . . . Johnny . . . whoever this guy was she'd met and talked with in the park. Call him Max. Forget the fact that he looked like Johnny. Their parting argument had mostly faded from memory. Instead, she kept circling around this intense attraction she'd felt toward him, the sense of connecting with someone who could really mean something to her. A soul mate.

"This is nuts," she said, unaware that she was speaking aloud until Joe shot her a quick look.

"What is?" Nia asked.

Zeffy turned to her. "How come I can't stop thinking about a guy I hardly know? Worse, he looks exactly like the last person in the world I'd want to have a relationship with."

"But he's not Johnny. He's Max."

"I guess . . ." Zeffy looked out through the windshield again and sighed. "What am I saying? I've only talked to him a couple of times. What do I know about him? For all I know, he could be worse than Johnny."

"He's not."

Zeffy smiled. "Like you're in the least bit objective, little miss matchmaker."

"You guys'd be great together. Really."

"I doubt he even knows I'm alive."

"I'd find that hard to imagine," Joe said.

Zeffy gave him a surprised look. "I didn't think you knew Max."

"I'll tell you what I know: You're not the sort of woman a guy forgets in a hurry."

Zeffy was happy it was so dark in the cab of the pickup – no one could see her blush. She cleared her throat.

"So," she said, hoping to change the subject. "How much farther do you think we have to go?"

Joe was silent for a long moment, then relented and followed her lead. "A few miles as the crow flies."

"And as the crow drives?"

He chuckled. "A lot farther. A couple of hours, maybe. The sun'll be up."

"Is Max going to be all right?" Nia asked.

Joe kept his attention on the road. "I wish I could say yes, but I won't make any promises I can't keep. Depending on who's been called up by whatever he's done, I can't even promise that *we'll* be all right."

"But we've got to try," Zeffy said.

Joe nodded. "That's the decision we made."

Meaning they could change their minds, Zeffy thought.

They could turn around right now and no one would know any different. Except for them.

"The sooner we get there," she said, "the sooner we can deal with what's waiting for us. So let's just concentrate on arriving in one piece and everything working out."

Joe glanced at her. "Just wanting it to work out isn't necessarily going to be enough. You know that, don't you?"

Zeffy did, but she didn't want to think along those lines. She wanted to think positively, to *expect* everything to be okay in the same way that they were expecting this riverbed road to take them to where they were going.

"But I'm choosing to believe it will," she said.

Joe smiled. "Good for you."

They drove from night into the morning twilight. For a long time the sun remained hidden behind the mountains, but the east side of the riverbank began to grow long shadows and slowly the light changed. The blur of the forest separated into individual trees. Lots of pine. Birch, cedar, aspens. Oak, maple. Zeffy was watching a hawk float high above the riverbed, when Joe killed the engine. The pickup rounded a corner and coasted to a stop.

Zeffy turned to him. "Are we—"

He put his fingers to his lips and nodded to the dusty length of the riverbed ahead of them. Zeffy and Nia looked ahead, then studied the banks on either side. There was only the forest and the dry bed of the river cutting through it like a road. Buddy stirred where he was sitting between Nia's legs. He whined and tried to clamber up on her lap to look out the window.

"Shhh," Nia whispered. "There's nothing to see."

Except there was. Two figures stepped out from between the trees on the west side of the riverbank. Zeffy stopped breathing. Never mind that this was the spiritworld and full of magics she'd already experienced, she couldn't believe what she was seeing.

One was a woman with a bison's head upon her shoulders, the other had an African water buffalo's. The pelt of the bison woman was a startling white, thick and curly on her head, her woman's body covered with a soft down fuzz. The other woman was a black brown with massive horns that her shoulders seemed too frail to bear. Her skin was hairless, her chest bare, a brightly colored cloth tied around her hips. The legs of both women ended in hooves.

"What . . . what are they?" Zeffy asked.

The animal-women pushed through the brush and raspberry bushes that choked the east bank and then disappeared in between the trees. Zeffy stared at the spot where they'd vanished, but couldn't seem to hold their impossible images in her mind. She turned to Joe, realizing that she'd forgotten the crow's head that had been sitting on his shoulders when they first met, forgotten the boar-woman and her friends in Santa Feliz. With the memory now fresh in her mind, his face shimmered like a heat mirage and she saw the vague image of a crow's head superimposed over his more familiar features.

"Buffalo-women," he said. "Old spirits. Very old and powerful."

Zeffy blinked and the mirage went away. It was Joe sitting there again, the familiar, human Joe. But she remembered exactly what he was now and wondered how she'd ever let herself forget.

"They were so beautiful," Nia said, her voice soft.

Zeffy nodded in agreement.

"Beautiful," Joe agreed. "And dangerous."

"Are they Native spirits?" Zeffy asked.

"They're native to the spiritworld."

"No, I meant like the spirits of the Native Americans from my world. You know, White Buffalo Woman and all that."

Joe shook his head. "Here in the spiritworld everybody wears the shapes most comfortable to them. The spiritworld doesn't belong to any one group; it belongs to everybody. You find here what you expect to find; you look the way you expect to look."

"How come we don't look any different?" Nia asked. "I mean, Zeffy and I "

"Because that's how you expect to look."

Zeffy gave a slow nod. "Except," she said. "I wasn't expecting a beach town – or to meet a guy with a crow's head."

"Sometimes your dreams go deeper than you remember after you've woken from them."

"But—"

"We've got it all here," Joe said. "Deserts, mountains, cities, villages. Mosques and churches and temples. Tundra, mesas and cyberspace. Anything you might expect to find is somewhere around – the good and the bad."

"So those buffalo-women . . ."

"Either got their shapes from some dream-walking shaman, or just happened to pick them on their own."

"I see."

Though she didn't. Not really. Not completely. It was more that something deep inside her reacted to what Joe was saying, recognized and accepted the truth, while the rest of her was left floundering.

"So the gods," she began. "The way they look. It's just arbitrary."

"Who's talking about gods? They're something that belongs to your world. I was talking about the cousins."

"But you told us about these vision quests and sacred journeys that people make to come here."

"That's right. But whatever wisdom they happen to pick up, they get from spirits. If they don't do what they should have done in the first place and asked themselves. Trouble is, people don't trust themselves, so they come looking." Before Zeffy could ask another question, he pressed on. "Some of the spirits you find here will help you, some will hurt you. Most won't pay you any nevermind. There's no accounting how they'll react to you, or why they're one way or another. Maybe they just take a shine to you, maybe not."

"Like you did," Zeffy said.

"Right," Joe told her. He smiled. "Took a shine and here we are. You want some free advice?"

Zeffy nodded.

"Got this from my granddad and it's the only piece I ever heard that makes real sense: Look inside yourself for the answers – you're the only one who knows what's best for you. Everybody else is only guessing."

He started the truck then. As they drove past the spot where the buffalo-women had crossed the riverbed, both Zeffy and Nia craned their necks to get another glimpse of them, but the buffalo-women were long gone. Joe rolled a cigarette one-handedly, lit it with a thumbed match. A mile or so on, he stopped again, took his last drag and killed the engine. Butting the cigarette out in the truck's overcrowded ashtray, he opened his door then and stepped out.

"We walk from here," he said.

Zeffy waited for Nia to open the passenger door and slid out that side. The dirt of the riverbed didn't feel quite stable underfoot.

"I'm feeling scared again," Nia said.

Buddy was Velcroed to her leg once more, his gaze darting nervously from one riverbank to the other, tail tucked between his legs.

"Me, too," Zeffy told her.

Joe came around from his side of the truck. "We can still turn back," he said.

She wondered if he knew how tempting his offer was at this moment. But she couldn't do it – nor could she explain why. It wasn't simply that she had this inexplicable attraction to Max – or maybe simply to the man Johnny had become. There was something else afoot, a – what did they call it in the old days? It took her a moment to recall the word. A geas. Like in the Arthurian stories. Something she had to do. A promise, only she couldn't remember making it, or to whom.

"How come you're always offering to take us home?" she asked. "You know why we're here."

Joe shrugged. "Just like to make sure. I feel a little responsibility for you, dragging you all the way out here."

"But it's been our decision to come," Nia said.

"Like I said," Joe told them.

He led them out of the riverbed. When they pushed through the raspberry bushes choking the riverbank, they found themselves on a narrow game trail that wound off between the trees. The ground rose sharply as soon as they put the river behind them, but the trail followed the contour of the cliffs that rose steadily higher beside them.

They walked single file: Joe, Nia and Buddy, with Zeffy bringing up the rear. When Joe suddenly stopped, Zeffy almost ran Buddy over. She only just caught her balance by grabbing the branch of a nearby tree.

"What is it?" Zeffy asked, pressing closer to see what he was looking at.

Joe moved aside a little so that she and Nia could see. There was a clearing ahead of them, created by the rocks and debris that fell from the sheer cliff face behind it. It took Zeffy a moment to see the two bodies lying on the stones in front of the cliff, one lying on top of the other.

"Is . . ." Zeffy cleared her throat. "Is that them?"

Joe nodded.

"Why are they just lying there like that?" Nia asked.

She started forward, but Joe caught her arm.

"Hang on," he said. He looked almost wolfish as he lifted his head, eyes narrowed, nostrils flaring as though he was testing the wind. "Okay. I think we're the first to get here."

He was talking about his cousins, Zeffy realized and shivered.

"Those buffalo-women we saw earlier," she said. "Are they on their way here?"

Joe shrugged. "Could be. C'mon."

He started out leading the way, but Buddy bolted ahead and ran toward the figures, paws scrabbling for purchase on the loose stones as he hurried. Zeffy watched him reach the bodies. He stopped and walked stiff-legged around them. By the time he dropped down to his belly and began whimpering, she was close enough to see for herself.

Beside her, a small gasp escaped from between Nia's lips. "Th-that's Max," she said. "Max's body . . ."

With Johnny Devlin lying on top of him.

They hurried across the stones, letting Joe bring up the rear now. Nia started crying when they reached the bodies

516

and threw her arms around Buddy. A deep chasm seemed to open inside Zeffy as she looked down. Max Trader lay with his neck and limbs twisted at impossible angles, as though . . . Her gaze went up the side of the cliff. As though he'd fallen . . .

"Oh no," she said in a small voice.

She knelt down and with Joe's help pulled Johnny's body to one side. He seemed unhurt, but he was a dead weight, arms and legs limp. Joe rolled back one of Johnny's lids, but only the white of the eye showed. He put two fingers along the neck, checking for a pulse that wasn't there.

"Shit," Joe said, sitting back on his heels, studying the bodies. "Looks like one of them went over the cliff in Max's body, then the other got sucked into the corpse when he came over to check things out." He shook his head sadly. "That's hard."

"D-do . . . something," Nia said through her tears.

"Nothing I can do," Joe said. "You can't call back the dead."

Zeffy refused to accept that. "There's got to be something." She looked at Joe. "This is the spiritworld, isn't it? So where's the magic when we need it? Why can't we just . . . just *expect* them to be alive again?"

Joe made no reply. He wouldn't even look at her.

Zeffy turned back to the bodies, her vision blurring with tears. She cursed every time they'd stopped to eat or sleep. They should have gotten here sooner. They should have . . . should have . . .

They should have saved the day. Hadn't that been what they were *expecting*? This was all wrong. Terribly, horribly wrong.

She leaned over Max Trader's body. Swallowing thickly, she reached out and closed his unseeing eyes.

XV • MAX

IHEAR the sound of the engine stop. There's silence for a long time; then I hear something scrambling across the stones toward me. It sounds like an animal – big, fast. Something's found itself a meal, I think, and I'm glad that I can't feel anything. But then I hear whatever it is begin to whimper. A dog.

Buddy?

It's the first thought that comes to mind, but I know it can't be. He's safe in Newford with Nia. But then I hear her, too. And ... Zeffy? I can't figure out what's going on. There's a third voice – a man's. Unfamiliar. But I hear where he's coming from.

You can't call back the dead.

Tell me about it.

Zeffy starts talking about spiritworlds and magic and how things are supposed to happen because you expect them to, but none of it makes any more sense than what they're doing here. They're crying now, both of them, Buddy whimpering. The man's silent. I feel like crying, too. Can't move, have no sensory perception at all except for my hearing. But I can feel. Emotions, nothing tactile.

And all the time, ghost impressions of the body's other occupants range through me, shadowy and vague. The bird, all confusion and panic, mirroring my own. Devlin. He's a little stronger. I get mostly anger from him, a little regret, but not for what he's done, only that things aren't working out his way.

I get the sense that someone's leaning over me. Zeffy. Don't know what makes me think that. I can't feel the weight of her hands, but I know she's touching me. All the fear and panic comes roaring up inside me and I start to reach for her, for her body, trying to slide into it the way Devlin slid into mine. I catch myself at the last moment, horrified at what I'm doing, and force myself back into my own skin, push myself away, deep and deeper, down inside myself, away from the temptation.

I'm gone so far, I lose my hearing now, too. I'm in my own body, but this is unfamiliar territory, the shadowland where artists go when they shut themselves away from the outside world. My panic's ebbing, even my fear. They're replaced by resignation and sorrow. I float in the darkness, thinking this must be what it's like in a sensory-deprivation tank. I wonder if I'll get the chance to go on – heaven, hell, be reincarnated. Whatever happens. Is it something you do on your own, the directions genetically set in you when you're born, or does someone come to show you the way? Or maybe this is it – you're stuck in your body until it rots away.

It's funny how quickly time loses meaning when you've no way to measure it. I might have been floating there for minutes or days, I have no way of knowing, when I sense I'm no longer alone. It's nothing definite. Like the passing of time, I can't measure it, but there's something here with me. I pray for an angel, some spirit presence come to lead me into the next world, but find only a ragged remnant of myself – the pieces that got left behind when Devlin evicted me, the ones that must have worked on him the way his impatience and tendency toward depression worked on me.

I gather them to me and find in them a memory of Janossy, a time when we were building a set of twin mandolins for a bluegrass band and got to talking about the state of the world. He was the first person I heard voice the concept "think globally, act locally."

"The way I see it," he said, "is the problems that face the world are the same problems that face an individual. If you're at peace, if you're happy, if you have a desire to help others, then the problems of the world disappear."

"I don't buy that," I told him. "You can feel as altruistic as you want, but that's not going to stop the war in Vietnam, or feed starving people in Third World countries."

Janossy sighed. "I'm not saying there's an immediate cause and effect. But the world changes any time one person changes. What we have to do is clean our own house and then – by example, through discussion, whatever works – help others clean theirs. Until we have our own peace, an understanding of ourselves and the strength to stick to our convictions, how can we expect others to meet our expectations?"

"You make it sound so simple."

"The most important things are simple," Janossy said. "We're the ones who make them complicated."

"So we have to know ourselves . . ." My voice trailed off at his smile. "Okay, what then?"

"It's not enough to know yourself. Think of *who* you want to be and then strive to attain that ideal."

That last phrase goes echoing through me, kickstarted by that sliver of memory until it looms enormous and unavoidable.

Think of who you want to be.

Who do I want to be? Not dead, for starters. Not trapped in this helpless, broken body that would make a quadriplegic's life seem like one of infinite freedom. But not who I was before Devlin came into my life, either. I did some good, but not enough of it – or not enough of it deliberately. I lived too much of a mole's existence, so wrapped up in the insularity of my own concerns that the world passed me by.

I had no enemies, but no real friends either. No great sorrows, but no great joys. I wasn't at peace, I was drifting. I wasn't content, I was simply making do. I had convictions, but what was the point of them if they made no impact on the world beyond the walls of my shop and my apartment? *Tch*ing over the newspaper or the six-o'clock news, but never once making an effort to do something about what I felt was wrong.

I wasn't a bad person. I coasted through a limited existence not much different from most people's – only the details varied. But it wasn't living.

Who do I want to be?

A man who lives his life. To be a man who takes nothing for granted, who not only accepts the challenges of every day, but looks forward to them. A man whose enemies would be complacency and ennui. And if I can't be that man in my own body, then I'll be it in Devlin's. I'll reclaim his skin guiltlessly. He chose to trade, not I. I gave him his chance to make things right, but he refused it. Whatever his fate now, he brought it down on himself.

I want to rise up out of the shadows, back into the light that falls on my broken body, but I can't. I can't find the way back. It's all the same. Up, down. Left, right. Front, back. I need a guide. I need someone who cares for me the way I am, borrowed body and all. Someone who trusts me implicitly.

And then I hear it. A howl that comes shivering down through the darkness and pulls me up and out. It's not a sound so much as an emotion. A need, a reaching out. And I reach back. Physical hearing returns, ears popping, and the howl's for real now, Buddy's sorrow filling the world with despair. But hope, too. For me, it's a sound of hope.

I see Devlin's body as a flare of light and reach for it with all the desperate need of a man long denied his own, finally coming home. I know living in Devlin's skin won't make me perfect. I know the intensity with which I've promised myself to live won't be something I'll be able to maintain every day. No one's perfect. But at least I'll try.

I start to flow from the broken body into Devlin's, the skin familiar, a perfect fit this time. I sit up, marveling at the breeze that touches my skin, at the glory of sight, the taste in my mouth. I barely have time to register my successful return when Buddy's all over me, almost knocking me down, licking my face. Then Nia's hugging me, still crying, and I'm crying, too.

Through the blur of my tears I can see Zeffy, studying me. There's a look I take for hope in her eyes, but there's also a stepping back, like she's confronting a zombie from some late-show monster movie, an undead thing that's just risen from its grave. And I know what she's thinking: Who's inside that skin?

XVI • ZEFFY

THE TELLING point for Zeffy were the tears in the eyes of the man in Johnny's body. That was when she was sure it was Max who had come back, not Johnny. Johnny wouldn't cry for anybody.

The way the body had sat up, hard on the heels of Buddy's desperate howling, had given her a bad scare – maybe the worst since she'd found herself mixed up in all of this. But now that she was sure, she was suddenly shy and found herself hanging back from the joyful trio Max, Nia and Buddy made. She noted Joe was hanging back, too. Sitting on a boulder now, rolling himself a cigarette, calm as you please, a look on his face like he'd known all along this was going to happen – like he'd maybe had a hand in it. The old faker, she thought affectionately.

Max finally more or less disengaged himself from Nia and Buddy. He sat with his arm around Nia's shoulders, free hand resting on Buddy's neck, fingers kneading the dog's wiry fur.

"How'd you all get here?" he asked.

"We were looking for you," Nia replied.

"Really?"

His gaze was on her, so Zeffy nodded. He looked embarrassed.

"Listen," he said. "I owe you an apology big time for the way I lit in to you back in the park. You, too," he added, turning to Nia. "I can't believe how badly I treated the both of you."

Definitely not Johnny, Zeffy thought. Johnny never apologized for anything – at least not with such sincerity. She could read it in Max's eyes. There was a real pain for whatever hurt he'd caused them.

"That's okay," she said. "I guess I know now you didn't mean it."

Joe had gotten his cigarette lit. He stood up, his gaze on the forest that edged the clearing. When Zeffy looked to see what interested him so much about the trees, she thought she saw figures flitting through the undergrowth. Nothing definite. More the idea of something being there.

"Joe," she said. "What are those things?"

"Kind of a sign that you folks should be heading back home," he replied. "The cousins aren't exactly here yet, but I can feel them getting close. Got a few little manitou watching us right now. Curious, mostly. But the others'll come."

"The buffalo-women?" Zeffy asked.

"Them. Maybe some others just as powerful."

"I can't go," Max said. "Not right away."

Zeffy wasn't sure she'd heard him right. "Say what? The whole point of our coming here was to bring you back."

"I know. But I left a couple of things at Janossy's farm that I need to get. And then there's that."

Zeffy had still been trying to work out what he meant by Janossy's farm when Max nodded with his chin toward the corpse. Nia wouldn't look at all and Zeffy didn't blame her. She returned her attention to Max and saw the bleak look in his eyes. He might be alive, she realized, but now he knows it'll never be the same again. He'll never get his own body back. She couldn't imagine what he must be going through, how it must feel.

"Okay," Joe said. "We'll bury the body. Pile enough rocks on it so that the scavengers'll never get a piece."

"That's not it. It's . . ." Max sighed. "I don't even know where to begin."

There was a long silence that Zeffy finally broke.

"Try," she said, her voice gentle.

XVII • MAX

I REALLY *don't* know where to begin. Anything I say is going to make me sound like a whiner. I'm so tired of feeling sorry for myself, and I'm doing such a good job of it that I really don't need anybody else to join in.

"We want to help," Zeffy says.

"Yeah, Max," Nia adds. "We're your friends."

"I could use a walk," the man Zeffy called Joe says. "I'll go pick up whatever you left at that farm."

I shake my head. "No. It's okay."

I take my arm from around Nia's shoulders and shift over to one of the larger boulders and sit so I'm looking out at the forest and can't see the body. My body. Except I'm not dead. I'm sitting over here in Devlin. Buddy shifts over with me, collapses by my feet, tongue lolling. At least someone's happy, I think as I wait for the others to join me.

"You brought me back," I tell him, holding his head between my hands and looking down at him. "Saved my life even when I broke my promise to you."

"What did you promise him?" Nia wants to know.

"That I'd never desert him."

There's not much to add to that. I find myself wondering what Zeffy's thinking. If I break a promise to a dog, how good are any other promises I might make? I don't even know why I'm thinking about her along those lines except she *is* here, came looking for me, and there's something in the way she looks at me that makes me think maybe there's a chance we could get to know each other better. Except we've got something else lying between us.

"The thing is," I say, "I don't know what'll happen to me if I go back."

Zeffy and Nia are looking blank, but Joe nods his head.

"I get it," he says. "You're worried about the guy who originally owned that skin you're walking around in, that he's going to reclaim it and then where will you be?"

I don't even ask how he knows that.

"That's partly it," I say, "but it's more complicated than that."

I fill them all in on what happened last night – that connection I had with Devlin, how it brought me up to the ridge, the bird talking to me, the two of them going over the edge of the cliff.

"That's hard," Joe says when no one else speaks, "but none of it's your fault. Let me tell you straight, you've got no worries about carrying on in that skin. Any karma comes down, it'll fall on the other guy."

"But what's to stop him from taking his body back?"

"Live intensely," Joe tells me. "Live big. The cousins have a saying: 'Walk large as trees, with the blood quick in you and swift-running.' In other words, don't let there be holes in your life where somebody else can creep into your head again. You get what I'm saying?"

I nod slowly. "That's what left me susceptible the first time. I was just drifting through my life instead of living."

"Not that drifting is a crime," Joe says. "But now you don't drift, you do."

"But . . ." I glance over at the corpse. "It doesn't seem right."

"What Devlin did wasn't right," Zeffy says.

"I know, but two wrongs don't . . ."

Joe puts up a hand, palm out. "Stop hanging on to the guilt. Devlin's dead, carrying all the bones and burden of his wrongs along with him into the next world. And if he's not dead, then he's stuck here, same as all the cousins. They can't steal somebody's skin without it costing them. Borrow it, maybe, with their permission – you know, make a deal – or just take it, if they're too weak. But that's serious karma and it weighs as heavy on them as it does on you or me. Get enough baggage like that dragging you down and you're not going anywhere."

"I don't think Johnny Devlin thinks anything through that carefully," I say.

"If he even knows about it," Zeffy adds.

Joe nods. He takes the time to roll yet one more cigarette, twists it into shape, lights it.

"Okay," he says, through a cloud of grey-blue smoke. "Then I see only one way for you to set your mind at ease. You've got to lay on the hands again and find out what'll happen. I'm saying nothing."

So we're back to courage again. It's a funny thing, I'd step right in if it was Nia or Zeffy or Buddy that might get hurt, step in and take the hurt. But this, when it's only me, when I could just as easily walk away . . .

"Thing you've got to ask yourself," Joe adds as though he's reading my mind, "is how badly do you want to know?"

Part of me wants to turn my back on the body right now and walk away. But I know I'll get no peace until I find out, one way or the other. I can't leave without knowing for sure.

Joe gives me a sympathetic look – I guess he knows how hard this is. I don't think either Zeffy or Nia quite understand what could happen to me. But Buddy does. He whines when I get up and reluctantly follows me to where the corpse is lying on the stones behind us.

It seems no more real than it did before. Still no smell, no flies. But I can barely recognize it now. It's like looking at a stranger, someone I might have gone to school with but haven't seen in years.

"Wait a sec now," Zeffy says. "You can't—"

But I do. I have to. I don't hesitate, but reach out to touch for it because I have to know.

Zeffy grabs at my hand.

"Let him do it," Joe says. "Unless you want him brooding about it for the rest of his life."

She looks deep into my eyes and that makes it harder still, because I can see she cares for me – for me, the guy inside, not Devlin. But she slowly lets my hand go. I reach for the corpse's cheek again, feel the cold waxy skin. I shiver, but I stay rooted in Devlin's body. When I take my hand away, I realize everybody's been holding their breath – myself included.

"It's okay," I say. "I'm okay now."

We raise a cairn over the body. It's hot, sweaty work, but it's got to be done. It completes the story, lets us put it away and get on with our lives. At the end, Nia takes her magic marker out of her pocket and writes on the top stone: JOHN DEVLIN, R.I.P. And it's done.

I stand there for a long time, reading the words she's written. I'm here, reading them, but I'm under those stones, too. There's a real ache in my chest when I finally turn away, a sense of loss that I'm not sure I'll ever escape. I remember being a kid and pretending to be somebody else. Now I look like somebody else. I get a little crazy, worrying at it. I guess I always will.

The spirits are still watching us, but I guess the big guns haven't shown up yet, or maybe we caught them in a moment of sympathy. Maybe they think we've seen enough hardship for the time being and deserve a break. Or maybe, Nia confides in me, it's Joe being kin to them. But they let us raise the cairn, flitting shapes, part animal, part human, watching us work from the shadows under the trees. And they let us leave.

We head back to Joe's truck. He drives along the riverbed for a mile or so until the trail we're all expecting shows up. Ten minutes later the trail gives out, but there's only the meadows that front Janossy's farm to traverse before we're driving into the farmyard and pulling up in front of the house. I collect the guitar I was working on, a case for it and my knapsack.

"This is for you," I tell her, handing her the guitar.

She shakes her head. "I couldn't . . ."

"I can't play both and it'd mean a lot to me if you'd take it."

She holds it with the respect the instrument deserves, having known the touch of Janossy's hands, and I feel bad all over again for what happened in the park. I smile as she sits down on the front porch and has to tune it up, try it out right away. She runs through a beautiful old-timey folk tune, finger-picking the melody, thumb picking out the bass line, a sweet high lonesome Appalachian sound. Right then, if I hadn't been sure before, I know I made the right decision in giving it to her. That instrument's going to get a lot of love and play.

"What's in the knapsack that's so important?" Nia asks.

"It's all I've got left of my old life. Pictures of my parents. A journal Janossy left me. Some tools. Stuff I can't replace."

Zeffy looks up from the guitar and shakes her head. "You've still got your old life up here," she says, tapping her temple. "Nobody can take that away. And everything else is waiting for you at your shop."

"It's not my shop anymore."

"So have Trader sign it over to you," Nia says.

Zeffy nods. "You can be the apprentice that nobody knew he had."

"I don't know. Devlin Guitars?"

"Keep the old name."

It feels good worrying about something so mundane, instead of what I've been going through the past few days.

I'm looking forward to normal, though I remember my promise to myself and refuse to get complacent about any of it.

Joe's ready to send us back now, but Zeffy asks him to hold on.

"I've been trying to decide on a moment to give you," she says to Joe. She smiles. "You know, one of those stories that'll make it easier for you to cross over yourself."

Joe shakes his head. "Don't you worry about me crossing over or staying here. I make do. Always have."

"You think I'm doing this out of charity," Zeffy says.

"No, I'm thinking it doesn't need to be done."

"Maybe I'd just like to know we might see you again."

"Look for me hard enough," Joe says, "and you will. I'm not that hard to find. The thing is, I'm not exactly the safest person to be around. It's a genetic thing – got too much Coyote in me. Now, you caught me on a good day, first time we met, and I took a shine to you and all. The next time we meet I might mess up your lives. I won't mean to, but I just don't think things through the way I should. That kind of thing happens around me."

"I don't care," Zeffy says. "The thing with friends is, you've got to take the good with the bad – treat them with the same openheartedness as how you want them to treat you. Nobody's perfect." She pauses for a moment, then adds, "You did mean that about being friends?"

Joe nods. "Yeah. but mostly I just wanted to see how the story'd turn out."

Zeffy gives him a long considering look.

"Bullshit," she says.

I have to smile. I do like the brass of this woman.

"Anyway," she goes on. "Like I said, I started thinking and the best moment I could come up with was at my very first gig. It was just a spot at a little folk club, the room held maybe forty people and it was only half full. I was so scared I could barely hang on to my guitar but after I got through my three songs and those twenty or so people applauded – not just politely, but like they'd actually enjoyed my performance – I realized that I could really do this. I could be a singer and write songs and play the guitar and it didn't matter how long it took, that's what I was going to do."

Joe doesn't say anything for a long moment. He looks away, across Janossy's fields. There's a shiver around his features, a flash of coal-black feathers, the spirit face I hadn't seen until just this moment; then the man's back, dark crow eyes looking at her, shiny in the bright sunlight.

"That's a powerful piece of medicine," he says. "You better hang on to it."

"But I want you to have it."

"You know if you give it to me, you'll lose it and you won't get it back?"

Zeffy nods. He hesitates a moment longer, then he puts a hand on either side of her head. She gives a small gasp, eyes widening slightly, and it's over. She seems a little unsteady, but recovers quickly.

"You okay?" Joe asks, worried.

"I'm fine."

Nia gives him a story, too. "I guess I'm a little young to have much in the way of life-changing epiphanies," she apologizes, but then she lets him take the moment she first heard Miles Davis, sitting in a coffee bar while she's waiting for her mother to get her hair done in a nearby salon, radio behind the bar tuned to a jazz station.

"I had no idea that kind of music even existed," she says. "It really spoke to me. It was the first time something like

CHARLES DE LINT

that ever spoke so directly, you know, reached right into me and helped me make sense of things I was feeling. So that was a way special moment for me. People – like my mom and the kids at school – think I'm into it and beat poetry and that kind of stuff just to be different, but it's not like that."

"Maybe you're an old soul," Zeffy says.

I think of how Nia has always loved to hear about Janossy, about his beat days and the poets and musicians he knew, so maybe Zeffy's right. There's always a reason we are the way we are and after the experience I've been through, I'm not so ready to toss out the concept of reincarnation.

I'm ready to give him a story, too, the most intense and meaningful moment, the most *defining* moment, I can call to mind: that feeling I had coming back into Devlin's body. But I'm looking at Joe and suddenly something twigs. I reach into my pocket and hand over the hickory-handled knife I've been carrying around with me – ever since he gave it to me.

"Thanks for the loan," I say.

He looks at the knife, lying there in the palm of his hand, then lifts his gaze to search mine.

"How'd you know?" he says.

"It wasn't any one thing," I tell him, "just a lot of little pieces that only added up now. Something about the way you carry yourself and talk – it's different, but not different enough. The way you referred to the animal spirits as cousins, not really including yourself in their number."

Zeffy and Nia are both starting to catch on.

"Crazy Dog," I say. "Now that seems a name somebody with a bit of Coyote in him might wear – or at least what people might call him. And Jenna – back in Fitzhenry Park – told me how you're always taking these mysterious trips and coming back with a look in your eyes like you've been someplace outside the world. Like here."

"Is this true?" Zeffy says.

Bones nods. Something shifts in his features and for a moment he looks the way he did when I met him in Fitzhenry Park, then he's back to looking like Joe Crow again.

"I start with a look when I cross over to here and it's hard to lose it till I get back," he explains.

Zeffy's seriously not happy about this. "So all this time, you were lying to us."

"Lying how?"

"Well, you . . . that is . . ."

"I came looking for you is all," Bones says. "Never told you a lie – just didn't tell you everything."

"You said your name was Joe."

"That is my name. Joseph Crazy Dog."

Nia gets an "ah-ha" look. "That's what Jilly called him," she says. "Remember?"

Zeffy seems reluctant, but she concedes the point.

"Took me a while to track you down," Bones goes on, "but then when I did find you, seems you were pretty determined to see things through so I decided I'd better tag along to keep an eye on you, make sure neither of you got hurt."

"Why didn't you just tell us who you were?"

Bones shrugs. "Because then you'd've always been looking to me for the answers instead of thinking for yourselves." He pauses, then adds, "I meant it about being your friend."

"But these stories we gave you . . ."

"The draw's deeper on me, here in the spiritworld. I really do need the stories if I want to spend much time on the other side."

"I should be really mad at you," Zeffy says.

Nia shakes her head, says, "I'm not," and Zeffy sighs.

"No," she says. "I guess I'm not either. Too much Coyote in you, huh?"

Bones shakes his head. "He gets a bad rap."

"This from the guy who tells us that the next time he meets us he might mess up our lives because that kind of thing tends to happen around him?"

Bones shrugs. He and I look at each other for a long moment; then I step over to him and give him that story I've been holding for him.

"How's that mojo now?" Nia asks, grinning.

"Burning," Bones says, his voice soft. "Dropped in me like hot coals." He looks as though he's going to add something else, but then sets to rolling himself a cigarette instead. "Time I got you folks home," he said, thumbing a match alight.

"You're not coming?" Nia asks.

"No. I've got a bit of unfinished business to attend to first."

He stoops to pat Buddy, then starts to shake Zeffy's hand, but she won't allow that and hugs him instead. Nia, too. Even me. But I'm thanking Bones, the man that helped me out in Fitzhenry Park, not this guy that Nia and Zeffy traveled across the spiritworld with.

"Guess maybe now you know why I never settled down," he says.

"Guess I do," I tell him.

"You've been good to us," Zeffy says. "Thanks for everything."

"You've been better," Bones tells her.

The old vertigo returns as he sends us back, leaving us all clinging to each other, Buddy whining, until we find ourselves in the snow that's covering the lawns of Fitzhenry Park, where we lose our balance and fall in a tangle of limbs.

Walking Large
as Trees

To discover who you are, first learn
who everybody else is – and you're
what's left.
– attributed to Ashleigh Brilliant

I • ZEFFY

Nia scrambled to her feet first, then took the guitar case from Zeffy while Max gave her a hand up. They were alone in the park except for an old man sitting on a nearby bench who appeared to be wearing at least two overcoats and three hats, so bundled up he looked twice his size. He was facing the white lawns that ran down to the tree line and hadn't seemed to notice their remarkable arrival, didn't know they were there at all until he heard Buddy. He looked around at them, then returned to his contemplation of the wintered park while Buddy ran in circles around the three of them, barking, throwing up snow. Zeffy smiled at his enthusiasm until the snow and cold registered.

"What's wrong with this picture?" she said as she took the guitar case back from Nia.

Nia nodded. "How can it be winter? We were only gone three days."

"Four," Max said.

"No, definitely three," Zeffy said. "I kept track."

"Me, too. We must have been on different time lines over there – at least until we met this morning."

"And a whole different one from here," Nia said slowly.

Zeffy knew Nia was worrying about her mother and

what she must be thinking. Disappearing as Nia had for a few days was bad enough, but what if years had gone by? Then another thought struck her.

"How do we know we're even where we want to be?" she said.

Nia gave her a nervous look. "What do you mean? This is definitely Fitzhenry Park."

"But is it the Fitzhenry Park we know, or one in some other world?" Zeffy rubbed at her temples with her free hand and grimaced. "This is making my head ache."

"*And* it's cold," Max said.

He led the way to where the park opened out onto Palm Street and stopped in front of one of the red metal *Newford Star* boxes. His face went pale as he read the date on the newspaper.

"Monday. February twentieth."

This was too scary weird, Zeffy thought. Rip Van Winkle scary weird. Maybe she'd gotten a little used to the magical way expectations worked out in the spiritworld, acclimatization and all that, but she hadn't expected the strangeness to bleed back into this world with them. How much time had they lost?

"What . . . what year?" she asked, not sure if she really wanted to know the answer.

"Nineteen ninety-five."

"That's . . . my God. We've been gone eight months."

It could have been worse, a small part of her mind tried to reason. It could have been years. A century. They might never have come back. But she wasn't able to take comfort from any of that – not with a sudden eight-month hole in her life. She'd missed her gig, opening for Glory Mad Dog. She'd have lost her job. Probably her apartment. What would Tanya have done? And all her things. Max's guitar . . .

540

Beside her Nia began to tremble, as much from shock as the cold. Zeffy wanted to comfort her – she went so far as to put her arm around Nia's shoulders – but the cold had lodged deep inside her as well and she doubted she had any warmth or solace to spare.

"We've got to get out of this weather," Max said.

He stepped to the curb and tried to hail a cab, but none of them would stop. Because of Buddy, Zeffy realized. Didn't want dog hair and slobber all over their nice clean, warm upholstery.

"Try it where they can't see we've got Buddy with us," she said, "and then we'll just bully our way in."

Leaving Nia's side, she took Buddy by the collar and walked far enough away from the others to make it look as though they weren't together. Max hailed another cab and this one stopped immediately. While Max got in the front seat and engaged the driver in conversation, Nia held the back door open for Zeffy and Buddy.

"No dogs," the cabbie said when he saw Buddy getting in.

"C'mon," Max said. "He'll lie on the floor – what's he going to hurt?"

The cabbie shook his head. "Don't want my cab full of fleas and smelling like a dog."

After all they'd been through, this was too much for Zeffy. She leaned forward, the guitar case pressing uncomfortably into her midriff, her face only inches from that of the cabbie, and glared at him.

"Look," she said. "We're cold and we're tired and if you don't get this car moving I'm going to tell the dog to sic balls, got it?"

Both Max and Nia looked at her in surprise, and even a little embarrassment, but Zeffy didn't care. She locked her gaze onto the cabbie's, staring him down until he slowly turned and pulled the cab out onto the street.

"Thank you," Zeffy said sweetly and settled back into her seat.

"Uh, where to?" the cabbie asked. His gaze went from Max to the rear mirror to look at Zeffy.

"We should get Nia home first," Max said, turning to look at Zeffy. "Then we can clean up at my place and get some warm clothes before getting you home." He turned a bit more. "That okay with you, Nia?"

Nia nodded. "Sure."

Zeffy gave Nia's knee a squeeze, knowing how nervous she was about seeing her mother again.

"We can come up with you if you like," she said.

Nia shook her head. "No. I can do this."

Zeffy gave her a reassuring smile, then looked out the window. She was suffering a bit of culture shock, what with all the traffic and people and buildings. Eight months, she thought. Having been through so much, the panic she felt now seemed beyond inappropriate. But the more she fought it, the worse it got.

Finally she closed her eyes and called up the melody of the song she'd been working on for Bones. Make that Joe. She smiled. Mr. Crow Crazy Dog. Now that she knew him better, a handful of lyrics began to slide into place. She concentrated on them, on being home, on being safe, and slowly the panic ebbed away.

II • LISA

L ISA NO longer overslept in the mornings. She woke an hour earlier than she needed and took that time to check a few teenage haunts on the way to work, showed Nia's picture to whomever she could, asked around, then used another hour on the way home to repeat the process in some different part of town. She had no luck, but she refused to give up hope. And she was getting better at holding back the panic attacks. The only time they were really bad was when she woke sometimes in the middle of the night, breathless and crying, but then she had Julie to hold her and soothe her fears.

Julie. Lisa had to smile. Considering how first meeting Julie had turned her whole life upside down, it was a little odd that Julie was now the stable, calming element in her life. She didn't mind the late dinners while Lisa was out looking for Nia – in fact, she usually prepared them. They worked very well as a couple – far better than the relationship Lisa'd had with Dan, though Lisa never regretted her marriage. Without it, she wouldn't have had Nia.

She sat on the bus, looking down at the photo of her daughter that she used to show around at malls, coffee bars, bus stations, wherever kids Nia's age hung out, slipping into a sad reverie that almost made her miss her stop. Getting off, she pulled her collar up against the wind and trudged home through Old Market's narrow streets. They were calling for snow again tonight.

On the way up the stairs to her apartment, she paused outside Max Trader's door, thinking for a moment that she'd heard voices, then forced herself to continue up the last flight. Yes, Trader had disappeared at around the same time as her daughter, but she'd come to accept the fact that there wasn't necessarily a connection.

The front door was unlocked, which was odd since Julie had this thing about always keeping the door locked. But before Lisa could wonder too much about that, she saw the small familiar knapsack lying on the floor, heard the voices coming from the kitchen. Her pulse jumped into overtime and she almost ran down the hall, not bothering to take off her coat. She paused in the doorway, her gaze drinking in the sight of her daughter, sitting there at the table across from Julie, a coffee mug in hand. Nia looked up, an odd expression in her features. It took Lisa a long moment to realize that it was nervousness.

"Nia," she said, her voice soft.

She couldn't seem to move. A thousand questions died stillborn. All that was important was that Nia was back. Safe. In one piece. There'd be time for answers later.

"Um, hi, Mom."

Lisa's gaze slid to Julie's and read the warning there: Don't push, don't make a scene, try to take it slowly. She took a deep breath, then sat down at the table with them, still wearing her coat, the snow from her boots forming puddles on the linoleum floor.

"Are you all right?" she asked.

Nia nodded. "I've met Julie."

Julie. Yes, of course, Julie. Oh God. She hadn't had a chance to talk to Nia about it, to explain how she'd fallen in love with another woman instead of a man.

"So," Nia said. "I guess I'll be calling her stepmom, right?"

Julie laughed. Actually laughed at a moment like this. But then Lisa felt herself smiling, too, and some of the tension left her body.

"Oh, please," Julie said.

"Are . . . are you okay with this?" Lisa asked.

Nia nodded. "After some of the stuff I've seen, this seems relatively normal."

Lisa's mind filled with visions of bizarre cults, sexual perversions, a hundred and one other parents' nightmares.

"I've got to ask you something, Mom."

It took Lisa a moment to get back from where her fears had taken her.

"Sure," she said. "What is it?"

"Who did I invite to my twelfth birthday party?"

Lisa looked blankly at her. "What are you talking about?"

"Please," Nia said. She seemed to be feeling awkward, but determined. "Just answer the question."

Lisa took a steadying breath. "Okay. You didn't have a birthday party that year and you haven't had any since. That was the year you convinced me that you hated them."

The reply seemed to relieve Nia, far out of proportion to what such an innocuous question and answer should have done.

"So what was all that about?" Lisa couldn't help but ask.

"Nothing."

But then Lisa understood. She remembered the strange man she'd met in the hallway outside her door a few days after Nia had disappeared. What was it that he'd said again? The words came back to her quickly, called up from the familiar pool of information holding anything and everything that might be a clue to Nia's whereabouts.

She's convinced that you're not really her mother any-more – that there's someone else in your head.

How do you reassure your daughter that you are who you are? she asked herself. But there was no need to take the question further. Nia stood up from the table and looked at her.

"I've missed you, Mom."

"Oh, sweetheart—"

"And I could really use a hug."

Lisa took her in her arms. "Me, too," she whispered into Nia's hair.

An odd scent rose from Nia's hair – a curious mix of wood smoke and something else, not quite definable, wild and musky – but Lisa forced herself not to ask about it. Take it step by step, she told herself. There'll be plenty of time later to find out where Nia had gone and why. For now she was simply grateful to have her daughter back. She hugged Nia tighter.

"Me, too," she repeated.

III • TANYA

"THAT WAS fun," Tanya said.

After two months on the West Coast of gladhanding and making nice at parties and premiers and wherever else Eddie could get her in – "You want people to think of you when they're casting, *capisce*?" – hanging out in a pub with Geordie where no one knew her and she wasn't expected to be all outgoing and vivacious had been an utter relief. The Harp was Geordie's local, almost across the street from his apartment, and now her local, too, since she'd moved into her new apartment five blocks farther down on Kelly Street.

For a Newford bar, The Harp was surprisingly quiet. A handful of Irish musicians sat in one corner, none of their instruments plugged in, playing the music for enjoyment, what Geordie referred to as the *craic*, instead of for money. There were people in the small smoky room out to have fun, to be sure, voices loud, laughter louder, but there were also corner booths where you could sit and listen to the music, have an intimate conversation. Heaven. They'd played darts. Hung out for a while with Jilly, Sophie, Wendy and Geordie's brother Christy when they'd dropped by after a show. But mostly they'd been by themselves, talking face-to-face instead of over the phone. What Tanya liked the best was that they both still had so much to say.

Geordie smiled. "I was hoping you'd enjoy it. It's hard to think of something that'll measure up to what Hollywood's got to offer by way of entertainment, so in the end I just thought screw it, and went to the other extreme, seriously lo fi."

They were walking back to Tanya's apartment through a light fall of snow, but she stopped now and turned to look at him.

"You don't have to worry about me and Hollywood," she said. "It's all glitter and BS there and not my scene at all. I'm only there for the work."

The work. Whatever Eddie was doing, he was doing something right, because she'd landed another role, small, but more lines than she'd had to date. It was a big-budget film and she was making more for the few weeks' work than she had so far in her admittedly limited film career. She was the female lead's ditzy girlfriend, wardrobe care of Goodwill, character just this side of that waitress on *Mad About You* who never seemed to get anything right. Anyone only familiar with her work to date would think it a serious stretch, but she loved this opportunity to play a bit of a klutz instead of the babe and knew she'd be good at it.

"I know," Geordie said. "I guess I just miss you."

Tanya leaned closer to him and gave him a kiss. "I don't deserve you. You're way too nice."

"Yeah, right."

She kissed him again. "But you are."

Arm in arm, they continued up the street to her building, sharing the sort of goofy small talk that would make people who weren't at the beginning of a relationship grit their teeth. At one point Tanya got a fit of giggles and buried her face against Geordie's shoulder.

"Ewww," she said, pulling back. "You're all wet."

Geordie laughed. "Well, what do you expect, when—"

He broke off as Tanya came to an abrupt halt. Her good humor fled when she saw who was sitting on the front steps of her building, so obviously waiting for her, despite the snow.

"Oh, shit," she said.

Geordie gave her a puzzled look, then turned his attention to where she was looking.

"It's Johnny," she told him.

There was someone sitting on the other side of him, but she couldn't quite make out enough of the person to recognize them. Johnny she'd know anywhere.

"Johnny?" Geordie repeated, obviously not making the connection.

But why should he? Tanya thought. Johnny hadn't made a career of screwing up his life the way he had hers.

"Johnny Devlin," she said. "Back to make my life miserable again."

"He's not going to bother you," Geordie began.

But then Tanya suddenly shrieked and ran towards the steps, Johnny, Geordie, everything forgotten except for the redheaded figure who stood up and opened her arms as Tanya came running up to her. Tanya and Zeffy stood there hugging, laughing and crying, until they finally stepped back and looked at each other.

"My God," Tanya said. "Where'd you get the clothes?"

They made the ones she'd be wearing for her upcoming role look positively fashionable: a couple of layers of over-sized shirts, a padded coat in which Zeffy was swimming, hugely baggy jeans rolled up because the cuffs were at least a foot too long.

"They're Max's," Zeffy said. "I can't seem to find my own."

"Max . . .?" Tanya turned slowly to look at Johnny. "So it's really true?"

Max and Geordie had been introducing themselves to each other. At Tanya's question, Max nodded.

"And Johnny?" Tanya asked.

Zeffy shook her head. "We don't know. Dead, probably."

"Dead."

Zeffy glanced at Geordie. "Jeez, Tanya. Don't tell me you're still carrying a torch for him."

"No. I'm just – this is horrible – but all I feel is relief."

"I can understand that."

Tanya stepped closer to Geordie and linked arms with him. "So where have you *been*?"

"It's a long story," Zeffy said, "that'd be way easier to tell somewhere warm."

"Oh," Tanya said. "Well, I live right here."

"I know."

"How'd you find out?"

"I tried calling Jilly first," Zeffy said, "but she was out.

Ditto, Wendy. Then I called Kit and she told me how you'd quit at the restaurant, turned into this big-shot Hollywood type — "

"Oh, please."

" — and she gave me your address, so here we are."

"Well, come on in," Tanya said, leading the way up the stairs. "We've got ages of catching up to do."

Geordie and Zeffy followed her up the stairs, but they all paused when Max didn't join them.

"I guess I'll just leave you with your friends then," he told Zeffy.

Zeffy gave an exaggerated sigh and came back down to collect him.

"Face it," she said, taking him by the hand and pulling him up. "You're part of the circle now, too."

"I didn't want to impose," Max began.

"I think the word you're looking for is join in," Zeffy said. "No, wait a sec. That's two words."

"Will you guys come in already?" Tanya said from the open door. "You're letting all the cold air into the foyer."

Zeffy ignored her. "Unless you don't want to," she said to Max.

"No, I want to."

It was weird, Tanya thought, seeing Zeffy all flirty with Johnny like this, though of course he wasn't really Johnny, he was somebody else, living in Johnny's skin, so that made it all right she supposed. She stepped aside as they entered the building, holding hands. Still, weird didn't begin to describe how this felt. It was enough to make her head ache.

"Tanya?" Geordie said.

"What? Oh right."

She closed the door on the snowy night and went in to let

her friends into her new apartment, apologizing for the mess as she unlocked the door.

IV • NIA

THE OPENING for a show that Jilly and Sophie had at The Green Man Gallery later in the week seemed the perfect excuse for a welcome-home party, so everybody got together, milling about in the small gallery with the usual crowd of artists, patrons and hangers-on, admiring Jilly and Sophie's most recent collaborations, listening to the jazz pianist playing in the corner, sampling the buffet, and of course, partaking of all the gossip.

"It's so cool of you to have invited me," Nia said when she was alone with Jilly for a moment.

Jilly smiled. "You've got to have your friends around you at a time like this, right? For the celebrations as well as the down times."

"Sure. I . . . I'm glad we're friends."

Jilly gave her a quick hug. "Me, too." She glanced over to where Nia's mother and her girlfriend were talking to Albina Sprech, the owner of the gallery. "How'd it go with your mother?"

"I don't think she believes me," Nia said. "I mean, who can blame her, really – but she's being cool about it. We've been getting along better this week than we ever have."

"I meant with her and – was it Julie?"

Nia nodded. "I'm happy for them. I don't get it, but Julie's really nice and, well, you know. It takes some getting used to."

"Seems like everybody's turning into a couple around us," Jilly said.

Nia looked around the room. Her mother and Julie. Max and Zeffy. Tanya and Geordie.

"I hope it works out for all of them," she said. Then she grinned. "Zeffy's staying at Max's until Tanya goes on location and then she's going to stay there. Max claims she's sleeping on the sofa – as if. I think they make the greatest couple, don't you?"

Jilly laughed. "Zeffy told me about your matchmaking. Maybe I should get you to fix me up with someone as nice."

"You don't strike me as the type of person that'd ever have any trouble meeting people."

"Ah, but what about the right people?" Jilly asked, but then she smiled.

"My trouble is I kind of live in assonance – my whole life is getting the rhyme wrong, do you know what I mean? Instead of finding the right rhyme, I'm just stringing together all these vowel sounds."

That seemed awfully sad to Nia. It was so much like her mother, never connecting with the right guy for so long.

"I guess you must get lonely," she asked.

Jilly shook her head. "No. Not really. I learned a long time ago to be happy with myself, so I'm pretty much okay with it. I mean, one day I might meet the right person, but I'm not counting the days or anything. If I get a little melancholy about it, I just keep myself busy and the feeling goes away." She cocked her head and regarded Nia with a teasing smile. "How about you? Any beaus in the near future?"

"Oh, please."

Jilly laughed. "Yeah, that's what I always say, too."

V • MAX

I'M STANDING with my hand idly fussing the wiry fur on Buddy's head, listening to Zeffy's conversation with a woman whose name I can't remember anymore when I catch my reflection in the glass of a print near the back of the gallery. The stranger's face looks out at me, Devlin. The same face that's waiting for me in the mirror every morning when I'm shaving. I don't know if I'll ever get used to it. I think Zeffy has trouble sometimes, too. I catch her looking at me, the flash of doubt in her eyes gone almost before it registers. Almost.

I thought I'd adjust better. I seemed to, before, after I got over the initial shock. But then I kept expecting to get my own body back, if not right away, then at some point. Now I know it's impossible and there's times when I can barely stand to be in this skin. I want to rip it off like the mask I feel it is. I want to be me again – the me I remember. I want to look in the mirror with a sense of comfortable familiarity and not get caught off-guard the way I still do. The way I probably always will.

"I've been thinking," I say later as we're walking back to my apartment. Buddy's on a leash, but he doesn't seem to mind.

"Oh-oh," she says.

"What?"

"The way you said 'I'm thinking' sounds too much like you're uncomfortable with what you're about to tell me."

"I guess I am," I say. "I don't want you to get the wrong impression – you know, feel pressured or anything."

"About what?"

"Well, I was going to say, I've been thinking that you

don't have to get your own apartment. I've got plenty of room. We could move all that stuff I've got in the spare room and you could have it. That way you'll be able to work on your music without having to worry about rent and stuff like that."

"What, like a kept woman?"

I don't realize she's teasing until I start to protest and she laughs.

"I'm sorry," she says, and I realize she's carrying around her own nervousness about how all this is going to work out. Her, me. Us. "It's really sweet of you to offer," she adds.

"Just think about it.

She nods and takes my hand.

"I think I'll still stay at Tanya's when she's gone," she says. "It'll give me some time to myself to work things out."

I get a warm glow. All I can think is, she didn't say no.

The first night she's at Tanya's I get a call around midnight.

"Hi," she says.

"Hi, yourself."

"Whatcha doing?"

"Nothing much," I tell her. "Buddy and I are hanging around. He's sleeping and I'm reading a bit – trying to get sleepy."

"Miss me?"

It's been so quiet in the apartment that I've had the radio on all evening. Hasn't helped.

"I don't know if *miss* is a strong enough word," I say, playing with the way she's always redefining words.

She laughs. "I know just what you mean." Pause. "So why don't you come over?"

I realize later that she wanted our first time to be on her own homeground – or as close as she can get to it with most of her stuff still in storage and no place she can call her own. We're lying in Tanya's bed after and she's running a finger along my cheek. Buddy's finally forgiven us for calling him a voyeur and making him get off the bed earlier. He's sprawled out at the foot again, snoring softly.

"I had to think about it," she says. "This whole business with you being you, but looking so much like Johnny."

"I understand. I'm not exactly comfortable with it myself."

"But I think I'm okay with it." She smiles and lays her head on my shoulder. "You're so *you* that I don't really see him anymore when I look at you."

"I wish you'd teach me the trick."

"It'll come," she says. She turns a bit so that she's lying with her head on the pillow beside mine, looking up at the ceiling. "What do you suppose really happened to him?"

"I don't think we'll ever know," I say. "I just know I'm not going to make the mistakes *I* made before he came into my life. I'm going to do like that saying of the spirits that Joe told us and live large."

Zeffy smiles and puts a hand down between my legs.

"Mmm," she says. "This is a good start."

Buddy stirs, looks up. He gives a sigh and gets off the bed without being asked this time.

Zeffy and I manage to put Johnny out of our minds and not think about him for the rest of the night. I think it's a very good start.

V • JOSEPH CRAZY DOG

BELYING THE cowboy boots he was wearing, Bones moved silently between the trees, ghosting through the underbrush like one of his other world cousins. Ahead of him, the undergrowth gave way and he entered a stand of hemlocks, the tall trees rearing cathedrally above him, their needles turning the forest floor into a soft carpet. He paused a few yards into their churchlike quiet and turned his head, dark gaze alighting on a black bird sitting in the lower branches of a nearby tree.

Sinking slowly into a cross-legged position, he rolled himself a cigarette and lit it. He and the bird regarded each other as he smoked. He'd told Zeffy he had unfinished business here, but that hadn't been entirely true. Mostly it was that curiosity of his that had kept him looking, needing to know the end of the story. That was maybe his greatest weakness – he always wanted to know how everything worked out after "The End" scrolled up on the screen or the cast had taken their bows. Long after the curtain had closed and the stagehands were sweeping the boards, he'd still be slouched there in a seat, wondering, And what happened *then*?

"So," Bones said after a while. "How'd you end up in the bird?"

Who the hell are you?

Bones took another drag, exhaled. "Nobody. Just got curious about what happened to you."

The bird cocked his head, regarding him with a gaze as dark as Bones' own. *I feel like I should know you.*

"Naw. We never met."

The bird perched silent, considering, while Bones smoked.

"So are you going to finish the story for me?" he finally asked.

I don't know how it happened, the bird said. It hopped down to a lower branch. *It just did. Look, you've got to help me.*

"Help you what?"

Cross back over.

"Not much use for talking birds there. You'll probably end up in a lab, getting cut up to see how the trick works."

I mean help me to get my body back.

Bones finished his cigarette. He put it out against the side of his boot, then stowed the butt in his pocket. Stood up.

"You only get so many chances," he told the bird. "Seems to me, yours are all used up, this turn of the wheel."

I didn't know what I was doing.

Bones raised an eyebrow. "Like that's an excuse?"

This isn't fair.

"But that's just it," Bones said. "It is fair. Everything comes down to courtesy and respect, you know? Seems to me, someone finally refused to take on the shit you were laying out and just spiraled it back to you. Thing you've got to deal with now is all that baggage you're going to be dragging with you onto the next spoke of the wheel."

Look, I'll give you whatever you want, the bird told him. *Name your price.*

"What've you got that I might want? A real bird, that'd be different. I could learn something. Birds are interesting. Shit, anything's interesting if you pay attention. But what am I supposed to learn from you?"

I don't get it.

"And that's the whole problem," Bones said. "You don't get it and maybe you never will. But until you work it out, nothing's going to change. You'll be here, and I'll be gone."

But you could—

"Listen carefully," Bones said. "I'm not responsible for what happened to you, Max isn't responsible, nobody else is. Only you. Now you've got to live with it."

You know Trader? Listen, just tell him that—

"This got old real fast," Bones said, cutting him off.

They regarded each other for a long moment, then Bones turned away from the bird on its perch in the hemlock and stepped back across the worlds. He felt swollen with story and thought he'd be able to stay longer than usual this time, all things considered. Maybe he and Cassie could even head out on a road trip somewhere, just the two of them, take in a few sights.

Lord knows he'd been missing that big-hearted, patient woman of his.

All Pan Books are available at your local bookshop or newsagent, or can be ordered direct from the publisher. Indicate the number of copies required and fill in the form below.

Send to: Macmillan General Books C.S.
                Book Service By Post
                PO Box 29, Douglas I-O-M
                IM99 1BQ

or phone: 01624 675137, quoting title, author and credit card number.

or fax: 01624 670923, quoting title, author, and credit card number.

or Internet: http://www.bookpost.co.uk

Please enclose a remittance* to the value of the cover price plus 75 pence per book for post and packing. Overseas customers please allow £1.00 per copy for post and packing.

*Payment may be made in sterling by UK personal cheque, Eurocheque, postal order, sterling draft or international money order, made payable to Book Service By Post.

Alternatively by Access/Visa/MasterCard

Card No.

Expiry Date

Signature   _____

Applicable only in the UK and BFPO addresses.

While every effort is made to keep prices low, it is sometimes necessary to increase prices at short notice. Pan Books reserve the right to show on covers and charge new retail prices which may differ from those advertised in the text or elsewhere.

NAME AND ADDRESS IN BLOCK CAPITAL LETTERS PLEASE

Name _____

Address _____

_____

_____

_____

8/95

Please allow 28 days for delivery.
Please tick box if you do not wish to receive any additional information. ☐